Charlotte E Ha
ONCE UPON

******

ONCE UPON A

An erotic novel
The first part of The Stained Duet
Copyright ©2017 by Charlotte E Hart
Cover Design by MAD
Formatting by MAD

All rights reserved

Without limiting the rights under copyright reserved alone, no part of this publication may be reproduced, stored in or introduced into a retrieval system, or transmitted, in any form, or by any means (electronic, mechanical, photocopying, recording, or otherwise) without the prior written permission of both the copyright owner and the above publisher of this book.
This is a work of fiction. Names, characters, places, brands, media and incidents are either the product of the author's imagination or are used fictitiously. The author acknowledges the trademarked status and trademark owners of various products, bands, and/or restaurants referenced in this work of fiction, which have been used without permission. The publication/use of those trademarks is not authorized, associated with, or sponsored by the trademark owners.

License Notes

Charlotte E Hart
ONCE UPON A

This book is licensed for your personal use and enjoyment only. This book may not be resold or given away to other people, or used for any other reason than originally intended. If you would like to share this book with another person, please purchase an additional copy for each recipient. If you're reading this book and did not purchase it, or it was not purchased for your use only, then please return to your favourite book retailer, or copyright owner, and purchase your own copy. Copyright infringement of this work, or any other works by Charlotte E Hart will exact legal proceedings. Thank you for respecting the hard work of this author.
ISBN: 9781981741861

Table of Contents

Chapter 1
Chapter 2
Chapter 3
Chapter 4
Chapter 5
Chapter 6
Chapter 7
Chapter 8
Chapter 9
Chapter 10
Chapter 11
Chapter 12
Chapter 13
Chapter 14
Chapter 15
Chapter 16
Chapter 17
Chapter 18
Chapter 19
Chapter 20
Chapter 21
Chapter 22

Acknowledgements

ONCE UPON A

By

Charlotte E Hart

"THERE IS ALWAYS CALM BEFORE A STORM."

Chapter 1

ALANA

"It's undeniably alluring how the human skeleton stretches under pressure," he says, rounding the prone body in front of him and tapping the flesh gently. "Muscles lengthen when warmed. Ligaments twist slightly, lending another inch of growth to the gratifying position asked for." He turns his head back to me for a second, scanning my dress and sneering, probably at the fact it's not see through. "The rapid intakes of breath and then sighs coming from her lips increase blood flow, resulting in yet more give to her tendons." He leaves the naked woman's side, travelling over the wooden floorboards and making me back away from his extended hand. "But it's the howl that finalises the posture to perfection." Really? My feet move me again, away from his still extended hand as my eyes flick around nervously. "Her groaned scream of agony." I feel my shoulders hit the wall, leaving me nowhere to run to, no room to manoeuvre at all. He smiles, obviously amused by my attempt at escape. "Haven't you ever wondered how that's achieved?"

To be honest, no, I've never thought of how they get these girls into extreme positions, or why the hell they put up with it in the first place, and this interview is just becoming more and more nonsensical by the second.

"Are you still breathing?" Barely. It would help if this one wasn't so damned attractive. He was last time, too, in the normal world where average people exist. In here, he's like a quirk I can't refuse. And why do they all smell so bloody good in these places?

One week I've been at this. I was supposed to be simply collecting data for research purposes. Just a quick sit down with a few of them. The first one, a Dominant called Wraith—yes, apparently that was his real name—was obliging and gave me a thorough breakdown of how the whole thing works, but then, at the end, he offered to give me the name of someone who might be able to help me a little more with the sadistic tendencies of the scene. The one thing I didn't expect to be delving into, when I eventually picked up enough courage to call the man in front of me, was the seedy underground side of what I'm trying to research. It has been reasonably useful, though, and he is hellishly attractive. Hardly a chore in reality.

"Would you like to try? We have another twenty minutes left before I have to leave."

I tip my chin up at him, signalling my absolute horror at the very idea of such a notion. Highly educated women do not, in any way, allow themselves to be strung up and potentially gutted like a pig. As the woman in front of me is currently doing. Although, she's not being gutted. Nor are any of the others I've seen as far as I know. In fact, her moaning is quite arousing in some way. Not that Mr. Beautiful here will ever know that's the effect I'm feeling.

"No, thank you." I wish that didn't come out as shakily as it did, but it did, unfortunately. It's only because of the moaning woman. Well, that and the fact that I'm pretty certain he's wearing Chanel under that suit just to enhance his muscles further. All the good looking ones wear suits. Good ones. It's utterly debilitating to professionalism.

"Is it all too dirty for you? The floor, I mean." Well, yes. Not that it would make any difference if he swept me off to a more 'high end' version of the same subject matter. I mean, I'm only writing a book. It's all the rage, you see. BDSM. Kinky stuff. Before this, the most kinky thing I'd ever indulged in was a vibrator I got as a joke one year for a friend. I didn't actually have the balls to give it to her, so I ended up keeping it myself and giving it a go. It was… different, and still quite useful when I get myself wound up through writing. Not that it happens too often lately.

"You're wet." What? Where's the water? I look down at my feet then back up to him. He winks, licking his lips at the same moment. Oh. OH. The flush of colour that rises through my whole body has me barging past him and towards the door before I know it. Bastard. How would he know if I was or not? Or am. *I am.* This is another unfortunate thing that keeps happening around these men. I think they have some sort of link to vaginas. I'm just not quite sure what it is yet. It needs more research, something I'm not currently prepared to entertain given this atrocious venue. Certainly not with this overly attractive one anyway.

"I can help you with that." I swing my head sharply, aiming for yet more abhorrence at his crude remarks as he walks behind me, chuckling.

"Do you think this is amusing? I'm a professional, not one of your…" I don't know what to call them. I wave my hand at the woman behind us, who is still moaning. "…things."

Professional. Very, actually. I nod at him, clamping my false smile in place and indicating my departure from this building. I've been writing novels under two pen names for around six years. Three actually, if you count the disaster that was Sci-Fi PNR. I don't discuss that, though. Anyway, Valerie Du Font writes romance. She's where I started in college. She does quite well—well enough for me to not be in this repellent place anyway. And Peter Halloway writes crime thrillers. He also does reasonably well, given that I'm a woman writing as a man, a trick another author turned me on to some time ago. Seems male readers prefer to read male authors. Who knew, right? Anyway, BDSM is the new thing. Unfortunately, it's a thing that neither Valerie, Peter, nor Alana know anything about. And if there's one thing I do, it's research. When this book hits the shelves, which is a long way off given that I've only just started researching, it will be as if I was the one living the scene.

"Is there anything else I can help you with, aside from the obvious, that is?" he says, his voice still full of glee at my disastrous predicament. Arse. Perhaps I should pop a tampon in the next time I see one of them, soak up the creative juices, so to speak.

"No, no, really. I think that will be enough for today," I reply breezily, waggling my hand in the air and lengthening my stride through 'The Pit'. Quite enough. My nod to myself confirms this thought as I continue through said Pit, trying not to stand on any appendage that presents itself en-route.

He rounds in front of me as I eventually reach the exit through the labyrinth of maze-like hallways, smiling again. He rarely smiles. In fact, it's only when he's got the upper hand that he seems to manage one at all. I've met him twice now—once for a coffee in a small restaurant in Manhattan, and then today when I met him at this address, which was unwise now I think about it, but thankfully, he does seem gentlemanly in some respects, as much as he can be in this situation.

"Actually, one final question if you don't mind?" I ask, sidestepping his outstretched arm as he guides us through the double doors out onto the pavement. He raises a brow as confirmation that it's okay to ask. This is another thing he does rather than speak sometimes.

"Have you ever been in love?"

For the first time since I met him, he falters, a frown descending to show through the normally unaffected expression of disinterest. It's a look that has me taking a step away from him. Not in fear, more like surprise really. I've never seen such a scowl on his face. "I'm sorry if that was inappropriate. You don't have to answer." Although, it would be nice if he did. All these books talk of men who've never been in love, never known a woman good enough, never been tamed. It all seems a bit unrealistic to me. I'd like to know that real dominants, the ones out here on the streets, are human, too. That they love and are as fallible as the rest of us.

"That *was* inappropriate. I'm not inclined to answer it," he eventually replies, backing himself away from me and taking hold of the door behind him again.

"Oh, alright." Clearly that's hit a nerve, one I'll need to understand in more depth.

"Do you need a taxi hailing?" he asks, all pleasantries and joviality lost from his tone.

"Oh, no, no, I'll walk. It's fine. It's the middle of the day. No problem at all."

He doesn't smile at me again. He just scans my dress again, allowing his slightly mocking sneer to develop as naturally as it did before, and then slips through the door back into the building.

Right. That went well, then. Wonderful.

Charlotte E Hart
ONCE UPON A

I turn into the bright afternoon sun, clutching my precious notes and laptop, and start the walk back to my one bed apartment. It might not be overly large, but it's mine. Bought and paid for. Being an author has done me proud. It's not what I thought I'd do when I was at college. I'd hoped more for vet or similar, and I managed to get at least three of the five years completed, but college loans needed to be paid, and it's just the way life has turned out for me. I made a fair profit off the sale of my first book, which led to me being snapped up by a publisher here in New York. I moved here, thinking I was some high-flying professional. That turned into ratshit, to be honest. While landing me with a four book deal, which seemed extremely exciting to a twenty-one-year-old, they basically ripped me to shreds financially. They took all the money, barely leaving me with enough to support myself over here, and laughed all the way to their bank while I ate noodles and rice for sustenance. Manhattan is extortionate to live in. Food was not a necessity at the time. However, that was what led to Peter being born. He worked independently to Valerie, giving me the ability to make money through him as long as I kept up my obligations to the publisher with Valerie. And the contacts I made, although I had to be quite secretive about it—penname and all that—helped me achieve more profits than Valerie ever allowed. Thankfully, by the time my new deal came around with Valerie, I was more savvy about the publishing world. So, she now writes for my publisher, making me a good deal in romance while they do all the marketing around the world, and that gives me the freedom to write Peter, and whatever I'm going to call my new penname, independently. I really need to think of a new name.

I snap out my phone and call the only real friend I have around here. Don't get me wrong, I have hundreds of friends, most of whom are in the publishing industry, but only one that I call an actual friend. She's also an author, an independent one at that, and she writes entirely in the male domain. Thrillers, fantasy, romance, all as men. She says it makes her more money and she can slip in and out of private chats unknown as the person she is. I think it's because she likes being a man, and if she'd actually admit she was a lesbian, it would help no end.

"Wanna have lunch, Bree?" I ask before she actually speaks because she hardly ever bothers doing that unless it's an absolute necessity. There's a grunt on her end, more than likely because she's writing three books, Facebooking and Tweeting at the same time. You should see her office. Three screens, all with open Works In Progress, and then she'll have another on audio playing in the background. She'll be editing that one as she goes.

"Where?" is her eventual human response, not that she inhabits the human world all that much.

"Bluties?"

"See ya in fifteen."

The phone goes dead. Pleasant.

I'm not even sure why I like her, but she's always been straight with me, which is something a lot of these other publishing people don't do. Don't get me wrong, I'm happy to help and be part of a team, always have been, but I'm not stupid either. Some of these people wouldn't have given a shit about me if I hadn't have made my way up the tree, so to speak. They would have trodden on or over me merrily to get to where I am now. So if they think I'll give one inch of help to their conniving little arseholes, well, they're wrong. I've learnt my lessons along the way, thank you very much. I've become stronger and more able to see the clearly, perhaps changed myself to see straight through the bullshit or at least accommodate its occasional virtues. It's a shame, but needs must. Trusting, happy, whimsical Alana is long gone. Perhaps swallowed up along the way so that this new version could survive the cutthroat business I'm in. Who knows? Control is all I know now. Control and methodical planning.

I turn along Madison, heading for Bluties, and feel the last rays of the autumn sun belting down on me with a smile. Summer's lovely in New York, not like the winter that's coming, which is, frankly, hell. The UK did not prepare me for winter in New York. It's freezing. The most we used to get over there is a few days of panic stricken roads, empty stores and then as suddenly as the white dusting arrived, it would all disappear. Maybe there would be a bit of sludgy stuff for a few days, but nothing more than that. I think I remember a couple of weeks of it when I was about twelve, but really nothing more. It's horrendous here. Five foot drifts. Women falling over in heels with their arses sticking up in the air, which always makes me titter, and then there's the wind. Jesus Christ, all these straight roads are like wind tunnels. I literally took off last year, arms flailing around like a banshee, my coat acting like wings lifting me to the sky. Fuck. It was terrifying. I now go nowhere in the winter without sturdy boots and a handy umbrella to anchor myself to something should the need arise. In fact, since I've been living here I hardly wear anything but boots and jeans, which is odd because I never used to. I loved dresses, summer ones with heels, but I suppose I've just drifted into casual because of how much time I spend at home rather than going out. I'm only dressed in this dress now because of my interview. Being an author means I can wear what I like when I like, and suits aren't it. I like to get dressed up, and I can certainly afford it, but on most occasions I spend my time sitting behind a laptop. Why would I get dressed up for that? Most of us are a mess, wearing nothing but old comfy gear and more than likely not even attempting make-up of any description unless we have to.

"Yo. Lana! The fuck is that?"

That'll be Bree, welcoming me into her arms with her less than excitable exuberance.

"Hey, Bree," I call back, lifting my head to find her standing outside Bluties, laptop in hand and her phone held high in the sky.

"The fuck you wearing?"

"I had that interview with the Dom."

"Yeah, right. You get all sexed up then?"

I don't know why she thinks I would have. She's not seen me with one single man since we've been friends. This has something to do with the fact that I don't do men. Clearly, I do *do* men. I do men quite a lot actually, but I do them on my terms, which usually involves a hotel, no exchanging of numbers, and a quick thanks very much. None of which I tell her about.

"He's research. And quite a gentleman, Bree. I've got to get this right. I'm not writing a bad one."

"How would you know what's bad or not?" she replies immediately, ever the logical and direct friend that she is. And she's got a point, one which makes me nod my head in acceptance of that very fact. It's one of the reasons I'm doing this research after all. "Not sure why you're not letting him show you properly. How do you expect to get accurate data unless you try it out for size?" The second part of her argument makes me frown at such a thought, regardless of his good looks. It might be a sensible thought process some ways, but it's not for me. I laugh, trying to lighten the moment as she stares at me, one hand on her dark tattooed arm that she's scratching, the other still flicking through her phone. "Seriously, Lana. How do you expect to be able to edit your way through the actuality of sensation when you've never experienced it? Sure, we can all write romance, but from what I'm gathering, being whipped ain't the same, you know?"

Unfortunately, no matter my near nausea at the thought, she's probably right. She normally is. It's the same thing I've been playing with for some time on and off. To try, or not? I was hoping that simply conversing with a submissive would give me the range of sensations needed for written verse. However, on talking with two of them so far, all I've got is breathy moans and something that is apparently indescribable. It's lacking to say the least.

"Let's just get lunch, shall we?" is my quick manoeuvre out of said conversation that I absolutely do not want to have.

"Or you could just go back and ask him to do his thing on you."

"No."

"Well, your shout, I suppose. Just remember that when the reviews start rolling in," she says, tucking her head back down so she can respond to something on her phone.

Bitch. Correct, but a bitch nonetheless.

~

Lunch goes according to plan, as does everything in my life. Pinpoint precision is key to strategic timelines. Do you know the amount of hours that go into preparing books? I think my readers assume stories magically pop into my head and then appear suddenly on paper. They don't. The first few did in some manner. I thought of a story, wrote some words quite effortlessly, ones full of vigour and youthful exuberance, and before I knew it I'd written a book. But the ones after that? Well, they take planning and preparation. Most books are well written before the reader even hears about them. I currently have six works open and four completed books that aren't even published yet. I've actually just released one that I finished writing fifteen months ago. That's how it works. Forward planning. There are calendars and spreadsheets, release dates planned years in advance. Word-counts to keep up with. Three rounds of editors to go through, sometimes four, even five on occasion for my crime thrillers. Publication dates to meet. Covers and teasers to release at the optimal times for marketing purposes. Paperbacks to produce with different graphics for different countries, although I never did really understand why. And don't get me started on events. I did twelve last year. One a month. Nine here in the states, one in Oz, and two back home in the UK, which gave me a chance to see Mum and Dad. I only do events as Valerie, obviously, but I've been toying with the idea of hiring a model to play Peter. I make a lot of money out of them, and believe it or not, it's nice to actually meet my readers, talk to them and get direct feedback rather than the constancy of social media. It makes me feel human in some way, I suppose. Alive. Not the robot I seem to have become to meet criteria and provide the reader with the ultimate story. It's like I've changed into something I never was before. Maybe it's because of the workload, or maybe it's because of circumstance, or maybe it's just natural evolution. I don't know, but something feels out of sync lately. It just all feels a bit messy and distant, like this current version of me is not comfortable with itself.

"So, when are you seeing him next?" Bree asks, still attached to her phone and not really listening to my answer.

"Thought I'd try a gang bang next Tuesday."

"Right, well that should work," she replies, totally engrossed in whatever she's looking at as I grab her shoulder to stop her from walking directly into traffic. "What?"

"The road, Bree," I reply, hovering my pointed finger at the onslaught of mid-day traffic.

"Oh right, thanks."

"Do you ever just look forward and take the world in? At all? See what's around you rather than focus entirely on what your next set of words are?"

"What the fuck, Lana?" she says, looking at me like I'm the biggest moron on the planet. "You know we've got no time for that. I'm six chapters behind on my current. Four more open that should be ready for Christmas. One novella going live now, and another two going live next week under pens. What the fuck time do I have to look up into the sky? My life is right here in this phone."

I let go of her arm and snicker at her distressed looking face, totally understanding where's she's at and remembering the fact that that's exactly where I am, too. Rightly or wrongly. It's probably the reason why I spend so much time stuffing amphetamines in my mouth, hoping that by not snorting it and rolling up bills like others do, I'm not actually addicted to the damn stuff. I mean, she's the same. There's nothing wrong with it. It's just our way of coping. It helps contain the noise, or at least channel it more effectively so we don't have to admit the issues behind whatever's going on in our heads.

"Yeah, I know, but when's enough enough? I mean you weren't even listening to me, not that you ever do. What about everything out there, life, you know?" Her face shoots up to mine, probably astounded at my audacity to question our life.

"I was so listening to you," she replies, still secretly tapping at her phone even though she thinks I can't see it. "I multitask." You bet your arse she does. We all do. At speed. I sigh and shake my head, knowing I've lost the discussion before it's begun. "What did you say exactly?"

"Gang bang."

"Really, when?"

"Next Tuesday." She scowls, lifts her phone again and swipes about a bit.

"Can't, got a deadline for book two in the Assessor Series."

"You think I want to gang bang with you?"

"The fuck's wrong with me?" she spits, ruffling her blonde mass of dreds about and shaking her booty like a hooker. I smile in reply and start us walking again. Nothing's wrong with her, nothing that being male wouldn't fix, anyway.

"Nothing. You're perfectly wonderful. Just not a man."

"You're gang banging with only men? Fucking go you. How many?"

The snort that comes out of my nose as we meander over to 57th can only be described as snot worthy. How many? As if I've ever done anything other than straight one on one. I'm the straightest straight person she's ever met. I can't even comprehend bent. Even the sight of those people in that club earlier was making me feel on edge, let alone one actually touching me, or, heaven forbid, asking me to indulge in their strange alternate reality.

"I've done two before. You need pointers?" she says, still attached to her phone and discussing this as if it's perfectly normal. No. I absolutely do not need pointers of any kind. Although...

"Have you?"

"Yeah. Long time ago. Off my head. Can't remember most of it, really."

"Well, that's about as useful as bugger all then."

We walk silently for a while, doing our best to avoid the rush of people trying to get back to work after lunch, all desperate not to be late for that next meeting. It makes me smile as I keep weaving in and out of them, hand on Bree's shoulder guiding her because she's still not looking at anything but her phone. One of the very fine things about being a writer is the ability to not have to conform to society's rules or work hours. We do what we do whenever we want to—restaurant, coffee shop, late nights, early mornings. I have a particular penchant for waking up at 1am with an idea and just opening up the laptop. It's not like I have to get to an office for 9am, so why not? I'm not convinced it was helpful when I first started writing, trying to do college at the same time, but now it works for me well enough. I just catch up on sleep at another time. Not that I get all that much of that. There never seems to be any time. It's like I never have any me time, no space for my mind to rest anymore. There are so many stories. So many characters. And it's become constant. It's a hive of other people's feelings, other people's emotions inside me. Murder and mayhem. Sex, love and romance. Beaches and holidays, wishes and dreams. I can't even remember my own dreams anymore. Maybe I never had any, or maybe they've been realized and I missed them while I was writing everyone else's happily ever afters. I don't know, but they're not here anymore giving me a purpose to all this. It's just a constant drive of forward momentum, barely giving me a chance to smell my own roses.

"Lana?"

"What?"

"I was asking about your Sexy Pants Dom."

"What about him?"

"Name?"

"I'm not allowed to tell you that. You know the ethics behind research," I reply incredulously, finally breaking through the throng of other people out into the small square where we afternoon sprint write sometimes. "And he is most definitely not *mine*."

In fact, I doubt men like Blaine Jacobs belong to anyone. He's the type who gives little compassion to anything but action. I can tell that by the way he peruses women as if they're pieces of meat to be tasted. I wouldn't say he's cold because he has quite a warm aura about him, welcoming even, but he's dispassionate, callous maybe. As if nothing is to be looked at with any other intent than study and interrogation. Everything he's shown me so far has been logical, as if it's methodically sentenced into its new position. There's no passion about his preferred entertainment. He touches skin as if it's not worth anything more than the chance to find its density or its durability. Maybe he's a scientist or a clinician of some kind in real life. He certainly doesn't come across as a man who's ever thought the idea of connection intriguing. Although, that love question threw him right off center.

Bree's already set out on the table by the time I've wandered towards it, notepad, tablet and laptop in the exact same spot she always has them. She sits to the right, accoutrements laid out to the left like an array of necessities to do her job correctly. And funnily enough, as I start unpacking my things, too, I end up putting them out just as precisely opposite her, never questioning my positioning either.

It makes me giggle beneath my breath, imaging Blaine and his craft. It's the same really, isn't it? We have little warmth for our craft now either. We write; that's it. There's no sense of confusion or mess anymore.

We don't live our characters in the same way we used to, scrawling them onto paper and enjoying their passion as if it's our own. I can't remember the last time I cried when something happened to one of them, not like when I killed—figuratively speaking—my first one off. I might be immersed in my characters' stories, might even be feeling them to a degree, but I just don't bleed when I cut them like I used to. It's something I've been questioning lately. It makes no sense to just see it all as a workload without any connection to their feelings. I'm lacking in empathy, not something the old me used to be.

"What's another word for 'delineate'?" Bree asks, her hazel eyes peeping up at me above her screen.

"Present, outline, depict. Depends on context. Draw, sketch? Characterize, detail—"

"And there she is, the fucking synonym queen of New York," she very kindly cuts in, breaking me from the thesaurus that opens up in my head every time anyone asks questions like that. It's like a freight train rips through my head, granting me each and every connection to any word that has anything to do with the particular phrase mentioned. Sometimes I wish I could shut the bloody thing off. I hardly missed a beat out of writing my own story as I answered her either. I just kept writing, not even looking at what my fingers were describing. You'd think it would be useful for a writer. Actually it is, I suppose, but it's the damn noise that drives me mad sometimes. It's never quiet in there. Never. There are no breaks from being a storyteller, not for me anyway. People talk of writer's block; well, I've never experienced it. Never. If I didn't work so hard on putting barriers around the stories, I'd be quite insane. I think it's why I don't feel the hunger in the substance anymore, maybe because I can't afford the emotional turmoil. At some point I put those barriers in place purposefully, making the characters stay in their boxes where they're contained and malleable for when I need them next.

"Pitch?"

"Slope, slant, incline. Modulation, frequency, tonality." *Tone.*

Mr. Jacobs certainly has a lovely tone. Its texture is like satin, with a sense of down covering the final endnote. I'd write it as lulling you maybe, or tempting. It has a calming quality, as if he's the master of his little universe and there isn't a thing anyone wants to do to leave it. In fact, it makes me question the sanity of the women under his hands in that place, or any other pair of hands, I suppose. Do they know what they're doing when they start off, or are they mesmerized into doing something simply because of the attractive men and their strange needs?

"I still don't understand why would anyone want to be whipped? Don't you find that odd?"

Bree's head pops up again, this time, actually for the first time today, her face appearing totally focused on my question.

"Yeah, I know. I've been thinking the same. I read that book by K D Ling the other month—The Enchantress—you know the one?" I nod, chastising myself for not getting round to studying the latest bestseller yet. "Her character explains it as a 'necessary requirement for expulsion'." I think I'm frowning, although my sense of intrigue at the statement makes me twitch in my seat a little. I'm not sure why my backside's so interested in the thought. "Now, you know me, it's not my thing, but when you read the context of the story, she seems to have it spot on. Makes me wonder if there really is something to it, ya know?"

"Do we know if she's in the scene? K D, I mean?"

"Well, Zachary Creed seems friendly with her, and we know he is, or at least he was when I saw him at the Book Bonanza Memphis Signing last year."

Zachary Creed is this last year's newbie on the block, bringing with him an instant bestseller, which launched him to stratospheric heights in the indie world. I know him, vaguely. I even thought about interviewing him for this next book, but we try not to pick each other's brains about context until we're closely linked friendship wise, like Bree and I. His book is damn good, though. Gives me an idea he does know what he's talking about, or he's done what I'm currently doing and researched hard. Although, in this world, one never really knows. It's not like any of us have ever seen each other in action. Most of us only know what the others portray, and the social media world is full of people pretending to be into BDSM. Apparent Doms creep out of the woodwork daily. Dick pics, dirty messenger conversations, and of course, the ever loving arseholes who like to skulk around in group conversations, dropping their pearls of wisdom. It's become a sad state of affairs on most days for me, making me feel incredibly uncomfortable with the whole scene in general and its ability to cajole. It's difficult enough having a penname of my own as a man. That in itself makes me feel like a fraud. It's something that tugs heartstrings I'd almost forgotten about, on occasion, making me question the whole set up, but at least I don't pretend to be a Dom and manipulate women.

However, regardless of my feelings associated, I am, have become, nothing more than a business lately, and readers flock to this new sense of adventure. It proves the fact that marketing wise it's a relevant strategy. And who am I to blame anyone who wants a little excitement in their lives? I don't have that right at all. That is, at the end of the day, what us writers should be writing for, to create passion and engagement, to give someone a new world to play in and enjoy. Something I appear to have lost lately. But what does infuriate me is the fact that this could all be so wrong. It annoys me that these pretend people could be getting the context and situation incorrect, inadvertently misleading readers into believing the scene is something that it's not. That's why I'm researching properly. I want to know the reality of what it gives these people. Why they do what they do. Why they need it, or apparently find comfort in it. I mean, why would anyone?

Chapter 2

ALANA

For whatever reason, our conversation on the matter seems to stop as we both drift back off into our stories. I'm not sure what Bree's currently working on, but I'm in the middle of a passionate but sweet love-making scene. Melany is about to lose her virginity to Gerald, who has been wooing her into the sack for the last few weeks. It's worked, and she's about to drop her drawers with little thought to the fact that she's not on contraception, but then Gerald is desperate for a family because his own first wife couldn't have children before she was sadly taken from the planet by way of a car accident. If I'm honest, it's the same story I've written for the last few years with Valerie. Different characters, different circumstances, but basically the same. Everyone wants a happily ever after in romance. It's the description of the atypical story. Man and woman meet, they fall in love through difficult circumstances, something happens that threatens their wellbeing, and then there's a happy ending. You can't write romance without a happy ending. Everyone has to be happy. If they're not, it's suspense. Or you can now be deemed dark romance if you want, which allows a little leeway with complete happiness. Valerie's more Mills and Boon, ready to fly the kite for anyone who wants to feel gooey by the end of the story.

I'm just finishing up my last line in chapter twenty-two as Blaine Jacobs arrives back in my head again, confusing me with his oh so calm demeanour. He seems so far removed from every other Dom I've read to research the genre. Apart from a few, anyway.

"Why are so many of these stories written about a Dom who's unbalanced? You know, bad upbringing, fucked up childhood, abusive parents etc." I don't lift my head or bother to look at Bree as I ask the question. We don't do that. We're both perfectly capable of multitasking our way through several things at the same time and retaining information. When we're interested enough.

"Everyone loves a truly bad boy, Lana. You'd know that if you ever dropped you panties below your knees for longer than ten minutes." What the actual fuck? My head shoots up at her, almost to the point of lifting myself off the bench. "And before you start," she continues, still not lifting her head so I can slap the face she's not showing me as she keeps writing. "I don't mean those stupid one nighters you do. You think you can assess depth from a one-night affair? Some would say you don't even know sex from the occasional quickie in some hotel room."

"Listen, Bree. I've had just about enough of your digging. I have sex. Often. Just because I don't choose to share it with you all the time doesn't mean that…" She lifts her head, a wry smile plastered across her lips as she pushes the laptop to the side and inches herself towards my end of the bench.

"Don't get those panties in a knot, now. You know I don't give a shit how you get your kicks, but if you want to know the substance of why the ladies love these big, bad bdsm boys, you need to understand how that particular variety affects the psyche." Why does she always do that? My irritated backside is instantly deflated into accepting mode again, reminding me that she is my best friend and, as always, she's mostly right.

"Okay, I sort of see your point. But I can't seriously have to get involved with this shit to be able to write a good book about it. Surely? I'm doubting Cassandra Evels has ever seen the broad end of a belt, and she managed that trilogy that sold off the charts."

She stands up with a sigh, digging out her wallet and pointing at the drinks vendor over in the corner of the square.

"You want a tea?" I nod, grabbing five dollars from my black trench coat and offering it to her, but she waves it off. "You need to have a hard think, Lana. 'Cause I'm thinking if you wanna get this right, you're gonna have to give the reader something a little different. This shit ain't some romance level that Valerie can sweet-talk her way through." That's the last thing I want to write, again. I want the excitement as much as readers do, but this, really?

"Seriously? You really think I should ask him to help me understand it in that way?" She smirks then dives into her phone, flicking through something until she holds up her screen at me.

"See that? That's my PA's account." She's one of her own PA's, even though she has a different name for that. It's very confusing. She swipes left, showing me a picture of a fully erect piece of manhood on display. "I don't know about you, but I get those daily, mostly along with some depiction or description of Dom like connotations." I roll my eyes at the thought. "Don't you want to tell a real story and know that you did your bit to help the real scene hold its own in the middle of this craze? 'Cause I'm thinking this shit ain't real."

"But that doesn't mean I have to—"

"Yeah, it does, Lana. Or I could slap you seven ways from Sunday so you know what pain feels like, but I doubt you'll get the same sexual thrill when I do it, ya know?"

She walks off after that, leaving me with my mouth hanging open as I try to find a sensible reproach to her argument. Sexual thrill. It's plainly outlandish. I'm not sure anybody gets a sexual thrill out of anything that happens in those places. It's more likely that they simply appease the man's need to be savage in some way. Men are, after all, hunters who are now limited to what a civilized world has persuaded them into. I mean, we all become a little on the excitable front when we have sex, throwing caution to the wind while saying and doing things that would normally be frowned upon. A nip on the neck, the occasional scratch here and there. We don't, however, strap each other into apparatus and beat each other with leather, no matter how bored we may have become. And it's not surprising it's mainly women who seem to take the brunt of this pain. We have a higher pain tolerance. That's fact. Still, it doesn't compute as logical or acceptable in my mind. And it certainly doesn't strike me, excuse the pun, as appealing in any way, regardless of this strange thing that happens around Chanel dowsed men in suits. Blaine Jacobs included.

"So, is it going to be me or him?" Bree says, dumping a takeaway cup down in front of me. My mouth is still hanging open.

"Because if it's going to be me, I need to gym it a bit. You're a big girl."

"Screw you. I am not."

Well, I am, but that's not the point. She laughs.

"Screw you back. You're touching six foot in those heels, and most definitely built for comfort."

I could be offended, but the raise of her brow as she performs some sort of pumping motion with her hips has me giggling before I've had time to close my mouth again.

"I am not built for comfort."

"You're not built for anything if you don't let something fuck you better than your one nighters do. Let him beat the story into you."

"Jesus, Bree."

She spits out another laugh and wanders herself around to her side of the bench again, sipping her hot chocolate as she goes. Which is topped with extra marshmallows and cream. Not that I'm jealous or anything.

"What's his name?"

"Not telling."

"Suggest you keep your mouth closed better next time. Blaine sounds intriguing."

"What the fuck?"

"You mumbled it."

"I did not."

"Yeah, ya did. When you were writing sex. It was all breathy and shit," she says, leaning her arms onto the table and grinning from ear to ear.

"I did not breathily moan out his name." I didn't.

"I didn't say anything about moaning. You're moaning about him, too?" I'm not winning this argument any time soon. I can tell. She's gone into attack mode. "He's cute, right?"

"Oh, fuck off," I splutter out, knowing nothing is going to stop the tirade of quick thinking perfection that falls from her mouth effortlessly when she's focused. And why does it matter if he's cute or not? It's not like there's any way I'm going to concede to this ludicrous reasoning regardless of his looks, no matter the intrigue that's building. "I suppose he's attractive. Pleasant in an impassive way." Which is an outright lie, one that makes me squirm to avoid looking at her, because he's absurdly good looking. A dream boat. The sort that makes girls believe they've won the damn lottery by just looking at his form. It's unfortunate for my well-being.

"And so the problem with fucking him is?"

"Do you have to be quite so crude about it?"

"Yep. No time for anything else." She's got a point. It's one that makes me sigh as she taps her fingers on her hot chocolate cup and she tilts her head at me. "Look, Lana, you've got one shot at making a new pen in this game. You know the crack. Fuck it up and you're a no one. You wanna run the risk of that?"

"Of course not," is my reply, as I sigh again, barely able to think coherently about the pressure that would cause to mount up. It's already enough that I can't move, think, or attempt anything other than what I need to do. Heaping more burden onto what I just about manage would be an impossibility. I'm almost done as it is, let alone adding more into the fold. There's just too much noise lately. It's all becoming too much.

"So, what's the plan?" I look back at her, neither knowing the answer nor understanding my want to throw this laptop I'm hovering over into the trash.

"You're really going to make me do this?"

"I'm not making you do anything. I'm just telling you what a sensible writer who wants to write the best book possible already knows," she says, shifting her body back along the bench so she can get behind her laptop again. Bitch. "We heading for seven or eight K today?"

Words. Eight thousand words. They seem so much easier than the thought of research all of a sudden, and yet so much harder than they've ever been before.

"Ten." With any luck, one of us will have come up with a better plan than me fucking the Dominant for research purposes by the end of it, hopefully proving it unnecessary.

~

Neither of us came up with a better plan than originally suggested by the time we had finished our sprint. In fact, I didn't even achieve six thousand words by the time she'd hit the target. The very thought of being strung up seemed to interfere with writing in a major way, which is interesting in itself. I can't remember anything interfering with writing for a long time, short of boredom. I've spent so long doing it now I don't even think about it that much. It just flows without real engagement. It's the editing that takes thought and true substance. Today, though, sitting at that bench and beginning to give real thought to letting him touch me, well, that threw all normal behaviour out of the window. Of course, that amused Bree no end. I heard her snickering to herself every time my hand hovered over the keyboard mid-stream. And, I swear to God she kept saying his name just to build the impetus, or I did.

Now we're here in my apartment, getting ready for a Publisher's Awards Convention at Carnegie Hall tonight. Bree's going as my partner, because I don't have anyone else I'd rather take, and because she, being indie and a woman writing as a man, which no one knows about, doesn't get to go to these things any other way. I'm not sure what she gets out of the experience. It's not like she wants a publisher. I think she just likes being around the writer types, even though she doesn't give out any information about who she is or what she does.

"You know, I don't think you get to fuck the Dominant. I think he gets to fuck you," she says, mid-way through yanking on a slim fitting black dress. "Pretty sure that's the way it works."

"Oh, for Christ's sake. Enough with the damned topic," is my slightly snippy response.

The more I've thought about it, and the more she's peppered the evening with comments about it, the more I'm thinking about just jacking the idea off as ill thought out. I cannot seriously contemplate screwing a man for research. It's ludicrous. I may have gotten ideas in my other one-night stands on occasion, but fiddling in this type of thing is not up my alley at all, regardless of my intrigue that keeps biting my arse. I mean, what idiot would do that for a book? Some of them are sadists—him included apparently. I'm pretty sure that involves huge amounts of pain, and bleeding, and things I don't even think are acceptable for humanity.

I pick up the end of my green evening gown, shrugging the end of the silk out to ensure it flows properly behind me before slipping my feet into my matching Louboutin's.

"It's not normal, Bree."

"Neither's your ass in that dress." What the hell's wrong with my arse in this dress? I swing around to her, just about managing to contain my breasts in the little covering they have.

"Why? What's the matter with it?"

"It's…obscene." This is a concern coming from Bree, given that she is happy to have anything on show most of the time. "The fuck have you strapped that in?"

I storm directly back into the one bedroom I have and try to get a good look at the back of myself in the full length mirror. Okay, it's fitted, probably a little more so since the last time I wore it given the amount of sitting on my arse I do, but it's not obscene. The boob thing is a little more worrying to be frank, as I pull on the halter-neck, trying to arrange them into some semblance of order.

"I'm more worried about my nipples escaping."

"I'm not. They could do with some licking. Your ass gets plenty of that most of the time."

"It does not."

"Does, too. You're going to be fawned over all night. Queen fucking Du Font, literary goddess of the romance world."

Sadly, she's right. At twenty-seven, I'm beginning to hit a rising peak in my career. I'm tried and tested, and so far I've had three offers from other big publishing houses to sign with them next time round, which is in six month's time. It's the main reason there's so much arse licking going on, something I despise for my own reasons. I'm starting to feel like a fraud at these events, one who simply puts fingers to keyboards and tells the same old same old because my publisher makes me do it that way. It's what the reader appears to want, well, wants from Valerie anyway, but I'm getting jaded with it for all the same reasons I thought would make it easier. Somethings changed since the first few I wrote. I can't work out what, or why, but something has. It's becoming more apparent every day. It's just a sea of the same words, synonyms changing the meaning on occasion, but fundamentally just a blur of similarity. And each and every time I try to go outside their boundaries, change the story or offer a different perspective, they damn well halt me.

"You know I'm not interested in that," I eventually huff out, making one final rearrangement to my boobs and turning back to her. "Hair?"

"Looks groovy. I'm digging the new purple tones." So am I. I don't know why I did them—perhaps its escapism, because writing doesn't appear to be providing that anymore, but blonde just seemed boring all of a sudden, and straight even more so.

"You like the curls?"

"Yep. For a white chick they look funky."

There's only one person in the world who could call me a white chick and get away with it. Breana Jenkins is that person, and she only does it because she's mixed race. Actually, that's not why she gets away with it. She gets away with it because she's my friend. Other than that, I hate all forms of separation in colour, creed or religion. I hate the sense that we even notice ourselves as different to each other. We're human, and should live happily together without allocating borders around ourselves. When I first started talking to Bree online I didn't even know her colour, or his at the time because I thought she was a man, obviously. It wasn't until he suggested a meet that I eventually found out who *she* was. It was the most bizarre meeting I've ever had, and to this day I don't really know why she decided to 'come out' to me in particular, other than the fact that we live close to each other, which she only knew as Manhattan when we first started talking. Anyway, meeting a black woman when I thought I was meeting a white man was highly amusing, and at the time made me question her choice of pen. We've since talked it through quite thoroughly, and it seems she doesn't sell as well as a black man. Her figures prove that point succinctly, which fucking annoys me no end, but I suppose that's still the world we live in. My aunt was black, and I watched the taunting my dad's family got because of it in a rural community, so I know how small-minded the world can still be. She's gone now, as is my uncle, but that doesn't stop the memory of it reminding me how closed people are sometimes.

    The thought makes me hover, suddenly unsure of my reaction to Blaine and the scene I'm researching. Have I been unfair? Made it seem as though I believe it a joke, or something that should be frowned upon for its eccentricity? I'm instantly disgusted with myself, my insides boiling at the very idea of discrimination of a kind. I stare blankly into the mirror, listening to my thoughts on his world, recanting words I've said to him, questions I've asked. I aimed for professional, needing to show my sense of control and ability, proving he and his world doesn't fluster me, but now, thinking back, did I just come across as rude? Shit.

"What's up?" Bree asks, for some reason slapping her cheeks as she stands in the doorway watching me. I'm a bitch, that's what's up. I've turned into a bitch. When the hell did that happen? It makes me shake my head and brush my dress down again, hopefully getting rid of the bitch lingering about that I do not understand at all.

"Why are you doing that?" I ask, deflecting the topic from my thoughts.

"It's like natural rouge."

"Oh, right." Interesting technique, seems like I could do with some of it myself. "You sure you don't want to go experiment in this BDSM world for me?"

"Fuck that. I'm not an idiot."

"And I am?"

"You're the one writing the book. How are you doing with that, anyway?"

I turn away from the mirror, grabbing my bag as I go and checking my earrings and boobs are secure for the last time, as we wander back into the lounge. How am I doing with it? I lift my glass of Champagne and stare out of the window to gaze at the facing buildings. Well, it's drafted, plotted. The story is sort of secure. It's just the practical nature of the acts I've described that I need more assistance with, if they're even possible. That, and the fact that I have no comprehension of what the feelings associated with the scenes or acts are.

"Fine, really. I'm not all that sure I need his input to finish it correctly."

She snorts behind me, reminding me that she is not a fool, I cannot lie to her, and that if I try, I will be burnt at the stake as she cackles gloriously.

"Right. Let's see then," she says, as I hear her footsteps move somewhere. I swing round, my feet ambling towards my office behind her as I continue to chastise my thoughts. I'm a bitch, it's an inconceivable thought to me. I don't even know where it's come from. Has it built? Become a part of me because of the pressure I'm under. I don't know. By the time I turn into the room, she's already staring at my open laptop, flicking through files to find a BDSM story.

"That's private," I mutter, leaning on the doorframe with no real intention of trying to stop her. It's a buried file; she'll never find it, and anyway, it's not even titled.

"Do you really have a novel called 'The Western Way'?" she says, chuckling to herself and scanning one of my current works. "Is Valerie now doing old school westerns? Jesus, Lana."

"It's in resurgence. Gotta keep up with the flow, Bree."

"You are so bored," she says, turning back to me, picking up my notes from the side of the desk and skimming through them, too. "And what's this 'gasping' section about?" Ah, the gasp. I smirk at her, finally enjoying the thought of a smile and shaking my head as I head back out of the office. "Gasping? Did Blaine make you gasp?"

Yes. Yes, he did. On a few occasions, regardless of how proficient I attempted to remain. I didn't even feel the gasps until they erupted from my mouth, giving away any element of professionalism I was hoping for. I still can't quite put my finger on why. It's the way he moves, I think. Slow, disciplined, as if he's so comfortable with his every thought that his whole purpose is to make someone else feel insecure.

"Of course not, Bree. It was a professional meeting. Nothing happened." Although, at this moment, and after several self-conversations about it, I'm beginning to question just how much of an impact he's having on my lucidity.

"Where?"

"What?" I'm stalling. I know what she said. I'm just attempting to direct the conversation away from the really quite seedy place I spent the morning in. "I think the cab's here. Shall we go down?"

With that, I don't give her time to question, dig, or even keep up with me as I grab my keys, take a quick glance in the mirror to check my eye make-up, which is pretty damn good for me, and then head out of the door for the waiting cab.

I've given up on the subway here. I cab everywhere at night or walk during the day. Frankly, the few times I tried when I first got here were fine apart from learning a new system, but then I did a few journeys late at night, missing stops and eventually ending up in places I didn't know. It scared the shit out of me as junkies hung around, watching me hurry through the stations and following me until I found some light again, hoping for the cops to be present. After the first bag snatch, and the next week's inappropriate gesturing from some man in a long mac, I made a vow to never use the things again, and certainly not at night.

"No amount deflecting is going to make me give up on this conversation, ya know?" she says as she catches up with me. I keep heading for the car, descending the steps from my two-apartment brownstone to the pavement.

"Remind me to send my edits back tomorrow, will you?" I say, once again trying to avoid her topic as I reach for the cab door. "I'm late with book three."

That's all I've currently got as she shifts the tail of my dress over so that she can get in behind me. I smile over at her as she raises her brow and waits for more of an answer, one she won't get. It's not that I don't want to talk about it. It's more that I need her to be more honest about her reasoning. She's not talking about me fucking a dominant because she wants me to write a good book. It's because she thinks I need a man in my life. I don't. I'm self-sufficient and happy that way. I've tried relationships, and they don't work for me. Men can be needy. They get clingy when you don't message them constantly. Stroking their egos as well as their dicks is apparently a necessity. Not for me, it's not. And there's not one part of me that wants to be tied down so I can fall in love and have babies. It's not the way I'm built, not now anyway. Maybe once upon a time I was, but whatever that dream was has gone along with the quirky version of me that used to exist. And besides, when you write romance for a living, as well as crime thrillers, what's a man got to offer in the way of excitement? I know it all already. There isn't a story, romantic interlude, situation, or happily ever after I haven't already written. I know all the endings. I know all the one-liners. I know all the ways men sweep you off your feet. I've told their stories a thousand times and every one of them I've ever had sex with has tried the exact same stories to lull me into a relationship of some sort. I don't want that. I don't want a man who thinks those cheese-ridden one-liners engage me. They don't. They make me roll my eyes in abhorrence, forcing my thighs to close the instant they open their mouths.

"What's the harm in fucking someone who's good looking and could give you a new experience?" she says as the cab pulls away for our journey.

Well, there is that school of thought, I suppose. Still, my non-plussed expression doesn't change as I watch her pull out her make up bag and start applying, because she hasn't done it yet. She was too busy answering emails and getting ready for her release to concern herself with looking perfect for these people. "I mean, you're the one always complaining that men are boring. What was the last thing you said? That they couldn't come up with originality if they were offered it free of charge?"

Yes, I did say that. I say that sort of thing a lot. It's entirely true on most occasions. "Perhaps this Blaine guy can show you something original?"

I don't doubt it. It would also be painful from what I saw of that poor woman strung up into some sort of torture position, and worrying for cleanliness given the sticky carpets.

"They really do hang people in those places. Did you know that?"

"What?"

"Hang them. From the ceiling. On hooks. They use carabiners and then they wrap ropes around the skin to create patterns. Shibari. Kinbaku." She looks a little shocked. I don't know why. She's read some of the books I've read. "And if you're not in to that then you can have a 'gimp mask' put around your face as someone pulls you across the floor for others to pee on." She pulls a rather nauseated expression, the same one I tried not to use when I saw it happening to a man right in front of me. "Mmm. Also, I touched the implements they use to cause pain. It's not Victoria Secrets' version, I can promise you. They're solid pieces. It's not a pleasure thing at all from what I can tell." Her frown has become more distressed than amused. "Still think I should let him show me?"

"Well..."

"Oh, and there's a place called 'The Pit' where you earn your right to be called a member. Can you guess what happens in there?"

"I'm not sure I want to."

"Let me tell you. It's apparently exciting, and the highest form of honour for a submissive." She shifts her weight around, giving me just a few moments of feeling superior in front of Bree's normal devil-may-care attitude to life. "You've already guessed, haven't you? Fucking happens. Lots of fucking. Men. Women. They all fuck the submissive, as if it's their divine right in the middle of their hedonistic fun to initiate the newbie." She frowns again, looking me up and down, probably trying to gauge my interest in such a strange initiation process.

"But surely that's not the only way? There are too many stories of committed couples and collaring. Isn't that the true BDSM lifestyle?

I thought that's what you were researching." So did I. Unfortunately, that's not what was presented. And, thinking back, it's no wonder I may have been bitchy about its atmosphere.

"Well, not according to Mr. Jacobs, who, from what I know so far, is one of the most respected Dominants in this particular club. He told me nothing of committed lifestyles or realistic endeavours. It just seemed like a den of iniquity to me." Although, he didn't seem quite right in that particular den. Still doesn't as I visualise him there, his body moving as calmly as a gentle wind through trees, completely opposed to some of the other men's loud, aggressive behaviour. He was, perhaps is, above what I witnessed. At least different to it somehow.

The statement appears to shut her up, thank god. It gives me a little time to attempt to rid the man from my mind as we continue through the streets. Tonight is reasonably important to Valerie's future. I've lined up a few discreet conversations with other publishers, all of which will have to happen away from my current publisher who will hover endlessly around me—either him or his son anyway. Oh god, I hope it's not the son. I'll have to endure the entire evening with him leering at me while I try to keep his fingers from my arse. It won't be fun. In fact, it hasn't been for the last few I've been too. It's becoming nothing but hard work, frankly. The events are filled with sycophants and bootlickers, none of whom have the foggiest clue who *I* am, what *I* want, or why *I've* become the person I have. They don't care about me in the slightest, not Alana anyway. All they care about is Val and how much money she can make them, or what being her friend might bring them. It's so damn exhausting. Even now I can feel the anxiety rising, telling me something is so very wrong with all of this. It makes me dig into my bag, sighing at the thought of yet another thing I'm struggling with and pulling out some of my happy pills. They'll help at least; mixed with some of this champagne, they'll do wonders to make this evening seem acceptable. Perhaps I should just get blotto and make my own fun, let the professionalism ebb out of me so I can just be me for a night, at least try to find me again. Bree can join in, no problem there. She finds the whole thing snot worthy most of the time.

"Did you bring your hipflask?" I ask, turning to see her applying her last layer of lipstick, my fingers reaching for her bag as I get two pills out.

"Yep."

Good.

Chapter 3

BLAINE

The pattern's as striking as it always is, intricately carving its way into flesh and enhancing the taste, but it holds no sense of realism. It labours in my mouth, less venomous than a snake in flight and as diluted in flavour as blended Scotch. It's cheap, weakened by overuse, and tainted with the scent of every other man who's fucked it lately. My fingers push the girl away, wiping my chin and running my tongue across my lips in search of something more palatable. She lingers patiently on the bench long after I've stalked back to my seat, waiting for another to enjoy his place at the feast I've delivered for them. Feast— it's such a desolate term. Nothing is worth feasting on. It's all empty, vacuous. Barely edible in reality. It stains my tongue, wrenching at old desires and haunting me with thoughts not meant for this innocuous venue.

Another man gets up and moves to the girl, his mouth open as he leans between her legs and begins his ministrations. I'd show him how to do it more effectively if I could be bothered, but I can't. This is a celebration of acceptance, one I've announced myself for all these students to enjoy. Why they think it's something to celebrate, I don't know. Some of them are Doms and some of them sadists in the making, ones who are yet to unfurl their hands on anything until I'm ready to let them.

That's all I do now, use this experience behind me to teach management and skills. It's containment, essentially. Something I used to get an amount of pleasure out of it. I'd grade their abilities against my own, remembering what I used to do and enjoying the weight of the thought. Perhaps allowing someone else to use their inclinations for me on occasion, relish its sound as it cracked the air, but now it's all as blunted as the thoughts I make myself labour in. They haunt the back of my mind, taunting me with visuals and images of sickening need, making me weak for my own desires. However, they're also the same sentiments that force my own repression into human familiarity, a rare aggressive kink allowed to break through and show amusement maybe, or debasement depending on your standpoint, but basically I'm now normal again, at least a pretence of it given my new career choice.

Still, teaching I can do. It's a tool I know well. I understand it. Bask in it. I enjoy its monotonous drone each day, maybe as a determination of self-worth, sanctioning it a draw on my own opinion of demonstrability in the middle of others' chaos. Teacher. Entertainer. Deliverer. All life has become is a ritual of empty encounters and hollow engagement, all of which facilitates the sense of emptiness to consume thought more and more by the day.

I sigh and shift in my seat a little, noting the dim lights that bounce around the room's sparsely populated interior. Five men in total, two women, one a Domme and the other an aged and appreciated sub, who is moaning her approval at the current guy's efforts. I'd rather fuck the guy—not that I'm gay, but the fact that Adam's a virgin to anal means the experience would be gratifying. Tight. I ponder the thought, arguing with myself about the uproar it might cause for me to unleash just a little temper into the space after all this time nurturing the brave. They've yet to see a sadist in full flight, any of them. I've refused them the privilege, not broaching the subject in fear of them pushing for answers I can't give. Not anymore, not after her.

A screech of orgasm crashes into the room, the little sub squirming as she tries, in vain, to break her bonds. She won't; I've taught the Domme too well, invested time with her when she showed an aptitude for rope work, met her often to enhance her skills. If I'm honest, she's the best one in here. The best Dominant, too, regardless of the heavier set men. She has a career in front of her should she choose it—lithe frame, accentuated by long arms that hold a crop firmly, and legs that broach athlete's standards when she crushes within them. She's good. Fuckable too. And she always has a high ponytail mounted on her head, one I long to rip from her fucking skull while my dick's driving into her mouth.

Adam makes his way back to his seat, his dick straining at his pants and the sub's juices glistening on his lips as he smiles. Seems he's pleased with his performance. I'm not sure why. The sub's still smiling. She shouldn't be. Fucking is an art form that should leave both too exhausted to move and barely able to breathe, let alone damn well smile. Smiling is for fools and romantics. It's for those people who harbour nothing more than fanciful adoration and some passage of self-obsessed relevance. Adam should have taken his wants and given them to her with neither regret nor instruction. She is there to be used. The man knows what he is; he feels it just as I did all those years ago. He's a sadist. A true and brutal sadist by the look of his grip on most things he touches. It's the very reason his tongue's efforts are weak. He doesn't want to please the sub. He's not bothered if she comes or not. What he probably wants to do is strangle her, watching the way her eyes dilate as she begins to die, just so he can push her limits further each time he tries again. But people long for pride to be bestowed, sadists or not. They lavish themselves with goods and merchandise to build self-esteem, rendering their borrowed time on this fucking planet worthwhile in some way. They look for people to appreciate them, nodding their approval at valiant efforts, something I do as Adam looks at me, waiting for teacher's acknowledgement of success. It's hardly success, more a failure if truth be told, but it's my failure because of my own inadequacies, not because of Adam's.

The thought annoys me, so much so that I'm standing and hooking a finger at the guy before the next one gets up to engage his fancies with the sub.

"Is that all?" I ask, watching as Adam frowns and takes a step towards me. "Is that all you want from her?" Adam doesn't speak. He just continues frowning, presumably because of the question at hand. "Don't you want to watch the light go out?" I move towards the girl, wondering how much she's endured under true duress before now, having never pressed this particular one. "It's easy enough to do. Isn't that what you really want?" Adam's face hardens. I'm not sure if it's from acceptance or excitement, but, just for once, I'm going to drive the man forward into his oblivion, irrespective of his confusion on the matter. "Look."

It only takes a second or two to find her pressure points after asking permission by way of a nod. She frowns at first, but eventually returns the nod, her lips already parting at the thought as I wrap one hand around her neck. For the first time in a while, a true smile breaks across my face as the sensation surges inside my veins, unfettering impressions I've buried because of *her*. Adam looks stunned, his hand reaching forward as the sub begins to squeal in my grasp. "Watch her eyes brighten," I say, as my fucking cock remembers the connection even though I refuse to look at what's happening in my hand. I can't, won't. I'm barely able to contain the need to drive myself inside her now as she fights and writhes against my hold. "Then dim." The debilitation should I gaze into weakening eyes is just not an entertainment I can divert myself with, no matter how much I long to see the lights go out myself.

Adam takes a step closer, as does the Domme and one other man. I'm not surprised as I scan the remaining two who hover in the background. Their faces seem confounded, a look a sickness rising on one of them. Good, the shorter one needs hardening up. He's weak for a Dom, always hesitating and proving his insufficiency. He's probably a switch in reality, something I've not spent long enough investigating. Delaney would have a field day with the psychology going on in that mind, as would I if I could be bothered with the prosaic nature of the task. I can't, though. I can't be bothered with anything these days. I chuckle at the thought a little, bracing my fingers tighter as the sub tries to wiggle her way from my grasp, and then turning back to look at my favourite little Domme.

"How long can they last?" she asks, her hand running the length of the sub's leg and eventually landing by her cunt to finger her way in. "Before they choke out?" My eyes close as she speaks the words, barely restraining the need to help her feel the sensation so she can know it herself. Instead, I let the pent up breath exhale from my lungs and open my eyes again, slowly glancing over the leather-clad woman and wondering if she will fight as well as I hope.

"Not long."

It's the only answer I've got to ensure most of the room will look after those in their care. The truth is, most don't last long enough. Some do, though. My Eloise had. My little fuck toy had lasted as long as I needed every fucking time, giving me the time necessary to fulfil my wants on her skin. And she fought valiantly, too, her body scratching out at me as her heels kicked me on for longer. I can still feel her now as this little sub's pulse begins to increase in my fingers, her squeals dimming to near defeated. Her perfume still resonates so intensely in my mind it makes all other scents seem pallid in comparison, but with Eloise's scent comes the visions of her broken body, too.

My gaze turns to Adam as he starts rubbing himself against the bench. The man's movements become sharper as he loses himself in his moment, hips grinding with forceful intent. His face is ashen, probably doubting his own sanity in the middle of sexual asphyxiation, and then the inevitable happens, proving my earlier thoughts true. The man comes, quickly, his body shuddering against the surface as he flicks his eyes between throat and cunt for discharge. The visions makes me smile and release my grip of her little neck instantly, allowing the sub breath again and turning back to look at her as she gasps and gulps for air.

"Never do that without me in the room with you," I say, firmly, stroking the sub's hair and then leaning down to kiss her forehead out of duty. "Any of you." She smiles up at me, weakly, then does the same for Adam as he walks over and admires her efforts. At least Adam gives a damn about her efforts; hopefully it'll instil the respect I've aimed to teach him. I don't. She's barely managed seconds. Hardly worth my fucking time at all. "You're not ready until I say you are, Adam. Never. You understand?"

"That wasn't long," the Domme snaps, sneering at Adam and avoiding going anywhere near him as she approaches, disgust etching her every move. The comment makes me smirk at her attitude, forgetting Adam for a moment as I remind myself to show her something that will last a little longer when asked.

"You will get yourself in trouble one of these days, Constance," I reply, watching her clean her glove on a rag and then cross back to the sub again with a damp cloth. "She lasts well enough for the likes of you four." Constance tuts at me, her hand finding its way begrudgingly to the sub's forehead and brushing off the sweat as she pulls the ropes away. It's enough for my own dick to rear at her, the thought of wiping the aggressive little bitch into unconsciousness consuming any form of suitable I'm hanging onto.

"Enjoy your night," I eventually say, as I open the door, berating myself for every thought involving my body's cravings. Eight other subs walk in, two of whom would be best suited in orgies, but I'm doubting Adam will give a fuck what he gets up to this evening after watching that. The guys cock is probably already hard again as he eyes one of them up. "Adam, not without me." Adam scoffs, but he does nod as he grabs at one of them and pushes it to its knees.

So I leave, discomforted with my thoughts, and desperate to find something to alleviate the strain I've put myself under. My cock's as close as it has been in some time, and more than ready to grate against something unwilling given half a chance. It's not until I manage to push through the crush of other guests, avoiding eye contact with anything that offers itself on the stairs and ground levels, that I finally feel myself calming down. I groan at the images still passing through my mind, allowing them a few more moments before I need to rid my head of them again. Times past filter in as I push through the door onto the street, sucking in breaths for clarification of the facts. New York. Dirty at this end. It not like the clean living I grew up with, or the family who would have had me providing a certain standard of life. It's as I like it now, letting me be who I am without consequence, other than the obvious, anyway. And that's of my own making.

Brushing off the front of my shirt, I stare out into the night as my cock finally begins to shut the fuck up. It might as well have screamed for attention as it burst at my pants, ready to rut hell into something that could take it, or not. I still don't fucking care when the old mood takes hold, the same one I've just let loose for reasons unknown, regardless of how antagonistic the inclination. My muscles are currently hostility personified, just as I've asked of them. All it takes is that one pinch at a neck, just the shortness of breaths, the slight squeal of fear. Just one small offering, one surge of strength set free and it's all here again, reminding me of how it feels to give my all to a woman. The antipathy heaves through my veins as I button my jacket and look into traffic, barely noticing it for the thudding of my pulse against flesh. Its rapid acceleration reminds me of skin broken and stripes of glory slashed into pale white surfaces. I can feel my fingers itching to trace welts again, widen them. I can feel it all as if it were only yesterday, hear it hollowing the recesses in my mind. The tears, the screams, the clank of metal, the sharp flick of canes and leather, the ring of a well-placed spanking resonating like never before. Over and over again, the sounds embed themselves, almost to the point of me turning back around and walking straight back into the building. It makes me lick my lips and swing my gaze to the door as it opens, just willing it to be another offering. It wouldn't take much now. I'm more than ready to give in to the noise consuming rational thought. However, instead of something useful, Richard walks out with his harem of whores hanging onto him as they head for an array of taxis.

"Blaine," Richard says, nodding his customary good night.

I don't reply. Richard's nothing but a high end car salesman with only the slightest penchant for rough and ready, something proved by the used models currently waving their cheap assess about for the world to ogle. Still, they'll be useful for slashing if this mood doesn't remove itself sooner or later. Perhaps two of them could be stitched together, their skin clamped via staples so as to broaden the landing of the whip. The thought makes me smile, imagining the squeals that would emanate should I get the chance to try. Something tells me Richard won't stick around for the viewing pleasure, as one of the whores grins back, waving her fingers at me inanely. If he did stay, he'd violate the floor with a stench best left for the inside of a person's guts. I raise a brow at the image, wondering what I can do with the thought and letting it idle as I watch the five of them get into their taxis, the one girl hanging back for another chance at flirtation. It amuses me as I let her enjoy her moment, all the time sizing up her weight, the distance it will take to catch her should she run, the amount of blood she has in her veins and how long it might take to drain from her should I choose that type of fun. The images make my damned cock rear up again, enough for me to look down at it with a smile and then press its girth to help alleviate the throb. She giggles, her finger hovering around her lips and then dipping inside, finger fucking her mouth and causing my feet to move towards her. It wouldn't hurt to have a few minutes. She'll come back inside, I'll do what I need to and then I can give her to one of the others to tidy up. Or perhaps I'll just leave her on the floor, bleeding out and screaming. Who gives a fuck? Cheap whores are ten a penny and not worth any more than the fucking she's asking for. Used, tired. She'll probably beg for the end when someone finally dims her entirely, sending her skank ass into the ground below.

Thank fuck for my brother, the one who will be here any minute now. The thought stops my impetus before I enter territory deemed unsuitable these days. She's nothing but another cunt, not even a particularly attractive one. Not that that has ever stopped me previously, but tastes refine with age. Few are worth tasting anymore, and even fewer worth risking my wrath on. They don't endure enough, don't connect. Their eyes are all as insipid as their flavours. Lifeless, showing nothing but vacant dispositions and blank willingness. This one would be more use to Cole, who would fuck her and then leave five thousand dollars on her body after the act, something he sees as a thank you for services rendered.

The car pulls up just as I'm stepping backwards from the woman, the distance between us more relevant than she knows. A few more steps and I might not have stopped. Another suck of her fingers and she might well have ended up in that back alley just behind the building, her lungs bellowing out the sounds of whores as I drove my fingers into every hole she has.

"Fucked anything yet?" I quietly slide myself into the car, dismissing the woman's still grinning face and closing my eyes to help me concentrate on my cock's excitement.

"You know I haven't touched anything for over a year." Not with any real sense of need, anyway. Nothing has been appeased. I haven't been able to dispense my venom on a woman since Eloise, which my cock still reminds me of as I will it down, again.

"For Christ's sake, Blaine. Why the hell not?"

I shake my head at Cole, wishing it were as simple as that. Unfortunately, people who aren't heavily involved in the scene have little knowledge of the actualities of it. Control is paramount when dispensing needs such as mine. A well-rounded, level head. One that's happy to deliver content to willing recipients, ensuring sense prevails. What's not needed is a screwed up sense of sadism, coupled with the memories of what happens when situations are plundered past wisdom's boundaries. The only things I play with lately are Dominants, new ones who require training, and even they fill me with tedium. Pretty boys turning up, pretending their little hands can deliver stripes warranting terms they neither understand nor are willing to totally employ. It is, has become, mind numbing. A point proved by the irrational act in that room I've just engaged in.

The clubs have become nothing more than moneymaking pits—somewhere I arrive into, teach, and then leave. They're somewhere reprobates wave their dicks around in to gain some kind of distinction, perhaps hoping for a sense of fulfilment. It isn't the scene anymore. Not truly. Yes, there is fucking, plenty of it, and multiple partners, and any kind of need you have will more than likely be fulfilled, but there isn't any sense of collaboration anymore. Not like it should be. Not like it was when *she* was there to temper my flow.

"It doesn't work like that," I mumble to myself, staring out into the night and just willing the car home before Cole starts with his 20 fucking questions again.

"Why not?"

The question makes me sigh and tune him out, not caring for yet another discussion on why I should or should not be fucking something. Why I ever bothered telling him I don't fuck anymore is confounding in itself. It's none of Cole's business who I fuck or when. The fact that I haven't had my dick inside anything for over a year isn't a discussion I need to have with my little brother, the same little brother who is eternally screwing anything that moves with little regard for the consequences.

"Melinda still pregnant, is she?"

"Don't start that bullshit," Cole barks, groaning out his sarcasm as the car pulls towards Park Avenue and begins speeding up. "I'm just worried, Blaine. It'd be nice to see you happy for a change. Get rid of a little tension."

I close down completely at the mention of happiness. I'm not worthy of it, nor remotely interested in feeling it. Happiness is for people who love and enjoy, not for empty shells of humans who barely consider life acceptable anymore. Certainly not for ones who have done what I have.

"Am I taking you to home or shall we go out and—"

"Home," I cut in, my eyes opening as we round corners.

Not that it is home. The place I call home now is far out of Manhattan, but this place does the job while I have to be here. The only other place I want to go to right now, I've recently banned myself from going to. I don't expect my self-imposed abstinence from going there will last all that long—the draw will be too strong—but for now it seems to be having an impact on my stability.

Cole nods, realising the brotherly conversation is well and truly finished as we carry on in silence, cruising the streets to get us back to the apartment. Until undisciplined adolescence takes over again, that is, interrupting my peace once more.

"How long is this going to go on for?" For fucks sake.

I sigh again, blowing the breath from my lungs and closing my eyes again in the hope that it will stop the constant badgering. As long as it needs to. As long as I want it to. Maybe forever. Who fucking knows? As far as I can tell at the moment, nothing is any better than it was eighteen months ago. Life is stalled. I'm neither moving forward nor suffering in the past. I just am. Stagnant. Lifeless.

"You know, Annie Renforth is still—"

"Stop, Cole," I grate out, quietly.

As if little Annie is the answer to any of this. I don't need an old high-school sweetheart interfering in my life, especially one who is too sad and lonely to find herself another dick to play with, let alone play with the sort I've got to offer her.

"I killed her, Cole. You think me doing another one in will help?"

That would shut the fucker up if I had the front to say it. Not that I truly did, not physically, although I still snarl at the reasoning. It doesn't matter how many times sense is applied to the situation; it isn't true. She's dead, and it's because of me. Her life was taken from the planet because she agreed to participate in the sordid capacities of my mind, loved me for it even. I close my eyes again and listen to the memory of her breathing beside me instead of arguing his point, her frame filling the gap I'd always left open before her. It wasn't love for me. It never had been, but it was something I'd never found before. Contentment perhaps. A body that would take me, offering me no consequences for the magnitude of my wants and desires. She'd needed it as much as me, begged me to give her more on every encounter, but then the day came when it was all too much.

My career had been ruined that day. My life, destroyed. Hers, obliterated.

"Perhaps if you talked to a psychiatrist about…"

I tune my brother out further, rendering the conversation obsolete and just giving her the memories she deserves, because now there is nothing but solitude, the pretence of amusement, and the haunted memories of her skin against mine. I'm not maudlin in the after effects like some lovers would. I didn't love her. Why would I have done? She was just a student, a beautiful one, yes, but just one who fell into the wrong pair of hands regardless of how much I tried to deny them. She'd been as screwed up as me, a godsend in some ways. Someone who held my hand and told me it was acceptable to be who I am. It wasn't, not with her anyway. I should have been stronger and pushed her away, perhaps been more of the man I am today. Controlled.

It hadn't been until after the event that I'd met Delaney, and then all that came with him. The man had given me a sense of realism, sadly all too late for Eloise's life. Still, at least I've learnt now to appease my nature in other ways, keeping the truly sadistic thoughts inside my mind rather than unleashing them on society. Mostly. "Or maybe just fucking something else might make whatever the fuck's going on in your head better?"

The statement rouses my attention again and forces me to finally make eye contact with Cole, hoping that my glare attached might stop the ramblings of a youngster in heat. What does he know of fucking? Nothing. Cole knows how to drive his dick inside something until his come drains out. That's all. It's not unlike the way he drives this car now. Efficiently, but not really testing the car's proficiencies, let alone toying with its mechanics until it falls apart.

"What? It's worth a try, isn't it?" No, it isn't. Cole doesn't know of the connection made in the middle of true fucking, or the unnerving sensation that courses through skin and bone as blood mingles and swears allegiance and responsibility. Nor does he even remotely comprehend the glazed look of fear that can be produced when human anatomy is dangled on a string to play with. Cole Jacobs just fucks. For him, fucking is a simple case of engage and release.

Caress and unload. There is no thought and no purpose to the event. I've watched it myself, trying to understand the ability to simply fuck with nothing but the finality in mind. Whatever that ability is, I don't have it. Unless I can deliver pain, there is nothing but a half stalled backward and forward motion. It doesn't produce pleasure or achieve anything, nor does it give any sense of realism or entertainment. I'd rather stick my cock in an oven than fuck something that won't let me cause agony to it while I do.

"Something's got to change, Blaine."

I turn my head away again and stare out at the road ahead, disdain proving more interesting than the effort involved in arguing. Why? Why does anything have to change? I don't deserve change. Eloise's lifeless, rotting corpse is proof of it.

"If you drove a car the way I fucked a woman you might understand. Until then, keep your fucking opinion to yourself." That's all I've got to say on the subject. Time has gone by, and the conversation has been well and truly worn out. There is nothing Cole can say to change the facts. We're just two different animals, regardless of the shared genes uniting us. Cole will never understand, and thankfully, he'll never have to control himself because of it.

"Well, fuck you very much," Cole replies, his foot pressing the accelerator to speed us forward again. I half chuckle, amused by the brotherly response to antagonism, but I'm not willing to be pushed into a battle I'll only win regardless. I've spent too long studying psychology to bother with more quarrelling, and I'd rather question why I've never told Cole the truth in the first place. Perhaps if Delaney hadn't come along so soon afterwards I might have needed to. Perhaps then all of this would be easier to explain, thus ensuring Cole never pushed again. But only Delaney knows. I assume, looking back, it was some misguided hope that absolution would come if I spoke about it. The man's response had been resolute and unwavering. He'd not flinched. He'd just listened intently over a glass of Scotch and then smiled, as if the morbidity of the situation meant nothing to him. It hadn't been absolution that came, though. It was more akin to a confession of sin, one a priest stood tall over and then offered hope to.

I muse the night to myself as we travel on, no longer caring for the speed at which the car is travelling and in some ways wishing the fucking thing would simply collide with a wall. Nothing makes any difference now anyway. I've got no right to be alive while she's dead. And the sight of Delaney in my mind, opening a door to a world I'd not known about before Eloise, while intriguing, had been as morose as the sight of her lax form between trees. It was all too late. The new visualisations shown, the sense of a place to be included within and steered by, celebrated even; it had all come too late.

"What about going back to teaching again? You could."

I snort in disgust, frustrating myself further with the thought of what I should have been doing for those in my care. Those days are long gone. I'm not worthy of any accolade currently bracketed on my own walls. Line after line of them, taunting me with what could have been had I not been so reckless with her. I just teach in a different way now, for some reason still needing the feeling of guiding regardless of my inability to control myself. Perhaps that's the point, though. Perhaps it's the necessity to ensure it doesn't happen to others. Who fucking knows anymore? It's all just a haze of dalliances, barely interspersed with interest unless something is screaming. Time just goes on, its interest as mundane as its lack of absorption. I simply dawdle in comparison to my past, neither fulfilling a requirement nor accepting its demise. I don't open up futures for people anymore, offering them career paths and ensuring fresh thinking slides in to the methods of psychological evaluation. I don't discuss years of study, guaranteeing that students learn the old ways, too, so they can mingle new innovation into the system's archaic ideas. No, now I hinder. I halt progress, or at least tame it. That's how it feels. I take sadists and Dominants and domesticate them into a mould, helping contain the anarchy inside their minds. Delaney calls it direction. Drake Contas, the guy who owns the club I've just been in, calls it safety enhancement. I call it monotony, which at least pays me handsomely for the only option of teaching I have left.

Time just moves on. That's all it does. It moves on.

Chapter 4

ALANA

After a dull evening of socialising with New York's finest literary agents, I find myself inebriated and completely in Bree's hands as she totters us out of the entrance to get to our waiting cab.

"Val," is called somewhere behind me. My head swirls as I turn towards the sound, wondering if he's got another drink to offer me, because that has been the only thing of interest happening for the last four hours of my life. Jesus, I wish it was like it used to be. It was fun then.

"It's Scuttler," Bree whispers, catching my arm and trying to tug me forward again. Fuck. Barringer Scuttler the Fourth—an irritating fuckwit who is completely focused on getting his hands on my goods. Annoyingly, he's also someone of importance in this literary world, his father being owner of Valerie's publisher.

"Val, wait up," he calls again, as I attempt to hurry my footfalls and avoid an uncomfortable conversation for the third time tonight. "Please, Val?"

Bree giggles, causing me to join in, too, as we clatter our way down the steps in unison.

"I mean, he couldn't even reach your tits if he stood on a box," she hisses at me, snickering again as we keep travelling. "You think his dick's as small as his hands?"

The thought of Barringer's penis has me immediately convulsing with laughter, drowning out the sounds of his continued calls behind us. I'm not even calling it a cock. I can't.

"That's really nasty. He could have a lovely penis," I respond as I chuckle around the thought, still desperate to get away regardless of whether it's lovely or not.

"As nice as Blaine's?"

My feet crash to a halt, tripping over themselves at the mere thought of what Mr. Jacobs might have to offer down there. She tugs me again, trying to keep our momentum going. Unfortunately, this, combined with both my thoughts of Blaine's cock and my lack of stability, causes my feet to give up on composure. My left heel tilts, flinging me sideways away from her, and regardless of my hopes of rebalance, I feel myself tipping uncontrollably towards the ground. My hands splay, my bag thrown into the air so I'm ready to break my fall, but before I actually hit the deck, a pair of hands pinches at my waist and hauls me back upright.

"Careful," he says, his nose resting in my chest as I finally put my feet back onto a solid surface. "We wouldn't want you breaking yourself, would we?" No. Absolutely not. Although, the thought of that rather than him near me is reasonably appealing at the moment.

"Oh, Barringer. Thank you so much," I reply, trying to unwrap his hands, which are still firmly braced around my hips as his mouth hovers far too close to my boobs for comfort. "Really, what a saviour you are in my moment of need." He smiles at up me, or rather leers.

"Anything to help you," he replies, at last removing one of his sticky paws, but then, in the same moment, wrapping his other further around my waist to pull me closer. Bree laughs again, near abandoning me in my hour of need as she disappears off down the remaining steps to get to our car. "When are we going to have dinner, Val? You promised me months ago," he asks, at least allowing me to begin walking down the steps now. Never. We are never going for dinner.

"Oh, you know me, Barringer. It's just so busy all the time. Go, go, go," I reply, just hoping if I fluff it enough I'll get away with it again for the fourth time tonight, probably thirtieth time in the last year. It's getting tedious to say the least. "It's your father's fault. You know how much he pushes me to get these books out for him."

"Perhaps I should have a word with him then. You do work awfully hard. We all need a bit of R and R every now and then. Some downtime. A massage. Weekend away?" Ewww. I've screwed my nose up before I can stop it, prising his hand away from its descent to my arse as I keep moving towards Bree.

"Barringer," I say, feigning shock. "You know how your father despises fraternization in the company." I pick the front of my dress up, hoping to speed my bloody legs up. "Surely this is inappropriate? And what about Anna Maria?"

"Father will be dead soon enough, Val." Real shock actually freezes me to the spot as I turn to him, for once on the same level now that I'm two steps beneath him. "And divorce is easy enough."

What little respect I had for him just disappeared out of the window, making my insides not only hate him because he's a sleaze ball, but also because he's a misogynistic pig. "Come on, Val. When are you going to let me have a go at your ass?" My eyes widen, stunned by his sudden lack of the refinement that I'm so used to from him. "Don't give me that look. I've read your books. You're a little slut really, aren't you?" I'm so dumbfounded by this statement that I just stand there, open mouth gaping at his boldness as I stare into his piggy eyes and watch his smile broaden. "You want me dirtier, Val?" No. No, I don't. I don't, in any way, want more than this attempt at dirty. Most definitely not from Barringer shitty arse the Fourth. However, Blaine Jacobs, quite unfortunately given the context of dirt, pops into my head with astounding speed, diverting my thoughts from unsuitable meanderings to downright unspeakable acts. It's enough for me to gasp, my hands flying to my lips for fear that Barringer thinks it's him that's caused the reaction.

"I think that's entirely inappropriate, Barringer. I'm appalled," eventually manages to push itself out of my mouth, thankfully replacing the diatribe that would have come had I not kept it in check.

"Val, you coming?" Bree shouts, breaking me from my staring match with Barringer, who is still endeavouring for sexy and intriguing. I swing my head between them, watching the way his smile is still firmly in place and wondering how the hell I get myself away from him without ruining my financial security.

"I'm a little drunk, Barringer. Perhaps we could pick up this conversation another time?"

"Perhaps you should think about your career a little more, Val. Brushing me off every time I ask nicely, like you're better than me, is pretty unwise for someone in your situation." Fuck.

Who the hell does he think he is? I take a step up to him, rallying my own set of balls from somewhere and grip my skirt to stop my hands slapping something.

"You think I couldn't sign with someone else tomorrow if I needed to?" He chuckles, lifting his hand and running his fingers across my cheek, which causes me to quickly back away again.

"I think you couldn't do anything without my father releasing you from contracts you know nothing about," he says, still smiling and putting his hands in his pockets like he hasn't got a care in the world. Fury bubbles in me, not only because of his not so quiet threat, but at the fact that, to a degree, he's right. I have neither the knowledge nor power to big myself up here at the moment. I might have become savvy about publishing, but even I'm not able to fight a major publishing house with legal contracts. So I plaster on a fake smile, giggling a little and pretending to stumble again, thus proving my drunkenness in the hope that he realises I don't know what I'm talking about.

"Oh, silly me," slips out of me, as I fake stumble one more time to get me further away from him. "Look at the state of me. Too many bubbles, I think," I say pathetically, still giggling and faltering every next footfall. "Was lovely to see you, Barringer." I continue on, my arm reaching for the safety of Bree as I get closer to the cab. "'Til next time then."

The moment I'm in the cab, I'm screaming, expletives of every kind coming from god knows where as I swear repeatedly at Bree in the hope she'll take it.

"Who the fuck does he think he is?" My tirade goes on as I kick at the seat in front of me and the cab rounds a corner. "I mean, fuck him, right? Little shit. How fucking dare he threaten me?" The stream of obscenities keeps coming, all the time helped along by Bree's nods of approval and joining in. What a wanker. I can't believe he would try to get me in bed by threatening me. It's not the first time that sort of thing has happened in my life, but from a senior executive at my own publishers? Now what? I've got to go and work with him and pretend it didn't happen? Make it seem like his behaviour is okay? Arsehole.

I can't breathe for the continued rant session. It's probably fuelled by the amount of alcohol in my system, and pills, but I couldn't care less. Barringer the Fourth. The fourth what? Dickhead in his family to treat women like muck to be walked over. "I've a good mind to go back there and tell his father to shove his contract up his arse," I shout, at Bree really because she's doing well at taking my venom.

"You go, girl. Screw the publishers, right?"

"Quite. Fucking little tosser."

I'm not sure this amount of expletives has ever come out of my mouth since college, not all at the same time anyway, but screw him. I'm on fire. More discourse pours from my mouth with little care for whether anyone else can hear it on the street outside. What? I'm supposed to fuck him if I want to keep my contract? Or renew it?

"You could always go all out indie, anyway." Bree cuts into my irritated ranting, making me acknowledge this as an actual option. It's not like I need my publisher. I could do this without them. I could. I might not make as much money, but what do I need that for? I've got my apartment. I can pay the bills without them. And if I can get this new pen going, I'll make more anyway, won't I? I don't have to have a publisher, especially one that appears to now have a fucking clause attached to it that I was unaware of before. "You've got me, and all your contacts. Fuck 'em."

She's right. I don't have to be scared of this crap. I'll ether go down to their offices in the morning and demand an apology from the little bastard, or I'll flat out refuse to write for them until I get one. I don't even like the crap they're making me write, or the little time they give me to write it. It's become a fucking nightmare in all honesty, making me question reality every day of the bloody week. I'm so damn tired of it all, It's constant, and now this? No. Enough. I don't even know who I am anymore.

I've calmed a little by the time the cab starts to meander through traffic along Bree's street. Or maybe I feel pumped by the fact that I really don't need them. I don't know, but the rain that's started coming down helps my mood no end. Its gentle patter on the roof lulls me into a sleepy haze, more than likely because of the alcohol, sheer fucking exhaustion at all the never-ending nights trying to achieve deadlines, and my rant.

"You wanna come in?" Bree asks, just before I see her apartment block come into view.

"No," I mumble out, half asleep and just wanting my bed, which I will get into on my own, as usual, and gratefully so. "I'm going to have a long lie in tomorrow and a day off, I think. Maybe go for a day out somewhere if you fancy something different." Because screw all of it. I'm so done.

The cab comes to a stop by the bottom of her building.

"Me? Something different? I don't think so. I have releases to prepare for. Marketing, you know? All the stuff you, with your publisher, don't have to think about too much."

I nod in reply, knowing that she would never have said yes anyway, and lean over to kiss her cheek goodbye. Bree never does anything outside work. Unless there's a chance of it potentially making her money, she doesn't do it. I used to be the same, but nowadays I'm just exhausted by it all. I just need a break, a change. Something.

"Okay. I'll call you," I say, watching her get out and hand me twenty bucks. Another thing Bree does all the time. She refuses any financial gain out of friendship. She's fiercely independent, never even allowing me to just pay for a cab. I don't know why. Not that I mind, but it's not like I can't afford it.

"Bye."

The cab waits until she gets to the door, like any good cabbie in Manhattan should do, then pulls away. So I lean back after I've told him my address, enjoying the few minutes it'll takes us to get there. I could have walked, I suppose. It's only a few blocks really, but it's late, I'm drunk, and my heels are killing me.

I end up just closing my eyes and letting the cab lull me further into sleep. It seems ages since I've slept properly. A good night's rest is what I need, certainly after that little encounter with a person whose father is the one who pushes me to meet deadlines permanently. It's the reason for the speed in my system, the same stuff that has obviously given up now, and probably yet another reason why I'm so fucking uninterested with my stories. There's no time for immersion in them anymore. It's all just so...

The sudden blare of a horn has me turning in my seat to see what's happened, barely registering anything but lights as I'm flung sideways and brakes are slammed on. And then the sound of metal colliding explodes in my eardrums, ricocheting around the car and sending me closer to the door with its shunt. My head bounces off something, the thud resonating as I try to protect myself from more harm, and wrap into a ball. I peer out from beneath my arms, realising the car is spinning as I try to steady myself and keep from being crushed into the window, but the screeching of tangled metal just gets louder, grating my ears as I try to find a way to stay alive and grab for anything. My legs push at a seat back, bracing me away from the window for fear of smashing through it as we keep spinning uncontrollably, and then everything happens in slow motion as I take a final gasp of air and watch the corner of a building coming at me. My head turns, desperately trying to stay away from the oncoming impact, my fingers reaching for the other door handle in hope as I scramble across, but all I see through the window is a pair of eyes staring back at me. They're as fear filled as mine as he grips his wheel and tries to get his car away from ours. It's lodged against us, the metal continuing to grind and grate, the cars battering on each other and pushing us closer to the building. Nothing's stopping this now, no matter how hard my hands brace this window. We're just spinning. Out of control. Both our eyes filled with terror at the thought as we go and there's not a thing either of us can do about it. I know it. He knows it. We're all going to die, and all I can do is watch it coming at me.

~

Sunlight blinds me as I squint my eyes open and try to move, my head pounding the hangover from hell into my brain. Oh good god how much did I drink last night? I clamp them closed, wondering if I should ever touch the dreaded stuff again, and reach for the glass of water that's always by my bed. It's only when I find nothing there, after several attempts of fumbling around, that I dare try again. It's a slow appraisal of eye opening, one I do with considered care this time given the amount of pain that came last time. The room slowly blurs around me, instantly reminding me to never mix vodka and Champagne again, but eventually I start to see shapes.

Unfortunately, they're not my shapes. None of them.

I stay stock still, knowing I'm on a bed and unsure whose it is. The dark grey walls climb around me, occasionally interspersed with a painting or two. Modern ones. Quite nice ones actually. Still, they're not mine, which means I'm not in my apartment. Thankfully, there doesn't seem to be anyone else in the bed with me—at least one good thing about this situation.

Gently turning my head a little, I notice a door at the end of the room, another one on the other side, both closed and giving me privacy. And then, out of the blue of that thought, I realise I'm naked apart from the scrap of a g-string still riding my arse. Holy fuck, I've slept with someone. It takes me no time at all to roll the covers further around myself, luxuriating a little in their texture regardless of the fact I have no idea who they belong to. Unfortunately, with this movement comes the realisation that not only does my head hurt, but most of my body seems to agree with the sentiment. My thighs ache, my right shoulder twinges every time I try to move it, and my back seems painful through my shoulder and up into my neck. It's painful enough that I stay still again, gently trying to move muscles about to ease the discomfort as I gaze around looking for clues.

There's still no form of enlightenment by the time I've lain here for a while longer. It's a masculine room, no doubt, but there's no sense of who he is or why I'm here. I've noticed my dress and shawl lying across the back of a small black sofa, my shoes neatly placed beneath them. It hardly looks like a stripping scene from some wild night of passion, like one of my normal one night pick-ups from somewhere.

Oh, my dress. I was at the Publishers' do. And that fuckwit Barringer threatened me. I crick my neck up at the sudden realisation, causing a bolt of pain to shoot through the rest of me and bring an agonised groan from my lips. My hand comes up to brace it as I heave on my tired legs to get them out of the bed. It's time to get out of wherever this is. Regardless of whether I've had a good time here or not, or who I may or may not have had sex with, that little shit is out for ruining me. I remember him now, standing on that step and sneering through his piggy little face, threatening me unless I slept with him. I can't quite remember what happened after that, but whatever it is it's done now and there's not a lot I can do about it, I suppose.

I trail across the floor gingerly, noticing that there's nothing wet down below as I go. I've either not had sex, or I had the afterthought, post fucking, to clean myself up. It was more than likely awful sex, then. I mean, no one cleans themselves up when they've had unbelievable sex. Limbs are too exhausted to move, let alone worry about cleansing oneself. Although I did write a book about a woman who used to douche afterwards, apparently thinking it would remove the sperm, thus removing the problem of pregnancy. Needless to say, she became pregnant by the end of it, hopefully proving to the masses who read that particular book that it does not work.

My fingers rest on the bridge of my nose as I hover in the middle of the room, still searching for answers as to why I can't remember anything and looking at my dress for inspiration. Nothing. Not a thing springs to mind. I can't even remember if I had sex, which means I seriously need to stop drinking vodka and Champagne, or certainly stop doing the aforementioned with speed inside me. Jesus wept. I'm a twenty-seven-year-old professional female who thinks inebriated one-night stands are acceptable? They're not. Well, they are under normal circumstances, but not when you're so drunk that you can't remember a thing the next day. Good lord, what the fuck am I going to tell Bree? That I just dropped her off after the do and then found some random guy on the street and slept with him? Maybe it was the cabbie.

That thought instantly brings visions racing back into my mind. The screech of wheels comes first, irritating my already pounding head and forcing me to fumble for the bed frame to lean on, and then the sound of metal clashing rattles, too.

"You're alive then?"

My body folds into itself, desperate to hide from the voice that's appeared behind me as I swing round, grabbing for the sheets. It's a scrambled affair, one that has me tripping over my feet and hurrying for the other side of the room, duvet wrapped around me. It's only when I take stock of my situation that I realise I haven't even seen his face. Regrettably, I don't think I need to. "We haven't fucked if that's what's bothering you." My eyes fly up at the comment, linking straight with ones I know all too well and pondering the correct response.

"I don't fuck people I research," I snap, flustered at his body in my space. His space. Whatever.

He smirks at me, and that combined with the waft of Chanel that's floating across the room is nearly enough to make me wish I had.

"Why not?"

"What?"

"You're writing a book about kink. Why wouldn't you fuck the person teaching you how it all fits together?"

"It's hardly the time to discuss..." My mouth seems to diminish its attempts at language as he takes a step closer to me. It still leaves an eight-foot gap between us, but that's nowhere near enough room for a practical conversation regarding kink when I have no clothes on and he looks too tempting for words. "You hurt people. And besides, you're not a teacher, you're research." He smirks again, crinkling his dark eyes at me and loosening his tie as he runs a hand through his hair.

"I am, actually. Professor, if you'd like to be precise. Psychology."

My mouth hangs open at the comment. I'd like to say it's only because of his revelation, but it also has something to do with the fact that he's removing his jacket. Why is he doing that? I back up again, coiling the duvet closer to me and aiming myself towards a seat.

"Why am I here?" My question is bolder than I feel given the context of this odd encounter, but useless behaviour in front of these alpha types infers inferiority, something I'm not, and never will be. Not even under his eyes, or lips, or voice. "I can remember a crash, I think. Were you in it?"

"Yes."

"Any more explanation?"

"No."

"What does that mean?" Seriously? He's not going to tell me what happened?

"How are you feeling?" That's not an answer either.

"Fine. Answer the question. What happened? Why am I here? And if you were in the accident, did you cause it? I mean, is the cabbie alright? The other driver?"

"Where in England are you from?" I stand up, infuriated with his lack of answers, and cross over to my dress. If he's not going to give me the information I require then I see little point in being here. Perhaps it's been reported to the police and they'll have a clue if the cabbie's okay.

"Mr. Jacobs, if you could leave the room so I can get dressed please," I ask, as politely as my current state of frustration will allow. "I have things to do today and this is getting me nowhere."

"What things?"

"What?"

"What things are more important than you understanding your subject matter correctly?"

"You're not my subject matter."

"Drop the sheets."

"I'm not—"

"Alana, drop the sheets. Or would you rather me call you Peter?"

"What?" How does he know my name, let alone any relation to my pen?

"Or we could continue with Valerie. Seems a little old for you, in my opinion, but I'm not against fucking a man either, so you can choose."

I'm gaping and clutching the sheets so tightly my hands are hurting. It might be related to the fear I'm beginning to feel, or it could be to do with the fact that no one knows about Peter, only Bree. No one else. I've had experts cover my Internet presence, ensuring that all the backgrounds are checked out. Profiles alienated, emails covered and logged over. There's no way anyone could know about him. I even have separate business accounts for banking, and that all goes to PO Boxes.

"I don't know what you're talking about. Who's Alana?"

He shakes his head, a flash of the expression I've only seen once before gracing his mouth as a slight sneer creeps along his jaw.

"I don't like games, and I don't like liars, Alana," he eventually says, backing himself to the door so that he can close it. "I research the people who come into my space and ask about me, especially those who want me to open up about matters that are relatively private to the outside world." And then he takes another few steps towards me, never once giving me a chance to look away from eyes that defy any sense of reason. "Drop the fucking sheets."

I have no answer for any of that. None. The only thing I'm moderately aware of is the fact that, for some unidentified reason, my hands are giving up their desire to hold on to the fabric in my hands.

"How do you…?" I mean, seriously, how does he? "And why should I…?" I can't finish any sentence. None of them want to actually come out of my mouth. This could be a metaphor for something I need to check out later. Research. I snatch a glance at the door behind him, wondering why he's closed it if we're the only people here. Maybe we're not.

"I'll scream if you touch me."

"I'm not going to touch you. I'm teaching you. You asked for information," he replies, calm as a summer ocean as he smiles again, probably at my misfortune and his superiority in the room.

"I'm not dressed for research."

"You're perfectly dressed for research." And by the look of the smirk accompanying those last words, he means naked.

"This is inappropriate," I say, reaching for my dress and wondering if I could get it on under the duvet while still managing to hold onto it. I frown at the thought. It was hard enough getting it on when I had an entire room's worth of space.

"I'll help you write your book, Alana, but I want something in return. At the moment, that's you naked and the truth about who you are."

"There was a crash." I don't know why I said that again. Maybe I'm trying to change the subject. "I hurt in places."

"Not nearly as much as you will do."

That's it. Last straw. He's talking about pain with a smile on his face while taking another few paces in my direction. I'm actually scared now. Like, shaking scared. It makes me snatch my dress without much fear as to whether he'll see me or not. I have to leave and regain some sense of reality. I mean my body is physically shuddering now. I can feel it as I step into the bottom of the dress, shunting it upwards in the hope that I'll manage this without my breasts leaping out and attacking him. Unfortunately, I'm not entirely sure if it's fear or excitement.

"If it helps, I was the one who undressed you last night."

Well, great. He's seen it all anyway. That doesn't help, though, as I stall mid-shrug. In fact, it makes the whole situation more uncomfortable because now I can't stop myself wondering what he thought of my body. Fucking hell. Jesus. I start shrugging and jostling again, desperately trying to clamp my arms onto the top of the duvet for privacy.

"Please, just leave so I can get dressed in peace, Mr. Jacobs."

"No. I'm intrigued by this dance of yours."

I roll my eyes at his accompanying chuckle, turning my back on him in an attempt at subtle aggravation. Whatever this might be, he is right to a degree. I do require information from him, and he's rather good at giving it succinctly, apart from in this circumstance.

"Could you be more juvenile?" I mutter, loud enough for him to hear. I mean, what an arse. I just want an explanation about the crash and where I am—about a lot of things actually, given his little dive into my private life. And god knows why my body's reacting to his voice in such a slutty way, but it has to stop. It's in no way helpful to anything.

Eventually, after much tugging, bouncing, and jumping, I hold the halter-neck fastening around the back of my neck and drop the duvet. There. Done. Fuck him and his drop the sheets. Sadly, it occurs to me as I look up and find a mirror reflecting my image at me, I haven't got a hope of zipping up the back. I hover, my fingers fiddling with the clips at my neck as I consider just wrapping my shawl around my mid-section.

"Would you like some help?"

"No." The word is out before I've given it any thought. I do not require help of any kind that might involve his hands anywhere near me, especially if they get here and bring more Chanel with them. "I'm fine."

"Yes, you are, Alana."

There's a pause in the air as he finishes his sentence. It makes me look back through the mirror at him without thought. It's been so long since a man's called me that. I've spent years having a different name for each encounter, never exchanging details or revealing who I am. I've almost been lost in a world of pennames and social media, occasionally being called by my real name if I needed to pay a bill or fill in something at the bank, but never with a man. Definitely not with any sexual connotation associated, anyway.

He moves again, crossing the carpeted floor slowly and continuing to stare until he drops his gaze to my backside and stops. I feel the moment my arms give way to blocking him, not that they have been physically doing so, but my mind has. In fact, since the moment I met him I've been blocking him. He's been research, that's all. The fact that he's everything I would generally drool over has meant nothing to me. Tall, broad, and full of that understated swagger. He's the sort of man who owns the world simply by residing within it, somehow announcing to the inhabitants of the planet that he will not be messed with, nor fooled. It makes me smile to myself as I watch the way he appraises what's in front of him. He's measured, disciplined, weighing up his options given the situation around us, and considering the correct approach to getting hold of me. At this moment, it wouldn't take much. I can smell him as he rubs his chin, stroking his finger across his cheek to his jaw, then pushing it over his lips. And those prevailing notes of wood and spice filter across to me from his neck, lifting any sense of appropriate out of the open window on a breeze of irrationality.

"You should leave," he says softly, finally taking the last few steps over to me and zipping up my dress without asking if he can. "You're right. This is inappropriate."

Not one bit of his finger dragging along my spine feels inappropriate. I wish I could say it does, but it feels exquisite, as if I've never felt such a sensation. His touch is dense, like I can feel it beneath my skin finding its way inside with little effort. And the callous that roughens the touch? The way it grates slightly and coarsens the moment, effortlessly changing the dynamic between us? It's deafening to my awareness of his proximity, showing he's in complete control of what happens next. I can feel his breath on the nape of my neck, the heat from his skin, the air continuing to thicken with every breath that falls from my own lips. I'd only need him to lift those brown eyes again and this would escalate into something I'd remember for the rest of my life, I'm sure. Because I can feel the weight of his hands, regardless of the fact he's removed them. I can feel their grasp, their flex. The way they'll harness what's inside him, turning his frame with skill and using it wisely for endless purposes. But mostly, I can feel the fact that they'll hurt when they take hold. I know that, irrespective of this gentlemanly exterior. I can feel it all with just one touch on my skin and the rapid response from my heart, its fear and excitement, lust and confusion. It's a heady moment. One that should be written onto parchment and sealed in blood for eternity, leaving it in the hands of millions of others to read so they too can feel true depth. One could fall in love with such a refined sense of beauty. In fact, one might well do just that. What the hell does it matter anymore?

Chapter 5

ALANA

I stare for precisely one minute longer before turning into his face and waiting for him to do something. Bree's right. I should let someone just take hold and lead. Show me something new. My life is all about being in control—times, dates, release fixtures, promos, and certainly how my sex life works. It's constant, even in the books Peter writes. And for once, here, now, I just want whatever happens to be in the hands of someone other than me. In his hands. I don't know why. Perhaps it's his aura or his looks, or maybe I'm going insane. Who knows? Who cares? I don't. I'm free of thinking for once, free of controlling my life and ready for whatever he wants.

Rather than initiating anything, though, he backs away. First one small step, followed by another longer stride, until he's standing four foot away and staring at my lips with frustration etched into every hard contour of his face.

"My brother was driving the car that crashed into your cab, badly. He's next door recovering and the cab driver is in hospital, doing fine." Oh, well that was a change of direction, I suppose. One that leaves me with a raised pair of brows and my body still aching to close the distance between us again. "My doctor looked you over last night.

There's nothing but some whiplash, which she's left you some pills for."

"Okay," I say, trying for sensible thought and failing as I reach for my shawl. He's right. I should go. This is… Actually, I don't know what it is, but it's not useful for research purposes whatever it is. And ten seconds longer in my scattered brain and I would have been launching myself at him, proving his beauty and my inability to think logically, which is something we researchers don't do. I shake my head at myself, remembering who I am and chastising my stupidity. I don't daydream of impulsive encounters, pretending that reality doesn't exist. It's ridiculous. I'm considered. Deliberate. It's what I've become. I've had too, to write a book that makes sense to people. It's probably just the heady concoction of drugs in my system still, I suppose. Or that combined with a bump on my head maybe. I don't know, but it's not right. Whatever I was thinking, I was wrong. This is all wrong, regardless of the ache that's still there.

I scan around for my bag, eventually finding it next to the bedside table as I slip my shoes on, and then smirk as I realise that's how he knows my name. He must have rifled through my bag for the doctor. Doesn't explain the Peter thing, though.

"You have your own doctor, huh?" I say, lifting the shawl and looking at him, trying to ignore the fact that I need something from him that I don't understand.

"As you said, I hurt people. It's necessary."

"Dodgy doctor?"

"Kinky doctor," he replies, seemingly uninterested in my question. Of course. It's a useful fact that I can use in the story. I'd never considered that these places and people would need a doctor, or at least someone with medical training to act as a backup. Presumably it's not easy to explain lacerations and rope burns to the hospitals if they ever need to go.

I fiddle with my bag as he stands there staring at me, unsure how one ends such a meeting or says thank you. And for what? Crashing into me? Not that he did by the sounds of it, but I'm okay, so what does it matter.

"Is your brother okay?"

"He'll survive," he says, completely devoid of any of the warmth he had. All joviality seems to have gone. All passion. He seems colder than I've ever seen him, making me question if I've done something wrong. And then he just opens the door, finally removing his gaze from me and walking out into the hallway with little emotion other than boredom. I eventually follow him with one last sweep of my eyes around the bedroom, checking for anything I've left.

"I assume this is your place?" I ask, wanting to find something to talk about, which is unlike me. I frown at myself, amused by my nerves around this man. Normally they're just there for my own satisfaction. One nighters. One nighters where I up and leave with little in the way of explanation or conversation. After several failed attempts at the relationship status everyone else seems to chase, I don't bother anymore. I certainly don't hang around for a tête-à-tête about our night's activities in the morning, if I even make it that far through a night.

"Sometimes," he grunts in reply. I don't know what that means. What a strange reply. How is somewhere your place sometimes?

"Strange response…" I can't believe I'm doing this. It's all me. Why can't I just shut my mouth?

He doesn't answer at all, just keeps striding along the hall as I grasp hold of my dress to keep it scuffing on the floor, my heels clipping loudly. We turn at the end, the wooden stairs funnelling us off down to the next level as I keep following and looking around. The house is sparsely decorated, masculine in appearance, not unlike the bedroom I was in, but it's more than that. It's like it's had stuff removed from it. The spaces are unbalanced, as if pieces of furniture have been taken away or moved to new locations, leaving a huge hole behind and nullifying whatever warmth used to be here. Perhaps that's what he means by sometimes. Maybe he's moving somewhere else.

My feet hit the hall floor as we reach the ground, and once again my heels seem to echo through a large kitchen space. It's strange given the fact that I can't even hear his. I look at his legs moving, watching the high-end brown brogues stride along making no sound at all.

"Your shoes don't make any noise?" Oh my god, could I sound any more desperate for conversation?

His head swings around to me, the angle tilted and questioning. He's right. That was a stupid statement. I instantly stare down at the floor, wondering if I could perhaps make myself any more ludicrous as we keep moving.

"Yours do," he says sullenly, as if my shoes making a noise is a problem. Well, there's nothing I can do about that, I'm afraid. They're shoes, expensive ones actually. They're supposed to make noise and flash their red bottoms about. Most men would find them damned attractive. Why is he so bloody grouchy all of a sudden? He's making me feel like I've done something wrong, when he's the reason I'm even here in the first place.

"Yes, there's this thing on the bottom of them called a sole," I snark back at him, irritated by my own pathetic response to this odd situation. I mean, whatever that thing was in the bedroom doesn't suddenly mean I'm someone to be walked over. "Why don't yours make any sound? Is it a kink thing?"

He stops so abruptly I crash straight into the back of him, my feet scuttling around the wooden floor for stability and hands grabbing out at the wall as I bounce off his frame. He doesn't even attempt to catch or help me. Instead, he watches me stumble until I grasp hold of a side table and regain steadiness.

"Your balance is abysmal," he says sharply, a slight smile forming around his mouth. "You spend too much time sitting down. Walk more." What the actual fuck? I glare at him, wondering if there's a gentlemanly bone in his body.

"You didn't think helping me was more polite than criticising?"

"Critique is what garners perfection, therefore—helping," he replies instantly, turning on his heel and walking back in the direction of the door. "You're a writer, aren't you? You should know that if you're any good."

"Fuck you."

The speed with which he turns and gets back to within an inch of my body is too quick for comprehension, and the sudden lifting of my body from the ground and the change of direction have my head spinning.

"Put me down." I wish my words came out with the sense of mild infuriation I'm feeling, but they don't. I'm more surprised than infuriated. Possibly excited in all honesty. "You will put me down."

He won't, it seems, and the fact that, in his eyes, I clearly weigh nothing at all doesn't seem to be helping my cause at all as we glide into the kitchen again. He gets to the back door, leaning on it with his elbow and clicking it open, then takes me straight out into a garden come patio area. I'm not hanging on. In fact, at some point I started trying to push him off me. Nothing helps, though, and the moment I realise what's coming I start screaming in the hope of a saviour. That doesn't help either as he keeps going, somehow managing to wrap his hand so that it covers my mouth.

"You're about to learn some fucking manners, Alana," he says, his arm hitching me into a different position and his hand tightening around my mouth again. "You're a stuck up bitch."

Manners? Me? At what point was I rude? And stuck up? Oh my god. I scream into his hand again, possibly attempting apology for swearing at him and kicking out for dear life.

Unfortunately, the feeling of leaving his arms is not as harmonious as I'd like. That's mainly because of the small pool coming at me. It doesn't matter that I'm clawing at his neck, or at his arms. His strength simply propels me into the cold water with little thought for my wellbeing. I hit it with such force I squeal at its impact on my skin, desperately trying to get out even before I'm fully submerged. It's glacial, as if it's had ice cubes lying in it for weeks, and as I splutter about, the water drenching my dress as it flaps around me, I can hardly get air into my lungs.

"Fucking arsehole," I manage to spit out, absolutely furious with him for doing such a thing. "How dare you throw me into fucking pool?" My arms slather me around, reaching for the side. My mouth gulping in breaths as the temperature decreases my core rapidly. But the water keeps sluicing around in my frantic fight, making the trail of my dress wrap around my legs and tangle me up. It gets to the point where I can't move, my arms stretching for the edges with little hope of reaching them as I begin to go under again.

His hand grabs my hair, physically ripping me up until it's just my mouth above the surface and then he just holds me there. I gasp out as I finally make eye contact, freezing and truly feeling thankful for his help even though he caused the problem.

"Speak," he snaps, holding my hair tightly and keeping too much pressure on me for me to be able to move. I'm still gasping, hardly able to verbalise let alone know what he wants me to talk about.

I reach my hand forward again, the other one trying to get the dress from around my ankles so I can separate my legs. "What do you have to say?"

Nothing, nothing apart from 'help' as it sputters out of me and I keep trying to untangle the dress. My head slips under again, water sliding down into my windpipe and making me choke a little.

"Help," I cough out as he pulls on my hair again and inches me closer to the side. It's not close enough to touch, though, and my arms thrash madly again, trying to grab onto it. "I can't brea—"

He lets go of me before I can finish the word, gently pushing me away into the water and then backing away from the edge. "I can't…" Breathe, I can't breathe.

I've never seen my death. I doubt many have. But in these few seconds, I see it. My thrashing doesn't work. It only makes the green of my dress undulate around my legs, wrapping ever tighter and pulling me down. And then my legs begin to give up their fight for life, as I let myself float, hoping that will work. It's doesn't, and I feel the water slipping over my mouth again as I dip below the surface once more and hold what little breath I have left. Nothing works, not even my last attempt at a struggle for life. I find myself just looking up at him through the murk and reaching, as if he's the only lifeline I've got. I don't even know him, but he is my only hope, isn't he? It's just him—him and the hope that he's not a killer, because he can save me, can't he? Or he can let me drown. No one knows I'm here. I'll never be found. It's just me and him and this pool of bottomless water.

The vision of his hand delving down to me is worthy of angels. It seems to take minutes to get to me, as if travelling through space to find me in the depths of murky waters. I don't even reach for it as my arms splay at my sides, somehow knowing I don't need to. It'll find me on its own, hauling me from this anxiety as it does. It's almost spiritual as it descends another inch or two and promises rescue, its form blurred as the water distorts its movement. But the second it reaches me and begins to lift me free, I know I've just felt something beyond usual. I don't know if it's the drowning, or the cold, or even if it's him, but this is closer to godly than I've ever felt before. And the climb up is treasurable, every split second longer just making me want to enjoy its tormented pull more. Perhaps stay down here even, linger in it all.

I'm dragged to the side slowly. There's no gasping or flapping about as the water calms. I'm not even sure I've taken my eyes off his hand as it hovers in front of me and he crouches behind it. I'm just breathing again, slightly shakily given the fact that I'm freezing, but I am breathing, and it feels like the first time I've ever taken a breath. Deep, long cleansing breaths pull back and forth through my body, reminding me what it's like to be alive as the sun belts down above me, birds chirping in the sky as they fly by. I just stare at his hand hanging from his knee, the water droplets gliding from his fingers as they take another eternity to drip down onto the poolside.

"What do want to say, Alana?"

His voice shocks me, as if I'd forgotten it was there, or that there was a real human attached to his arm. I look up, suddenly gasping for air again and broken from a moment of peace. There's not a hair out of place. His body is still perfectly put together as he frowns down at me and offers me no help in getting out.

"You have to ask. It's all about you asking me."

I don't know what he's talking about. I'm just here in a pool of freezing water, having nearly drowned because he put me in here. I thought he wanted an apology, but now he wants me to ask him something? I inch my way along the side of the pool, hoping to reach a point where I can touch the floor, all the time barely looking away from his focused gaze. Deep brown eyes, a frown covering them, his wet fingers now reaching for his chin and rubbing at it as he keeps looking. There's no smile, no amusement. He's deadly serious about this, whatever it is.

"I don't know what that was," I chatter through clenched teeth as I keep sliding away, still hazy but as focused on him as I ever have been on anything. It's unnerving. Strange.

The moment my foot hits the step of the pool and I start to climb out, I realise I've got no shoes on, my expensive shoes. If there's one thing that won't be happening because of this, it'll be me losing my shoes. My beautiful shoes. The one piece of loveliness I allowed myself to spend stupid amounts of money on. I stare back into the water, watching the way the two black Louboutin's gleam at the bottom, reminding me of myself a few moments ago. Before I know what's happening, I hear a small splash, then notice him lowering himself into the water and straight under it. He doesn't falter or shiver as he comes back up again. He just walks the length of the pool, slowly pushing the waves out in front of him until he reaches me and holds up my shoes.

"I..." He's wet. Beautifully wet. His usually roughed dark hair is slicked back, sharpening angles on his jaw I'd not noticed before, and his muscles are suddenly all on display beneath his white shirt, possibly announcing how he creates pain. I can't speak. Floored. Not only at this god who has appeared before me, but... he throws me in the water, nearly drowning me because I've been rude, and then he goes in to rescue my shoes? "I..."

"Unless you're going to ask me for something, don't speak."

"But I..." The apology, and thank you. That's what he wanted, wasn't it? I don't even know why any of that happened anymore. He holds a finger up to his lips, staring at me so boldly and with absolute intention to cause harm that I blush, regardless of the glacial temperature.

"You looked so beautiful," he says, his body rising from the water as he walks forward. He just stops there and looks at me again, his body beginning to lean in until his fingers reach for my face. I can't move, I'm fixated on his gaze, my mouth still chattering a little as I consider his words. Beautiful when? When I was drowning? And then he just leans in further, his lips coming down to mine slowly, the look of them more inviting than anything has ever been in my life. "Ask me, Alana." Oh god, I can't focus on denial any more. I just want them on me. I do. I need them. And they're so soft as they land, barely any force attached. They tease the edges of my lips, creating the same feeling I had under the water, furthering it even as I hover beneath them recklessly and let him lead me wherever he wants. They're like a summer breeze across me, whisking me off somewhere as his hand holds me firmly, guiding me perhaps. I'm mesmerised, my lips matching his, trying to create more intimacy than his softness allows. It's a moment I fall into without care to any repercussions, desperately hoping that he's going to take me further away. Fly me like a kite maybe. But then he just stops and backs away, the feel of his lips leaving me far too quickly for my liking as I watch him rise up. I just gaze back, longing for him to continue as I see his frown descend, until he absentmindedly wanders past me, my heels still in his hand, and then heads up to the house without another word.

Eventually, having sat here for a few minutes rubbing my lips, constantly flicking my gaze between the pool and my shivering fingers in utter confusion, I turn to see if he's still there. He's not. I'm alone. I'm actually alone and bloody freezing, enough so that I crawl to my feet, picking up the weight of my soaking dress as I do, and then head for the door to the house, too. What I'll find in there, I don't know.

The air is thick with tension as I finally push the door wide and look around for him. He's nowhere to be seen. It's just a kitchen full of the usual bits and pieces with a long, dark wood, beaten up table in the middle, completely juxtaposed to the high end furniture about. Yet I can feel him here. I can feel his presence somewhere. It's like those few moments in the pool, and the kiss, have changed us, transforming the air into a connection he seems to murmur at me.

"Blaine?" I whisper, barely able to say the name out loud for fear of it being too personal, perhaps solidifying something I don't understand. No response, only the sound of silence. "Blaine? I need..." I trail off when I realise I don't know what I need. It makes me turn to look back out through the window, noting the perfectly calm water again. Something happened out there. Something inexplicable. I nearly drowned, and for some unknown reason I allowed it to happen, enjoying it in some odd way. It's all so unlike me. It was spiritual. Calming. A bolt of something sent for a purpose I don't comprehend. So instead of speaking, I just stand by the window, letting the water drip onto the floor as I shiver and muse over what the hell happened in that pool. It floods me with thoughts, plots, and images of sex scenes—love, the promise of a story untold. Even paranormal stories begin driving through my mind, ones filled with heaven and hell, vampires and demons. Angels and their muses, lost in a world obsessed with despicable acts and atrocious behaviour. If only I had my notebook. I'd be writing things down so fast I could hardly keep up with the visions. Notes, dates, times. Venues and countries. I can see them all so clearly. Even the names of the characters are beginning to creep in. They're talking to me loudly, telling me who they are and what they want. I fling my eyes around wildly, searching the countertops for paper and a pen. I need to write this. I have to. It's bleeding from me like nothing has for months. It has to come. It's actually desperate to come.

My bare feet run around the kitchen, sluicing water everywhere as I open drawers and cupboards in search of paper, until I eventually find some in a small bureau just before the hall. I grab at it, snatching a pencil as well and then heading back to the table. Oh my god, so many stories and visions. They're pouring from me as I sit and start scribbling down notes. It's all there, making me smile and giggle as my pencil scratches harsh lines to amplify points.

"Here," he says, breaking me of my moment in thought. I wave my hand at him without lifting my head, so focused on my task that nothing is breaking my train of thought.

"I just need to get this down," I mumble at him, annoyed at the interruption as I continue scribbling, drawing mind maps to enhance my little new world of sin. "It's amazing, see?" I don't know why I followed through with that. Perhaps I want him to see what he's helped me create. No one's ever helped me create anything. Well, maybe some have. The occasional person in the street as a character, or a sentence a random woman said at a shop, but no one's ever given me this. This is astounding. It's a whole world of inspiration. There's a series here. A big one. A trilogy at least. I push the second piece of paper to the side of the first, joining the sprawled writing so I can double its path. "Look, see what you've done," I say, smiling again and furiously doodling more words and plot alternators.

I feel his body rather than see it as he comes to the side of me and looks over my shoulder. I'm still too engrossed in my new lead man, who happens to look reasonably similar to Blaine. It's only after I half hesitate at that thought that I realise the real version is naked, short of a towel wrapped around his waist and another one in his hand.

"Fuck!" The expletive drifts from my lips as I try not to look at him. Naked is not fair, and something I can't deal with at all, regardless of my scribbling and being lost in my own little bubble. His hand reaches for my paper as my pen hovers above it, suddenly unable to scribe a bloody thing because of his nakedness. He turns the paper, running his fingers over my words and following the mind map with astonishing ease given the fact he's not a writer. And all of that would be so much easier to comprehend if I wasn't desperately intrigued about his cock, which is hiding just to the left of me, practically begging me to do something with it.

"Clara?" he says, his finger tapping the name of my new lead character. I nod, my only response to the very real threat that I might do something stupid any minute now. Like fuck. Which is plainly the most stupid thing possible, regardless of the pool scenario. I mean, we've already discussed me leaving. I should. He chortles to himself then unhooks my halter neck so swiftly I can't stop the material from falling before I catch it. "You're wet." You don't say. I swing my head to him, clutching my breasts, remembering the last time he said those words as my eyes travel along the ridges of his body before reaching his face.

"You're hard." It's my best, stuttered response to the effect of his masculinity assaulting me without physical touch. He is. It's all hard. I drop my eyes from his amused smirk and look back down at the stomach in front of me. There's not an inch of fat. Anywhere. Sinews and veins erupt from his skin, lining routes to that abdominal V we all like to put down in our books. The fuck contour as some describe it. All roads lead to it, apparently.

He watches me for a second or two, his eyes purely focused on mine and calmly searching me for something. It makes me feel insecure immediately, reminding me of wobbly bottoms and lips that don't fit my own bloody face. I look down, flicking my eyes back at my paper for a safer place to play. The imaginary world, that is. I'm in control there, happy to deliver anything without consequences to the emotion of my own life. Or lack thereof. It makes me realise how much I live my life through my characters, never stopping to endure the emotions myself in the real world.

My fingers smooth over the paper, nervously trying to find sense again, but Bree is right. How can I know any of this if I don't experience the sensations myself? What happened in that pool was extraordinary. The kiss – debilitating. I don't even know why, or what, or how, but he did that, made me feel something I've not experienced before. And it was nothing to do with pain, or even pleasure really. I was drowning for god's sake. Lost, but happy to be so.

"Dry yourself," he says, dumping his extra towel on the table by my writing and turning away from me. "I'll find you some clothes and call a cab."

"No." The word surprises me as it springs from my lips. So much so that I cackle to myself, looking at my writing for support of some kind. No. I don't want to leave. I want more of what he has to offer. I stare at my words, scanning the way the story has flowed so easily. It's entirely new, nothing like the story I've already drafted. "You... You did this, Blaine. I don't know how you did it, but I need you to do it again. It's brilliant, don't you see? That thing in the pool just now," I say, stabbing my finger over the bullet points and looking up at him. "The kiss." The sound of the word makes me look down, blushing slightly at the thought. "It's what I came to you for in the first place. Help. Research." He turns back to me, his sunken brow seeming angered by something as he begins to turn away again, shaking his head. "No, Blaine, please…"

He halts in the hallway, his head hanging low as I watch his back muscles exhale and inhale slowly. It's quite a moment, one of deep thought and confusion. If I wasn't so enamoured with it that my mouth was hanging open for a response, or the possibility of just going and licking his spine for the sheer intoxication of it, I'd be scribbling it down too.

"I can't, Alana. You need to leave," he eventually says, beginning his walk again and denouncing a conversation of any kind. Screw that. I need him to do this. Actually, I might need more of him, but that'll have to wait. He just has to help me. A new pen needs a book like this, and if I'm going to have to leave Val behind because of Barringer, I'm desperate to get this right.

I'm up and marching towards him instantly, grabbing at my notes and scrunching them into my hand. He's halfway up the stairs by the time I've caught up, dragging my wet dress with me as I go.

"Please, Blaine, I need help. Your help. You said you would, that you didn't have anything to hide." He just keeps ignoring me, his brow furrowed as he opens a door and walks into a bedroom. "It's not like it's hard for you. This is what you do, isn't it? They said master, didn't they? So just show me. Show me more of whatever that was in the pool." Still he just walks around the bedroom, opening draws and grabbing clothes, then shutting them and moving somewhere else. "Blaine, come on. It's not like I need you to work hard. It's your job, isn't it?" I continue, wandering quietly into the room and trying not to drip more water all over his carpet. "What harm can it do?" None that I can see, and if it gets me more of those feelings as well, then bonus. I'll deal with any consequence to my heart along the ride. "I'll pay if that's the problem." The mention of money seems to stop him in his tracks. His body swerves towards mine, bringing him within a foot of me and making me back up a step from his annoyed expression. "I don't mean like a prostitute," I splutter out. That's not what I meant. Although, I suppose that is what he would be doing if I paid him. He stares at me, still full of fury. "Look, I don't mean everything. Just whatever that was in the pool. What was that? What did you do? I need to know more about what that was? I couldn't think properly. Logically, you know? Everything was distant and weird. And the kiss. It was …" Amazing. Beautiful. Soul wrenching. Oh god, it was so soft. Tender. I shake my head at stupidity. I can't think about the kiss. This just has to be business. His eyes narrow, briefly skimming my body and then rising back to my face. Nothing comes out of his mouth, though, as he stands there, barely able to contain whatever is happening in his head. "I mean, you threw me in a pool for what? Punishment? And then I found myself wanting to stay under the water and drown until you came for me." Which still sounds utterly ludicrous, and quite frightening now I'm in the middle of discussing it rather than experiencing it. I stare down at my notes crumpled in my hand, wondering if this really is worth my life. "You did that, right? It was because of you."

I look back up at him, imploring him for answers as I search his face. He doesn't talk; he merely glances me over again, frowning and making me feel like a stupid little girl in the middle of something so much larger than myself. Eventually, he pulls in a sigh then blows it out, one hand resting on his highly toned hip as he brings his other up to his brow.

"That wasn't me. That was you."

"What?" That makes no sense.

He shakes his head, leaving me in the middle of the room again as he goes off in search of more drawers. Screw the drawers.

"Blaine, what's me?" I hear the huff of irritation directed back at me and couldn't care less. "Hey, I deserve an explanation if nothing else." Because I might even be able to write an entire book around that very experience if I get a little more clarification about it. I can embellish the rest, make it up as I go along if him showing me is such an issue. "And anyway, you're the one who told me you could help me out with my problem when I was wet the first time around, aren't you? Where's that cocky fucker gone?" The sharp turn of his frame has me backing off a little again, slightly concerned for my own wellbeing as he begins tugging at his towel. Death by orgasm springs to mind—not an entirely unappealing idea, although I'd rather not die from the sensation. Having said that, needling him seems the only way forward. "Well, you said I had to ask. I'm asking. And I am wet. So, do something to help with my state of arousal." I raise my brow at him, waiting for a response and considering lowering my halter-neck from my clasped hands. Maybe a little tease is necessary.

"Before you let that go, think carefully, Alana. Because no matter how much you tease, slut your way around, or try to push me, I will not show you what you're asking for. I can't." Oh, that's not useful at all. I frown at him, wondering what's so bad about me that I'm not worth enjoying for an hour or two. "I will happily fuck the breath from you, though, if you're asking."

That's not what I'm offering. I don't think I am, anyway. Actually, maybe I am.

"Screw you."

"Another lesson in manners?" Yes, if it'll give me that other sensation again.

"Fuck you." He frowns immediately, his body seeming to move backwards regardless of the fact that his feet don't. It makes me stare at him more, wondering what I have to do to get this out of him. It's like the man downstairs, the one who filled me with sensation and lips softer than air, has disappeared, leaving me with a shell who won't engage again.

"You don't know what you're asking for," he eventually says, flicking his gaze around the room as if he's uncomfortable with something. I don't understand what. It's not like this isn't his area of expertise. He should be used to dealing with women who challenge him, shouldn't he? This bit should just require lifting me, or making me kneel, or one of the many other things I've read about.

"Do you need more expletives? I've got quite the repertoire. I'm a writer, you know…synonyms and all that."

"Have you?" he says, throwing what appears to be jogging bottoms and a sweatshirt on the bed beside me, still frowning and seemingly bored as he turns away. "What other ones do you have?"

"Wanker." He smirks slightly, nothing more than that as he continues in the other direction. "Cunt." His body turns back to me, pitching through the waist as he fiddles with his towel. He clearly likes that word, enough so that it makes him lick his lips and slowly walk a step in my direction again.

"Why don't you tell me about yours?" Another step closer, making me check how close the wall is for potential escape routes should they be needed.

"What?" I'd like to say I'm still in control of this conversation, but my face must be as shocked as my tone, and the mere mention of cunts has my own considering his lips again.

"Talk about it, Alana. Tell me what makes it burn." My eyebrows shoot up, totally agog. Nothing makes my private area burn, apart from overuse, which frankly never happens.

"What a strange question." Who asks that sort of thing? And why is he moving forward again? His proximity makes me shiver, reminding me of the glacial water downstairs, and the fact that I'm still soaking wet. In more ways than one now thanks to his lips. And then he just pushes me backwards to the wall. It's only a small shove, but it's one that takes me by surprise as I thump against the plaster and stare in shock at the brunt of the impact.

"It's honesty. What you're asking for is all about honesty, Alana. You tell me about your cunt, and I'll consider your request a little more seriously than I currently am doing."

What the hell does one say to that? I'm sure the look of utter disbelief is flashing loud and proud on my face as I try to think about my privates in intimate detail. It's not like I can't be descriptive about them. I write it all the time. Just not about my own.

"Overuse?" I stutter out, barely able to contain the sudden mortification that's threatening. He moves in another step, only a thin layer of air separating our bodies as he hovers there and looks me over again.

"Your cunt knows nothing about overuse. It knows about ten minute drives of inadequacy, I should think," he replies, his arm suddenly bracing itself against the wall beside my head as he breathes deeply. "If it knew any better, you wouldn't be asking for my help, would you? Talk." I scrunch my nose up, accepting that fact to a degree and searching my mind for more plausible specifics.

"Teasing."

"Hmm. Better. What else?"

He says that as his hand skims the side of my arm, dragging a single finger along it as he decreases the space between us a little. What the hell else does he want me to say? A sharp tug suddenly breaks my grip on my top, making me aware that he's removed the halter neck from me and fully exposed both of my breasts. I wish I could stop the excessive breath that seems to come with this realisation, but my panting continues nonetheless. "Will me sucking these make you more talkative?" Fuck, yes.

"No."

"How about fucking you, Alana? Do you want me inside you?"

"Yes." Shit, I said that out loud, didn't I? I look away, gazing at the wardrobe for something to look at as he chuckles, running the tip of his finger down the front of my chest until it reaches my nipple. And then his other hand sneaks its way behind me, finding its way straight to the zip on my dress and beginning to lower it.

"You think fucking is going to give you the answers you want?" I'm not sure, but it's a damn good start at the moment given my panting and his mouth in front of mine.

"I..." Yep, I've lost all the words again, more than likely because he's lowered his mouth to my chest now, breathing his hot air all over it and skimming his lips around. Oh good lord it's all so dreamy, making me think of Val's stories and romance. Sort of. Actually, not at all.

"You don't know, do you?" he says, sliding his other hand to the back of me as well and tugging sharply again. The dress rips. I hear it tear as I gasp and feel the freedom from the restriction it normally delivers. It removes any thoughts of Val, reminding me about the hands currently holding me, and what they could do. And then he rips at it again, shredding the fabric and tightening his hold on my arse as he does. "Tell me that's the sensation you want, Alana." I don't know what I want. He's right. I don't even know what I'm doing apart from being a slut as I clutch these notes in hope, half bracing myself away and half totally absorbed. I look back at him, watching the way his eyes narrow as he pushes his body into mine and crouches a little to get better purchase on me. "You want me inside your mind, tearing it up from the inside, don't you?" Maybe. I'm not sure, and the fact I can hardy hear over my own breathing as he whispers is beyond frustrating.

"You're just a bored little cunt wandering in a world of clichés, aren't you?" His fingers move from my breast, travelling the length of me until he rucks the fabric up and draws it up my thigh.

He just hit the nail on the head. I am. I'm so full of stories that end well, happily, dreamily, pleasant and acceptable. It's all the same—love, connection, admiration. And that downstairs, those blissful moments by the pool, were beyond compare. "You want me to fuck that out of you?"

Oh god, his hand is near my crotch, flicking gently and moving my g-string out of the way. I can't think. Fuck it out of me? If I could speak it might help, but the sensation of him breathing and moving his hand closer, dragging his finger over my mound and slowly starting to dig inside my knickers is too consuming. I could come without thought. In fact, my hips are grinding with no help from me, welcoming his fingers even though I hardly know who he is. "Ask me to do it and I might." Ask him, yes. All I have to do is ask. He told me that downstairs. Just ask.

"I want you to..."

I haven't got all the words. For once in my life, and because of him, I haven't got all the words I need to explain something. It's foggy, unpredictable. I don't know what's coming or even what I'm asking for. And as his finger slips inside the material, the very tip of it skimming my clit as his lips touch my neck, I couldn't give a damn what I'm asking for. It's in his hands. That's what I want. He's my answer, I think. This right here is going to give me everything I need.

Chapter 6

BLAINE

A bored little girl with too many happily ever afters in her head to be affected by them anymore. The thought makes me wait for more to come from her mouth, enjoying the lilt of her voice as she half Americanises her British accent, but nothing more comes. She just stands and offers herself nervously. If it was nerves associated with pain, I'd be profoundly disinterested, but it isn't. It's fear of the unknown that tests her resolve, nothing else. She's the fierce kind. Wild with her mouth and rightly so given her intelligence. It makes me finger around her clit some more, listening to the hesitation in her breathing and waiting for her to ask. She doesn't. She just hovers there, her arms neither engaged in the moment nor pushing me away from it as my lips skim her chest again. It takes everything I've got not to just take her body and do with it as I choose. She smells of sex, her perfume wafting between us, the chlorine of the pool not diluting any element of passion that's pooling around my fingers. And she's as stunning as she was the first time we met. Her ass is as firm as I thought it would be, her hips as womanly as they ought to be. They're hips that need wrenching open, her legs spread wide so I can devour what little sense of realism she has, replacing it with the very thing she begs for. The vision makes me smile as I trace over the edge of her nipple, considering how she'll scream if I bite into it hard enough for blood to seep out. She'll yelp, I'm sure, but she'll buck against me, too, her cunt grinding for something she has little comprehension of. She has enough guile to warrant the pain, which is as interesting as the way she pants in front of me now.

She's riled me carefully, crafting her route to getting what she wants without deliberation or remorse. It's stimulating, and my mind's already engaged in thoughts of manipulation, enough so that I've barely been able to keep myself from fucking her where she stands as this damned cock throbs beneath me. What isn't as stimulating is the way she looked beneath the pool. The vision reeled thought back from places I'd hoped buried. Thoughts of connection, ones dowsed with the reality of being bonded in truth, being aware of commitment. Trust. It makes me haul in a long breath, giving her a few more seconds to make a decision and breathing her uncertainty in. Still she doesn't offer her words, but it doesn't stop the ache from building inside me. If anything, it heightens the need.

Eventually, I find some moral fortitude and reluctantly step away from her again, backing my footsteps slowly until I've put adequate distance between us again. Nothing about this should happen, irrespective of her need for it. Or mine.

"Put the clothes on, Alana. I'll call you a cab." Not surprisingly, her look of unadulterated sin turns to one of shock again as she steps a foot towards me, provoking more thoughts.

"But you said—" She doesn't finish that, which interests me more by the second. For a woman who can rally off a string of words without pausing when motivated to prove her worth, she's useless at it when sexually enthused.

"What did I say?"

"That you wanted to..." She trails off again, shyness creeping over her flawless features as she tries to look anywhere but at me. "That we should..."

"Fuck? Is that the word you're looking for?" She nods quietly, trying to push her dress up to cover her perfect breasts. "I didn't say we should fuck. What did I say?" She frowns and looks around the floor, perhaps searching for an answer. She only needs to roll back a few minutes and recall the actual words that left my lips. I know we should fuck. I'm more than engrossed in fucking her, but I won't be doing it anytime soon. I don't fuck anything anymore. It's an unsafe venture, certainly with something that interests me as much as this one does.

"That you'd..." She fidgets again, slowly taking hold of her dress and clutching it to her body as she moves over to the bed and looks at the clothes I've put out for her. "They're women's?" I don't answer her surprised question as she looks back up at me. I've got no intention of discussing why I have women's clothes here. I wouldn't have had any fucking intention of bringing a woman here ever again if we hadn't been twenty yards from the doorstep when Cole crashed fucking the car. Idiot.

Instead I grab my own clothes from the wardrobe and walk into the bathroom to get dressed, ready to forget any of this has ever happened. She won't come back to the club. She's too flighty to actually see this through, regardless of her need for the information. She's also too pompous in some ways. Constantly looking down her nose at the scene as if it's dirty or sordid, as she grips her notebooks. Talking haughtily of things she's knows nothing about. Perhaps she thinks the clubs are dens of heinousness, only propagating filth mongering and dissention from society. I couldn't fucking care less. She's wrong. They're places to be free and believe in your right to exist as you need to. Places of safety, to a degree.

"Do you bring many women here? Is it a thing your kind do?" she calls.

Her tone makes me glare at the mirror as I pull up my pants. My fucking kind? Am I a fucking alien all of a sudden? If I wasn't so preoccupied with my cock continually leaping about at her words, I'd go and show her the back of my kind's hand. "I mean, presumably you're all quite loose about who you do it with?" My temper and frustrated tension makes me grab on to the vanity unit, fear of doing something incomprehensible beginning to rile me further. I glare at myself again, taking in sharp breaths to calm my cock's wayward thoughts. For the first time in over a year, I want to fuck. It wants to fuck. Not the fucking I was tempted by three minutes ago. This is the old sense of fucking, the one I've pushed away for so long. It wants to batter something until it bleeds. Ravage it. Lose control in it. Specifically, the little madam who is presently half naked, sitting on my bed and waiting for instruction. I look down at my hands, watching the way they grab incessantly, as if even they know this is the wrong thing to do.

"I assume you do it a lot, really. I mean, your kind get up to all sorts, don't you?" It goes silent for a minute or two, giving me room to keep pulling in breaths in the hope I can contain the need to fuck her mouth 'til that bleeds, too. Why the fuck did I tell her she only had to ask? Why? And fuck, why did she look so good in that pool? No one has looked like that since... "And I'm assuming, as a Dominant, you just do what you want, don't you? From what I've gathered in other literature I've read, you're allowed to put your dicks in anything that moves without consequences. Acceptance or not." Fuck that.

I storm into the room, barging the door out of the way to get to her before she utters another word that demeans my community. The vision that hits me halts me in my tracks. Enough so that I grab onto the dresser for support and scowl at her.

"Take those off," snarls out of my mouth, not daring to walk another foot.

"But, you gave them to me?" she questions, glancing over the clothes she wears. She's right, I did, but I put no store on how seeing *her* clothes on a woman again would make me feel. I shift my feet, trying not to look at the way her breasts fill the t-shirt perfectly, or the way her legs are hugged by the material, just as *hers* were.

"Off." It's all I can get out of my mouth. And if this fucking cock wasn't indulging itself before, it certainly is now, confusing everything tenfold.

"Blaine?" Why the fuck does her voice sound so good when she breathes her B's, let alone allows the rest of her mouth to wrap around my name.

"Fuck you. Take them off." That isn't even a logical thing to say. It makes me furious with myself. So furious that I turn and rage from the room, slamming the door behind me and rubbing my head for clarity. Jesus fucking Christ. One of the clubs—that's what I need, and something in it. Leaving and getting out of this house is the first thing, the house I hardly ever come to.

I lengthen my strides down the stairs, aiming for the door, hoping fresh air will lesson this madness, then remember I can't fucking leave Cole alone. "Fuck."

No matter how much I want to shout that word out loud, I don't. I mutter it instead, standing stock-still by the front door and glaring at my shoes for not being on my feet so I can run from the little bitch upstairs.

"Blaine?" her voice says again, this time from not too far away regardless of my attempt at leaving. I swing my head around, catching a glimpse of her purple striped hair hovering at the top of the stairs as she leans over the banister. "I don't understand what you want me to do." Neither do I. For the first fucking time in over a year I feel downright out of control in front of a woman. "Tell me what you want me to do." The statement isn't useful. She means about taking the clothes off, I know that, but the connotation of dominance is all over her lips as well, whether she knows it or not. She wants it all taking from her. I could feel it in the way she drifted beneath the water, just waiting for someone to rescue her. Her whole being screams for help from someone. That person is not me. It isn't. It shouldn't be. I'm too much for someone like her. Too severe.

I turn from the door and head for my phone, hoping that simply getting her out of here will be enough to dowse her from my mind. It isn't, no matter how hard I squeeze the phone, and the need to walk back up those stairs overtakes my judgement. Her startled face gazes at me as I slowly walk the stairs back to her, both feet labouring each pace, neither in control of myself nor caring for the outcome. And her mouth quivers as her hands begins to hold themselves up, her feet backing her away at the same time.

"Changed your mind?" I ask, a sneer developing on my face as muscles prime for use. She looks behind her, possibly for where to run to. There isn't anywhere to run. "Push, push, push," comes from me, musing her continued asking rather than her body begging for a fucking it doesn't understand. "Here on the floor?" She shakes her head, her feet still moving away. It makes me chuckle and imagine her chained to the radiator as I drag my hand around the last of the banister. I could leave her there to wallow in her temper tantrum maybe, just as Eloise had done once before. Perhaps then she'd know who she was asking for help.

"I…" I don't stop my movement as she scans my body, her fingers sliding over her hips nervously as she looks around again. "Blaine?"

She has no fucking idea what's hurtling through my mind. The blood—its taste. The sight of it weeping, and the way my cock currently aches to have it on my tongue again. She doesn't know the pain either, or the nature of its sensation for deliverer or recipient. The thought rallies all those engagements to collide inside me. Dominance. Sadism. Control over something willing to take the brunt of me. The temptation of an innocent overwhelms the indecision inside, almost instantly bringing with it a calm for me to pitch against. I grab at the back of my shirt, pulling it over my head and throwing it to the floor. She watches it go, her hands outstretched again as she continues backing towards the third floor, her feet hitting the first steps. Stupid little brat. I smile again, remembering what's up there. It's the last place she should be leading me to. No one knows she's here. No one even knows that we know each other, apart from a few at the clubs, and not one of them will say a word. I could just keep her here for a week or so, show her the evolution of a story she could write, quickly. Let her feel the ramifications of cheeking a sadist. Let its effects sit on her skin for a while. Entertain myself.

"Blaine, I don't know what's happening here, but I don't like that look in your eye," she whispers, her feet faltering on a step and her ass falling to the floor because of it. Her face shoots up to mine swiftly as she rights herself, her eyes boring into mine filled with exactly the fear I crave. But there's something else there, too. I don't know what. Resolve perhaps. Tenacity even. She appears, regardless of her fear, aggressive in her demeanour. It's the most provoking presentation of honesty I've seen for some time, and it somehow snaps my mind from its calm, making me lick my lips and stop the forward momentum.

"I need you to go," I grate out, infuriated with the thought as I watch her panting, and yet overcome with the decency I've worked so hard to achieve all this time. "Get up, and leave before you have no choice left to make."

She has to go. I won't have her back at the club again. I won't meet with her again. I certainly won't engage my cock in its amorous intentions again. She's a liability, one I won't put my soul through the pleasure of. Once was enough for my mind to manage; twice is not of use. I can't do it again, no matter how hard my dick beats for her to be pinned against something and fucked until she screams.

She slowly gets up, her body sliding between the banister rails and me to get past, not once removing her eyes from mine as she goes. Good girl. Astute. Sensible. Fucking perfect, actually. And still filling me with indecent images and visions. She reeks of come now, the stench of its excruciating taste floating around the air and making me ache to stop her retreat. "Keep going," I continue, allowing her distance before I follow her descent to the ground floor carefully. When I finally get to her, my hands shoved into my pockets to disable their advance and my eyes landing on anything but her body or eyes, she just hovers by the door.

"I'll get you another research partner," I mutter, still transfixed by the sound of her breathing and the way her scent lights up the hallway, regardless of the fact that I've turned from her.

"I don't want anyone else," she replies, slowly manoeuvring her way in front of me. I try to keep my eyes away from her, desperately wanting to keep a safe distance between the two of us to make it easier, but she bats her fucking eyes knowingly. Without thought, I feel my mouth curve upwards at the gesture. She's such a clever little thing. It isn't surprising she can write a story so well. She appears to know all the correct tactics for engaging a man's interest. "I won't trust anyone else but you. Please, Blaine." She trusts me? Unwise. It makes me snort cynically and pick up a lock of her hair, barely restraining myself from tasting her lips again as they quietly tremble in front of me.

"You'll trust whoever you want, Alana," I reply, twirling the blonde edges and smirking at the purple highlights as I flick some of them away with a smile. Rebellion at its finest. "You're the one who needs the information. You'll ride whatever takes you to it. I'll find something else to fuck it out of you." She steps back, frowning at me and snatching the rest of her hair from me as she waves a hand around in my face.

"You don't have the right to tell me what to do," she spits out. I've told her nothing as far as I can tell, only that I won't help her any further and that I'll find someone else, regardless of my first offering. It's best for both of us. Practical. And she won't get hurt—physically or mentally with someone else. Not as long as I find her the right type of partner for her adventure. "Who the hell do you think you are?" Temper, temper. *Push, push, push.*

I smirk some more, enjoying the way she practically begs for a firm hand on her ass. I've seen all this before, hundreds of times. Watched the beginnings of a frayed woman's nerves get the better of her as they raise their voices and begin spouting forth diatribes of fury. She does just that as I watch the way her face contorts, removing the splendour of it and replacing it with tension and strain. It makes me tilt my head in thought, intrigued, wondering what would have her wound so tightly. And then she opens the front door, surprising me and lifting her chin as she readies herself to deliver more hostility, no doubt.

"Your loss," is all that comes from her mouth, though, her feet backing away from me and turning, a mocking smile trying to break through her frown. "You don't know what you're missing. You clearly don't know how to live."

I look straight at her ass as she slips her heels on. I know exactly what I'm missing, and I'm suddenly so enthused with reminding myself that I nearly grab for her belligerent little body and shove something inside it. And then she waggles the fucking thing in my face, cocking her hip and folding her arms as she waits and taps her foot. Brat. "If you're not man enough to help me then I'll find someone else on my own." Man enough? The thought infuriates me again. I feel it rise again so quickly it surprises me further, announcing my need for her more than I'm willing to admit.

"Good luck." It's my best response, and after checking she has her bag in her hands, I close the door behind her. It's the right choice. The only sensible choice. She's correct in her analysis of the situation. Someone who has little to no effect on me I'm willing to play with. Guide. Her, I'm not. The door knocks again instantly. I glare at it, wondering why she won't take the fucking hint, until eventually curiosity gets the better of me so I open it. Stupidly.

"Well, screw you," she spits out, grabbing the handle and slamming it in my face again.

I stand, stunned, and then realise I'm smiling so widely my face begins to hurt. It causes a chuckle to reverberate around my chest, reminding me of a long lost happiness and contentment. I can feel a sense of closeness wrapping around my hands, almost sense her in my hold. Still, I let my feet back away, allowing the wood beneath them to ground some logic into the circumstances regardless of her tantrum until her form disappears and I'm left alone again. The breath that huffs out as I accept her leaving is galling, making me chastise myself for some reason I'm not aware of. Perhaps I'm irritated with my lack of reasoning, or too much of the fucking emotion. My cock isn't happy about anything in any case, and I find myself staring at it, willing it to shut the fuck up.

"You're of no fucking use here," I mutter at it, wondering why it's so excitable. "She's just another woman." The damn thing disagrees vehemently, swelling further and batting around the inside my pants. "Your taste in women is terrible." And now I'm smiling again, which is the only workable response to talking to my own cock, and has nothing to do with Alana Williams and her wide, soft mouth that's in need of filling. She's gone. It's done.

Striding forward I launch myself up the stairs, hoping that half an hour with my brother might induce sentiments of the normal variety. Tedium.

"Cole?" I ask, rounding the corner into the guest bedroom. "You still alive?"

"How come you know the girl," is the response that comes from the bathroom.

"She's a researcher."

"Of what?"

"Research."

"What sort? 'Cause I know you're not doing psychology lessons anymore." I'm always doing psychology lessons. That's all this world is anymore. Self-abstinence may have removed the physicality of life, but the mind still remained occasionally engaged.

"None of your business." Cole strides back into the room, naked, a toothbrush perched in his mouth as he scrubs and glances him over.

"Why is your cock on display?" I will the damn thing down again, getting nowhere near making it happen. "Brother, you're interested," Cole mumbles around his stuffed mouth as he walks to the dresser and yanks out some of my old clothes. "Why? She's cute, but nothing special." She fucking is. She's beyond special. I cock a brow in response because cute is the least of my concerns where Alana Williams is concerned. Cute I can handle appropriately. She isn't cute. Cute depicts workable, easy to play around with. From the first time I saw her I knew I should have turned around and walked away. She was just waiting in the restaurant when I arrived, fiddling with her phone and smiling about something. I'd waited by the window for a while, watching the way she moved her hands through her perfect hair and wondering whether they'd wrap around my cock sufficiently. And then I'd noticed the way she snickered, lighting up the room with a devilish grin that defied normal amusement. It wasn't until I actually took her hand by way of greeting, though, that I noticed her need for more than she knew. She crackled in my grasp, just as she did earlier. Shivering and shuddering. She'd begged me then without even knowing she was doing.

"You thinking about starting again?" No.

Although, standing in this room now and thinking about the way her cheeks had blushed in the club, the way her body had quivered at the mere thought of more, and the way her blues eyes had shone with unknown need when she first saw a woman's ass strapped is tempting rational thought no end.

"No," I eventually reply, walking away from the conversation and out onto the landing again to grab my shirt from the floor. "I don't do that anymore. I teach." The ending of my statement is muttered with lacking finality to it, regardless of sending her away. I know it, and Cole will certainly know it. It makes me quicken my strides to get away from more interrogation, regardless of the fact that I'm peering out of the window the entire way looking for her. "I'm leaving in ten minutes."

The fact I have to have Cole tagging along with me all day is frustrating, but with family comes loyalty, and when Mina had visited last night, checking the pair of them over, she said that he wasn't to be left alone in case the knock to the temple had done more damage than she could see. I huff as I round into the lounge to get my keys. More damage? The guy is already out of his fucking mind. Driving with no licence. Getting women pregnant with no sense of remorse. Cole Jacobs is a dick—a dick I happen to be related to. One I vowed to protect from the moment the little fucker was born, regardless of the never-ending drama the bastard causes. It doesn't contain the stupidity that Cole is one of the most eligible twenty-eight-year-old bachelors in the city, or that he has more money than he knows what to do with. Women fawn over him, throwing themselves at him in the hope that he will settle down, produce children, perhaps be the man our parents had wanted him to be. I frown at the thought of my mother, snatching my keys off the coffee table and remembering the look on her face when I'd got my first position. Pride. Being a professor was good for a politician's son, a worthy cause, one I'd studied long and hard for from a young age. She'd been so proud standing there with my father, the pair of them mingling with society's finest at the induction of new students for their first semester. If only she'd known what lay beneath my veil of respectability as the students filtered past, all the girls batting their eyelashes at the dashing professor who smiled and nodded at fresh new skin. It was the hardest year of my life, tempting me with anything that moved as I dodged the daily advances for fear of showing my true self. The notes, the apples, the pleas for extra help after hours. She would have been so ashamed, so repulsed at what I really was inside the shroud of pretence. Not that any of it matters now, anyway. They're both dead and buried, the plane crash still as vivid in my mind as the day I watched it unfold on television. The money in both Cole's and my bank accounts now is just a reminder of a society I used to live in, one Cole flagrantly abuses, one I deny on all counts because of the wealth they left me.

I look up in the lounge and stare at the rows of framed commendations and degrees lining the wall, all neatly cornering the study area into its own space, and sigh. All that work, all that hope, gone in an instant, along with the reason I risked it all for.

"You ready?" Cole asks from behind me. I just keep staring at the walls, remembering the daily lectures and the enthusiasm the youngsters had, all the time wondering if it might ever be possible to rid myself of the guilt, perhaps go back to teaching again. The thought makes me snarl at myself, lowering my gaze and taking a final glance around the space. I won't be coming back again anytime soon. We should have been heading home instead. My own home. There's nothing here but old memories and pain. Pictures still litter the surfaces. Cushions I now despise lay unused on the sofa, a book on one of them, *her* perfume still lingering on its pages, no doubt. I smile a little at the image of her reading, her glasses perched on her nose as she licked her finger to turn a page. "Blaine?"

I turn, shaking my head at the vision of her in my mind and barely missing barging into Cole as I walk out towards the door then down the steps.

"You called a cab?" Cole asks.

"You can ride the subway like any other human," I reply, jogging down the steps to the pavement and buttoning my suit jacket. "You trash your car again, this is what you get." Cole snorts behind me, his feet halting.

"You're the one who denies the money, Blaine, not me. Fuck you and your subway rides." I swing round to watch him hailing a cab at the side of the road, my own jeans and t-shirt sitting as comfortably on Cole as they always do. Fucking idiot. He's like a pubescent schoolboy—horny, lazy, and without cause or hope.

"When are you going to grow up, Cole?"

"Never. You should try growing down, brother," Cole shouts back, clicking the handle on a waiting cab and stepping inside. I cock a brow again, smirking at the connotation of being less sensible with my decision making process. "Fucking something without thought would do you good." Without thought. Not something I've done in a long time, and certainly not fucking something without it. "Get in the cab. Spend some of that fucking money you've got holed up doing nothing. Christ, Blaine. I'm not the only eligible bachelor in town. You're not dead yet." I flick my gaze to the road again, watching the rush of traffic going by, and then stare up into the sky, hoping for a sign to wing its way down from above. "You coming?"

No, I'm not, but I want to. I want to fuck and come. I want to live. Perhaps it's Alana Williams' words, or perhaps its Cole's words—

I don't know, but for the first time in a long time I want to live. *"You clearly don't know how to live."* Those were the words she used, her contemptuous mouth smiling around them as she snarled out her scorn.

"No, you go. I've got something to do," I reply quietly, my strides already heading in the direction of Drake's club. I don't know what it is that I want to do, but it doesn't involve Cole, and I can't be bothered with the tedium of looking after him either. "Stay awake," I call back as an afterthought. Family duty or not, this feeling inside is making my feet wander of their own accord, reminding me of desires that simply take hold without thought. And the sight of Alana is still firmly imprinted, her lips trembling as she sat on the step, unsure of what was coming next.

"Can you even fuck without hurting someone?"

The thought pops into my mind as I amble the pavement and stare blankly into the clutter of people coming at me. It was Cole's continued discussion in the car before the crash, regardless of the fact I tried every way of shutting the fucker up. *"No."*

It had been my only response to the question. It was honest. Truthful. Sure, I can fuck, but I can't come, never have been able to while fucking. There isn't a debilitating story to tell about old injuries or abusive behaviour. I've had a normal family, normal upbringing. Loving and comforting. I shouldn't be any different to Cole, but I am. I can jack off, be jacked off. Sucked off. But fucking, letting my seed go inside someone else? Impossible, unless they either screaming or nearly unconscious. Years went by with me thinking I was a pervert, or that something was wrong with me. I fucked everything I could in college, hoping to find one it worked with. I even tried men, but that didn't worked either, not until it was a man who wasn't sure if he wanted it or not. It had been a struggle, both of us almost fighting our way through fucking. It was the first time I'd ever come in anything, bringing with it a sense of discharge I'd never found before.

I continue onwards, my hands in my pockets as I wander the avenues letting the memories come and imagining the smell of the guy as I'd held him against the locker room wall. It was some high-end dick, one who came from wealth, shorter and weaker than me at the time, and one who was too friendly for simple friendship's sake. Not that I'd given a fuck about friendship at the time. Or rights and wrongs. The guy had been a hole, nothing else, just something to try on for size.

Crossing by the lights, I find myself smiling at a woman as she gazes back, a sexy little half smile telling me of anything but the meeting she's heading to. I hover her there for a minute, just letting her stand in those few seconds and remember she's attractive, relatively anyway, and then I let her go as I turn away. The magician's trick, Delaney calls it. *"You're like a fucking magician."* No, just a good professor of the mind, one who enjoys to taunt every now and then. I care little for the mechanics of people's everyday life anymore, relegating them to ineffectual content. They all long for something more intriguing than they have, all the time wasting themselves away in their drone of monotony. That's why I do what he do, I suppose. I make money teaching and labour forward, occasionally stalling with something of partial interest and offering them a new vision. Not that I need the money, Cole's right, but that isn't the point. I feel comfortable in this guise, enjoying the way my type of people open themselves up, accepting each other's foibles and relaxing in them. It's the psychologist in me, I assume—that or the sadist who wants to taunt and taint the world.

I watch more ordinary humans pass me by as I turn the roads, all of them limited by their inability to question themselves. Not one of them will grow without conscious effort to strip and be stripped. I doubt anything makes most of them groan or cry in pain, other than the daily grind of bills and life. Nothing makes them suffer consequence as a primal act or real fear should. They just keep filtering past, restricted in their outlook, and all bound by the constructs they build around themselves.

By the time I reach Drake's club, I've had nothing but visions of Alana haunting me again. It's annoys me as my mind reels over the possibilities of another sense of companionship. Perhaps Drake's will be a good detour for a few hours. I can sit, drink. Perhaps get drunk and watch the world go by so I stop imagining her constantly. Or maybe I'll beat something and continue imagining her face instead. Maybe that will dull my cock's enthusiasm. Long legs, full breasts, tight ass. Lurking evil eyes behind a soft frontage, ones she switches to a devil's glare without too much effort. I suppose if I couple that with the way she riles me, tossing her holier than thou attitude around and making our people appear dirty somehow, I'm not surprised she's become all-consuming to my world of analytical problem solving.

My own fucking fingers fumble with the lock as I envision her ass high in the air, or her hands bound into cuffs. Writing a fucking book about me and my people? How fucking dare an outsider even attempt the thought let alone call me at a club and ask for guidance. I eventually walk in and travel through the back corridors, a sneer on my face and not understanding why I currently ache for her so much. Nothing else has been as interesting since Eloise, and yet here she is, sparking something of consequence and waking my cantankerous cock up again. It pisses me off, enough so that I head straight for the bar, hoping to douse the feeling with Scotch and rid myself of it.

When I arrive, the cavern of back corridors eventually breaking out into the main rooms, I hear sniffing coming from a corner. I ignore it for the first few minutes and reach for a bottle of Drake's finest, assuming it's a sufferance something has been put under, but it eventually turns my head as I sink my first glassful. A woman's there, huddled beneath the stocks, her legs tucked into herself as she tries to get further into the shadows. I look back to the room, searching for an owner or someone of significance who can tell me why she's there. Nothing seems interested in her. No one watching or caring for her endurance. I tune the rest of the noise out and listen to her murmurs. They're fearful, not remorseful. She isn't apologising; she's frightened. It makes me stand and wander over, unconcerned with anyone's reaction to my involvement.

"Adam," Drake's voice says before I make it another step forward. I twist my head to look at the guy, a brow raised for explanation. "Got a bit carried away, apparently." Did he. I snarl at the thought, ready to tear the little shit a new asshole for this kind of behaviour, then walk on to crouch in front of her. Bruises litter her skin from collarbone upwards, her make-up, what's left of it, is barely covering a scrape to her cheek. She twitches in my hold as I tip her chin, her fingers scrabbling for grip on the blanket she's tugging closer.

So I pull it away slowly, briefly noticing the fingerprints around her throat before she grabs it back again.

"And you thought you'd just leave her here like this?" I ask, as infuriated with him as I am with Adam for such disrespect. "She needs care, Drake. Look at her."

"It's not my responsibility to manage this," the guy says, walking past me and away from the scene towards the next set of rooms. "I balance the books. That's it. I fucking pay you for a start and you do worse than this." I spin on the guy, ready to tear him another fucking asshole, too. Never once have I done something in here without being asked, apart from last night. I teach; that's all, and this is apparently the result of last night's teachings. "She's just another pain slut. Let her weep, Blaine." The thought sickens me as I stare back down into her eyes, perhaps trying to calm her down as I push the rest of the blanket towards her. One show of true sadism from my own hands for the benefit of learning, and this is what has come of it? One small weakness. One moment of captivating blindness to show the possibilities and Adam has acted without sense? Fuck. The vision causes me to shake my head at myself, chastising my own flaws and castigating my inability to control them. I've made this happen, regardless of Adam's involvement. This woman quivering in front of me, frightened for her life and in pain, is all because of my sadism, not Adams.

"You'll be alright," I say, smiling slightly and trying to control the lecture that wants to propel me away from her towards wherever Adam is. "Do you know where he is?" She shakes her head, tucking the blanket higher to her chin and trying to back away from my hold. She's lying; she knows exactly where he is. She's just too scared of the man currently holding her to say anything at all. I'm not surprised, but her fear of me isn't necessary at this time. I don't own her. She has nothing to be scared of. "Up you get. Come. I'll show you some magic." She frowns, her head still shaking as I pull on her arm and force her to her feet. "'Shall I let him know what it feels like?" She looks around nervously, her body shivering as she slowly balances her feet and covers herself with the blanket. "You can watch." I need to beat something anyway, and this will be legitimate. I can imagine Alana's eyes instead. "Just tell me where he is." She nods slightly at the stairs, slowly, her face quickly lowering to the floor again in submission as her feet scuttle her away from me. "You have nothing to be scared of here, not from me," I say, swiping the bottle of Drake's finest, along with the glass, and heading in the direction she's indicated. I pour her a large shot as we climb the stairs, handing it back to her and letting her keep pointing the right way.

"Sir?" she says, her voice barely a quiver. "He won't touch me again?" No, Adam won't be touching anything for a while. The thought makes me smile, possibly amusing myself with the potential image of what has happened to her, even if it is unacceptable. She looks a mess—rightly so if owned, but she isn't, and I told Adam not to touch anything aggressively without me present. "You... You're a trainer, aren't you?" she asks, her voice finding itself after a sip or two of Scotch. I nod in reply, knowing they all know who I am and what I do. "Then, you taught him to do this?" My feet linger on the landing as she passes me, anger working its way through me again at the thought. "He hurt me, and you showed him how to do it?"

She quivers there in front of me, her lips trembling around the words as she asks me for answers. It infuriates me further. Enough so that I nearly grab her and show her real pain.

"Where is he?" I bark out, unable to answer the question and growing more incensed because of it. She jumps backwards, my hand reaching for her at the same time before she falls down the damned stairs. "Where?" Enough with the fucking pleasantries and coddling. I snap her to me then push her in the direction she's already indicated as I point at the doors. "Which one?" She cowers instantly, her body lowering to the floor, presumably attempting the crawl she's been trained into by some other Dom. I couldn't care less for crawling, or kneeling. I'm certainly not charmed by its positioning beneath my feet. I just want Adam. That's all.

"There, Sir," she says, her voice beginning to sniff out sobs again.

I roll my eyes at her, bored with her melodramatic reaction to my question, and then open the door leading to one of the dens. The light's dimmed, only just basting the area with a low red gloom. And the stench is intense. It's come filled, the salty tang of it permeating the room as I gaze across the languid bodies looking for Adam. I find him in the corner, his hand ferreting about in something of no importance as they all roll over each other, an orgy carrying on regardless of this girl's discomfort. I turn back out again and grabbed her from the floor, dragging her in and upturning a discarded chair in the far corner for her to sit on.

"Stay there and hold that," I snarl, handing her the bottle and covering her with her blanket again.

Three strides across bodies and I heave on Adam's half naked frame, my fingers digging into the cunt's ass the moment I've got him upright. The surprise is clearly enough to give me a few second's grace, and that's plenty of time for me to have chained the little fucker face down on the table in the middle of the room before he gets a chance to move away. The clunk of the third lock wrenches the bastard's right leg wide, my own hand helping the momentum by way of the pulleys. The whole fucking thing makes me chuckle as Adam grunts and I keep manoeuvring the locks into place, all the time avoiding his thrashing arms.

"The fuck are you doing?" Adam shouts. The sound of his voice rouses other bodies to begin turning. Good, they can all have a little fucking show about how not to get on the wrong side of me, too. Most of them are degenerates anyway, from what I can see, and they're all in need of discipline one way or another.

"You disobeyed me, Adam," I reply, kicking a woman by my feet to get her to move out of the damn way. "What did I say to you?"

"What?"

"The exact fucking words I left you with last night—what were they?" Adam goes still on the table, presumably thinking. It's not quick enough, though, causing me to walk back over to the girl and offer my hand, asking for the bottle, which she hands over slowly. "What were the words, Adam?" There isn't much of a response, not one worthy of my consideration anyway. Some irate mumblings maybe, but nothing more, so I pull the guy's pants down until one leg comes off, yanking on the left pulley at the same time to spread him wider. "This is going to hurt, Adam."

There really isn't any more to be said. Nothing I care to say anyway. Entering a man's body is as easy as a woman's, as long as you know where to aim for. Unluckily for Adam, it's been a while since I've invested in the act, which just means the yell that sounds through the air is louder than expected as I begin shoving the bottle in his ass. People stare. I don't give a fuck. In fact, it turns me on as I keep twisting the fucking thing and shoving. It's a show. That's what I do. Entertain and teach I'm glad they'll fucking enjoy the lesson. Perhaps it'll make the lot of them think fucking twice before they decided to hurt something in their care.

"You pissed me off, Adam." Adam seems unamused, his body squirming on the table as he tries to break his bonds. It's a shame, because the vision's extremely humorous, comical even, enough so that I get my phone out and take a few photos as I sit on the velvet seat. "I'm not friendly when pissed." I lean back, putting my feet up on the table within in an inch of the glass bottle currently twitching about, neck deep, from the asshole.

"I don't know what you…"

Already uninterested in the conversation, I look back at the girl, smiling at the way she still quivers in her corner, her blanket neatly drawn around her as she gazes at the bottle, her feet tucked up again.

"Go around the front," I suggest, wanting nothing more than for Adam to see what he has caused himself. He needs to see it, and he needs a definitive negative response to the action, one I'm happy to deliver. She doesn't move, she just sits and quakes more. "Go." I growl it the second time, resulting in a more enthusiastic response as she gets up and slowly inches the perimeter, her body weaving quietly through the throng and eventually ending up in Adam's eye-line. "What did I say to you before I left, Adam?" I tap the bottle, nudging it further in and then watching it pop back out a little with a smirk. "I could have sworn I said not to touch anyone." I tap it again, harder this time, listening to the taut, pained grunt that results from the impact with a smile. "She looks like she's been touched to me."

Something's said. It could have had please attached to the end of it, or it could have been someone else protesting about the behaviour. I barely hear it, or care. This is a lesson in discipline, not a conversation about why. They'll learn with barely any words involved before someone gets truly hurt. The girl's face is becoming more interesting as she begins smiling at me, anyway. Which is diverting. She hardly sees the man in between us anymore. She just stares, a mix of awe and wonder tracing her eyes. She looks pretty with her tear-stained cheeks and her bruises, her fingers still gripping the blanket as she waits. Fuckable. Just a waif of a girl really, not my type at all, but she trembles so beautifully as she stands there. She'd be an entertainment for a while, one that would fall into my hands with just one click of fingers.

"Drop the blanket. Show him," I murmur. She does, slowly, causing my eyes to travel ravished skin hungrily. It might be a fucked up reaction, but it's mine, still. The stripes and scratches arouse me as I skim her outlines and transfer my cock's intentions to Adam's prone body instead.

Just the thought of aggression makes me raise my foot a little more than I should, nodding at Adam to get the girl to look into the face of the man who has hurt her. She does that too, already in my spell as I slam my heel onto the end of the bottle, repeatedly. Bellows and pleas for mercy ring the air. Chains shake, rattling and scraping the table's metal surface. The girl's eyes widen as she gasps, possibly in fright. Who fucking cares? I'm awakened as people in the room scatter across the back wall, some of them retreating to the corners in fear. Their whispers and mutterings just heighten my scene, making me look at a few of them, wondering which would take the most pain if I chose to carry on. I'm not concerned anymore about the initial issue as I continue slamming the bottle. At some point I've become provoked, absorbed in more than simple disciplinary repercussions. The thought makes me imagine Alana Williams and her lips again. That vision only enhances the room's equipment ten-fold as I gaze around it and catch glimpses of several subs. Perhaps I could lose some time here, become involved in what my hands harbour, show Adam what real sadists choose to do with their time.

The sound of the crack makes me tilt my head and stop, my eyes following the fissure that runs a rivulet along the base that's still protruding. Done.

I stand and wander around the front, buttoning my jacket again and instantly smiling at the tears that course over Adam's cheeks. They're as provocative as the girls have been in some respects, more so given the fact a man can take so much more, but still not as beautiful as Alana's trembling lips or the taste of her snide skin. For once, Cole's right. She has sparked my interest. I could almost say I've become invested in the idea. Alana Williams, rightly or wrongly, is a thing that needs attending to, regardless of how she made me feel in that pool or the concerns that came with that thought.

I pull in a long breath, accepting the inevitable, and nod at the girl as she smiles meekly, her tears now gone as she looks at Adam and fidgets. I simply hand her the key to the locks on the chains and begin leaving the room, happy to let her have the final say on what should happen to little cunts who don't follow my rules.

"It's about to shatter," I say, tapping the glass one final time as I walk by and then glaring at a new man who stands between me and the door. "One more shove and magic happens." I stare at the dick in the doorway, willing him to try something and provoke me further. What would be next? A stripping? A beating? The lash of the nine tail hanging beside my head layered over flesh for an hour? This dick's cock in a vice? I tilt my gaze at the guy, licking my lips in thought and wondering if this one likes magic, too. Unfortunately he moves, his body making room for me to leave and lessoning my fun as he does. "Next time, do as you're fucking told, Adam. I won't have this conversation again."

Chapter 7

ALANA

I can't stop writing. I'm fucking possessed. And not like with normal Valerie books. Oh no, I'm involved in this. It's pouring out as if I have no idea what I'm writing or where I'm writing to. It's normally so planned and mapped, like I know the story well before I've started. Lines drawn, chapters made and noted out, but this—this is like it was when I started writing. It's higgledy-piggledy. A mess. I can't concentrate on any one bit. My hero's an arsehole. My heroin's weak as piss as she flaps around not knowing what to do with herself. Oh, and sex scenes. Wow. Whoa. I almost had to go for a shower at one point, which would have been nowhere near as inspiring as my dip in the pool at Blaine's house.

The thought of him makes my pen halt halfway through a word that I now can't remember. Everything's gone blank apart from him and his mouth. What is it with his mouth? It's either delivering filthy words or smiling, no, smirking at me. And oh god, that kiss too. So soft. So warm. Nothing like I expected, not that I know what I should have expected. The frown's good, too, almost edible. It makes me want to lick it off his face and run my fingers through his dark hair.

I haven't even changed out of this old running outfit since I got back. I'd like to say I'm pissed off at the way he shut the door in my face, and I suppose I was in some ways, until he opened it so I could slam it back in his just to prove my point, but I'm not really. I'm not pissed at all. I'm enlightened by something. It's making me excited to write again, just like I was in his house. Notes are scattered around me over my small kitchen table. Names, dates, times—it's all here. I've no idea where it's leading me, but it kinda makes sense, to my mind anyway. And it's all because of him.

Standing up, I stretch my body out, letting the pen fall to the table for the first time since I got back and looking around. Things look different for some reason, as if they're too perfect for me. The kitchen area is immaculate, but the small dining area I'm in seems lacking in warmth, and for some reason, even the lounge looks scant, which is normally the way I like it. It all just seems deficient in some way. Lacking homeliness. I scan the rooms again, walking about as I have done a thousand times in my own home. The light blue tone seems cold suddenly, and the pale creams and yellow accents that I chose to match perfectly now seem devoid of any heat at all, and then, as I look over my beloved grey, chesterfield in the middle of all this modernity, I realise even that seems empty. It's not. It's got a few cushions scattered over it in greys and blues, but it seems huge sitting there all on its own by the cream coffee table. My face scrunches up, not understanding where this new sensation is coming from. I spent time and money here, creating the look I loved and filling it with not too much so as to construct peace around me while I write. Maybe I need a makeover.

ONCE UPON A

My fingers run along the walls, as I head towards my bedroom, already knowing the sensation will be magnified once I reach it. If anything's lacking life in this house, my bedroom certainly is. It's a place of rest; that's it. Nothing else happens in there. Never once has a man been here. I've purposely made it so. I don't really know why. It's not like I ever had a really bad relationship, or someone did something unacceptable. No rape incidents. No off my face and doing something stupid. I just haven't seemed to like men very much over the years. Of course, I *like* them, and some of them have been reasonably entertaining for an evening, but they just don't appeal as something I need to complete me. I've tried a few weeks, one a month or so, but it just doesn't work for me. There's nothing about them that makes me feel they're needed or that they'll give me something that adds to my sense of life. I am complete. I have done all this on my own, without the need to hang from a man or have his opinion alter my course. They seem unnecessary normally, something I can either have or leave alone. Unfortunately, nature calls on occasion, tempting me into its bidding. That bidding tends to end up with me feeling reasonably satisfied with the experience, but not overly bothered if it happens again. Frankly, the vibrator that's hiding in one of my matching cream bedside cabinets is just as useful, if not more so. It doesn't ask me to divulge information or give away emotions. Not that I have too many to give away. I'm reasonably happy, reasonably sensible, mostly calm and calculated about decisions. Occasionally something sets me off kilter, ruining my chakras or whatever, especially lately now I come to think about it, but nothing really gets in my way or hinders me to the point of frustration. I'm what you'd call settled, I suppose. Settled and happy to continue being so. Rushed and hassled about deadlines permanently, of course, and constantly in need of my little pick me up pills, as I like to call them, but mainly I'm on track. Or I was, until I started thinking about what else is out there.

I turn from the room, a little irritated at why my perfect cream look suddenly seem devoid of anything interesting, then make my way back to the table and smile. It feels so good to want to write again. So good, in fact, that my hands graze across the paperwork, finally believing in something other than what my publisher asks for. This is me, right here in front of my eyes; this is what I started doing it for—passion, suspense, a love story based on something beyond the usual. So many times I've written the same words, changing up the storyline obviously but then always coming back to the same ending, but this… I don't know what this is. This seems darker, a mix between Peter and Val. A new type of intrigue. To anyone else this would look a jumbled mess. Chaos. But to me it's littered with brilliance, ready and waiting to be pieced together harmoniously—if I can actually make that happen without him. It's a shame, because it reeks of something I wouldn't have gotten close to without being shown or experiencing something new. In fact, now I really think about it, it reeks of Blaine Jacobs, his abs and mouth included.

The thought makes me plonk my arse down on the chair, wondering how the hell I'm going to be able to pull all this together without his help. I know he said he'd find me someone else, and I know I told him, basically, to go screw himself, which was kinda stupid, but no one else is going to cut it. I trust him. I'm unsure why given what happened on his landing, which was quite odd and a little scary, but I do. It's some kind of pull. Something is real and tangible with him, as if we're just out of reach but lingering in readiness nonetheless. I've read snippets of it in some of the other books I've leafed through for research. A sense of connection unlike anything else, they said. And the subs said the same thing really, with their sighs and moans. If what happened with Blaine is anything to go by, they're right. It's a draw, an enticement that makes me want to give him something. I'm not sure what. I don't even think it's me, not physically anyway. It's more emotive than that, more poignant. Oh god, I don't know. It's just something that's more than I've given before.

My phone bleeps, dragging me back from my musings as I shift another piece of scribble covered paper around. I don't look at it. I haven't got the time or inclination to bother. It's probably just another hassle I don't want to deal with. And anyway, I've got more of this to do. It's my way. Knuckle down and get on with what's flowing. There won't be food or bathing until I'm satisfied I've achieved enough for the day. I just need to get all of this into the laptop, at least in some semblance of order, and then I can worry about how I'm going to make Blaine show me more. I gently lift the pages, keeping them in order as I make the first run over to the office. It has to be placed correctly. In order. If it's not in order then I'll lose my way. It's already disturbing enough in my mind, making me try desperately to contain it in its rightful place and find a current for it to travel along. The last thing I need is for it to start falling over on paper, fucking it all up before I've had chance to plot it properly.

Just as I'm about to go back for the next lot, my phone bleeps again twice, tempting me to have a look. I snatch it up, ready to switch it off for its interference, but notice Blaine's name and freeze.

- This is not going to be enjoyable for you.

What isn't? And why has he said that?

My mind searches the words for some hidden meaning, as if he might be trying to convey something in between the actual letters. Nothing's forthcoming, so I scan the next one.

- Pack a bag and be ready for 9pm.

I don't know what that means. What does that mean? 9pm? Why?

- Wear an evening gown.

An evening gown? What sort? What?

If messages could be vaguer, I'm not sure what they would say. My fingers scrabble back a reply asking why, what sort, and why I need an overnight bag. I refrain from asking who the fuck he thinks he is, or telling him that a please might be nice. Not because I haven't got the balls, more because I haven't got a choice. I need him for this. I need what he has to offer so I can get this book done. And regardless of how much I might hate to admit it, the flutter of nerves in my stomach is mind-blowing. It's that mouth of his, isn't it? It's the way it connected with mine, making me feel al gooey and significant in some way. The thought makes me stutter as I swear at the phone, at him really, for some reason unsure if I'm even allowed to swear in my own home.

He doesn't reply swiftly as I sit here for ten minutes staring at the phone. In fact, it seems there isn't going to be a response at all. Great. It's not going to be enjoyable for me, I need a bag, and I need an evening gown.

I check the clock, trying to imagine what's in my wardrobe as I do. 1pm. An evening gown? What do I have? We must be going somewhere posh. My favourite high-end thing is still in his house, ripped, from what I can remember. Why did I leave that there? I loved that dress. It was me. I look down at the tracksuit I'm still wearing and consider just tipping up in that. Perhaps that would show him who's in control of this relationship. Not that we're in one. He's just research. Research. For god's sake. A relationship? What is wrong with me? I need Bree.

I've sent a message to her before I reach my bedroom, telling her to meet me at Saks in an hour. It's not like she'll have anything else on. She never does. Apart from yet another release, which she can do on her tablet, anyway. But what Bree does have in bucket loads is style. It pours from her. She's the sort that throws stuff together, somehow making them look both ingenious and elegant at the same time as sexy. I need sexy. Properly sexy. I need more of what he did to me. I need to feel the same sensations so I can write them.

I get one single letter back as a response.

- K

It's all I need to propel myself into the shower, discarding the tired old tracksuit into the bin as I go. It might have been comfortable but it's not nice. It makes me wonder why he had women's clothes in his house at all. That thought, for the first time, makes me halt my furious scrubbing and consider whether he's actually got a partner. I've assumed not from his behaviour. No one talks about cunts and fondles breasts if they've got a partner, do they? Or maybe they do in his world. I stare at the tiles, watching the water splatter the wall, and wonder what the hell I'm doing. This is supposed to just be about a book. That's all. Just information gathering, no feelings involved. No thought other than getting what I need from him. If he's got a partner, what does it matter, I suppose? If he's happy to initiate that sort of thing then it's either okay, or he doesn't care, in which case, I shouldn't worry. I won't worry. Whatever's going on in his family life is nothing to do with me. I've asked for his help. This is obviously his way of giving it. Why that involves me wearing an evening gown, I'm not sure.

I'm out of the shower, dressed and walking to the front door without much more thought on the matter. I don't really care in all honesty. It's not my problem to deal with. I grab my bag and slam the door behind me, checking my phone in case Bree's cancelled. She hasn't, thank god. And then I start thinking about it again. It wouldn't be surprising if he's got a partner. I mean, he's gorgeous. He could have several of them dotted about. One in every port, so to speak. He's the type we all write about. Bad boy with an attitude. Or intelligent man with unfairly good looks to boot. And psychology professor? That was an interesting little nugget of information, one I haven't really given any thought to either. How does a psychology teacher get involved in BDSM, let alone become what they call a Master of it? I'm still not sure what that accolade entails.

I hurry along the sidewalk, suddenly full of enthusiasm for life as I go. I'm like a new me, or the old me. I'm full of verve, so much so that I could skip if I thought about it. I don't, clearly, but the thought does make me smile widely as I keep avoiding the oncoming masses of daily walkers. Ladies with their dogs, men with their umbrellas, all ambling along with their own minds wandering as mine is. It makes me remember the joy I took in each step when the publishers offered me a contract. It was my first time here. New York was so large, huge in comparison to the small town I grew up in. I'd flown over on my own and then made my way into the offices on my own to sign my deal. It felt like the first time I'd done anything on my own. It felt good. Really good. I remember feeling elated, as if I could conquer the world. I suppose I did in some ways. I've made my way, survived the big city's wolfs. I only went home for two weeks to bag my belongings, which wasn't a lot. Yes, it was tough at first, really tough given the shitty contract I'd signed, but then things got easier, and then the real money started coming in. Life, while unfair at first, has been damn good to me here. It's only the last year or so that has been a little odd. That's been nothing to do with money or success, though, but personal goals. They've felt deflated in some way, or maybe not even thought about. Life has become so monotonous. Not today, though.

Turning onto Columbus, I head over towards the Plaza, dodging the stream of traffic as it crawls by, honking and blaring sirens at me. One thing I have learnt about Manhattan is that the traffic doesn't give a damn if you walk out in front of it. It'll slam you down without thought. It's half the reason I cab everywhere, but today, well, it's a beautiful day. The sun's out. The sky's blue. Birds are chirping. And me, well, I'm just feeling bright, excited. Ready for life to throw something at me that I don't know about. New beginnings, or ridding myself of this stagnation I've been in.

By the time I've reached Fifth Avenue, I'm ready for anything, new adventures included. Just the thought of this book, or him maybe, is making me ready to take the world on with less venom than I normally would. I want to flow with it again, amble within it, taking in the unusual as I go.

"That's a serious smile you're wearing there."

I swing round to see Bree walking behind me, her hand on her hip as she mutters into her phone at the same time. She stares at me, covering the mouthpiece on her phone and smiling. "Yes, *your* smile, Lana." I smirk a little at her, trying to fathom the smile that is indeed plastered on my face. "Well, send me the bill and I'll pay it," she snaps. I assume she's talking into the phone this time. "Fuck you." She stabs the phone, then slips it into her bag, which is the first time I've seen it detached from her hand in god knows how long.

"In your bag?"

"Yep. What we doing here?"

"Shopping for evening gowns."

"Right. Why?"

Ah yes, why. I scan over her clothes, noting the way she's managed to make it all look effortless in a grungy way. Blue ripped jeans, a beige shirt with a cardigan over, baggy on the thigh and a belt pulling it taut. Long brown boots and a tan bag. Her dreads are down, scooped up slightly at the sides with a clip. Fabulous. It makes me look down at my own combination in dismay. It doesn't look bad, but I wish I had that sense of charisma when putting my outfits together. They just don't hang well on me, not the way they do on her anyway.

"I don't know."

"What?"

"I don't know why. I just need a gown. I'm going out somewhere that needs a gown."

"What are you talking about?" Quite. Even to my own ears that needs more explanation. "Who with?" Apparently I don't need to answer that, because her brows rise, a wry smile tipping her lips upwards as she slides her arm into mine and starts us walking. "Him?" I nod, lifting my chin to show I'm in complete control and this is not something I should be concerned about in any way. "So we need a dress that rips off easy, yeah?" If only she knew. My feet halt, immediately turning me back to her with a look of horror on my face. It's fake. We both know it, and her smirk at my dramatics only highlights that fact as I break out into another smile. "All for research, obviously," she says, tugging me to get me moving again. "Tell me about him. I need data for the dress. You got a picture?"

We turn into Saks as I wonder what I can say, bypassing the make-up brands and chemical layers of perfume to get to the clothes. It's not like I know anything about him really. He's fit. Good looking. Around six foot two, I guess. Built like an athlete, one everything looks perfect on.

"What do you need to know? I don't really have any—"

"Dark or blonde?"

"Dark." Not that I'm sure what difference that makes.

"Tall?" I nod.

"Taller than me in heels."

"Naughty?" What? He's into BDSM. I would think so given the club I've already been in, not that I've actually seen him do anything. My bemused stare as she picks up a red dress is barely noticed. "Yeah, but I mean, cheeky naughty, as in red, or dark and nasty, as in black?" she says, fingering the material and flicking it away as if it's cheap tat.

"I'm not sure." Her face fills with scepticism as I think about that kiss, and then remember the slight deviation from lovely when he had me backing up the stairs.

"You've been in a kinky club with him and you're not sure?"

"We didn't do anything. He just showed me round and we talked."

"But you must have got a sense of his type?"

"Not really. He's…" I'm not sure what he is. He's not cheeky, that's for sure, but nasty? I didn't feel nasty when I was under the water. I felt calm. Nasty would denote a real fear I haven't felt in his company at all, even on those stairs. Uncomfortable, yes. Chastised and belittled maybe. Slightly apprehensive even, but not frightened. There's a darkness inside him, I'm sure. It lies beneath the surface of his façade, but it's not madness or criminal, or it doesn't seem that way to me at the moment. Cheeky isn't a word that fits, though, not in the slightest. I'm not getting the comedy feeling. "Dark."

"Dark? Right, we need black then," she says, walking away from me and weaving through the brightly coloured dresses towards the back. "And hot." Well, yes, that would be preferable. "The sort of thing that screams fuck me slowly." I'm also not getting the feeling Blaine Jacobs does anything all that slowly, and her language in the middle of Saks makes me flick my gaze around, concerned we're about to be banned forever. Three haughty looking assistants glare back. Actually, they're not glaring, more looking like dog shit has walked in to demean the place. Screw them. Bree does a typically Bree thing and heads straight at one of them, her eyes refusing to budge an inch from the woman's face. "Everything black that you have. Evening gowns." The woman sticks her nose in the air, apparently refusing to acknowledge Bree but walking off to search for dresses nonetheless.

"Where's he taking you?"

"I told you I don't know. I just got this text," I reply, handing her the phone and watching her look through the messages.

"That's not a lot of info."

"No. I know." She grabs her phone out as we wander over to the sofa area and sit down, waiting for miss haughty to deliver us some dresses, and then starts inputting his number.

"Better safe than sorry, right?"

"What?"

"Lana, you know shit about this guy other than the fact he's into kink. I mean, who is Blaine? That was his name, right? Blaine who?"

"Jacobs."

"See, never heard of him. He could be a murderer for all we know and you're going out with him to god knows where."

"You're not filling me with confidence. You were the one who said I should—"

"Screw him. Yes, but maybe at yours?"

"Oh no, that wouldn't work. It's not the way for me to understand this," I reply, shifting my weight around on the leather and lowering my voice a little. "It's his aura, and how could he have the same one if he was put into a new situation? No, it needs to be somewhere he's comfortable so he acts like him, you know? It's like when I was at his earlier and he—"

"Wait, what?" she practically shouts in the middle of the store. "When were you at his house?" Oh, I'd forgotten I hadn't told her that.

"The cab crashed last night, after we dropped you off. I woke up in his house. Apparently his brother was driving the car and—"

"Sounds suspicious to me."

"No, it was just a coincidence."

"All of New York and he happens to crash into your car? Were you naked?" Yes. Obviously, apart from the g-string.

"Well, yes, but nothing happened."

"How do you know?" Oh for god's sake.

"I know if I've had sex, Bree."

"Yeah, but what about if he touched you?" He did, but that was later. And I asked for that, not that Bree needs to know about our little interlude of near orgasmic proportions. I can still feel that. It makes me muse the moment, staring out into the store and remembering his hands on my skin, the hesitation in them, and the way they tore at fabric like it was rice paper.

"I'd know."

"How?"

"I'd be bruised."

"And you're not seeing anything wrong with what you've just said?"

Her words make me question why I said I'd be bruised. I don't know why I said it, but something tells me it's true. I halt my quick fire responses, wondering what sort of idiot would say that out loud and feel as okay about it as I do. It makes me look at my own knees, for some reason feeling the need to brush the black cotton down, perhaps hoping to rid myself of this odd sensation he delivers rather than smiling about it warmly.

"I can't explain it," is all I've got. She tuts at me, not giving away anything other than that as the woman arrives back in front of us, laden with dresses.

A parade of dresses ensues. Full-length ones. Fish tailed ones. Strapless, backless, two piece. Tight fitting, loose. I'm not even slightly concerned as she walks around, swishing the fabric to show its finery. I'm more bothered about why my mind just got comfortable with the thought of bruising. Most of what's happening in front of me is a blur of black, matching my sudden change of mood exactly. Black and dark. Foreboding is probably the most accurate description of where I am right now. Half an hour ago I felt like I could float on air, and now, having spoken with Bree about this, I feel lost.

"That one will do," I mumble out, watching the way the woman flaunts the silk in front of us.

"No it won't. It's fucking awful."

"It's *Yves Saint Laurent*," the woman states, as if this should be enough for me to acknowledge its beauty regardless of whether I like it or not. I don't. Not really, but I just can't focus on any of them at the moment. I'm trying to process information, find a bond, a route, anything to help me understand the connection I felt in that pool with his lips on mine.

"He threw me in a pool and I wanted to drown," I mumble while I stare at the array of dark fabrics and really acknowledge that fact. She gasps, her hand waving at the woman to tell her to leave. "I gave up, Bree. I just waited for him to come for me." I feel her slide up against me, her arm linking with mine. It's not supposed to be comfort. That's not how Bree and I work. It's just support. As if even though she doesn't understand, she'll hear me out regardless. I turn to face her, my head hanging slightly under my own contemplation. She looks as bemused as me, her furrowed brow highlighting that fact. I'm not surprised. If she'd said it to me I would be dragging her off to the local psych wing.

"What do you mean you gave up?"

"I don't know. I can't explain it." I smirk at my own confusion, remembering the way it all felt so peaceful and quiet under there once I stopped fighting for air. And then the way the writing and mapping poured out of me because of it. "I knew he'd come for me. All I had to do was ask." It still doesn't make much sense to me, so how Bree's supposed to understand any of it I don't know. But I know. Somehow I do. I know something anyway, something that feels factual regardless of logical reasoning.

"You don't even know him," she eventually says, a huff of disdain following the words as she gets up and wanders towards one of the dresses hung on a peg. She glares at the still hovering woman until she backs off and walks to the counter. I'm not sure why. It's probably her way of feeling in control of the situation, ever the logical choice maker that she is. It would have been my response too, snatching a chance to have a go at someone, making me feel better about myself in some way, but not in this moment, not in this situation. I just want to sit in this haze and let myself want to know more of him, really understand him. It might be stupid given it's only research, and nothing else is ever going to happen regardless of his mouth, but I don't care. For now I'm just going to brood on my thoughts and let them invade.

Chapter 8

ALANA

We returned to my apartment after Saks. We just bought a dress I liked, somewhat blindly given I didn't even try it on, and then headed back here for coffee and a chat. Unfortunately, I may not have spoken the entire way back here, giving Bree plenty of ammunition for more interrogation on matters concerning Blaine.

"You sure about this?" She asks, deliberately stirring her coffee slowly. She does that when she's considering life's abundant flaws and complications.

"No." Because what right-minded person would be? He's moody, temperamental, inexcusably good looking, and somehow able to make me do things that seem ludicrous when I walk away from the situation at hand. "But the book, Bree. I want this to hit home. It needs to be right. You said so yourself. It has to be representative of the facts." And I want those lips again, I do. It's annoying.

She picks up her drink, turning her body around to face me and leaning back on my fridge.

"I know, but drowning?" I chuckle at her, realising how stupid that sounds in the broad light of day, not that it is anymore.

"I wasn't about to drown, Bree. He pulled me out." And saved my shoes, quite gentlemanly really.

"Still," she says, kicking off the fridge and making her way over to me on the couch. "If he can do that with a pool, what the fuck is he going to do with handcuffs and ropes?" This is something I've been considering on our route home. "And what reason did he have for putting you in a pool in the first place? Because you swore at him? Sounds slightly psycho in my opinion."

I snuggle myself into the cushions, watching the way she waits for me to respond. I've got nothing to respond with. How would I know what's deemed rude or not with these types? She's right in some respects. When I actually have to explain, it all seems unwise. But, for whatever reason, I'm still smiling at the thought of it all. Him especially. "I imagined it would just be a bit of rough and tumble. You try some pain, comprehend its effects, and then you're able to write it more succinctly, having fucked someone a little interesting. This, Lana.." she continues, her legs pulling up so that she's cross legged. "This is fucked up stuff." She's possibly entirely correct.

"I can't explain it, Bree. And at this moment in time, I don't want to. Honestly, you should've see that table this morning," I say, pointing over at my small dining area, once again devoid of any mess now that I've reorganised. "It was brimming with notes and plots. Not like my normal MO. All neat and tidy, shelves and appropriate boxes, you know? No, it was covered. It's like it used to be when I started in college. You remember, don't you? Those first books? Ideas, characters, flow. The way it just takes off without any planning involved."

"Yes, but—"

"But nothing, Bree. Just that one experience and I'm back there. Val's gone. Peter's gone. There's something new in here now," I say, tapping my skull and feeling the excitement build again. "Sparks, you know?" I'm fidgeting now, almost like I can feel the story inside my blood. "He does that. I don't know how. If I did I'd explain it better, but I…" I can't. I can't even find my own sense of rationale in it, let alone tell her. I search the air again for inspiration as I look around, hoping it'll give me something to cling to other than a feeling. "He's…" Bolder than the sum of his parts? Good looking, yes. Built, yes. Everything I would normally drool over, absolutely. But that's not it. It's in his eyes, in his smirk. It's in the way he moves, somehow countering anything that normal attractiveness dictates. There's an energy about him. It might be dark, but it's healing, too. It's... "He's…" Yep, still nothing describes the way he fills a space, announcing his intention to own it without ever moving his lips. "And then when he..." Speaks? I don't even know if its speech, more likely the anticipation of what might leave his mouth, or what he might do with the thoughts he's not actually delivering via speech.

"You scared of him?"

"No." My tone is almost offended at her question.

"Why not?"

I scrunch my brow at myself and pick up my coffee, staring at it as if it will answer my own questions.

"I suppose I'm afraid of what he could pull *from* me, but not of what he could do *to* me." That's about all I've got in the way of reason.

Not that it's reasonable or sensible. "It's about me, Bree. Not him. He said it was me." I'm smiling as I remember his words. *"That was you."*

Bree laughs, but I'm not sure why. It makes me lift my eyes from my musings to look at her.

"You're falling for him."

"Oh, don't be stupid." No one falls for someone this quick. "He's just research, Bree. Nothing more." If I keep saying that enough I'll remember it myself, hopefully forgetting my need to taste those lips again and lose myself in them. "Besides, he's not exactly the sort for settling down with." I snort at the thought, my hand brushing nothing but fluff off my jeans as I muse that image, too. I mean, what a ridiculous notion. Blaine Jacobs, husband. Although, he might be, I suppose. "He might already have a partner for all I know."

"Yeah, right. I believe you." She picks up her phone, ending a sudden buzz before it even really begins. "And you know what? You're right. You need the info for research purposes." Indeed. That's all it is. Research and technical data, regardless of slightly dream like happenings. "And anyway, I've got his number now so I'll just give him hell if I don't hear from you by tomorrow night, right?"

"Right." The thought of Bree giving anyone hell is enough to make me feel concerned for his wellbeing, to be honest.

"So, shoes and shit?"

"Got them. He saved them from the pool." She rolls her eyes, probably at the inane smile that's suddenly attached to my face.

"Hair?"

"Up."

"Bag?"

"Gucci."

"Jewellery?"

"My pearl choker," I reply, amused at my own thoughts as I giggle around the words. "It should give him something to focus on, don't you think?"

"You're not wrong there," she eventually says, having spluttered most of her coffee out onto her top. "Fuck's sake, Lana. You're really gonna do this?"

"I think I really am."

~

The afternoon ends up turning into the evening as we exchange coffee for wine. Apparently I'm in the mood for a little loosening up. By the time it comes to actually getting dressed, I'm a little looser than I ever intended to be. I can tell this mainly because every time I try to apply make-up it ends up on the wrong part of my face.

"What proof is this shit?" Bree says, holding up a bottle.

"What's that?"

"Gin, I think. Or vodka."

"I thought I was drinking wine?"

"Yeah, we ran out of that so I changed it, or mixed it. Not sure."

"Jesus Christ, Bree." I try to move my drink out of the way, wondering if I should have more coffee in the hope of countering its effects. Unfortunately, I end up taking another sip rather than applying sense. "I seriously don't need to be lathered for this."

"Lathered?"

"Pissed. Drunk. Off my head." Fits of giggles ensue as she trips over her own feet, bypassing the dresser, just, and then collapses on my bed as she snatches up her ever present phone.

"I think that's precisely what you need to be for big dick Blaine."

"I've not seen his dick."

"Bet it's big. In fact, I'll ask, shall I?" She's attempting to type. It's worrying.

"Bree..."

"Or maybe it's a weasel dick. Maybe I shouldn't put him off his stride."

"Bree..." She throws her phone on the bed again, thankfully.

"Or maybe its immense and he'll whip you with it." I'm nearly crying, attempting to keep my face straight to stop my make-up falling off any more than it already has done. "Maybe that's what he does with it." For fuck's sake. "Whippy dick." That's it. The snort that leaves my nose forces out gin, or vodka, bringing it up from the depths and almost making me sick.

"Bree, shut up."

"Why?"

"He has not got a whippy dick."

"How would you know?"

"I..."

"See. Whippy Dick Blaine Jacobs. Master in cock floggery. That's what they call it, isn't it?"

I shake my head at her, having never heard of the term cock floggery before, and turn back for the mirror in the hope of finishing my dark and sultry look. I'm thankful for the amusement in some respects. That she's managing to keep all this light-hearted and funny is perfect. If I thought about any of this too much, alcohol or not, I might well call him up and say thanks but no thanks. It's crossed my mind several times as we've fussed about. Should I, shouldn't I? Is this really the sane thing to do? How far should I go in the pursuit of the perfect story? I'm guaranteeing other authors haven't decided to go under the hands of a Dominant just to get the right groove going on. Well, maybe some of them have. A light caning potentially, but not what I'm considering, not that I quite know what that is yet, but I'm doubting there will be anything 'light' happening. "Is this him?"

"What? Who?"

"This?" she says, practically falling off the bed as she makes her way over to me and holds up her phone.

"Ewww, no," I reply, pulling my eyes away from the sixty-something man looking back at me. He might be reasonably handsome for his age in some respects as he stands at some function, an equally attractive older woman on his arm, but he isn't my Blaine.

"It says it is. Archibald Blaine Jacobs. Look."

"Well, it's not my Blaine."

"Your Blaine, hey?"

"Oh, fuck off."

She doesn't fuck off. She spends the next hour revving me up into a mass of hysterics and more near vomiting situations. She even puts on some music, opting for the relaxed tones of the *Gangnam Style* because, apparently, the dance moves should offer me an insight into sadomasochism. I'm not entirely sure why until I see her parading her body around the lounge, her arm swinging in the air calling whippy dick at the top of her lungs.

Eventually she collapses on her arse, barely managing to land on it as she skims the corner of the sofa cushions and grabs hold of the arm for support.

"I'm trashed," she coughs out, her legs splaying around as if she has minimal control of any limb.

"Yep."

I, thankfully, am not. At some point in the last hour, regardless of my gigglesnort sessions, I've managed to contain the fuel she was force-feeding me to a minimum of sips and tasters. It's not like I'm not in the mood. I am. She's definitely made me feel like a good drinking fest is in order, but the very thought of Blaine's whippy dick has suspended the need to feel completely blotto.

I find myself watching her and running my hands over my dress for the tenth time, checking that I look okay. Everything's in place, and luckily the dress fits like a glove as it glances my calves and then fishtails out, but for some reason I feel nervous. Overly so.

I feel the sigh leave my lungs, effectively loosening the midsection of the dress as it does. Bree didn't have any problem at all lacing up the back of it, ratcheting the thing in too tight as she did and forcing my boobs out of the top. She did it as she sang, or rather attempted to sing 'Smack my bitch up.' I'm still not sure where she found that track, or has even heard of the Prodigy.

"You look great, Lana. S'up?"

I'm not sure what to answer her with, so I don't. Instead, I stand by my kitchen table and stare at the door to my office, willing it to give me another kick of inspiration that might leave me able to end whatever's happening tonight before it starts. It doesn't. It just hangs there, taunting me with nothing at all as it stays stationary and empty without his guidance.

"You know, you don't *have* to do anything, right? You have the choice to say no." She somehow manages to pull herself upright as I look across at her, her top falling back to cover her exposed stomach as she does. "I'm pretty sure all this BDSM stuff is all about consent." She's right. He told me that the first night we met. In fact, it was one of the first things he said. I nod at her, still unable to remove the nerves regardless of her soft smile. I could have some more happy pills; they might shift these nerves or at least sort my head out into some sort of practical and logical order again. "So that means you have to say yes, yes?"

"Uh huh."

"So, really, Alana Williams is in complete control of anything that goes down," she calls, as I dig two tablets out of my bedside cabinet and sink them down with a quick sip of gin, or vodka, or whatever it is. "As long as she's not too fascinated with whippy dick to not think straight." My snort at the term forces one of the tablets back up, making me cough out and swallow again rapidly to send it back down. Fuck. But fascinated - it's a good term for how I feel. Spellbound is better, rapt, even.

"Can we please not call him whippy dick," I say eventually as I right myself and walk back out, hoping for controlled and sensible again. "I need to be on my game for this. The last thing I need is that term flying round my head all night." She leans back on the arm of the sofa and taps her head, smirking at my predicament and sipping her drink.

"You need analytical and controlled Lana, yeah?" I nod as I watch her steadying herself, somehow rallying the Bree I need back into the room, just as she always does. "Then you're gonna need an espresso or two before he gets here." Jesus. Wine, gin, vodka, happy pills and coffee? This could go spectacularly wrong. But she's right. This whimsical version of me he creates is useless for this sort of encounter. It'll only force emotions forward, ones I can't afford with him, making me nervous and edgy, lost. I do need my serious game on, or at least my less fanciful one. "What's the time?"

"Eight-thirty." I know this because I've been watching the minutes ticking away for the last thirty-six of them. It's been excruciating, frankly, reminding me of the nerves I do not like. I nod at the offer of coffee anyway, flicking my hand at my own thoughts and assuming no harm can come from yet another drug in my system. It's not like my body's not used to them by now.

"How's he know where you live, anyway?"

It's a good point, one I've given up trying to work out. Similar to how he knows about Val and Peter, too, the latter being something I haven't told Bree about. She's a stickler for anonymity. She's built her whole career on it. There's only her sister and me who know anything about the fact that she writes. If she knew he knew who I was, she would be telling me not to go. She'd find it too personal. Tell me I was being rash and thoughtless. Believe me, there's nothing thoughtless about any of this. Quite the opposite, actually.

"I told him in the text."

"That was stupid. Why not meet him there?" Shit.

"I wanted you to meet him." I didn't, but it's the quickest answer I've got to get her off my back. She screws her face up and folds her arms across her chest, clearly suspicious.

"Why?"

"Safety, right?" She stares, narrowing her eyes and suddenly sober as a judge. "If you've seen him then it's another thing we've got in case things go wrong."

"Like you drowning," she says, her head tilting at the image in her mind. "Or being whipped to death by large dick blunt force trauma." The thought makes my guts churn, or maybe that's the pills. Lord knows. Whatever it is, it's enough that I ignore the fact that my thighs tremble, too, followed by my crotch clamping on air beneath this dress, highlighting a slight problem.

"Yes, Bree. Like me drowning," I reply, rather than explaining any of my current state.

Having stared some more then looked over my dress and shoe ensemble, she pushes off the sofa and moves towards the kitchen with a huff.

"You know, he better at least be good looking," she calls back, starting to clank things around in my pristine space. Oh, he is.

"He's okay."

"Fuck off with your okay. For you to even be considering this he must be hot. Tell me about him."

I blow out a breath and meander over to her, trying to think of enough superlatives to describe Blaine Jacobs. By the time I reach the chair beside her and sit on it, gratefully resting my vibrating legs, I still haven't got any. Most times it's easy to describe a man—height, weight, eye colour and all the things that usually define a look—but with Blaine it's about something other than that. It's about the way his hand hovers, the way his body moves, and the way he manages to delve into my mind without doing a damn thing. "You know," she says, having watched me not finding any words at all. "I was in love once, Lana." Was she? I look up at her, noting the slow stir of her coffee as she puts mine down in front of me. "Drink."

I pick it up, sipping it and waiting for her to deliver what small snippet about her past she's willing to give. "She was indescribable." My smile widens, glad to finally hear her talk about being bi, or gay. I don't care either way as I watch her dark lips stretch into a grin. "I could never find the words to explain how she made me feel, or even what she looked like."

"You could have talked about this before, you know?" I reply, sensing a shyness about her thoughts creeping in as she gazes out of the window.

"Hmm. I know, but it was a long time ago. Hardly worth talking about. And she was white. Her parents wouldn't…" She stalls, looking back at her coffee and sighing to herself. "Well, I'm black, right?" She chuckles in contempt. "Gay was okay, but mixed race wasn't. Go figure."

What was a broad smile slips into a grimace of sadness. Who would do that? Why?

"How old were you both?"

"She was twenty-four and I was twenty-two. I thought she was it. First time I'd really acknowledged being gay and gone with it. She was everything that love should have been."

"I'm sorry." It's all I've got. There's no point attempting a long and meaningful conversation with Bree because it won't happen. She's given what she's prepared to, and probably only done that because she knows I'm going out and can't prod any more than ten minute's worth. "We can talk about it again if you want?" She shakes her head, brightening her mouth back into a normal smile and crinkling her eyes as she shrugs off any thought of love. I can see it visibly leave her, as if it's the only way she knows how to deal with it. "What was her name?" I ask, sipping my coffee and letting the rush of caffeine do its job.

The sharp sound of the intercom buzzer going off in the room startles me, causing me to stand up so abruptly the coffee cup falls from my hand and smashes to the floor.

"Fuck," I cry, my breath shaking around the word as I stare at the splintered shards of porcelain and watch the dark brown liquid ooze on the beige linoleum. It doesn't take me long to notice my hands as I step back. They're trembling, too, as I check my dress for any splatter.

"You are scared," Bree says immediately, rounding the surfaces to get in front of my face and making me look at her. "You tell me you're going to be okay or I'm going down there and telling him you've changed your mind."

"I'm fine, Bree. The noise just surprised me."

"Did it fuck! Look at you, you're shaking."

I turn away from her and cross the room for my bag. Whether I'm shaking or not is completely irrelevant. I've got information to find and a book to write, and the man downstairs is the answer to that challenge. Like it or not, I need him. I need his mind. None of this is anything to do with the feelings or emotions I'm having. It's work. That's it. My trembling hands will just have to sort themselves out. I grab at my gold Gucci clutch, checking its interior for all the necessary items, keys included, and then turn for my shawl.

"Come on, Bree. I've got to go now. He's here."

She narrows her eyes in response, slowly taking hold of her bag and slipping her things inside it one by one as she continues drinking her coffee. I push onto the intercom, telling it I'll be down in a minute and waving my hands at Bree to hurry her up. She's clearly not in a rush. "Bree, come on. I don't want him waiting."

"Why not?" she says, putting her bag down and leaning on the countertop.

"What?"

"Why don't you want him waiting? The Lana I know always makes men wait for her."

Her words halt my flapping hands, making me question what I am doing as I panic about the situation. I do make men wait. I *always* make them wait. There hasn't been one meeting, one rendezvous, or one encounter at a bar where I haven't made them wait. It's almost always been that way. I scan the floor for thought, wondering why my normal reaction isn't there, then grab at the notebook by my door, scribbling thoughts and feelings down onto it so I don't lose them.

162

"Research, Bree. Business," I mumble out, furiously scrolling the pen with no real inclination to make sense of the words at this time. This is nothing to do with research. This is sensation, one he's somehow created in me without even being here. How's he done that? "I'm never late for business meetings. It's rude." Rude it might be, but that's not why I'm never late for them. I'm never late because I'm too organised to ever be late for anything. "Come on."

I open the door, flapping my hand at her again and smiling to get her moving, eventually going back into the room to drag her out instead of waiting for her.

"I call bullshit," she says, pulling her arm away from my hold and chuckling about something as we get outside the door. I slam it to and shove my overnight bag at her. "You're hooked on him."

"I am not," I protest as I lock the damn thing and fumble with my keys.

"You can't even lock the fucking door." My huff of attempted disregard doesn't go unnoticed as I swing my black, silk shawl around my shoulders, artfully trying to arrange it. It doesn't work, something to do with my still shaking hands as I head for the stairs.

"Besides, it's not possible, Bree. This isn't one of Val's books. I'm writing factual this time." I wish I meant that with as much definition as it sounds like, as I quicken my steps and hurry down towards the main door. "Well, fictional factual. " She giggles behind me as I lift my dress, worried for my own safety given the height of my heels and the angle of the staircase we're descending. "Honestly. You think this heroine's about to get whisked away in a high-end car towards her knight in shining armour? You're mad, Bree. This isn't a fairy-tale. He's no prince charming."

"You sure about that?" Yes. No. Oh god, I don't know.

My hand reaches for the door, the other still attempting to position my shawl in some semblance of elegance as I fiddle with it and swing the door wide to find him.

Rather than Blaine, I'm greeted with a small portly man who's dressed in a suit and smiling at me.

"Oh," comes out of my mouth as my feet halt in their tracks.

"Nice opening," Bree says behind me, chortling away to herself and nudging me in the back, which makes me turn and scowl at her.

"Ms. Williams?"

"Yes," I say, higher pitched than I would have liked, indicating stress levels I wish I didn't have.

"Mr. Jacobs asked that you meet him there," he says, holding out his hand towards a silver Mercedes that's idling by the side of the road.

"Thank fuck," Bree cuts in.

"What?" I ask, looking back at her.

"Well, I thought this was him." Oh, right. Ewww.

"Bree!" I'm astonished. This chap has to be at least fifty-five. "Really?"

"How would I know?" Fair point, I suppose.

"Really, though?"

"You're the one unable to describe him," she replies, an incredulous look on her face as she moves past me, wanders out onto the street and dumps my leather overnight bag on the pavement.

"Ma'am, if we could get going?" the man says, interrupting our conversation. Right, yes.

"I'm sorry," I say out of courtesy, given the fact that we've just been talking about him in a less than pleasant way.

"No problem, ma'am," he replies, stepping away from me to grab my bag and pointing for his car again as I pick up my dress to follow. Nice. Great way to piss off the driver.

"You really gonna get in a car with a complete stranger?" Bree asks, her face a picture of distrust as she scribbles the car's licence plate down and peers in through the windows. I haven't been given much of a chance to think about it, but now I do. It's a fair question, one I currently have no answer for as I look the chap over. "And what's your name?" she asks, aiming the question at him.

"Stone," is the reply.

"Mr. Stone, or Stone something?"

"Just Stone, ma'am."

"That's not a name," she mumbles, apparently now drawing a picture of him on her police notepad. I roll my eyes at her as I approach, watching the way her hand creates quite the likeness of Stone.

"That's good."

"Thanks, I'm doing illustrations now, too."

"Ma'am?" Stone coughs, probably at my stalling. "We should really get going."

"Where to?" Bree asks.

"The location is undisclosed."

Both Bree and I stare at him, a look of bewilderment on our faces as he drops my bag into the boot and walks to the driver's side of the car. He can't tell me where I'm going? That's not alright. I need more than this. For a start, I expected Blaine here, not a nameless driver who's been told to take me somewhere.

"I think it's best if I don't go then," I say, making my way to the back of the car to retrieve my bag. Need him or not, I'm not putting myself in danger for anyone. The thought makes me snort at myself as I imagine what I was thinking about doing in the first place. BDSM does not come in this format, I'm afraid. I'm not writing about the same thing as all those other books. I want the real meat of the situation, not whatever this is. I thought the dress was over the top enough, lovely as it is, let alone being driven somewhere 'undisclosed' for surreptitious adventures with people I don't know. Blaine is what I need, not this.

When I'm done with my thoughts of intrigue and slight irritation, and as I'm tugging at the boot that won't open, Stone hands me a phone. I stare at it as it rings, mystified as to why I should answer his phone.

"It's Mr. Jacob's, ma'am. For you." The only wording on the phone is J; that's it. Nothing else to indicate who it might be.

"You sure?" He nods. I'm not sure why I asked in the first place. I take it from him, ready to tell Mr. Jacobs that I won't be coming anywhere, regardless of how important he is.

"Hello," I say, quite sharply given my confusion as I continue tugging at the boot of the car. There's no real response at first, just a hushed rumble and something that sounds like classical music in the background, or perhaps a band. "Hello?"

"I have zero patience and you're already fucking testing it," eventually comes back at me, very nearly snarled through his normally bored tone. My brow shoots up at this new tone of anger, followed by my knickers considering desertion. How did that happen? He's not even here. "Good evening," he says, his voice suddenly brighter and full of charisma. I go to say something, not understanding what it means, but before I'm given a chance, he talks again. "Get in the damn car, Alana." His tone is full of malice again, nothing like the charming one I just heard. I back up, as if I'm trying to get away from his voice. "Speak." Yes, speak. Why can't I speak? I should tell him to go screw himself, or ask him what the hell he thinks he's playing at. I look at Bree, who's still busy drawing Stone, then glance at the man whose eyes are trained on me as if I'm the only thing worth dealing with. "Stone will give you thirty seconds after I end this call to make a choice," Blaine huffs out, the sound of raucous laughter in the background carrying on, along with the start of a new song. "You asked for my help, Alana. Take it or stop wasting my fucking time. I don't care."

The phone goes dead the instant the last word leaves his mouth, and in the same moment, Stone picks up his arm to look at his watch. There's no emotion, no sense of coercion coming from either Blaine or Stone. No one wants me to go other than me. I was right; this definitely is not a fairy-tale. It's as much about business for Blaine as it is for me. He might not be making any money out of it, but I'm clearly offering something of value nonetheless. I can only assume that something is me—that I'm something to play with for a while.

"Okay," I say as I move a step towards the car, possibly without my true consent. Bree hurries to my side, her hand grabbing my arm to stop me. It's the right thing to do; we both know that, but it won't get me my story or his mouth on me again, will it? And I need both now for some reason, much as I might hate to admit it. "It's okay, Bree," I say, gently removing her hand and reaching for the car door. "He's meeting me there."

She narrows her eyes but doesn't try to stop me. She knows once I've made a decision it's usually a sensible one—one that I've considered, prepared for. Everything in my life is always that way. It has to be. The chaos of it would be overwhelming if I wasn't so concise about keeping it tight, irrespective of the occasional meltdown, and the need for drugs to help keep me in order. My decisions, my rules. Only this time, much as she might believe I've made this call with sense applied, I haven't. He just has. He told me what to do and I'm doing it, willingly.

Chapter 9

BLAINE

I sigh and turn for the road again, choosing to seat myself on the nearest bench rather than follow the fray back into yet more perfect smiles and deliberations. Games of chance I'm willing to play on occasion. Games that involve pretence and deception are not in the least bit appealing, certainly not in relation to a room full of high-end kinksters. I've been there, done that, ridden the waves that push and pull boundaries ever closer to the edge of stability. The only reason I've come here is for her to see a new version of the scene, one that should make it abundantly clear that 'my kind' are something more than just dirty backstreet clubs.

Minutes tick by, and I begin wandering the road again, kicking up dust and checking my phone, until eventually I see the car pulling onto the top of the drive. It travels slowly, twisting the corners precisely just as Stone, Delaney's driver, always does, and finally ends up by my feet. Stone gets out, rounding the car and walking to the back door to open it, and then I get my first glimpse of her leg as she pushes it out. It instantly makes me tilt my head, enough so that I smirk at myself as the rest of her follows, the picture of elegance. Her evening gown clings in all the right places as she straightens it down, highlighting that exceptional chest of hers and elongating already lengthy legs.

"Hi," she says, a little unsure of herself as she gazes around the area and runs her fingers through her hair to perfect it. She doesn't need to. Its stark purple stripes are perfectly aligned, rising up into the diamante clip holding it in place. I stare for a while longer, happy to simply watch her move and falter in her discomfort as she continues glancing around. "Is this okay?" she asks, pointing at her dress, presumably trying to break the silence I'm purposely creating. It makes me smirk again, amused at her nerves and enjoying her torment as I gaze at her face. She's truly beautiful. Not like the others here. They all hold a pretentious lilt to their manicuring, as if they've been at a salon for hours forcing beauty and dressing like sluts to achieve admiration, but not her. Alana Williams is a vision of impeccably flawed splendour. A woman who neither denies her attributes nor flaunts them to attract imbecilic men who aren't able to deal with her. "Are you going to speak at all?" Possibly not if she jitters as a result. The unease is titillating, entertaining, and cock hardening. It reminds me of the slight fear she had earlier as she fell on her ass in my hallway. "Because this is going to be very dull if you don't," she quips, digging into her bag for something then starting to apply a new layer of dark red lipstick.

"Wipe it off," comes out of my mouth, quicker than even I expect.

"What?" she says, her hand hovering the lipstick at the edge of her mouth.

"It stains you. If I want you stained, I'll put it there myself."

"Oh," she says in response, her face suddenly unsure of what to do. "But I can't just... Well, not here... I need a mirror and..." I take a step into her, pulling out my handkerchief and offering up my hand to within a foot of her face. She looks as surprised by the move as I feel. Normally, as with other women, I'd have made her wipe it off, forcing the smear and enjoying her discomfort all the more for it, but with her I feel courteous—a suggestion of it, anyway. "Okay," she says, beginning to take it from me. I shake my head, lifting it away from her fingers and watching her frown increase.

"Mine to take, Alana, yes?" I ask, moving my hand towards her mouth and relishing the small gasp that comes from it as my fingers brush her skin. I stare at her eyes for a moment, watching the way the pupils dilate, their rim expanding until it almost eclipses the blue iris. "It's the way this works." Her eyes flutter closed slightly, an escape of more breath quietly moaning out as I press firmly onto her lips to dab the colour off. I continue wiping, easing myself close enough to wrap my other hand around the back of her neck to hold her head still. "Don't wear it again."

"Why not?" she muses, half unaware the question's left her lips. It causes me to smile wider as her eyes close completely, remembering a time when women questioned me.

"I'm a sadist, Alana," I reply quietly, still musing over her lips and what I can do with them. Her eyes shoot open, her feet nearly falling over themselves to put distance between us both, which makes me chuckle. "There are no borders to our fads. Lipstick included."

"Yes, yes of course you are." she says, her body at odds with itself until she regains her composure and stands her ground again, defiance written all over her frame. "And I suppose all this stuff," she says, waving her hand at Delaney's grand hall behind us. "Is some sort of gathering of your kind? A club?" My blood boils at her comment, just as it did the last time she belittled my community. My kind? She's more my kind than she could ever imagine. She simply doesn't know it yet. I've seen it in the pool, felt it in the way she let me carry her, smelt it on her when she tried to deny interest in the first club she'd been in.

"Do you know what my kind is?" I ask, rotating away from her and walking towards the building, toying with all kinds of ideas to help her understand what she is. She doesn't answer, but hurries to catch up with me, her heels clattering against the pavement and distressing my nerves. Fucking sound. "My kind is *your* kind, Alana."

"It's not," she snaps out, desperate to validate her regularity in society's categories.

"Yet your cunt's wet again," I snarl back, stopping and letting her crash into me. She gasps as she rebounds off me. It's a good look on her—one that makes her seem less superior, which I like, regardless of it not sitting comfortably on her frame. "Should I hitch that dress up and test my theory? Put my hand inside you?" Her mouth stays open, momentarily attempting speech and then stopping again. "Our *kind* is only a form of honesty most won't entertain as acceptable." I back away from her this time, putting distance between us as I look at her. "Be careful who you look down on, Alana. You could be judging yourself without thought."

I look up at the building I come to two times a year as I walk on. Delaney's little gatherings are usually farcical. Comedic even. I come more out of respect for him rather than the entertainment, but this time it feels intriguing to be here, probably because I've brought someone to it. And I suppose the building is charismatic in some ways with its insidious little rooms waiting for use, if not a truly archaic version of the new bolder scene that lines backstreet avenues.

"But I'm not your kind, if I was I would know, surely?" she says, suddenly appearing by my side and sliding her arm through my crooked elbow. I stop and look at it, bemused at her audacity in increasing our proximity again but apparently unable to remove her from my arm irrespective. "I mean, you must have known the first time you had sex—that you were different?" I shake my head, chuckling at her straightforward way of approaching questions, no matter how uncomfortable I might make her feel, and then start walking again. "Because this honesty presumably applies to oneself, as you said, so you must have understood your need early on, right?"

"You ask questions like a lecturer would," I reply, ducking to get through the low hanging lights in the arched foyer and remembering standing by my board, this rise of seats spread out before me full of students. "Ever thought of a career change?"

"No, I like what I do. Actually, why don't you teach, if you're a teacher? Or do you still?" she asks, staring around the room as we enter. "What college were you at? I can't find you on the internet anywhere." I'm not surprised. I spend a fortune keeping myself off it.

"I used to teach. I don't anymore, not psychology anyway. I do—"

"Is that a jester breathing fire?" she suddenly asks, her eyes focusing on the stage. I feel her let go of my arm, her body turning to step into the fray with little care for her safety. "Oh!" She looks straight back me, her eyes widening as she stares at the rest of the room and notices some already bare bodies starting early. I nod, a smile broadening on my mouth at her quizzical gaze. She really is quite the beauty, especially in her interest. "But this isn't what I thought." More than likely not. I still can't truly understand why I've brought her here either. She probably expected another version of the second place we'd met. "It's incredible. Look at that." She wanders further in, her body weaving through the throng of couples, soaking in the atmosphere, turning and spinning on occasion. Farcical it might all be, but I have to give it to Delaney; he can throw a party better than most. The hall is filled with black and blue visons, half the guests matching the décor, and the opulence is just as exquisite as it always is.

I follow her as she keeps mingling, sporadically bumping into someone who won't appreciate the awkwardness. The third time makes me move in and glare at Robert Harris before the bastard swings his hand at her. It's probably because she knocked his drink over as she bounced off his sub's kneeling form, and normally I'd have ignored the response, rightly so, but not with Alana. Not yet. Robert nods and recalls his arm before it engages with her, all of which a still stunned Alana is oblivious to as she keeps moving forward. I snort at her astonished gaze, admiring the way she's suddenly become so open to what's in front of her rather than sullying it with reproach. She seems in awe of the venue. Perhaps it's the architecture, or the sense of showmanship that has been applied to its structure, changing her opinion of dirty liaisons and making her see sense.

Vast floral arrangements embellish the old hall's entrance lobby as we walk through, Alana still several feet in front of me and forging her own path onwards without my help. I find myself charmed by her confidence as she touches objects and stares at the iniquity beginning to evolve around her. On occasion she stops her feet to really mentally engage with an act, perhaps needing to smell the air as she integrates the vision into her mind, before moving on again. It amuses me. In fact, it tempts me more by the second, filling me with thoughts of howling screams, ones that appear clouded with sentiments involving her mind.

I've swiped two glasses of Champagne and caught up with her by the time she reaches the staircase, not the slightest bit ready to disclose such thoughts yet wanting nothing more than to talk.

"How does it all make you feel?" I ask, watching the way her small smile increases as I approach. She takes the drink, sipping it quietly as she scans again and lifts her dress to walk up the stairs.

"More interested than the other venue did."

"That's because you don't believe you're part of this. In time, the location will mean little."

Her smile widens, bringing with it an exquisiteness that holds no place here. Smiles like hers are reserved for moonlight walks and virile encounters, not for venues such as this. It makes me halt my momentum and gaze at her, wondering why she affects me so.

"You okay?" she asks, her head slightly at an angle. No. Something's at odds, just like it was when she was beneath the water and begging to be rescued. I can see it again now, warning me of storms that shouldn't be considered. It forces me to tense my hand inside my pocket, willing the sensation away as Eloise haunts my memories with her screams.

"Yes." *No.*

A raucous outburst breaks us free of the moment, causing her to swing her eyes to the floor below us. I don't look. I can't. I feel bewitched by this moment, her splendour bridging a hole inside me I don't want bridging as she moves into me to look downwards. She fills the staircase, the hem of her dress dropping three steps down as if she covers everything around us, including me. I can't stop the urge to touch her skin and run my fingers along her arm slowly, watching her reaction to it carefully.

She looks back sharply, narrowing her eyes and blowing a breath out at the contact, still not ready to admit what she needs.

"I'm not for playing with, Blaine," she snaps, anger pitching her voice regardless of not truly believing the words herself. I smile again anyway, a small chuckle leaving me as I lose myself in the thought of playing with her. Not that I should.

"Yes, Alana. You are."

She backs a step upwards, picking her dress up once more and glaring as she keeps climbing. It intrigues me further as I tip my glass at her and picture her replete the morning after a fucking session. I can smell her exhilaration from here, regardless of the sudden snooty effect produced by her stance. It seeps into me, reminding me of skin that handles my kind of bruising and gasps for last breaths of air.

"Where does this lead?" she asks, a slightly softer tone now she's checked her temper, her face turning from mine to dismiss our connection.

"Bedrooms."

She doesn't look back, but scrunches the black silk into her grasp and redirects her unknown need into it as she continues climbing.

The vision makes me chuckle again as I follow and nod at another a Domme wandering down the stairs, a human dog attached to her wrist. Alana looks and huffs, causing the Domme to raise a brow and turn, her crop ready to do its worst to disobedient little subs, no doubt. I shake my head at the woman slowly, flicking my hand back down the stairs to warn of potential repercussions as I walk by.

"You want me involved?" I ask, enough threat to send the woman on her way laced in my tone. She sneers in reply, one final backward glance directed at Alana's ass before she descends again.

The moment makes me deliberate being here with her, together, in front of all this, as I watch the Domme leave. It could be considered the most careless thing I've ever done. Although, it does show a pretence to the rest of the guests, which might keep the other subs from my feet for the night. Why I still want that, though, I'm not sure. I normally find something of partial curiosity here at least. Delaney always ensures something will be suitable for use should I want it.

"Blaine!" Her voice shouts at me, from where I can't see. I turn, irritated by my own lack of concentration and launch my feet up the few remaining steps to find her. My eyes search the others ambling around, looking for her purple stripes above the crowd, only to see nothing but everyone else. "Blaine!" It's louder this time, and with a sense of fear attached to it.

I push through the people milling around, anxious to get to her before something happens I'm not in control of, peering in rooms. Finally Lazarus points me in the direction I'm after, his finger inclined towards one of the bedrooms and a smile firmly in place. The help causes me to slow my steps and listen, wondering what I'm about to walk in on and smiling at the thought.

I hardly stop the laugh that wants to come out as I enter the space. She's over a man's lap, her dress about to be rucked up, and fuck is she hissing out. Her body's squirming like it would kill anything that dares touch her. So I lean back against the wall and sip my Champagne again, watching and waiting for what will happen next.

"Wild," someone says as they rest next to him. Maybe. Not untameable, though. And the tightening of the Dom's hands prove it as her body begins to give in, regardless of her mind's fight.

"Blaine." She shouts it again, like a final scream for help as her eyes flick around the room in search of me. I don't move to intervene, and when she finally locates me in the room, she glares with such malice it sends my cock into spasms of need. The Dom that has hold of her searches for me, too, our eyes connecting as he lessons his grip on her back.

"She's yours?" The guy next to me asks, the Dom holding her mirroring the same question with a simple look. Mine? I don't own anything anymore. Those days are long gone. I smirk into Alana's face, amused that she's on the back foot and still squirming erratically.

"No," is my reply, crossing my leg and taking another sip. She isn't. But I am protecting her. Nothing will happen here that I'm not content to allow. She wants a thrill for her story; she can have one. Her previous brattish behaviour deserves the contact anyway, and I doubt she's ever taken a spanking before, so now is as good a time as any for her to try the sensation out.

The Dom holding her is immediate in increasing his grip on her again, presumably effectively wound up by her squirming and grinding on his cock. Had she simply lain still, he probably would have become bored with her already, but nothing provokes a Dom more than a sub behaving like a terror, especially a juvenile one like the man currently rucking up her dress again.

"Blaine?" It's more a question this time, spoken with uncertainty as it trembles out of her.

I grab at a woman walking by and pull her in front of me, then pushed her down to the floor in front of my feet. She groans and assumes the perfect position for a sub, displaying the servitude some require and, with any luck, showing Alana how to behave. She'll enjoy it if she does. The squirming has probably made her wet already, wetter than she already was, and the way her eyes widen at the vision by my feet tells me everything I need to know. It makes me nod at her and lick my lips, tipping my glass at her again to let her know I'm here and that she's safe. Nothing will happen that I'm not in control of. Nothing.

It doesn't take long for the Dom to continue. Her dress is raised higher, her ass on display for the room to see. She writhes at that thought, too, trying to twist her body out of the man's hold once more, until the first spank lands. Her mouth opens immediately, a sigh quickly following it as she stares at the floor in disbelief and raises her ass again with little thought. The next one only furthers her arousal as she stills and takes it. It's all there in her eyes, waiting to be explored and invaded. She needs the impact, relishes it after only a short introduction. She already seems more pliable in the guy's hands, and my own fucking cock rages for escape at the sound that rattles the air in the room. It sends waves of wrath through my own soul, throwing ideas and images at me, ready to do their worst to unblemished skin. I know because of the way my fingers itch for her across my own lap. And I know because of the way I'm willing the younger Dom on for a firmer handing on her ass. She's begging for it without any noise at all. I can hear her, her body already opening for use should it be asked of her. She wants it more than she knows. Her breath is rapid, her compliance quick and relatively easy to achieve given the complete strangers staring at her. She pants now, still lifting her ass even after the fifth strike lands. I scour the room, looking for something stiffer to land on her skin, knowing she needs more than the youngster's achieving and desperate to give it to her myself. A cedar paddle catches my eye, tempting me with irrationality in the middle of this decadence, but something stops me before I push off the wall. I look back at her, sensing something other than compliance in the air for some reason and gaze into her eyes for explanation. She just lifts her head to me, a sadness creeping over her features regardless of the way her ass continues to rise in the Dom's hands.

 I've walked to her side before I've thought, her melancholy affecting me more profoundly than anything in this room ever could.

 "Enough," I state, my hand reaching for the dress and dragging it back across her ass to the floor. The Dom glowers at me, presumably trying to look threatening. I just hold my hand out to Alana and wait for any repercussion the fool thinks appropriate. She takes my hand quietly, shrewdly realising something is happening in the four feet surrounding us as she clambers back to her feet.

 "You said she wasn't yours?"

"She's not," I reply, suddenly confused about why that sentiment irritates me more than I'd like to admit. "But she's not yours either. Are you, Alana?" She frowns in response and lets go of my hand as her feet start backing her out of the room, her eyes darting to the other people around her.

I turn and follow her, dismissing the growl that emanates from the younger Dom.

"They can't know, Blaine," she says, quietly, backing her way from the room and rubbing her ass as she goes. "No one can know who I am or why I'm with you."

"Why would anyone here know who you are?" I ask, bemused that she would say only that rather than feel the need to talk about what just happened in the room.

"But you're a… and I'm… Well, I've got different names, haven't I? And you can't call me them here. I didn't think…" She starts to babble her words, still walking away from me and back towards the stairs. "This isn't right, Blaine." I frown at her back as she starts her descent and follow her mysterious ass as she picks up her dress and her speed.

"What's the matter with you?" I ask, pocketing my hands as we reach the bottom and enjoying the way she collides into several objects, humans included.

"Do they know who I am? All of them?" she snaps, hitching her dress further to aid her ability to move quicker. "I shouldn't be here." She mumbles the last of it, which amuses me no end given her desire to write a book about the lifestyle.

"What are you talking about?"

"Is this a fucking joke?" she hisses quietly, still wildly scanning anyone within twenty foot of her and rubbing her ass again. "Jesus, Blaine, of all the fucking places to announce my involvement in your sordidity."

"Sordidity? That's not a word," I reply, watching the way she twirls through tight spaces, her ass continuing to ram anything remotely close as she heads for the doorway.

"It is now. I've made a new one. You deserve it." I almost choke on the snort that leaves my nose, chuckling around her innovative word and moving in to decrease the space between us. "And that fucking hurt in there. I mean, who does that? I didn't even enjoy it."

"Yes you did. Make up another one," I say, my mind suddenly fascinated with her ire as she lets the black silk travel along her tanned legs again, fluffing it out and swinging her glare back to me.

"What?"

"Another word up for me, and watch the—" She doesn't watch anything. She tumbles, regardless of me reaching for her. Her legs splay first, clipping the edge of the bench, her arms flailing as she begins to fall backwards. I might have moved quicker if I hadn't seen a fully masked and cloaked Delaney coming up behind her, his arms catching her and righting her onto her feet again.

"You let me fall," she snarls, slapping out at Delaney's grip on her ass and wincing in the same breath as she spins back to me. "Get off me, will you, whoever you are. Jesus Christ." There's an amount of huffing from her mouth after that, followed by what might be brat like stamping feet. "Fuck." I smirk again, just about managing to contain the laughter that wants to echo out into the night for the first time in however long.

"Nice ass," Delaney chimes in, still sporting a shit eating grin and looking her over.

"Well, it's not yours either, or that man's upstairs, so fuck off," she spits out, tossing her head as if her hair is down, clearly venomous.

"That's not friendly. Have you brought an unfriendly one?" Delaney asks, eyeing her up with no interest in the answer. Good or bad.

"Neither are you. Are you one of him too?" she snaps in reply.

"Who?"

"Him," she says again, pointing her finger at me. "Sordid."

"I am. I'm very much like him." He's nothing like me. He's all pleasure and amusement, sordid or not.

"You're nothing like me," I eventually cut in, having watched their conversation and decided the only place it's going to get any of us is irritable, worked up more than I currently am, and more than likely giving Alana something she's not asking for. I extend a hand to her instead, asking her to take it so I can get her attractive legs and heels back on solid tarmac, away from Delaney too.

"Is it free for use?" The man himself asks. Alana scowls, furrowing her brow and sneering at the suggestion, amusing me with her reaction as I consider the thought.

"I'm one hundred percent certain anything here *should* require compliance and a certain sense of charisma attached to the one asking. The second of which you have none of," she says, shrugging her hand from mine and tucking her hair back into place. "And the first of which he has just enforced without my consent," she snaps, swinging her eyes back to me with another glare of disdain. She sucks in a breath and rubs her ass again as she turns back to Delaney. "Unless you've got a huge dick in there... Have you?" My own mouth might have gaped at the comment, and Delaney, for once in his life, looks blank. "Well, come on, big boy, whip it out. What does it matter anymore?" Fits of giggles start to come from her mouth, to the point that I actually stare in bemusement, too. She keeps on going, covering her mouth and finally finding a way to contain her mirth as she swings around to look back at me, her eyes scanning my tux. "You might as well, too. Let's see it. If I'm going to play with it anyway, I might as well have a look. Come on whippy?" Whippy?

"Is it drunk?" Delaney asks, still seeming as mystified.

I don't know whether to be affronted or charmed as I watch her haughty expression return, and it takes me some time to conjure up a response worthy of such a blatant display of insanity.

"As and when you deserve my cock, don't worry, you'll get it," I eventually answer, moving towards her with every intention of warning her of the inevitable should she continue with her mouth. She knows where she is and should assume that cockiness will get her nowhere at all but cunt deep in a misfortune she isn't ready for. "Until then, I suggest you take your schoolgirl tone and wrap it up before it gets you in trouble."

"You can't talk to me li—" I'm so quick to smother my hand over her lips she has no hope of removing herself from my hold, as my eyes snatch a glimpse at Delaney, flicking my head at the same time to get him to leave. Our host just chuckles, amused at the frivolities, and then wanders off as I tug her towards a more private area. She struggles a little, but it's hardly a fight, nothing that denotes real fear anyway, which pisses me off.

"I'll talk to you however I want," I growl, barely holding in the need to fuck the sass from her given what I've just watched upstairs. "Do you know what I want to do to you because of what I've just witnessed, Alana?" I ask, weaving us through the maze of pergolas and wooden struts around the terraces. "I want to get my tongue inside you." Her breath hitches behind my hand, her body tensing in my hold. "See how long you can keep using that filthy fucking mouth when I do." I manoeuvre her into a partially hidden corner, pulling at her dress as I aim her for a stone table. She mumbles behind my hand, spit leaking onto my skin as she does. "You want to say something?" She nods, her body twisting a little as she does, but still not struggling with any real violence. "I don't want you to say another word unless it contains begging for my cock." She gasps a little, her ass beginning to grind into me regardless of the red still imprinted on its surface. "See, this is the way it works. You beg. I play. How's that cunt doing?" More saliva pours from her mouth, pronouncing her need long before her mind accepts it. "Is it still wet for me?" She keeps her head still as I push her down, levering her at the waist to stick her ass further into the air. "Had this fucked?" I ask, my fingers digging into her ass as I slowly slide my hand from her mouth. I doubt it. Too prissy for anal. "You scream, shout, or do anything other than beg and I'll give you the quickest break down of sadism I've ever delivered. You understand?" She nods again, her cheek resting on the dirty table's surface as she keeps her gaze to the side and away from me. "Good."

That's all I've got for the moment. I'm too busy trying to assimilate sensations I haven't felt for too long. Anticipation wracks my bones, drawing freed thoughts from the depths of me and begging me to expunge fantasies I've long since abandoned. My fingers draw the length of her spine, testing her strength, labouring on her muscles and pushing at them to trial their durability.

"Tell me why you floundered up there in the house," I ask, wondering what set her off as she grinds herself back towards me. I immediately move away, giving her the room she needs to feel exposed. Intimidated. She needs to understand, and this is the quickest way for her to learn about rewards.

"I didn't think…" she replies quietly, sneaking a look back at me and murmuring the words rather than speaking them aloud. "I thought this would be something else. Dinner maybe. A discussion." I gaze at her neck, a stray purple stripe falling free of its constraint, enjoying the way its length brings on visions of fucking and biting. "You're supposed to be research. I didn't think about how to play the occasion. Who to be." I raise a brow, amused by her analogy as she lays her head down again and sighs. "I wasn't prepared to meet those people. I wasn't prepared to interact with others and be called by my name." Her body relaxes completely after the final explanation as I move back to smooth my hand across her skin again. I watch it settle, smiling at how quickly she freely gives information in this position, how much softer she becomes in her tone.

"You were scared?"

"No." She shudders as I reach for the hem of her dress again and run my finger along the inside of her calf, its silky texture causing my own shiver to race through me. "Unprepared. I'm never unprepared. It makes me tense, flustered."

"And this doesn't? Stay there." I drop to my haunches, rucking the fabric higher and letting her scent drift across me. Long toned calves, shapely thighs bare of stockings, just as I like them. I dare my lips against her skin, remembering the taste of a woman who attracts my time, and hear a small moan leave her. "You're not flustered by me?"

"I'm prepared for you, for this. There's nothing you can do to fluster me here. You're just research."

Research. Hmm. I smile again, letting myself rise to my feet to back away as the fabric falls down her legs. And then I just watch her prone body as it fidgets a little, waiting for whatever reaction she might offer to help me see her more succinctly. She's submissive; that much is obvious, but she's less than ready to offer her soul on a plate because of a quick display of strength. And she's too intelligent for that approach anyway. She's devious; she's clearly had to be. Presumably multiple pennames and fake accounts has provided a myriad of hidden depths, causing brattish behaviour, all of which is occupying more of my thoughts than it should be.

"How much do you want from me?" I eventually ask, smiling at the way her feet part slightly the moment I speak, her heels widening for no other reason than her own needs. "For your research?" Fucking research. The thought aggravates me for unknown reasons, make me back away and check the fury that wants to erupt on her skin.

"Everything that he started upstairs," she muses, quietly.

I back away further, my eyes still trained on her shivering ass and the way the silk flutters in the breeze. *Everything that he started upstairs.* That I can do. And more. With pleasure.

Chapter 10

ALANA

"Then we should go back to the party," he says, suddenly by my side and holding his hand out like a gentleman, as if the last ten minutes of being hauled, prodded and poked never happened. I stare at him, not ready to move for some reason and letting my body try to understand why. I'm leaning over a table, having been dragged here, and yet something about the whole situation feels fine. Relaxed even. And I'm not even trying to work out why I was ready to let him fuck me with no thought for protection, or voyeurism. Or why I enjoyed a complete stranger spanking my arse as much as I did. I'm evidently enchanted by the entire debacle.

"Why?" I mean that. I do. We could just stay here and carry on with this, or he could kiss me with those lips of his, rather than just letting them skim my thighs, which caused all sorts of reactions—ones no other man has ever managed. "What's in there that I need to understand?" I find myself lifting my arms onto the table in front of me so I can rest my cheek on them, still staring at his magnificence and resting myself on the stone as I smile. Perhaps I'm flirting. I don't know. Or maybe I just want to get on with the research that's relevant to my book. Or perhaps I'm just dreaming that last part is true and I'm not feeling butterflies in my stomach that have no right to be there.

"It's a part of who I am. You said everything, Alana." Christ, he's handsome. And the dark skies around him only multiply that. There's a soft twinkling of lights highlighting the sheen to his hair, the shadow of them reflecting back at me from his eyes, only deepening his handsome façade. One could easily fall for such an animal if one was stupid. I'm not. I can't afford to be. He's the sort I write about, the sort we all write about. Mean looking, dirty, but with an air of class that announces his right for women to tumble at his feet. It's an air that makes one do unusual things, without thought or opinion. Something I appear to have done up those stairs under another man's hands, quite irrationally. For Blaine.

"I don't need to understand who you are, only what you can do with your hands, which appear useful." God, that sounds brash, but it has too. There's nothing else here. There just can't be.

He frowns, brushing at the lapel of his tux and dropping his gaze from mine.

"Is that your version of a blush?" His mouth quirks a little, perhaps amused at how forward I'm being with him. He might be a sadist, but he's also a man, one I need to feel relatively in tune with for this to happen. "Because it's adorable if it is." He bursts into a small chortle, closing his eyes and then looking up at the sky.

"Adorable." It's not a question, more a reiteration of the word, one that makes me question why the hell I would use that term given the way he's shoved me about. But there is a sense of instability there somewhere, as if he's confused about something, perhaps questioning what he's doing with me at all. "You're going to be trouble for me, aren't you?" The continuation causes my smile to broaden. It's unlikely I'm the one who's trouble here. He's the one who creates pain for fun.

"You think I'm trouble?" I eventually say, finally moving my body to an upright position and stretching my arms. "I'm just writing a book. That's all. I'm here to learn. I'll take everything you have as long as it's relevant to my story." He nods, his eyes darting over my frame again as his cuteness recedes, flattening out to his more normal expression of detachment. "I won't fight or give up, Blaine," I say as I rub at my arm, still feeling his grip on it long after his fingers have left my skin. "I don't need romancing with grand gestures." Not that I think I'll get them anyway. "This is work for me, and not hard for you, I assume. Treat it like a job." He pockets his hands, a frown beginning to encroach, proving I've offended him somehow. I don't know how. I thought he'd want it this simplistic. Easy. "I just need my story and then you can go back to whatever it is that you do with your time." I say that with a finality I'm not sure I believe is true, but regardless he needs to know that's all I want from this. There's no romance here. I don't expect it. There's no story that needs to evolve or be considered, only what's significant to my novel. Whatever this is, and whatever his abilities in and out of the bedroom, I don't want him thinking I'm going to be a hassle.

I wrap my arms tighter around myself, watching him watch me, and wondering what's coming next. There's no need to go back in there. I'm not interested in his friends, or any sense of who he is or where he's come from. I'm not affording myself the possibility of falling in love with this sort of man, and I'm doubting he wants anything like that from me anyway. He's just a research requirement to me and I'm a job to him. He has to be that way.

"Are you on any medication?" he asks, completely out of the blue. It throws my confidence, wondering what the hell that's got to do with anything as I contemplate my answer. I'm not, nothing other than the pill and the amphetamines anyway, and they're definitely not prescription. In fact, I doubt the little guy who gets them for me has any medical qualifications at all. And I can't tell him about them anyway. It's illegal. Not that I'm sure what these people do is all that legal either.

Maybe I should tell him.

"No." It's the sensible response. It's not like he needs to know. We're not a couple, are we? And I haven't got a problem with it. I could stop anytime I like. I can't really see its relevance in all honesty. I flick my eyes around until they land back on him, hoping my lie goes unnoticed. He just keeps staring, a deliberate threat engrained in his eyes that might have something to do with more spankings. He more than likely knows I've lied, doesn't he? Perhaps I should tell the truth? Or perhaps not. "Well, only the pill," shoots out of me, my hands waving in boredom to pronounce my righteous assertion. "You know, for pregnancy?"

He just continues to stare for a while, making me feel more uncomfortable by the second as I attempt to stare back. It's an interesting feeling, bringing with it an underlying sense of discord that makes me want to look away. It's something some of them seem to have about them, Blaine especially. As if they're purposely trying to put you off balance, weaken you. Not something he's going to manage with me, not for this type of research anyway, but I'm sure he has with others. Maybe that's what some women want out of all this. Weakening. Although, I don't know why.

"You look beautiful tonight," he says, cutting off my musings and suddenly offering his hand again. A compliment? Nice. Mind you, given he had his hand up my skirt a minute ago, maybe it should have come before the act itself. Either way, I don't take the hand as I make my mind regroup itself from the peculiar wandering it's been doing, again. This isn't a playground session of love and commitment, much as I might be have been thinking otherwise at times. It's business, that's all. So instead, I walk past it, heading up to the party again for reasons I'm yet to understand.

"I don't really want to go back in there," I mutter, looking at the display of wealth draped around the building. I've seen inside now, and while stunning, it's not helping me attain more knowledge. Well, short of the spanking, which ended up feeling a little humiliating regardless of how arousing it was. But really, all this is just a display of glorified kink. Better than the last venue, no doubt, but I've dealt with money for quite some time now. I know it. It's all fast cars, this time laced with kinky people ambling around. Their spouses, or whatever you call them, dressed in odd clothes, some crawling over the gravel to show their ownership. "I just don't see how it's applicable to my work."

He stares at me for the longest time, his body switching between relaxed and tense as he paces around in front of me. He stops at one point, turning to face me and opening his mouth, a frown etched in as if he doesn't like his own thoughts, only to close it and move again. It makes me nervous, which is absurd given the spanking I just took, and the manhandling he delivered after the event. So I just wait for him to settle, wondering what he's trying not to say. Eventually, he stands still again and looks at me.

"We can leave if you prefer," he says, a completely emotionless expression gracing his face, as if he's shut me out of understanding anything, not that I understood anything anyway. "Are you ready?"

"For what?"

"Understanding who you are."

"I'm learning who you are, not me, aren't I?"

He smirks, turning away from me and heading towards the car park as he tugs at his bow tie. I follow, not really understanding why he's smiling but reasonably sure it's something I'm going to find out soon enough.

We arrive at a dark grey sports car, which doesn't surprise me in the slightest. It's long and low, fast looking, just the sort of thing I'd imagine of him. It makes me question the amount of reality anyone really wants to read, whether they're actually interested in a normal guy, one who's sweet and well mannered. The sort who holds hands because that's what he knows of love, rather than one who does it because it's required of him for some display of macho intention.

"Are you getting in?" he asks, leaning across his seat to look at me. He's got that undone look going on as he sits there, beauty and masculinity pouring from his being as he raises a brow. Yes, I suppose I am, rightly or wrongly. I gaze out the window as the door clunks into place beside me and he reaches across me, grasping hold of my seat belt to help me put it on. Sweet. I smile a little, tickled at this offering of chivalry, given his proclivities.

"Quite the charmer, aren't you?"

He smirks, but it doesn't reach is eyes. In fact, something seems to change the instant the seatbelt engages into its hole. All warmth drains from his features, not that there was ever that much. Something hardens. His eyes maybe, or perhaps his jaw as he hovers in front of me and looks at my lips, licking his own.

"You know what you're doing, Alana Williams?" I nod in response, not entirely sure I do, but needing my book regardless as I watch his smile peter out to something infinitely more nasty than bored.

He leans back away from me, sliding on some driving gloves and then reaching into the glove box by my knees for something. The vision of him in the gloves makes me titter, as if we're in the nineteenth century about to drive off on an adventure. And now he's probably going to offer me chocolates, or a drink, maybe even make me remove my knickers and give me a vibrator, something to give myself an orgasm with as we drive to our destination. What he pulls out throws me—a small bottle and a handkerchief. I watch as he empties some of the liquid onto the material, rubbing it together to increase its spread. "Breathe it in," he says, offering it to me with no emotion attached to any feature as he winds down his window. My face screws up in astonishment. Breathe in unknown liquid? I don't think so. I look back at him, my mouth gaping at his boldness and ready to leave unless he finds some explanation for this insanity. There's a slight lift of his lip, one that doesn't fill me with any confidence at all. "You want a story, let's give you one." My story? He's doing this for my story? I shift about in my seat, glancing between his eyes and the material in his hand, wondering why this has anything to do with my unfinished manuscript. "I want you unprepared, Alana." My brow furrows as he lays it in my lap and switches on the engine.

"Is that chloroform?" I eventually ask. Although why my mind's even considering any of this, I don't know. Could it be any more ridiculous?

"I'm not telling you what it is. You'll have to trust me." He engages reverse, leaving me with nothing but the low growl of the car and the feel of leather beneath my backside. I glance at him again, watching the way his hand spins the wheel around. "Trust is the first thing you'll learn about *our* kind, Alana. You have to trust."

I pick it up, glancing around the car park as we begin to drive out, and looking for other normal people, all the time wondering what the fuck I'm even thinking about this for. This is abduction, isn't it? And even if it isn't, I have no idea where he's going to take me, or what he's going to do to me when we get there. Trust. Quite the word given what he's asking me to do.

"You're asking me to knock myself out for the sake of my story?" He starts to increase our speed as we leave along the gravel driveway, stones clipping the edge of the metal work as we go. He doesn't look at me, but keeps his eyes trained on the dark road in front of us, his foot speeding us further into a night that appears to have an ending I don't know about.

"I'm not asking you to do anything, Alana. You're the one who asked for my help, not the other way around. Either do it, or I'll take you back to your average existence. Your choice."

The screech of the tyres as we round a corner and head out onto the open road is powerful enough to have me glued to the seat, trying to maintain my balance as he increases the speed and I watch his arm changing gears. I look at the material again, already starting to smell an acetone chemically scent waft under my nose. He's right, I suppose. I'll just have to trust him.

"Do you often do this? I mean, it was in your glovebox." He doesn't answer that. He just keeps on driving without even acknowledging I've spoken. I glance around again, looking for something in the car that might help make this seem somewhere near acceptable. There's nothing. It's as devoid of expression as him, which only furthers my nerves, but I do need my story. He's right about that. How can I truly appreciate sensation and feeling if I'm prepared for it? I can't. That other guy nearly gave me the same experience upstairs, and that was because of the unknown, I'm sure.

I lift the material, gingerly sniffing at it as it hovers about a foot from my face. I'm sure this is stupid. It's one of those things people tell you never to do. But this is Blaine Jacobs, not some faceless stranger who's grabbed me in the middle of the night. He's right. He is the man I've asked for help. I said no one else would do, that I trust him to do this. How bad can it be?

"Closer," he says, now with a small sense of frustration lingering in his voice as he revs the car again, pushing us further into the dark and swinging us onto a country lane. "Breathe it deeply. Cover all of your mouth."

I widen the material from its scrunched position, looking at him as I do and bringing it up to my lips as I watch the world flash by behind him. The chemical has a sweet tinge to it as I take in my first deep lungful, and the second pull leaves me slightly breathless, my head buzzing as if I've had too much to drink. The third seems to increase my pulse, sending a shock of panic through me and making me pull my hand away. He reaches over, his eyes firmly fixed on me as he pushes my hand back into place so I can keep breathing it in. There aren't any words from him, no sense of reassurance or passion, only that slight lift of his lip again as he stares at me and not the road. It's all I see as an odd sense of sickness takes over. I feel woozy, and the car's quiet all of a sudden, almost silent, its noise disappearing until all I can hear is my own heartbeat thundering inside. His eyes narrow as his hand increases the pressure again, my own hands feeling lax all of a sudden as they begin to tumble away. They're just slits of shadow now, matching the sky behind him and blending into one with it, the occasional flicker of a star dispersing the blackness, and then they're gone, too.

That's all there is. Black.

~

It's quiet here, peaceful. So much so that I can almost feel the sun beating down on me, reminding me of all the holidays I haven't been on. Why haven't I done that? I've got money, enough for me to travel to most places if I choose to. I should holiday more, live more. I don't know when that stopped. It must have been after my second trilogy. I went home to England, and then travelled Europe for a while, enjoying my first experience of real money and spending it accordingly. I went to Paris first, then the holy land, then Denmark I think. I can't remember. It was lovely, though. I travelled on my own with a backpack and nothing else to hinder me. I wasn't stifled or ordered. There weren't any deadlines. I slept when I wanted to, ate when I wanted to, relaxed when I wanted to. I wrote *Bailey's Scorn* while I was there, allowing the sentimentality of the holiday romances to take me off into hot nights of passion under clear blue skies. The book still does well. Seems people like a good old fashioned holiday fling. Perhaps it's their way of escaping reality's mundaneness. Something I've given up trying to achieve. I just write it for everyone else now, for some reason forgetting that I might need it, too.

    My head lolls back against something, probably a beach towel. I don't know, and in this fuzzy state of consciousness I don't really care. I'm just happy to stay here, relishing the temperature around me and thinking of things I should change as my feet dangle in cold water. I'm not sure how long I've been here, or even where I am. It smells of salt air, though, possibly a lakeside, or the sea. How did I get here? I try to open my eyes, crinkling the corners to purge them open, but they just stay shut, the light that was around me seeming to disappear into darkness. They're sore, as if they've forgotten how to open, or they're glued shut. I pick my hand up, ready to rub the sleep away, but hear a clunking sound and then feel something grating against my wrist, hampering my movement. I stretch my face, opening my mouth wide to help my eyes free themselves of the sleep, but nothing happens. I tug my arm, wondering what's holding it down, and then try to move the other one instead. That's the same, held back by something, and once again the movement causes a clinking sound of some sort.

"Hello?" My voice sounds weak as I try to call out, scratchy, unlike my own, and my throat stops the sound before it really gets to any useful level anyway. It's dry and parched, as if I haven't drunk water for weeks. I try again, but this time nothing really happens at all as I continue trying to prise my eyelids open. Nothing works. Why doesn't anything work?

It slowly dawns on me that I'm sitting, the wood of a chair making my arse ache and my spine tingle with painful spasms. I look around, naturally trying to see where I am until I realise my eyes are still shut. What the hell's happening? I drag at my arm again, letting the metallic sound clatter around as I try once more to get my fingers to my face. It still doesn't happen. Perhaps if I moved, shifted my body towards whatever's holding my arm back then I might be able to reach. At least if I can see I can understand what's going on.

The moment I try to push on my legs, they give way, their normal ability to lift me seemingly evaporating as my weight sinks back onto the wood again. Something's not right at all. Where was I before this happened? On a beach? No, in a car. I was in a car, driving. We were driving fast. Where to? I wasn't driving. There was a man. He was handsome, with black eyes, long lashes. I remember long lashes and stars, the world whooshing by behind them. I shake my head, rattling the metal again and scrunching my eyes. Over and over I twist them about, stretching for a way to get my fingers to my face, until I feel my thigh slip, its strength barely able to stop the fall that follows as I thump to the ground below me.

"Fuck." That word is barely audible either, the end of it scarcely leaving any sound hanging in the air.

A sigh escapes me as I test the floor with my fingertips. It's cold, just like my feet. Whatever dream I was having made me think they were in water, but they weren't. They were just on this cold floor. It's stone, or polished marble. There's a glasslike quality about it as I slowly run my hands around, searching for whatever's holding me in place. I eventually find it. It feels like a hook or ring in the ground, securely latched onto the chain I can feel holding me down by the wrist. Some sort of cuff or lock. I don't bother looking for the other one, assuming it will be the same as I reach for the chair again and try to remember what's going on.

"You're awake."

My brow furrows, the voice reminding me of something I can't quite place. Maybe it's someone I know, or someone I've heard before. "How's your head?" He's American, but his voice is refined, perfected by schooling probably. I open my mouth to reply but nothing comes out, not through lack of trying. I'm just so weak, tired. Everything hurts. It's all heavy and laboured, as if my body's given up trying to move me about.

"I…"

"You what?" There's a small chuckle attached to the back of his question. He's amused by me. It seems wicked, cruel even. "Are you ready?" Ready for what? I don't know where I am, or why I am. I rattle the chain again, trying to remember anything that might help and pushing myself to my feet. The moment my calves give me any propulsion, the room starts to spin, my mind whirring inside and instantly making me feel sick. Try as I might to contain it, I can't. Vomit races from my gullet, bursting through my throat and out before I have a chance to stop it. It spits out of me as I cough and heave, dredging up the last of it and filling my nose with its putridity as I fall back to my hands and knees again.

"Elegant," he says, his shoes clipping across the floor in front of me somewhere. A hand catches my chin, forcibly holding it in a certain position as he tips it upwards towards him and pinches into my throat. "Hold your head still. You'll remember in a minute." I don't know what that means, but the voice does sound more familiar, like I've spent time with it, laughed with it maybe. And then liquid drips onto my face from somewhere, slowly inching a cool flow towards the corners of my eyes. "Don't try to open them immediately." I can't help it. The water seems to seep into them, a freezing chill attached to it as they start to sting and burn behind my lids. "The more you force it, the more it'll hurt." His hand increases its grip to the point of causing pain to rip through my neck as he yanks me to something hard and pushes my head onto it. "Not that it'll bother me much." Then, as the last of the liquid seeps further in, he presses his fingers onto my eyes, stopping me from opening them any further. The pain intensifies, feeling as if it's singeing my eyelids and burning the rims off my face.

"Please," I splutter out, causing yet more pain to attack my throat, the itch so uncomfortable I shuffle about in his hold again.

"I was going to keep you blind, but now you've soiled my floor you'll have to clean it up," he says, massaging his fingers into my eyeballs until I finally feel the lids starting to peel away from each other.

The light blinds me as I get my first glimpse of the world and the hard thing leaves my head, followed by his hold. It's blurry, as if my eyes have never seen before. I go to rub them, then feel the chain holding my hand in place still, and for the first time I get a look at the thing restricting me. It's not a heavy chain, more like a dog lead really, but it's linked into a solid square bracket on the floor.

"What...? Why?" I'm still barely able to get words out as I slowly lift my eyelids again, trying to focus on the man in front of me as he backs away. I blink several times, letting the liquid seep through again as the burning sensation seems to peter out into a dull throb.

"Because you asked me to," he says from above me. Asked him to what?

"I don't..." Remember. I don't remember anything other than his voice and some sentiment attached to it. It's not fear. I'm not scared. Maybe I am a little, but I feel safe in some manner, perhaps as if this is okay. I don't know. It's all hazy, obscure, like I can't quite access the reason I'm here, or cotton onto its meaning.

My hand suddenly skids forward, throwing me off balance, my fingers gliding into something wet in front of me and making me fall forward.

"Careful," he says, laughing lightly. I raise my head again wearily, wondering what that means. Careful of what? It's only when I slide my fingers back, finally watching his frame come into full view as my eyes start to focus properly, that I realise I've stuck my hand into my own vomit. It makes me heave again, repeatedly. My back arches as I skate myself backwards away from it, trying to flick the sick off and get away from it. He laughs again. It's a menacing chuckle, not one I remember at all. It brings with it the need to cower slightly, concerned for my safety all of a sudden. "By the time we're done, you'll eat it if I ask." My head shoots up, cricking a spasm through my neck as my brain rattles inside my skull, the thought alone making me heave again. "Seems that gag reflex works just fine."

I stare in shock, trying to place the man in front of me. I know I know him. I've seen him before somewhere, spent time with him. He's touched me; I know that too. I can almost feel his hands on me now. My eyes drop to them, watching the way his finger and thumb rub together.

"Blaine?" The name pops into my head, but nothing else follows, only the thought of his lips.

"Mmm."

"What? Why?"

"You've said that before."

"I know, but I..." But I what? I don't know what. My mouth flails around for words as my own hand rubs against the black material on my body, trying to remember why I'm wearing an evening gown and desperate to get the sick off my fingers. It's high-end, designer. "We were..." I tug at the chain again, trying to hold my brow to help me glean information. "You were driving, and..." No. Nothing.

"Do you know who you are?"

"Of course I do," I reply, irritation lacing my tone as I start to find my voice again.

"Do you know what you do?"

"I write books." I know I do that. I remember it in my dream, or whatever it was that I was doing.

"Helping any?"

No. Nothing's helping. It's all just a blur.

"Take these off," I snap out, becoming maddened with my confusion as I feel my strength return a little. He doesn't respond, so I look up at him again, putting the pads of my feet to the floor to lift me up. I only get halfway upright, maybe chair level, before the chains stop me from straightening my back fully. "What the hell is this?"

"And there's my little brat. Welcome back." Brat? Fuck him. "This is what you asked for, Alana Williams. Or Valarie. Or Peter." He chuckles again as I stare at him, my anger beginning to turn into real fury. "Who are you today?"

"Fuck off," I spit out as I tug the chain again, violently. "Take these off, will you?"

He pulls his hand out of his black pants pocket, opening his palm to reveal a small key. I snatch a look back at the lock on the square bracket, realising it's the right size, but he just holds it there, about ten feet in front of me, taunting me with it.

"Well?" I say, holding my wrist up, offering it to him.

"You've done nothing worthy of having them removed yet." What? I glance around the room, looking for windows or doors, ways out. This can't be real. Who gets locked up in chains and can't remember anything? My back screams at me as I try to move again, barely able to gain any leverage against the metal holding me in place. "Perhaps you should sit on the chair again?" I ignore the comment as I scan the room again, checking out my surroundings. It's a large room, brightly lit with a cool blue marble floor, a Greek emblem running the outside edge. Some pieces of modern furniture are placed accordingly.

No soft furnishings, though, not even a sofa or chair other than the plain dark wooden one behind me. A small table sits to my right, about four-foot square, one that seems to be the same carve as the chair. There is one large window, covered with heavy brocade gold curtains, and a heavy set ornate door at the other end of the room, seemingly at odds with the modern cabinets and fixtures.

"How are your fingers?" Why? What's wrong with my fingers? I look at them, worried something's happened to them. Nothing has. They function perfectly, if not a little slowly given my aptitude for typing. He does nothing other than chuckle again, and then after a few moments, he crosses to the white sideboard and places the key on it as he draws out a phone and calls someone.

"Bring a cleaning kit," he says before ending the call and walking towards the door. He looks back at me, scanning my body as I wait for him to say or do something, like take these fucking chains off me. "Clean the floor. I'll be back in a while." That's all I get as he smiles, puts his phone back in his pocket, and then leaves me alone in the room, quietly closing the door behind him.

I immediately drag the chair back into place, giving me something to sit on as I begin yanking at the chains. They don't budge, even with my full weight behind them. I try levering one against the other, using my body as an anchor to create more power. That doesn't work either, so I wrap one of the chains around the leg of the chair, hoping the wood has more strength than me, but nothing happens. I'm still locked in place. I end up slumping back into the chair, staring around me for something that I can use to free myself. Of course, the key continues to taunt me from fifteen feet away, glittering against the surface as rays of sunlight filter in behind the curtains.

"Fuck," I mutter. "FUCK!" That was screamed, but I don't care. Maybe it'll get him to come back and take these fucking things off me. It would help if I had the first damn clue why I was in here. It's still foggy, though. There's something there, a conversation about a book. A kinky book. He said he would help me. I know that much. I remember him asking me if I was ready for something. What, I don't know. His smile suddenly flickers in my mind. It had a warmth about it. It's nothing like the version of him that just stood in this room. Nothing about that smile was calming or trustworthy. It was slightly creepy, if I'm honest. Chilling.

The door opens as I continue pulling at the chains, not really putting any effort into removing myself but continuing nonetheless. A man walks in. He's tall, not unlike Blaine, but he has none of Blaine's superiority. He seems non-descript as he walks towards me in a cheap suit, carrying a bucket and a rag, his shoes scuffing the floor loudly. I glare at him then flick my eyes to the vomit still about three feet in front of me.

"Clean it up," he says quietly, dumping the bucket down by my legs and slinging the rag into it. "You don't want to piss him off, love." Love? I'm not anyone's love. Certainly not this person's, whoever he is. And why don't I want to piss Blaine off? He's just a guy, one who happens to be attractive, but in my books at the moment, he's a dick who won't take these chains off.

The smell of disinfectant wafts under my nose, instantly bringing with it a thought of chemicals. I halt the abuse that was about to come out of my mouth and stare straight ahead at him, searching my mind for more answers.

"Chemicals," I say. "Sweet, like fruit."

"Huh?"

"There was a chemical." He shakes his head at me and turns away, showing me his back and forging another vision as I watch the way his suit jacket hangs against his trousers. "And a party." I look at my dress, remembering my shoes as I glance at my bare feet. "Where are my shoes?"

"Better get your shit together, love," he says, his head twisting back to me for a second before turning away again. "He's not a patient man."

"Jacobs." He stops, his feet grinding to a stop from his slow lope out towards the door. "That's his name, isn't it? Blaine Jacobs. We were at a party." I remember. There were lights and terraces. A huge party. People were there. Lots of them. Tables decorated with flowers and colours. A band, I think. I can't see any faces, but it was loaded with money. I remember the dresses and tuxedos. And kinky things, jesters. I was spanked over someone's knee. Blaine watched it. People were laughing at me while it happened, some applauding and shouting encores. I felt embarrassed. Awkward.

"Clean your mess up, love." I look up, startled by his interference in my mind musing and frown at him as he starts walking again, his head hanging low and his hand reaching for the door. "Before he comes back and finds you've disobeyed him."

I narrow my eyes at him, trying to stop the blurring and dizziness that keeps coming in swathes, and not understanding a damn thing happening to me.

Chapter 11

ALANA

I don't clean up my vomit, because I'm not a fucking slave. It's not that I'm not happy to clean up vomit—it is mine after all—but I'm not being ordered to do it, and I'm certainly not being scared into doing it, especially while I'm in chains. I don't know who that other man was or why I'm here, but the more I remember, the more realise who Blaine is. It's all coming back now. The party. The way my arse stings. No wonder it's uncomfortable on this chair, making me twitch about. His friend in a mask, most of them in masks actually. The way he manhandled me into a corner and whispered dirty things, his lips travelling my legs as he did. The chloroform, the car. The fact that I, quite stupidly by the look of my current predicament, covered my own mouth with the fucking handkerchief. What was I thinking? It was possibly one of the stupidest things I've ever done. I might want to write a decent book about BDSM, but I'm pretty sure this isn't the way to do it.

So instead, I'm sitting here waiting. I'm not here to be manipulated or scared. I'm here to learn something, and he said he'd help me. He said all I had to do was ask. Well, it seems knocking myself out with chemicals as he gazed at me was asking. It's not like he's really going to hurt me. He's Blaine Jacobs, the man I asked for guidance. This is all more than likely a rouse, something to keep me on edge and make me believe that fear has something to do with their needs. It can't. If it was about being scared, no right minded person would enter into it in the first place. Well, I assume they wouldn't. Although, there have been a few stories about rape and non-consent, which now I'm thinking about it does have my nerves a little on edge regardless of a sight sense of interest.

I scan around again, probably for the thousandth time, and try to get any sense of where I am. There's nothing to help me, nothing apart from the slight smell of salt still lingering in the air. It's the same as it was in my dream, reminding me of beaches and holidays. But given that I was in Manhattan a while ago, I can't see how I can be at the beach. Mind you, I have no idea how long chloroform works for.

I frown, wondering why I've never used it in one of Peter's books as I stare at the key on the cabinet again. I've done murders and mayhem, deaths, suicides. Huge complex plots involving crime and corruption. Mafia genres. The thought makes me smirk, remembering The Case series. I always loved that one. It's full of drama and intrigue, dirty politicians and… Oh. A snort leaves my nose, nearly making me burst into giggles as I replay the soundtrack in my mind, imagining horse's heads and bloodied hands. Perhaps I'm in it now. Perhaps I'm in the middle of a new book. After all, that's what he said he'd help me with, isn't it?

The sound of footsteps echoing outside the door brings me back to the moment I'm in, rather than the dizzying heights of tragedy and conspiracy I'm presently visualising. It's all completely irrational. Not that sucking chloroform through my nose wasn't, but there's no way anything really terrifying is going to happen here. Why would it? I'm a civilised professional, and Blaine is obviously a sane man, one I trust, regardless of these proclivities he indulges in.

The door cracks open then widens fully, and my brow rises at the entrance of the man himself. He's still just as attractive as he's always been, and now he's also draped himself with another expensive cobalt blue suit. He doesn't look at me as I attempt to cross my arms, showing my displeasure at my circumstances. Unfortunately, the chains stop my effort, clanking awkwardly as I let my hands rest in my lap again. He looks at the floor instead, a slight sneer cornering his wide lips until it breaks into a grin.

"You haven't cleared your mess," he says, taking another step in my direction but still not looking at me. "Stupid girl."

"Take these off," is the best response I've got. It's ludicrous that I've got chains on. What civilised human wears chains and sits in a room full of nothing. And I need to pee, anyway, which is going to be rather difficult in this position without a toilet.

"No." What?

"Screw you." The speed of his strides increases, his face turning into the one I saw earlier, which I'm sure should scare any rational personal. Not me apparently. "What? You're going to beat me? Fine way to show your dominance. This is all utterly ludicrous." He stops, his face half shocked by my outburst before he replaces it with an expression of annoyance. Good. I cross my legs instead of my arms, letting the black silk declare my superiority in the room. This is not a free for all at Alana. I will be shown respect while this happens, whatever it is. I'm here to learn. That's all. I will not be treated like some fuck toy or disregarded as pitiful and malleable. This is a professional engagement, regardless of my foolishness with the chloroform. The only thing I need is a sense of what Dominance is, and what it is to submit to that. Anger and fear are not part of the game plan as far as I'm concerned. "And I swear to god, if you lay one aggressive hand on my body I will have you imprisoned by the end of this."

"Mmm." I'm not sure what that means as his mouth quirks around the sound.

"I need to pee." We might as well get that sorted before anything else starts.

He wanders closer, skirting my vomit on the floor with some kind of grin developing. I don't know why. I'm talking about needing to pee, for god's sake. Nothing is funny about that as far as I can tell.

"You'll need a vessel then."

He bends, his fingers reaching for the bucket beside my feet. I'm not sure what to think as he lifts it. Perhaps he's going to swill the sick away. I don't really care in all honesty. I just need to pee and then we can get on with whatever is going to happen. It's only in the half second he swings it back that I realise what's coming. The sluice of it straight into my face makes me scream out loud. It's freezing, drenching me and dripping into every crevice. It makes me stand up, shocked and horrified that he would do such a thing as I dance around, trying to get it off me. He's fucking chuckling, like saturating me is funny. Fuck him. I swipe at the material then try to scrape my hair back, which I can't fucking reach, as I choke on the chemical taste that's exploding in my mouth.

"Fuck you," I splutter out, spitting out the sluice as I try to get the disinfectant out. "What the hell is your problem?" My dress is soaked, and I'm shivering as I try to get my feet away from the water beneath them.

"You are," he says, calm as fucking day. Me? I'm his problem? What the fuck is he talking about? I glare at him, stupefied by his answer as he takes a step away from the water that's encroaching on his brogues. "There's a vessel," he continues, dropping the bucket onto the floor beside me again. "Piss in it." I don't even know what to say to that. My mouth opens, but nothing comes out of it as I gape at him, wishing I could actually straighten my body. "You'll learn, one way or another, Alana, that this is not a fucking democracy anymore."

I'm still gaping as he backs away, his eyes hard and drilling into mine as he pockets his hands, so much so that I half forget about the water still running down the inside of my thighs until it tickles me, reminding me of what just happened.

"How dare you throw fucking water at me?"

Two steps forward. Just two, bringing him within three feet of my face, and then he stands still again and draws one of his hands out to rub his face.

"Apologise well, or I'll make you learn how to do it properly." Screw that.

"What for? Swearing? Fuck you."

I don't know what happens next. The speed of it has me on my knees before I have a chance to speak, my face being pushed into the water that's still sluicing around as he holds my neck down. I try to fight back for a second or two, writhing my frame around to gain some leverage, but he's too strong for me, and his grip is bruising as he grinds me into the floor. The chains clunk about, my hands grabbing out for purchase on anything, all to no avail. The water smells of disinfectant, the vile taste of it seeping back into my mouth.

"I despise swearing from a woman's mouth. Do you understand?" I nod, my cheek rubbing against the wet marble. I feel myself do it and hate the fact. Who the hell is he to tell me what to do? If I could get my body around I'd spit at him for doing this, but his hand on my arse makes my whole frame still beneath him instead. It's not tender or relaxed. It's hurting as he grabs at it, rucking the material of my dress and pulling it upwards. The fabric strains at my thighs, digging into me as he yanks it again to try to expose me. It's enough for me to start bucking again, attempting to get him off me once more. He's not having his hands anywhere near me in this circumstance as far as I'm concerned. I might not be terrified, and I know this is all for show to some degree, but I'll not be forced to do something I'm not ready for.

The chains somehow loop themselves as one of his hands works them, criss-crossing them to shorten their length to a foot or so. I watch as they buckle into each other, holding me down in place and not allowing any room for escape. It doesn't matter how much I turn, twist or try to kick out, he's just there, covering every attempt and halting each panicked movement. He's so damned heavy as I feel the buttons of his jacket scuffing my spine. He's like a blanket of pure male, drenching every attempt at freedom with nothing but himself. There's no threat. No weapon. No snarl of aggression. He's just there on top of me, offering a sensation I've never felt before and breathing into my neck.

I begin to feel myself giving in, just like I did in that damned pool. It makes me wonder if he's doing it to me, or whether I'm doing it myself. I don't know. I'm confused all of a sudden as I start relaxing into his weight on me. I'm smothered. Cocooned. And the more I let myself give in, still pitching the occasional weak roll at him, the calmer I seem to become. Relaxed. Quiet.

"Now, I suggest you apologise correctly, or I'll happily make this more painful for you, Alana."

I'm not sure what to say to that. I'm still too busy trying to assimilate the sensation of him on top of me. I've given up, haven't I? Again.

I suck in a breath of air, letting the watery disinfectant fall into my mouth, not disturbed by it too much anymore. I don't understand that. Why wouldn't I be fighting this? It reminds me of rape scenes I've written, being pinned and under the influence of something stronger than me. I should be battling him, forcing him off me. Screaming and shouting out in terror. But I'm not. I'm just here, breathing. And his hand is still roaming my arse, the material higher than it was before as I feel his fingers grazing in between my thighs. He's so close, close enough that I should be worried about him putting them inside me, certainly questioning if I want them there, but I'm not feeling either concern. I'm willing them inside without too much thought about why. It just feels okay, desperate in fact. Like him doing this will cement something in me I've not processed before now.

"I... I'm sorry." I don't know why that came out. I'm not sorry, not for swearing at him anyway. It makes me frown and mouth the words again to myself.

My eyes seem to refocus on my surroundings the second his weight lightens on me. He doesn't get off, just moves to the left, his fingers still lightly flicking at my barely covered nether region.

"Good girl," he says, his other hand slowly releasing the pressure he had on my right shoulder. "Shall we see what you've got inside you?"

My eyes creak round to his as he leans on his elbow beside me, his suited body lying in the water along with mine. I find myself gazing into them, as if it's the first time I've done so. I know I've looked at him before. I know I've noticed how attractive they are, but I don't think I've ever really seen into them. There's something so old about them, which is a useless description. He's not old, maybe mid-thirties, but at this moment I can see depths there I've not discerned previously. They have a small pinprick of light in the middle of the dark walnut brown, a black contour rimming the edge of his pupil, darkening the colour to a pool of murk and gloom. I stare, transfixed by his gaze, both of us simply quiet in the middle of the wet floor and breathing as my hands stretch out into my chains. That's all there is really. No thought. No concerns. No sense of the outside world. It's just me and him and this quiet he's created.

"Blaine..." It comes out so quietly I barely know it's left my lips, but the small lift of his lips tells me he's heard it.

"Open your legs."

I don't feel anything until his fingers inch inside me. I hardly knew he was moving them, or that my legs opened of their own accord, and the gasp that leaves me echoes against the floor between us. It makes him smile some more, his lips curving up into something quite beautiful. So beautiful that I sense my legs widening further to give him better access, just to get another glimpse of such a thing. His eyes soften, the pupil dilating further and rendering another gasp from my lips. And then he shoves his hand, his fingers driving in deep and causing me to groan at their impact. It hurts in some way. It's not a pain I can't take, but it's not delicate or gentile either. It's bruising with no attempt from him to make it any less so.

"It will all be like this," he says, a slight hitch to his words I've not noticed before now as he keeps watching my face. I gaze at his mouth moving around the sounds, not really hearing his actual speech as he slowly glides his hand out and then shoves it in again, putting pressure on my bladder as he does. "Painful. Can you take that?" I think I'm nodding as my head lolls on my upper arm, my legs widening again to let him push in once more, and the broadening of his smile tells me that's what he wanted to hear. He braces his head on his hand, his other one forging inside me as if he's testing me out. Each touch is like a dull flash of lightening, some making me gasp and moan, others making me cringe as spasms of pain shoot through me. My frown descends again, as my body searches for an orgasm that's nowhere near. I've never had someone do this so methodically. It's like I'm a test case. It's not fumbled. I'm not being mishandled by some juvenile. He's clearly intimately acquainted with the female anatomy. It's just measured, as if I'm being shoved around and probed. It makes me look away from him eventually, sensing no intimacy at all and beginning to feel like a toy for his amusement. "Look at me again. Learn, Alana."

I slowly creep my eyes back up, embarrassed by this whole thing as his hand keeps foraging around, his thumb beginning to stroke my clit as his pressure increases. Learn what? That I'm nothing to him? That this is just an entertainment?

"Of all the others who've ever been inside you, how many took the time to understand you?" There's a sense of passion about his voice now. It's only a quiet husk of need, one that fills the space between us with some degree of warmth again, but it's there. "Who are you, Alana?" It's not disrespectful or rude, and not a philandering question. He expects an answer, one that's honest. "How many dug in deep enough to find you?" I gasp out again as his fingers suddenly do something I've never felt before. They grind at something inside of me, pulling my crotch towards him as I slide in the water. "Our kind understand each other." There's another shove, followed by him beginning to push in and out of me, building a rhythm I've never encountered. It's unique, and tempering the edges of me with a madness I'm not sure is normal. My body starts to writhe again, my groin helping him build the momentum. My breath begins to labour, a smile widening further on his face with every gasp that comes from me. "Your cunt's delicious." He tugs again, sliding me further into him and dropping his hand to wrap me into his hold. "Give me your mouth. I want that scream that's coming." Oh god, it is coming now. I don't know where from, and the pain is so intense, making me buck and groan, but along with it there's a sense of ecstasy. It's coursing through me, my mouth hovering around his as he licks his lips and rubs his cock into my leg.

"Fuc…" He swallows the end of the word, our mouths meeting and sending me delirious with the need to come. Teeth clash viciously. It's animalistic as I try to move myself into him more, filling me with visions of nakedness and biting. I don't know where that comes from either. It's like a dream as I climb higher, focusing on his fingers as they hitch me around, rubbing and pushing at bits of me I never knew were there. And then he just stops. He just holds me in this moment, leaving my insides aching and reaching for something I can't get to on my own. His hold is tense around me, bruising, hanging me in seconds that I can't come down from nor climb higher into. He doesn't speak, doesn't move at all. He just lets his mouth arouse me further, nipping at my lips, creating a bite or two and lengthening the time we roll our lips together, and then finally, just when I don't think I can take the pressure anymore, he twists his hand. The orgasm that crashes is instant, blurring me with shivers and moans. There's no light exploding. No sense of elation. It's just dark and obscure, with flashes of his eyes and mouth joining the chaos in my mind. I'm panting, the air unable to find its way inside me because he's still there, filling me with thoughts of decadence and need. It's something new. Something in my blood. Perhaps like a heartbeat bursting out, maybe even giving up. Quieting. It's the most visceral feeling I've ever had, flooding me with emotions I can't deny as he begins to pull his mouth away.

It eventually leaves me completely, rendering a loss I've never encountered. I'd touch my lips if I could move my hands to check that they were still there, but I've somehow ended up on my back, my arms stretched above my head, still restrained by the chains. They yearn for him, though, still reaching themselves towards him in the hope he'll drop his own lips back down to me. The thought makes me question my rationality. It makes me question life itself, let alone if I'm awake or not as I gaze up at him and watch him settle himself over me, a strange look on his face.

"What was that?" I ask, barely able to form thought around the whole experience as I feel his weight on me again. He looks bemused immediately, a slight smirk appearing.

"An orgasm. I assume you have had one before."

Well, yes, but not like that.

"Yes, but it was connected. We were…"

His slight smirk almost immediately disappears, stopping me mid-flow and leaving me wondering what I've said wrong. It's replaced by anger, or at the very least resentment. For what? Me saying we had some sort of link, some moment of beauty in the middle of whatever this sleazy thing is? I gaze at him as he moves, his hands bracing himself above me before he finally shifts backwards and stands up. I'm in the middle of my transfixed gaze, wondering what's going through his mind when I realise he's looking at my body rather than me, specifically my open legs. A blush rises through me, clearly telling me I should close them, perhaps stop them lolling around, but I don't. Something makes me feel empowered or emboldened here. It's not me or my ability to feel sexy. It's something about the room, or the fact that I can see his eyes on me, travelling the length of my body and then slowly meandering back to his starting place. I think it's him in general, actually.

He eventually moves a step away, still frowning and not giving me any hint of happiness or contentment. I don't suppose he should. It's not like we're a couple. For a brief second I imagine my last one-night-stand, his copper hair flashing in my mind as I watch the water dripping from Blaine's suit onto his hand. I'd left in the middle of the night, unimpressed with the best efforts of a reasonably attractive man. He didn't give me a stitch of the feeling I've just had. In fact, it was barely conscious compared to this. The whole act was ineffective. The fucking was insensitive, normally just the way I like it. The orgasm, weak. His hands, light and only attempting sensuous. Nothing about it was desperate or involved. Not like this. Not that anything about Blaine seems desperate. I, on the other hand, am very open to suggestion. I'd take him now if he got on with it, but something tells me he's not going to. He might have done if I hadn't mentioned connection. I saw it in his eyes, felt it in his weight on me, but not now. For now, it's done.

"Clean the floor," he says quietly, picking up the rag beneath his feet and tossing it near my thigh as he walks away. The splash of water spits at my face causing me to turn away from it, rolling to my side with one arm still stretched behind me by the chain. "Before your vomit encroaches on your cunt."

If there was any way to destroy a moment's beauty, he's just shown me how to do it. It instantly sickens my stomach, making me question what the hell I'm thinking. I'm here, on a floor covered in disinfectant, rolling around in my own vomit while he finger fucks me. What is wrong with me? The thought brings a tear to my eye as my nose snuffles in the water, my legs pulling up into my body in an effort to shield myself from him. And then the door slams, showing me how little care he really has for me or how I'm feeling, more importantly how he's made me feel. Why has he done that? Perhaps I was alone in my moment of connection; perhaps it was nothing but a woman and a man, one who knows exactly what he's doing with my body. After all, that's what I asked for, wasn't it? For him to show me something. Presumably that's what he's done. Nothing other than that.

It takes me a few minutes to stare at the floor and feel sorry for myself, clamping my legs together hoping to rid myself of the memory of his hand inside me. It doesn't work, and no matter how much I chastise my ridiculous mind, I find myself glad it doesn't. I've never felt that sort of thing. My body still remembers it now. I can sense his hands still there. My clit's still throbbing, numb with that need to be flicked and awakened again. And my stomach's sickness is nothing to do with my own vomit filtering through the water I'm in. It's to do with the fact that I can feel cramping inside me, clamping perhaps. Like I'm empty, unfulfilled. There's suddenly a void in there that's screaming to be occupied. It's never been there before. I've never screamed for a fucking. Nowhere near it. But I am doing now. I'm internally screaming for him.

Finally, I pull myself to all fours, scanning the blue marble through the water beneath me and trying to balance myself around the chains. It's quite beautiful. Grains of darker blue etch through it, creating patterns and waves. It makes me feel almost gentile as I trace my finger along a line, following it until it brings me to the empty black bucket tipped on its side. The sight of it crushes the calm moment I was having, reminding me of my situation as I stare at its barren existence. And then actuality rapidly descends again as I reach for it, a small snort of contempt snickering out of me and the right chain restricting my movement. What the fuck do I need a bucket for anyway? It's as empty as I am. What was once full is now nothing more than a vacuous vessel. There's no water there to use. No disinfectant left either. The water is already spread around me. I look at it covering the blue expanse, the occasional ripple as I move highlighting its depth. It's too thin to do anything useful with and already soiled by my own expulsion. Useless because of its ferocious discharge.

I slump onto my knees, sensing the metaphor and fingering the wet rag by my hand. *Too thinly spread to be useful.* If I had my notebook I'd write that. I'd let the thought consume me and delve into the whys of that statement. Are we all too thinly spread, barely able to give full effect to any one thing because of our responsibilities and deadlines? Perhaps we are. I certainly am. For once, being here is focusing my mind on something as simple as a bucket of water and a blue floor. It's calming, passive in some way. Annoying too, but at least fluid rather than forced.

I pick up the rag, hoping to maybe mop the swill back into the bucket, refill it somehow. I don't know why. It seems relevant, like it'll make me understand what's important here. Like this bucket is the answer to something I haven't even asked myself yet. Why? It halts my movements as I wring the rag out into the bucket and look at the door. He's doing this, isn't he? How?

"Blaine?" I say so quietly he'd never hear it. I don't even know if I want him to anyway. I just needed to say it, had to let it through my lips so that it was real. Not that any of this isn't.

I mop again, swirling the water and watching as, foot by foot, the liquid gets lifted from the floor and squeezed back into its resting place. I'm almost smiling as I see the level rising, for some reason feeling accomplished. Empty vessel, and then a little more, and then more, until nearly full vessel. I find myself reaching and stretching against the chains to get to the final few feet of it. I can't get to it, though. It's been spread out of the range of my bonds, making me strain at the leash for finality. I become so incensed with managing my task, with making everything neat and tidy again, that I hiss at the pain that shoots though my wrist, desperate to gain another few centimetres of range. I'm so infuriated, in fact, that I end up squeezing my dress instead, wringing it out into the bucket, hoping for another few millimetres of liquid. I don't know why, and at the moment I don't give a fuck. I just need the bucket full. Perhaps I'm going mad, or perhaps I'm just so focused on filling this bucket that I'm delirious. Who knows? At the end of the day his hands inside me on the middle of a vomit covered floor was ludicrous, but I allowed that. He didn't force it. I'm pretty sure I moaned for it, actually. And then there are these chains. They're hideous, reminding me of slaves and their years of turmoil, but I'm still in them, regardless of the fact I could have made more attempts to make him take them off. Who the fuck wants chains around them, restricting them? Why would anyone do that? Ask for it even? I tug at them, annoyed with myself for allowing them there and yet oddly comforted by the way they focus me on one small area. Bucket, rag and chains. That's all there appears to be. That, and my task.

I eventually rock back onto my knees, surveying the outskirts of my reach. It wasn't far enough, not by a long shot, but it's got most of the liquid back in the bucket. It's all I can do, and for some reason that leaves me feeling incomplete, inadequate. I scowl at the floor, trying to understand the sensations and give them some semblance of meaning. It's just a bucket and a wet floor, nothing to be concerned about. But I am concerned.

The door clicks, lifting me from my thoughts, and I watch as the other guy carries a large box in. A box? What the hell is in the box? I scuttle backwards as he approaches, a dull, uninterested look on his face.

"Don't worry, love. You're not my type," he says, a small laugh directed at me as I stretch my hands out to move myself further away. I'd swear at him, or tell him to go screw himself if I thought it prudent, but for some reason I'm not sure that's going to get the best results out of any male around here. "'Sides, the boss would have me shot." Shot? My eyes widen, my arse trying to scamper away again as I glance about, not that there's any further I can go. "And look, you're behaving better already."

I might not be opening my mouth, but that statement doesn't sit comfortably at all. My snarl at his face as he puts the box on a table doesn't go unnoticed. I couldn't care less. I might behave for Blaine, but there's a reason for that. It's called career enhancement. Well, I think that's all it is. Whoever this fuckwit is, though, he has no hold over me, and I don't appreciate his tone in the slightest. I follow him with my stare, keeping my snarl perfectly formed as he chuckles and begins using a knife to slash the side of the box open.

"Good." Blaine's voice shocks me, making me swing my head to the door to find him leaning against the frame and surveying my cleaning work. "Wasn't that hard, was it?"

I don't reply as he just stands there, his very being annihilating the other guy in the room. I just watch as his feet eventually lift and start propelling him in the direction of the table. Some guys move just because they need to travel, their feet landing one in front of the other with no other purpose than to arrive at their destination. Blaine doesn't move like that at all. He stalks. I'd hardly noticed it before. The only thing I'd noticed was the lack of sound coming from his shoes back at his house, something that's not happening here, but I'd not noticed the deliberation in every move. It's what makes his aura different to others. It's like every single footfall or manoeuvre is prepared long before he delivers it. In fact, his hands move like that, too. Slowly. There's no excess flamboyancy or exaggeration. I can't even call it monotonous because it's fascinating, really. Each and every movement is precise and calculated, still fluid, but like he moderates himself, restricting bursts of energy that want to escape.

"You move like you're in chains," I say before thought catches up. Fuck. What a thing to say. He smirks, thankfully. He doesn't make eye contact, though. He's far too focused on his box, but he does look at the floor by my knees, widening his smile a little and then re focusing on his box as he blocks my view of it.

"I have a gift for you," he says as he grabs the back of the chair and turns to face me. Really, a gift? A towel would be nice. Actually, why aren't I cold? I'm not cold. I should be freezing. It's September for god's sake. I look down at my sodden body, wondering why I'm so hot.

"You should enjoy it." "What?" He just moves sideways, his hand waving at the table behind him.

Chapter 12

BLAINE

If only she knew how much I restrain myself. Chains are the least of her concerns, and if she mutters one more moan or groan when I have my hand inside her, I'll let her see just how restrained I'm being.

To see her here, kneeling, is almost too much. It reminds me of times gone by, times I neither care to analyse nor ponder over any more than I already have done. Of all the places I could have brought her, why here? *She'd* been the only one to come here. The only one I'd ever relaxed with, taken stock of life with. Eloise. The thought of her makes me draw in a long breath as I watch Alana gaze quizzically at me while I think of another woman and consider her posture.

"A typewriter?" she eventually says, her mouth hanging open in surprise. I turn from her and look upwards, scanning the hooks and then turn to Tyler.

"The blue lengths," I say, dragging the chair towards her and nodding at the cupboard on the right of the room. Tyler does as he's told swiftly, like a good little boy. It makes me snort lightly, admiring the man's newfound gait as he crosses the space. Once upon a time Tyler was nothing but a frustrated teenager, gangly and immature. Now he's more akin to a calmed predator, hardly tamed, but learning his trade nonetheless.

"Why a typewriter? It's barely useable," she continues, her eyes following me as I reach for her hand to help her stand. She frowns at it, possibly scared of what my next move will be. Good.

"To write, Alana. That's what you came for, isn't it?" She looks perplexed, still avoiding my hand as she tries to push herself up. I've shoved her back to the floor before she has chance to make it upright, and then offered my hand again as she squirms further away from me.

"What the…?" She falters, her mouth recalling the expletive before it leaves her lips. Good girl. Quick thinking for someone so outspoken. I smile at her, watching the way her mind ticks over the possibilities of what to do. She should just accept my hand, learn to trust it, depend on it. By the time she leaves here, she'll understand exactly what my kind are all about. There are no insane connotations here. No adolescence. No unnecessary concerns of youth and bad upbringings. There is only acceptance and involvement—pure, unadulterated immersion.

"I shouldn't need to explain what I'm suggesting, Alana," I say quietly, rubbing my fingers over the pad of my thumb and then opening my hand again for fear of doing what instinct tells me to do to her. "Take the hand." Her brow furrows, her body fidgeting as she thinks about her options. Her thought makes me tilt my head, interested in what she thinks her options might be. She only has two. Accept my hand and continue, or ask to leave. The latter choice inexplicably saddens me, but I'll honour it irrespective of my desires. "You came to learn, didn't you?"

A few more minutes pass as I watch her blinking at me, her fingers fiddling with her dress. She looks away a few times, her eyes focusing on the door behind me, and then she slowly lifts her arm. The chain glints and shimmers in the light, amusing me with its reflection in her eyes. She's exceptional, especially in this degraded state. Her mascara runs in black streaks down her cheeks, smudging her unblemished skin. And her mouth is still devoid of lipstick, the hue of natural pink coming through and highlighting wide blue eyes. I take her hand and feel the shiver descend through my own bones again, linking with the same one that caresses her skin. So I hover her, my hand keeping hers at a certain level just to let the sensation dig in deeper. It's an impression of fascination I've not forgotten since the first time I touched her, one I haven't felt before, irrespective of Eloise's lasting memory. This new awareness surges through me, reminding me of hopes I've never thought possible. There the same ones I'd given up on long ago after finally accepting my natural disposition to cause pain. And because of that very notion, every disciplined moral tells me to let her go immediately, because I've known this was coming since the house in Manhattan. I'd felt it between us then when I kissed her, and then again when I'd watched her smother her mouth with chloroform, offering me everything she has without realising she was doing so. I should have driven her back to her home and watched her until she woke, only to tell her I wouldn't help after all. Instead, nature is taking over, rallying me with patience-testing resolves and unwanted sensations bellowing for escape. It's all as profound as the touch of her fingers in my grasp now, her prints mingling with mine and hoping to join. And the spark between us, that's as instinctual as light and dark, mesmerising me with unwarranted futures and soothing nights in the arms of acceptance. She, this, is as captivating to me as the feel of her cunt on my skin, burning my hand and rendering me incomplete without the soul attached freely.

"You won't hurt me?" she asks, breaking me of the exploration into my own mind as I keep staring into her eyes. Hurt her? I'll destroy her given half a chance.

"Of course I'll hurt you. That's what you came to experience, isn't it?" I reply, still musing my other thoughts rather than what she's asked. She gasps, a small expulsion of air parting her lips again as she stares back. I smile, perhaps enjoying the majesty of her questioning, or the way she never once removes her gaze and challenges me, the tone still questioning long after the words have left her lips. I eventually let go of her, choosing to stop my wandering thoughts before this all becomes a game of push and pull again, one that will spiral into madness the second I let it consume wisdom. Control is the only sentiment she requires for her story. Mine and hers.

"But what about..." I turn back sharply, daring her to talk about the connection we'd both felt on that floor again, willing the conversation on. She can damn well feel what it truly means to me if she likes. Only once has something come close to that sensation, and that ended in death.

She steps back a little, her legs crashing into the chair. Good, perhaps the impact will stop the stupidity that's threatening her mind with images of love and contentment. There's none of that here, not the kind she imagines anyway.

"It needs inking. All you need is here," I finally say, backing away from her to stop any urge continuing further than it should.

"What? What do you mean, inking? I don't know how to do that? It's ancient." She looks at the contraption then lightly fingers the keys, depressing one until it achieves a clunk. "No one types on these anymore. What do you expect me to be able to do with it?"

How would I know? I'm not the writer, she is. I assume she doesn't need help with that, only that she requires sensations she doesn't understand. She fiddles again with the machine, her fingers twisting and turning levers, her eyes scanning for how it works.

"Typing is not my field of expertise," I say, remembering the lady in the antique shop who offered all kinds of information on how it should be put together. Which ink to buy, where to get the correct paper from, all irrelevant as far as I'd been concerned.

"No, apparently pain and humiliation is." It's a mumbled reply, one she says into the table rather than facing me head on. I smirk at her, enjoying the way her mouth can't help itself from delivering smartass comments, and knowing it won't take long before I feel the need to broach the vile contents of her lips with the back of my hand.

"You learn, then you write," I say, swiping the rope from Tyler's hand and signalling that the guy should leave. I'm infuriated enough with the fact that I've brought Tyler in at all, but needs must, and having another person present when I'm wound sufficiently tight is practical.

I put a foot onto the table to push myself up to reach the hook, watching as Alana's sense of welfare begins leaving the room and wondering why I've sent him away.

"What are you doing?" she asks, backing away as she gapes up at me and tries to move further.

"Creating tension." In more ways than one. Albeit, there's already enough tension in my body for all to see, no matter how much I'm holding it in. Tyler will already be concerned for Alana's safety, perhaps pondering his own introduction to submissives and sadists, which was the very point of having him here at all. It makes me question my own sanity as I carry on, flicking my gaze between Alana and Tyler, willing him away in one breath and hoping he'll challenge me in another.

The rope slides through as easily as it always does, reminding me of Eloise once more. I've not done this for so long. Dabbled, yes. Taught others to achieve their balance more than once, but prepare myself, feel the flex in the cord and let the ache embed itself? I've haven't done that since Eloise. Not once. Why I'm doing it now for Alana is a quandary yet to be realised. I should have made Tyler do it. Or asked Delaney to be here instead, given the job to someone else.

"Sit down," I say, glancing at her as she loiters as far from me as the chains allowed.

"Why?" I stop my hand working the knots and widen my stance on the table to look down at her, pondering whether the questioning will ever stop of its own accord.

"Because you don't understand how this works." She screws her face up, a slight sneer directed at me. "Let me explain so a four-year-old could grasp the thread of order." She tugs her chain, rattling it and warning me of the storm coming. I chuckle at the thought, my fingers itching with the prospect. "I say, and then you do whatever is asked of you." Still she stays disinclined to accept the train of thought. I admire her for it some respects, remembering the first time I'd watched a woman fighting her way through independence so she could finally feel free of the unending turmoil associated with it. "The more you deny the order, the more you lose your chance of freedom."

"I could walk out of here any time I like," she snaps. "Well, I could if you'd take these chains off me, which you should do, by the way. I didn't ask for them."

"And then you'd be free?" I ask, amused by her innocence and tying off a slip rope to jump down from the table. I land at her side, the clunk of my shoes sounding heavily on the marble, causing her to scuttle again at my proximity. The chains clatter as she moves and glares, defiance echoing through her every feature, again. "Free to go where, Alana? Do what?"

"Anything," she replies, her face as confused as she probably feels. "Go home. Take a bath."

"And that's freedom?" She looks bemused again.

"Well, it's better than being fucking chained and…" I slap at her cheek, hard enough that the impact reminds her about her offensive little mouth and sends her reeling away from me again. It causes yet more sensations to shiver through my own insides, a smile developing at the feel of her in my hand again.

"You hit me?" she snaps, her own hand moving to cover the area.

"You deserved it." Her eyes widen to the point of disbelief. "And you'll get it again if you don't behave appropriately."

"You can't go around hitting women." I smirk again, shaking my head at how little she understands and relishing the prospect of teaching her, should she sit her little ass down. "That's... That's assault."

"In here, you're nothing but something who needs to learn. Barely an animal." Far from it in actuality, certainly from wherever these feelings are emanating from inside of me, but that's what she needs to hear for her story to evolve.

"But..."

I wait for whatever revelation inspires her to argue further, my hand ready to catch another tirade of profanity should she choose that option. She doesn't speak, just flails her mouth around more unspoken urgings and then sees sense enough to keep them to herself rather than voicing them.

"Alana, listen carefully. I don't care what colour, creed, religion or sex you are. You swear once more and it'll be more than a slap. Do you understand?" She frowns, gently dabbing her fingers at her cheek and finally looking to the floor. "You have a world of words in that mind. Use them more exclusively than simple mechanical ramblings." I don't care if she understands or not. The fact is, if I'm honest with myself, I savour the prospect of disciplining further than I already have. I feel it in my slightly clenched fists, in my hardened cock, in the way her parted mouth begs for something to be driven inside it until she's gagging on it and vomiting again. The thought amuses me further as I glance her over and then turn from her again, offering my hand to the chair for the final time. "If you don't sit, I will make you sit without your consent."

She sits without further fight or conversation, her wrists unable to reach the table because of the chains, so I push the table in closer and move behind her to fix her in place. And then she stares in bewilderment at the rope dangling above her head as she ducks to avoid it, her eyes hardening again as if to begin more argument. The slight sneer of her lips makes me lower it to chin height and pull it taut in front of her with a snap of warning. She doesn't move or shake her head. She just remains still, occasionally tilting her head, but letting me begin the process of binding her in.

"Tight," she mutters on one instance. It makes me smile behind her, half stopping the process and choosing to trail the rope beneath her shoulder blades and back up to coil around her neck. It is tight; I know it is. I've been taught to do it this way. The looser the rope, the looser the contact. The looser the contact, the weaker the Dominant. It makes no odds that I enjoy the fear it produces in her, that's not the entire reason for such tension.

"It's an extension," I eventually say in reply, helping her understand the point of it. "It suggests I'm around you. Holding you." The last of the words irritate me, reminding me of feelings I choose to brush aside as my fingers caress her left arm.

She doesn't speak again until I round her and stand in front of the finished effect. She appears calm, relaxed even, which surprises me given the bonds I've wrapped her in. Her head's level, her back straight and held in place by the pulley above her head. Her neck is looped into the web, and only affected if she moves from her current elevated position, which is strained, but achievable.

"Balance," I say, my cock still constricted in my pants and wanting nothing more than to shove itself inside her mouth, or cunt, the latter of which is becoming exceptionally probable if she tries one more argumentative debate. "Put your hands as if you're typing." She does, again without brooking quarrel. It makes my eyes narrow, searching for devious intent because of this new sense of compliance. "Are you playing games, Alana?" She shakes her head briefly, still not venturing words or conversation, or even looking at me. "The only loser will be you if you are." She frowns, a small indent of confusion marring her beauty as she looks at the typewriter and then the paper and ink around her. "No? Are you sure?" I smile at her as she looks back at me, her lips trembling as she struggles to hold herself in the position I've forced her into. Comfort is an enemy here, and she'll eventually realise why. No one can write what she wants to unless they feel it, and no one will understand the merits of such discomfort until she learns how to convey it succinctly.

"Ink it, and then write about my hand in your cunt."

I'm not sure what the expression is that comes back at me from that statement, but one of amusement seems to deliver some content of reflection.

"I'm not sure my cunt can remember," she replies, the corner of her mouth lifting by only a few millimetres as she reaches for the pot of ink. She fusses with it for a moment then scowls at the machine, ratcheting a lever to gain access to the mechanism and wincing as something cuts her.

I watch for a while, musing her legs widening in response to her own words and barely restraining myself from offering a reminder of my hand inside her as she sucks the finger. She teases efficiently, her lips enveloping her bloodied digit with little care for the outcome of such follies. Perhaps she's given up caring for her safety, or perhaps she's simply goading, unable to contain her need for something she neither understands nor is ready to admit. Either way, I'm so close to ripping at my pants, regardless of how ready she is or not. The weight of my fucking cock strains against the material hiding it, scarcely hindering itself from bursting through and taking what it wants.

"You tease like a little girl."

"I am a little girl." My brow shoots up at her instant comeback, my cock commencing the same upward scramble for escape as she fiddles with her machine again and eventually finds the entrance she's after. "Are you my Daddy?" The question almost makes me come in my pants. In fact, I'm so shocked by it that I falter half a step backwards, pocketing my hands to hold them in place rather than allow them any forward momentum. And her fucking legs widen again as I do, locking themselves around the base of the chair to enable her to reach further. "I'm thinking fucking would be useful, Daddy." My own mouth fumbles for a retort, ready to forget words even exist. "I felt your cock against me earlier. Ready for me, is it?" She looks over at me, her sexy half smile turning into something I've not seen previously as she unscrews her inkpot. "I can feel your hand in there still. Was that the plan? Make the little girl ache? Surely there's more than that to all of this." I stand, bemused as she widens her smile into something gods could crave. "How does a little girl need to ask for her fucking?" She dips her finger in, carefully scooping up a dab of black liquid and then dripping it onto the paper. "How does one become so stained one forgets normality and delights in the extraordinary?" I feel my mouth twitch into a smile, breaking through my confusion, irrespective of how I'm trying to hide it. Little girl she isn't, not by a long shot. And much more of this and I'll happily forget any amount of tuition I'm attempting and go straight to the type of discipline brats like her enjoy.

"Interesting analogy of your situation."

"I came here, didn't I? Smothered myself for this. I'm far from a child, Blaine. Teach me," she says, her voice hovering at a level I've only heard once before as she moans the words, echoing them as if they come from her depths. It makes me remember the feel of her cunt around my hand again, the taste of her lips. "This is irrelevant. Show me what it feels like to be fucked by you. I rather enjoyed the slap." My feet step backwards, my eyes still watching her as she fingers the paper and draws circles on it with the black ink. It riles me further, making me think of instinctual thought rather than the kind she needs for her story, because madam is pushing buttons she has no idea about. "What's the matter?" she asks, her finger rising to her chest and drawing the ink through the middle of her cleavage. "Not ready to show baby how to act like a grown up?" She fucking pouts, bringing with the look connotations of degradation she hasn't even contemplated let alone heard of. If she winds much further, she might well get a deliverance of pain that scares her senseless. I can feel it in the back of my spine, straightening me as my hands come back out of my pockets ready to grab at her. "Baby girl needs staining, Daddy."

"Boss?"

"What?" I shout the question at Tyler, swinging my eyes to the guy standing in the doorway and snarling at the fact that he's still fucking here. "Get out." My fists clench, my jaw following the action as I look back at Alana and try holding myself away from her.

"You need to leave, boss." Fucking leave? There is nothing presently as important as showing this little girl what real women are made of. And I'm pretty sure she already knows, anyway. Fucking coaxing and goading. Pushing buttons. *Push, push, push.* Winding up the damn air between us. Time madam was shown a real lesson or two to ensure she understands the fucking dynamics.

"Fuck you." I'm not sure who I'm saying it to, it's possibly myself.

"Ah, naughty. Watch that mouth, Daddy." Fuck her, too.

If I could swing my hand to reach her, I would. The thought penetrates areas of my mind I've forcibly closed, so much so that I grind a step away again, my brogues clanking the fucking floor and raising the sound around us all.

"Will you haunt my dreams, Daddy? Make me come in my sleep?" I snarl at her, outraged at her ability to aggravate me, then glare as she dips her other finger back into the ink again and fiddles the ends of her hair. Black streaks appear, mingling with the purple ones and causing a riot of dirty images to collide in my mind. "Should I do it myself?" she asks, lowering her blackened hands and heading them for her thighs. "Can one stain oneself with need?" No, she can't, not if she wants to continue breathing. It causes yet more resentment to build inside of me, widening my sneer to the insanity I'd once felt with Eloise. And then she hitches her dress, flecking the ink across her thighs and digging her nails into it to scape upwards to her cunt. "Baby needs you, Daddy."

"Stop." It isn't an order as it leaves my lips, or perhaps it is but I hardly mean it. The need to fuck her is becoming unbearable, something I'm willing forward with every swipe of her fingers as they drive into her skin, announcing the need I know she has. What's happened to change her I don't know, but I'm so fired up about the outcome I can do nothing more than exhaust myself with another footfall backwards, hoping to stem my flow.

"Why? Is Daddy scared of what he'll do to me?" Yes.

"Miss, you need to shut up or—"

"I'm not sure you get to speak in here," she cuts in, not once removing her locked gaze from mine and lifting her dress higher. She squirms in the seat, the coil of rope around her neck inducing more writhing, heightening the already tense mood. "Does he, Daddy? Tell him to leave us so you can stain me properly."

"You need to stop this attitude." I mean it this time. She does. She's not ready, isn't capable or strong enough. And my needs have been confined for so long I don't know how they'll explode on her skin. Perhaps it isn't her. Perhaps it's me who isn't strong enough, still. So long I've kept this all at bay. Nothing has tested my resolve like this. No one. Not since… The thought of *her* eyes staring back, vacant and lifeless, makes me back away again, my body suddenly hitting the wall and not allowing the escape I need.

"Daddy's scared," she fucking mewls, licking her lips and landing her fingers exactly where they shouldn't be. "Baby girl's too much for him." Her fingers move, her head tilting back into the rope and allowing the sensation to take her off to the precise place I'd hoped she'd find. It's all I can do to think, let alone act. It's all becoming too much to contain. She's in complete control of the room, her body claiming everything she needs from a simple wrap of rope. Fuck. The thought alone makes me weak, my arms trying to reach her without any thought for wellbeing or care. I shift forward, my feet leading me to the very thing I crave. I do want to fuck her. I'm desperate to. And I want to stain her pretty skin with everything I have to give. She's right. I want to bruise her, mar her perfection and then enhance its integrity until she shines brighter than before. I want her panicked screams and her pain. I want the dulling of her eyes, the open mouthed gasp in the final few seconds. I want her life should I ask for it, because in this moment, I'd happily give mine for just one fucking taste of her. I'd fall from cliffs. Walk in front of cars. Decimate all sense of living if I could just bite into her flesh and feel it breaking beneath his teeth. There's no fucking point in life without that sensation anyway. I'm lost without it. I have been since Eloise. I just exist, barely enjoying taste or flavour without actual physicality to endure my wrath. Just one taste. What would be the harm? She's asking for it. Begging. Provoking and riling me. She needs it, doesn't she? I know she does. I saw it in the water, watched her beg for it then. And how she fucking moaned beneath me, her body gliding against mine, fitting perfectly into my hands and proving her worthiness. She wants it, and now it's going to happen. I'll deal with the lasting damage tomorrow. After I've finished ruining her, just so I can put her back together, slowly, piece by piece in my own fucking time. That's what she's come for really. That's what she needs for the perfect little story. Deliverance and liberation. Escape from the illusions she creates. Reality is what she needs. Real fucking tears, something to hold inside her and remember for its true worth in a world full of fake drama.

A hand suddenly touches my shoulder, digging in and bringing me from my fantasy of pleasure-seeking decadence. I damn near rip Tyler's arm off for daring the physicality as I glare back at him.

Fuck. I close my eyes to either torment, switching off her groans as she begins masturbating though her underwear. And instead of doing what I need to, what my muscles scream at me to do, I do what I should do. Just as a good fucking sadist should. I turn and walk from the room, nodding at Tyler for intervening and ready to beat the shit out of him for it in the same breath.

The conundrum is so baffling that I bite the inside of my cheek as I walk along the corridor, attempting to stifle the need to lash out in aggravation. It doesn't work. It only harbours yet more necessities, renting out the aggression in a different form. My hand swipes at the hall table, sending vases and objects crashing to the floor as I continue biting into myself, tasting the blood. And then I turn again, my body driving itself back to the thing I want most without my mind agreeing to the event. "Fuck." I just manage to keep the power from my voice, muttering instead it as I kick broken shards of ceramic along the floor in front of me. "Why now?" I'm not sure who I'm asking, possibly the little bitch in the room behind me who I'm still glaring at.

The irrationality of the whole fucking thing makes me sigh out and spin again, my feet walking from her possibilities rather than allow my body the response it wants. And eventually, I burst out into the midday sun, instantly drawing in long slow breaths, hoping to rid myself of the need to turn straight back around and go finish what she's started. Fucking groaning. Desperate mewls and wandering fingers. Blood and bindings. I've needed it more and more since she's appeared in my life. Why? I fucking know why, much as I hate the thought. She's new. Special. Untouched. She needs releasing and using until she's raw and panting for the unobtainable in civilised society. And that fucking connection I'm denying, the one that forces itself through my guts and offers hope to vicious hands, it's debilitating to reason. If only I hadn't taken her call. I could just be relaxing now, ready to let my sadist lie in its quiet dwelling, occasionally letting it dabble with things open for use.

"I don't want this," I say to nothing other than the sea in front of me. I swear the ocean laughs back at me, heckling me into remembering Eloise again and the way she took everything I had to give. It's enough to shame me, the sight of her vacant eyes flooding me with reminders and loathing as I glare out at the calm waters gently lapping the cliffs.

"She's a wild one."

I spin on my foot, surprised at the voice of Delaney as he comes out onto the deck. Wild? He's fucking right she is. The words makes me lick my lips as I stare at him and wait for information as to why he's here, glancing over the man's casually dressed frame. Not that I care. I'm too busy trying to control the eruption that crawls my bones as I analyse the situation at hand.

"She's…" I don't know what she is. Fucking idiotic is a good word. Stunning. "Ignorant."

"Doesn't look it."

I growl, snarling at the man and turning back to the ocean to abandon the conversation before we start debating her merits like she's a piece of meat to be devoured. She isn't. Not by Delaney anyway. That thought alone is unsettling, let alone the vision of what I want to do to her. It makes me jealous, an experience I've also not felt since Eloise.

"It's acceptable for you to fall again, you know?" No it isn't. Alana's here to learn. Nothing else. Why she's decided to wind me up rather than stay in the context of the situation is mystifying, but I'll give her thirty minutes calming time and then start again. It's the sensible approach. The one she needs to make this story of hers work. "She's clearly more than a fancy for you to have come out here with her. How long has it been?" I snarl to myself this time, remembering Eloise in the exact same room, her naked body opening the French windows onto the deck for fresh air. The cross she hung from. Her skin, stripped and weeping as she waded into the sea to bathe in the salt. Her cries as the sting cut in, causing yet more pain and making me smile as she wandered deeper.

"Why are you here?"

"Thought I'd pop by. The one way mirror was a diversion on the way through." Pop by? Delaney doesn't pop by anywhere. I turn again, scanning the man for deceit and eventually giving up trying. Whatever he's here for, it's good to see him again, and it isn't like I don't trust the guy. I do. He's one of the only people who understands, and one of the only ones I can talk to, have talked to, on many occasions. "How invested are you?"

"I'm not," I reply instantly. Although, for some reason, I smile at the thought as I walk back past Delaney and into the house, patting the guy on the shoulder and sighing out a last breath of frustration.

"You're just going to leave her there fucking herself?" I keep walking, rounding the corner and down the steps into the main lounge.

"I'm going to let her think about what's she's doing, yes." Delaney heads straight for the bar, immediately tipping out two large shots of Tequila and returning to sit on one of the large couches.

"You mean you're going to give yourself time to calm down before you give her what she's asking for anyway?"

"I mean I'm going to allow some sense to prevail before I forget what happened the last time I lost control and indulged myself in something I shouldn't."

"Mmm. Why?" I roll my eyes at the man, wondering if anything will ever shock the guy into sense. He hadn't flinched when we'd talked of Eloise. Death, it seems, means little to him. "Seems a waste of enjoyment to me." Probably true, but then Delaney has a handle on his force, mostly, or he isn't quite so bothered about the outcome of it.

"She hasn't come for that. We're not together."

"What?"

"She's researching."

"What? How to push a sadist's buttons?" I sigh, acknowledging that that is exactly what she's been doing, too effectively for rationality to be employed. At least I've managed to walk away.

"A book," I reply, picking up the shot and downing it. Delaney laughs.

"You're serious?" he asks, pulling off his jacket and laying it out on the arm of the couch as he heads back to the bar. "Interesting research option." It is; the man has a point. "And even more interesting that you agreed to the request."

"Mmm."

The ending makes me gaze out at the ocean for a few minutes more through the window, considering the best route forward and trying to work out why I've thought any of this acceptable. It's not as if I've done anything like this before. I've taught others on many occasions, of course, but this is personal, Delaney's right, something I've not had to consider since Eloise. I chuckle at myself, irritated and yet in some way enamoured with my own confused state of mind. Normally everything is so artless. The lack of emotional involvement makes touching flesh predictable in its absence of care. Now, though, with her, I can feel again. I can almost taste her still.

"She's like Eloise was," I mumble, mainly to myself, but it's not shocking that Delany laughs again, amused, no doubt, by the thought of the professor upturned.

"Obviously. You wouldn't have brought her here if not." My brows rise at the comment as I blow out a breath in defeat and wonder why the fuck I did bring her here. It just happened, perhaps instinctively or rashly, but it had felt right at the time. There isn't any point trying to hide or cower from the precarious situation I've put us both in by bringing her now. I know it, as does the man sat behind me. And as I stare out at the ocean still, rallying every control technique I have and failing to employ them effectively, I feel myself resigning to the inevitable. "You should just get on with it. See where it leads,"

Delaney continues, still laughing as if this is the funniest diversion he's had in some time.

"You don't have to be so self-satisfied about it."

"I'm a priest. It's what we do." I snort again, remembering night's that the idiot's dressed as one, dabbing crosses on women's heads before he whips them halfway to hell, apparently absolving their sins with every strike.

"There is nothing priestly about you. It's just a fucking name."

"Good confessional, though."

"Mmm." He is; that much is true.

"Look, I know you, Blaine," the guy says, coming over and standing beside me, a smile still attached to his too fucking attractive for his own good face. "You're a good man beneath it all. She'll be fine. You've learnt from your past." I'm not so sure that's true. The thought of delivering pain again is unbearable in ways I've not had to think about for some time, freeing too, but fundamentally insane given Eloise's dead body. "Just do whatever you brought her here for and stop chastising yourself for being a man." Being a man isn't the problem. Being the sort of man I am, with the needs I have, is. "She's a pretty thing. You're going to be interested, aren't you?"

"It's more than that," I reply, still staring at the marine blue sea and considering any other options that might tame my cock. "You know it as well as I do. As you said, I brought her here."

"You could give her to me instead. I could teach." I grunt at the thought. If there is one thing Delaney Priest can't do, it's teach. Break, yes. Cajole, certainly. Train for research purposes, no.

"You go anywhere near her and I'll kill you."

"See? Invested," the guy says, another laugh reverberating around the space as he backs away and heads for the bar again. "Just do it. Start her in the church if you want. I'll watch. Keep you on the straight and narrow." It isn't the most comforting sensation, but it is a level-headed idea. At least with Delaney about there is someone to counter the mood, someone who is more able than Tyler to judge content. "Mostly." I turn and snatch my keys from the hook by the fireplace, deliberately letting the sharp end sink into my grasp to try to stop the continued battering of my pants.

"She's not to be touched," I snarl out, staring the guy down to ensure the correct response will be met to that threat. "She's not a nobody from the streets. She's here for a learning trip only. That's it." Delany nods, a smirk still hovering across eyes that don't give one fuck about any form of threat I'm delivering. "Delaney, I'm serious."

"Of course you are," he replies, another shot drained from its glass as the man pours another one and then widens his arms on the back of the sofa. "Deadly." Sarcastic bastard.

"I need your help, not hindrance." I try for that approach instead, willing the man to at least acknowledge some resemblance of care for her. "My fingers itch." That should be enough to clarify the importance of the situation. Delaney just smiles again, his body lounging with little intrinsic interest to anything other than the further goading that will come.

"Anything you need, Blaine. You know that. Confessional's always open here."

I roll my eyes and pull in air, knowing that the one man who can help probably won't. Or maybe he will, and then I'll have to deal with the ramifications of falling again anyway. Either way, my fingers do itch, painfully. And the little thing possibly still fucking herself down the hall will do well to meet a priest. It might just calm her offensive little mouth to something that isn't as questioning as it is. Thus improving my odds of not strangling the disobedience out of her. "Bring her to me in an hour or so." Delaney just smirks, his hand raising his glass as he lounges back against the sofa again and watches me move to the door. "Is Tabitha there?" A broad smile forms on the guy's mouth, one that tells me everything I need to know.

"My little Tabby cat's always ready to help."

Chapter 13

ALANA

My hands are covered in ink. It looks like it's bleeding out of me through my fingertips and onto the typewriter keys. It's another metaphor I've not quite worked out yet. None of it makes sense. My behaviour certainly doesn't. But it's like he made me do it. He did. I have to believe that because there's no way in hell I'd be talking about Daddies otherwise, or sinking my hands in between my thighs. I don't know why that came out of me. I must have read it somewhere, and in the middle of my odd tantrum decided to give it a go, hoping it would spur him into more action than just watching and leaving me with a fucking typewriter. Perhaps it was just the way he looked at me, or maybe it was the way he acted so calmly, like I wasn't interesting enough for him to play with again. Not that I want playing with, I don't think I do anyway, definitely not emotionally. Actually, maybe I do. Christ. I need to stop that. I just, well, I need to know more about what makes me act the way I do in front of him and no amount of tying me up in ropes is going to make that happen. Or maybe it was just his attitude when he slapped me, the kind that made me feel like a misbehaving schoolgirl who couldn't work out whether to comply or rebel. I didn't even come after he left, which was irritating. I couldn't. The moment his eyes left me I lost it, the feeling leaving me as quickly as the irrationality took over.

My neck cricks in this strange sling he's put me in, making my back ache further as I try to get comfortable. It's been too long now, or at least too long for my own comfort. I don't know how long people stay in these contraptions, but I'm tired of it. It's scratching at me and making typing harder as I strain to reach. I have to give him the fact that being like this is helping me write, though. I've typed up all sorts of scenarios I couldn't possibly have put together without this circumstance focusing me into it. There's a sense of threat here. It's uncomfortable, making me feel on edge, but it's laced with a slow burning security somehow. I know that sounds outlandish, but it's here nonetheless, making me feel I'm in a state of sanctuary as I keep pressing keys and letting the words come. It feels almost like a safe-haven, a writer's retreat of some sort. It's weird, and would be confusing me beyond all belief if I weren't so intent on relaying the thoughts on this machine, regardless of my inked and bloodied fingers.

Looking at the stack of papers I've already done, I eventually let my fingers calm down and take a breath. I've done all I can for now. So much so that I stretch my stained fingers around, hoping to lessen the cramp that's been winding its way into them. It's not like a normal laptop. The slant is pitched high, making me ache from the act of continually depressing the ceramic letters. I'm exhausted, hungry, and still in need of a pee. That bucket's been looking more and more tempting as I've been sitting here. I've contemplated it on a few occasions. I could easily hook it over, but then I'd have to hitch it underneath me where I sit. It's not like I can move any further than this rope sling and these chains will allow, which is only about as far as the typewriter. Oh god, I'm so tired. I could quite easily sleep here if I didn't need to pee so much. In fact, maybe I should just close my eyes for a few minutes and relax, try to ease the ache from every part of me that's beginning to scream for freedom.

"You are a pretty little thing, aren't you?" What the fuck? Who's that? My eyes fly open again, barely ten seconds after I closed them. "Tired, are you?"

I stretch my eyes again, searching the man in front of me and looking around hoping to see Blaine beside him. He's not there. I'm just alone in the room with another man I don't know, one who's looking me over as if I'm nothing more than lunch in a tatty dress. He's the same height as Blaine but prettier and less aggressive in nature, with features that more than likely beguile most of the nation's female population. Blonde haired and blue eyed, and his gait is relaxed, lacking any sense of urgency, more a relaxed amble than a measured stance. In fact, the more I watch him, the more I think I do know him.

"Where's Blaine?"

"Gone."

"What? Where?" What does that mean? Why would he leave me? My fingers dig into the edge of the table, ready to lift me away from it before the rope around my neck reminds me I can't move.

"He's left you with me," he says, wandering his way around the room and apparently checking out the fixtures and fittings. I watch the way he moves, a sudden realisation setting in that I do know him as he walks. He was at the party. He caught me when I tumbled over the bench. He was masked, but I recognise the voice. He was jovial then.

Funny even, but here there's something about him that makes me fidgety, like the calm is just a veneer. He fingers a picture on the wall, making it swing back and forth, and then meanders away again, not bothering to straighten it. "I remember the last one he had in here." I don't know why, but that statement immediately makes me feel a sense of jealousy, which is quite preposterous. What did I think, that I was the first one? "She's dead now." My mouth gapes, not knowing what the hell I'm supposed to say to that. Dead? "What's the book about?"

I'm still too busy gaping to have a rational thought about what he's just asked. Dead? Why would a woman be dead because Blaine had her here? He strolls past me until he reaches the curtains on the far side of the room, and then swipes the key from the surface of the cabinet that Blaine left it on.

"What do you mean dead?" Sometimes I wish I could stop my mouth moving. Really, I do. I should just stay quiet. Shut up and not get involved in conversation with him about dead people. It's hardly relevant to what's happening here.

"Dead. What else is there to explain?" he replies, a quizzical look on his face as he walks back over and slides himself into the small space between the table and me. "Do you want a rundown of how she ascended to her heavenly dwelling?"

I shake my head, attempting to scoot further backwards to get away from him, as far as the rope will allow me, anyway. Something about him is not at all right. He seems too calm, too peaceful, as if the world is beneath his abilities and he's just waiting for a reason to watch it all burn around him.

"What's your name?" I ask quietly, watching his fingers turn over themselves in contemplation as he gazes at me. He smiles, titling his head and then reaching for the length of rope above my head.

"I'm just your priest," he says, his smile turning into more of an amused sneer as he slowly pulls the rope towards us, slackening the tension on my back. "Come to absolve you of your sins before you enter the lion's den." He's clearly insane. Or just strange. There's nothing that seems honest about him. Nothing reliable or even relatable. He's not like the funny version of himself I met at the party, the one I told to get his cock out, stupidly by the look of this situation.

"I'm not religious."

"They all say that. It doesn't stop the screams for God coming from their mouths, though," he replies, his fingers reaching for the side of my face. I snatch it away from him, the slight slackening allowing some movement again. "I'm trying to help, nothing more at the moment." He doesn't wait for me to agree. He just takes hold of my chin firmly and then yanks at the rope. The instant he does, all pressure keeping me aloft dissipates, sending my frame into a spiral downward. Everything begins to collapse. My muscles give in, exhausted by their fight to keep me upright, and if it weren't for his hand on my chin I would have doubled over instantly. Pain crashes though me, as the aches seem to cramp in on themselves, magnifying in intensity. I hang in his hand, my neck unable to hold itself up without his support regardless of how much I might want to move. "See? Now say thank you." I nod weakly, still panting my way through the excruciating sensations racking my whole upper torso. It's hardly thank you, but at the moment I'm too breathless to get anything out. He just holds me there for a moment or two, letting my body adjust and balance itself back into normality. Whatever his creepy nature, he was right. He is helping. Unfortunately, it doesn't stop me feeling weirded out by him. He's got no sense of believability, like I might have to second guess everything he ever says, making my own mind up about what he's actually about to do or say.

"Thank you," I manage to say eventually, trying to extricate my face from his hold. He doesn't let me move, proving he's not to be trusted in the slightest. He just stares at me, his smile turning to something nefarious, possibly indicating his intentions. "Really, thank you. You can let go now." I'll try for civil. It's not like I have many other options given the chains around my wrists, and the fact that he's the one holding the damn key.

He eventually smiles again, brightening his face into the same look I saw at the party. There's no denying he's handsome, but that's not what he is, not underneath. I can still feel the grab of his fingers long after he lets go of my chin. It bites in, still creating a pinching sensation. It's nothing like Blaine's hold, which while firm, isn't sharp. It's more blunted than that, giving it a sense of being enthralled rather than forced. This feeling still haunting my skin is bitter in its quarry, enough so that I just keep staring at him, nervously ducking my head a little and waiting for whatever he has to say.

"You look scared, pretty thing." I am, for the first time since this whole thing started. Blaine doesn't make me feel scared. He seems to wrap me up in a blanket, enveloping me with a sense of realization rather than making me feel frightened by the thought. This man doesn't do that. He darkens the scene, making it feel more like a murder mystery than a book about kink.

"Are you taking me to Blaine?" I ask, nodding at the key in his hand and hoping to deflect the conversation away from wherever he's wanting to take it.

"Mmm." His eyes go vacant again, his leg moving slightly closer to me as he reaches for one of my pieces of paper and begins reading. It makes me more nervous than ever. The thought of him reading my words has me panicking. I don't know why. I don't even know who he is. I certainly shouldn't care for his opinion, but I do. He's the first person in the scene to read them.

"You have too much sense of love here," he says, chuckling as he picks up the next one and starts reading again. "What makes you think love has anything to do with us?" I don't know. The thought makes me frown, wondering why I wrote it like that. I did. I remember the feelings associated with the words as they flowed out. They were consuming, as if one would have those harboured desires only in the context of love. "We fuck the way we do because nothing else makes sense, not because we have feelings for someone." He drops the sheet back down, carelessly letting it flutter to the floor as if it's rubbish. It instantly deflates me, making me question the entirety of my last few hours work as I gaze at his lips. "Someone hasn't experienced the real thing yet, I think." Perhaps not, I suppose. I haven't been in the middle of the club Blaine took me to. I haven't practised that sort of thing, which, now I think about it, didn't appear to have much to do with love. But with Blaine it does seem deeper, like it means something more than just fucking, as he says. It's connected. Merging both sensation and sentiment. "Shall I show you?"

No. That's not going to happen.

My head shakes in response as he leans forward and starts unlocking my chains, hardly touching my skin as he manoeuvres the steel around, like he's choosing to avoid contact deliberately. It makes me question his intent given his demeanour around me. Why would he choose not to touch me? Perhaps he's been told not to. That would make more sense than a man like him not just getting on with whatever he wants to do.

"There we are, all free."

"Thank you." I rub at my wrists, glancing down at my wrinkled dress and wondering if there's any chance of a shower, or even a change of clothes. "Do you think I could change before we go?"

"Why?"

"Because…" I wave my hand down at myself, indicating the state I'm in, and then holding up my blackened fingertips to cautiously wiggle in his face. "I could do with cleaning myself up."

"Why?" Oh, for god's sake. He might seem strange, but he isn't an idiot.

"I'm tired, in need of a change of clothes, ready to use a bathroom, and probably desperate for a new layer of make-up."

"Bathroom, you say?"

"Yes."

"You can do that here."

"What?" He inclines his head at the bucket. "I'm not going to do that in front of you."

"Yes, you are." He grabs at me too quickly for my brain to catch up with let alone do anything about as he hauls me upright and moves me two feet over towards the bucket. "The choice is yours. Here, or hold it." I stare, open mouth gaping at the idea of doing this in front of someone I don't know. He can't be serious. He just smirks, as if this is funny, or strangely erotic in some manner. I'm not sure which. It's neither for me. I can't think of anything worse than doing this in front of another human. I don't even go in front of Bree, let alone strangers. But I do need to go, and now he's started whistling, helping the need to go quicken further as I squeeze my thighs together in hope. He backs off a step, nodding at the bucket and then just staring again, tapping his foot to show his impatience.

"Do you need help? I have tricks." I bet he does, and I'm sure they're not enjoyable to endure. I look at the bucket again, knowing I'm not going to be able to hold it much longer. Perhaps I could wait 'til we get to Blaine, though. Maybe he'd let me... What am I thinking? He was the one who told me to pee in the bucket in the first place. I can't believe I'm thinking about this, but the bouncing carries on as I cross my legs and scan him again.

"What do you think I'm going to do, pretty? Rape you while you're pissing?"

Possibly.

I feel the moment my body gives way to the idea the second I feel a little bit escaping from me. It's quite vile, making me curse human physiology and then glare at him as he smirks again at my predicament. His lips purse again, another whistle leaving them, high pitched and long. Fuck. I'm so quick to hook my fingers into my g-string I hardly count the moments between them coming down my legs and the pee flowing out of me. It's almost orgasmic as it comes, my insides sighing out in relief as I watch every fucking move he makes.

"You could at least turn round," I snap, hovering my arse over the bucket and wishing the sound wasn't quite so loud.

"Well, that wouldn't be any fun at all." Fuck him. If I had even the slightest bit more nerve I might say that out loud, but given my peeing condition, I don't. So I just keep my eyes locked with his, hoping it's enough to show he doesn't scare me, even if he does. The second the sound stops, he takes a step into me, his hand reaching forward. It makes me scoot away, hauling my knickers back up my legs, nearly knocking the bucket over, and then glaring at his advance for fear of him trying something. He just chuckles again, pulling his hand back and turning for the door.

"Trust. You have to ask first, Alana. We're not all rapists and lunatics." It doesn't fill me with confidence, regardless of his offering of courteous intent after the act. And what does he mean by *all*? Does that mean some of them actually are? "They all ask for what we have to deliver." Really? Well, I'm not asking, not from him anyway. "Most beg." The thought doesn't surprise me given the attractiveness of the man, or Blaine. I still don't want this one anywhere near me, though.

"Are you coming?" he asks, his body gliding across the room as if this is all perfectly normal. I walk after him barefoot, at least thankful that I've got the pee out of me. A shower would have been nice, though, given I've been rolling around in disinfectant and vomit, which has now dried onto me. "If he does offer you a shower, I'd consider leaving the make-up off." My eyebrow quirks at the information, remembering Blaine not liking lipstick as he turns us out into a corridor, ambling his way along it and pointing out at a side window. "It matches your eyes," he says, carrying on and not even glancing at the view. What does? I grind to halt, mesmerised by the sight of the blue waves crashing against the low cliffs in front of me. Where on earth are we? It's glorious, spellbinding. I'm so in awe of it that I just stand here, transfixed by the thought of going down to the beach and dipping my toes in. I could wash all this off me and come out cleansed. Wet maybe, but at least I'd be clean. It's all so blue and vibrant. Beautiful.

"I wouldn't bother. He'll only get you filthy again," Priest says, suddenly standing beside me. Yes, I suppose he will. It's not like he appears to care how dirty I am.

"How long have you known him?" I ask, glancing at him and then back to the ocean.

"Long enough to know him. Not long enough to talk to you about him." He smiles a little, his hand reaching for mine and lifting it to draw on the condensation in the window as I fight his hold. It makes him hold tighter until the word draws out, but I don't need to read it. I knew it by the second letter. *Blaine.* He lets me go as the word finishes, leaving me to just stand there as the water drips along the surface, falling downward and creating long streams of droplets from each letter. "That's all you need to know about him, for now," he says, walking away and chuckling to himself again. I turn from the word, watching the way Priest's body seems so in tune with him. He's so confident about his movements, as if he owes the world nothing more than what he chooses to give it. In fact, the more I watch him walk, the more I feel at ease with his presence. The thought makes me frown again as I look back at the window to see Blaine's name dispersing into nothing but stains on a window pane. My fingers automatically draw up to it again, blending the letters into each other and brushing over the word until it's nothing but a blur. "Tears run deep when he delivers them, pretty thing. Are you ready for the outcome of such confessions?"

I don't know what that means. Confessions of what? I've got nothing to confess. I've never done anything wrong, short of writing dirty sex scenes my mother is mortified about.

"I've nothing to confess."

"We all have something to confess." I leave the window, hurrying to catch up to him as he turns another corner and disappears from view.

"Well, I don't, and if you…" My body slams into him as I round the corner, his fingers wrapping around my neck and drawing my lips to his before I've even got a chance to pull back. Everything happens at the same time. I'm pulled and then pushed, my body deposited against the hall wall with little ability to move away. And my damned mouth, regardless of my brain's disagreement, just follows his as he mingles us together and leans his weight into me. I feel so small. Tiny. And barely able to breathe as I let him kiss me, partly fighting his hold on me. I'm not even battling as his tongue licks its way over my teeth and then gently pushes in. I end up grabbing onto him, my fingers digging in at the thought of fucking without any real thought to why I shouldn't be doing any of this. And then his knee nudges my legs open, his hand hitching me into him as he pushes yet more weight against me and breaks his mouth away.

"You'll be begging before you know it, little thing," he whispers, his mouth running over my exposed chest and hovering around the top of my breasts. I'm panting, and if this feeling inside my body is anything to go by, he's probably right, much as that might infuriate me. I struggle again, exciting myself with the prospect of it getting physical and enjoying his weight countering me every damn time. It's similar to the sensation with Blaine, the same sense of desperation regardless of me battling against the strength, but it's not right. It doesn't have to connection, or the warmth.

My mouth opens as it tries to say no, or perhaps protest in a way that shows my own fortitude, but my body betrays me too quickly. I'd let him fuck me here, even with his peculiar sense of foreboding. It's as if I want him to just take me, rape me even. Something about him makes me feel deprived of air, just as Blaine does. Whatever it is makes me tip my head back against the wall, my legs widening further as he pushes into me again and chuckles. "Still nothing to confess?" Apart from the fact that I want to be used here? That I want a man to do whatever he wants with neither consent nor fight? No. I pant again, a sharp and glorious shiver gliding through my crotch and promising me relief from the tension Blaine created.

"I just..." I don't know what I want. This is all wrong. So wrong. I came here for Blaine to show me something, not this man. I shouldn't be doing this. It's not him I want. It's not. It's Blaine that I want. Blaine made this happen. He deprived me of himself earlier, leaving me desperate for something, anything. The thought makes me gasp at the realisation that I want more than simply teaching, as I struggle again and push back at him. "I'm..." Desperate. Absolutely and irrevocably lost to what he's making me feel about Blaine.

"Ask me." Oh god, that was groaned, his voice dripping with sex as I feel his hold come up to my chin. It echoed with my own inner voice, the one that's fraught with need for Blaine to make this sensation go away. "You have to ask, pretty thing." His eyes look into mine. There's no backing away, no moving from his stare, just the damned awareness that I want someone who's not here. His eyes are luminous as the colours swirl, almost laughing at me in my state of disarray. "You're not mine to take until you ask."

"I'm..." I'm not fucking functioning, is what I am. I push at him once more, letting the dull ache pivot away as I tug my chin from his hand, all the time longing for Blaine's there instead. "I'm not interested in you."

He immediately backs off, almost to the point of my body tumbling to the floor without him supporting it as he leans on the other wall and smiles.

"Now you have something to confess." My eyes snap up to his. No I don't. Nothing happened. And it shouldn't really matter if something did or not, anyway. I don't belong to Blaine. We're not engaged to be married, for god's sake. "Although, rape isn't as unusual a request as you might think." I clamber myself upright again, straightening what's left of my dress and running my fingers through my hair in an attempt at strength of mind if nothing else. How he fucking knows I deliberated that sort of thing, I don't know. And it's not relevant anyway. This is simply a research mission, one that, when I regain full control of my wits so I can think again, I'll find he's probably just helped me with in some way.

"You're hardly a confession, more a bump on the journey. A lesson learned perhaps."

"Oh, pretty thing," he says, shaking his head and turning from me to amble away, hands in his pockets and arrogance smothered across his every feature. "I'm not your confession." What? What does that mean? Nothing else has happened. What other thing do I have to confess? "He'll have his fun tearing you apart."

I want to scream a fuck you at him, but I don't. So instead, I just follow him, keeping myself a few steps behind and trying to understand how I fell into his hold so easily. It means something—something I'm not aware of. It's the same as when I rolled on the floor with Blaine, letting thought disappear to nothing but sensation. The same as when I let myself drift beneath the water, simply waiting for rescue rather than scrambling my way out myself. It's all meant to tell me something and the only thing I know is that it tells me Blaine is necessary in some way. That I want more than just the teaching I asked for.

I watch the swing of his gait as he eventually turns another corner, then opens wide doors letting the wind whip into the entrance hall we've arrived in. He looks back, a smile still hovering around his mouth as if he's amused at what he's taking me to. The very thought makes me glance around the outside of the building, looking for threat or concern. There's nothing there but a blue sports car and the view of the ocean again.

"Take a good look, pretty," he says, making me swing back to him, my arms wrapping around me at his sudden sneering tone. I'd like to say he repulses me, or that I'm in control of the way my body reacts to his stance, but I'm not. He looks almost edible stood there, his frame filling the doorway with a strange aura of control. It's unlike Blaine's, though. It's calmer. Less palpable in the air. And as the wind whips me again, fluttering what little dress I have left, I realise the difference between them. He's less violent, regardless of his current tone. He's not hiding anything at all. He is exactly what he seems. It's all on display with little in the way of concealment. I bet if I asked him whether he'd ever been in love, he'd answer immediately with no lies attached. "It'll be the last nice thing you see for a while."

"Quite the romantic, aren't you?" I say, smiling to myself and remembering the way his lips caressed my skin. There was nothing obviously heavy about them, not like Blaine's. No teeth biting in. No cruelty in his grip, no matter my initial thoughts on his demeanour. There's no sense that he might explode any minute. He just is. It's quite refreshing compared to Blaine's intrigue. "I'd say you've loved on several occasions. Passionately." He quirks a brow at me, then shakes his head and walks to the car, pointing at the other door as he does.

"Cunning little thing, too."

That's all I get as a response as he gets in and starts the engine. The only other thing I get is a piece of black silk handed to me. I stare at it, not knowing what it's for until he offers it up to my eyes and nods. Oh, a blindfold. Really? I stare at him again, wondering what the hell that's going to help me with, then assume it's another thing that may cause a sensation of use so slip it over my eyes. The world goes dark as

I tie it around my head and the car pulls away. It's all I get as we drive to wherever we're going. We drive in complete silence. No music. No conversation. It's just a meandered drive through what feels like country roads. Bumps and turns, the occasional heavy breaking, causing me to shift and slide about, which is apparently funny by the sound of the sporadic chortling beside me. It seems to go on for hours. Complete silence, only accompanied by the rush of other traffic passing us by every now and then. And, after a while, all thought of concern leaves me as I relax back into the seat, letting the wind take me wherever this man blows. I'm going to Blaine; that's all I need to know. Whoever Priest is, I have to trust him. He could have raped me back at the house. He could have done whatever he liked without applying much more pressure to me. He didn't. He's either a gentleman, and given his romantic bones it wouldn't surprise me, or he's under orders not to do anything to me, the second of which I'm doubting he cares anything about. It makes me smile to myself as we round another corner, strengthening my sense of understanding as I listen to his breathing and wonder where I'll end up.

"Priest?" There's no answer. "Why do I have to ask?" I say, musing over those other books that seem to delineate all Doms as freaks or sadistic arseholes who lose control at any given moment. Priest seems nothing like that to me now. He seems anything but, in all honesty. "Should a power exchange not be taken, rather than given."

"Those who take have less capability than those who are asked," he says softly, a slight sigh leaving his lips after the response. Right. I turn my head to him, not able to see but feeling better for looking in his general direction.

"Why?"

"Little things can't be liberated when forced. Compliance is essential for progression."

My brow shoots up behind the silk as his words sink in. He thinks this is freedom of some sort? I'm blindfolded, not knowing where I'm going, having been drugged to get me here in the first place, and then chained. It's hardly freedom. Let alone liberation. Although, I suppose I did ask for the help, therefore I can't say I'm being forced.

"If I asked you to take me home, would you?" He chuckles, his hand suddenly stroking across my face, causing me to jump a little.

"Do you want to go home?"

"No, I just want to know that I can if I ask."

"He'll let you go if you ask. I won't."

"Why?"

"You're not my obligation, you're his." Right.

The car goes quiet again for a minute as I try to assimilate the information and find use for it. Layers begin filtering through my mind, a sense of obligation I hadn't thought of before creeping to the top of the pile. Scenes unfold, ones that offer a connection through responsibility rather than simple matters of love or passion. I've read that sort of thing, and always wondered how the Dominant feels about his requirement to protect at all costs.

"But, presumably you're taking me to him, therefore you're currently responsible for my wellbeing because he's asked you to be, yes?"

"Mmmm."

"So, if my wellbeing is best served by letting me go home, then you have to take me. That's your position at the moment?" He chuckles again, the car turning a corner and pushing me into the doorframe a little.

"No, no, pretty thing. You're not getting this, are you?" Apparently not. "Your welfare is best served by me taking you to someone who can make the best decision for you. That's what you asked for, I assume." Did I? I don't remember asking Blaine to make decisions for me, only to show me how this all works. "It's why he brought you out here, to his home." That's where he lives? "Seems you're worthy of true consideration." I really don't understand that reference. It causes my brow to furrow under the silk, searching for an answer to what consideration I would be placed under. This is a job, nothing more, one we both have a part to play in, both Blaine and I, but it's not a relationship.

"And what about my opinion? Where's my say in all this?" I think the question is more mused than actually asked. I'm not entirely sure he'll answer, and even if he does, I doubt I'll understand the answer anyway. It's all just a blur of inaccuracies at the moment, neither defining answers nor exposing truths, other than the slutty ones my body's reacting to anyway, and the occasional pumping of my heart in completely the wrong direction.

And then there's a silence for a while, making me wonder what he's thinking about as I settle into the seat and begin listening to the rumble of the wheels instead of waiting for his mouth to offer a response. They're calming in some ways, reminding me of the silence in the room I've been in, the dull clunk of the typewriter keys causing a rhythm of sorts. And after a few minutes or so, I seem to give in to the noise, letting it lull me into another dreamlike state of near arousal, or infatuation. Perhaps it's physical exhaustion, or maybe just mental fatigue. I don't know, but it is what it is, somehow comforting me as my heart inclines into thoughts it shouldn't dare. I feel safe here in some ways, cocooned by men I don't know. It makes me smile as I drift off, knowing that I'll be with Blaine again soon enough. Whatever this all is, has become, is becoming, it's what I asked for. Kind of. I just have to believe that time will tell me why.

Chapter 14

ALANA

"Alana?" What?

I peel my eyes open, my fingers reaching for the blindfold only to realise it's not there and it's actually my eyelids struggling to open again. Oh god, I feel so tired. Still. My mouth yawns, my arms stretching high and knocking into the roof of the car as I attempt to wake up. Everything's blurry, hazy, as if I've forgotten how to function. I could use some of my pills. Several, actually. When was the last time I had some? Christ, I can hardly even move my shattered limbs I'm so exhausted. I hope my bag's been brought with us.

Eventually, I turn to look at Priest and find him sitting quietly, smiling, and filling up the whole car with a look that could be considered dangerous to my libido. "We're here."

I peer out of the car past him and am astounded to find a church looking back at me, although why, given his name, I'm not sure.

"That's almost laughable." A church, really? I mean, I'm not religious, but the suggestion connected with it still leaves me feeling uncomfortable. The sudden thought occurs to me that he might really be a priest. I don't know what I thought beforehand, when I had his mouth locked on mine, but I don't think I ever thought any of this was real. It makes me look back at him, for some reason scanning his hand for rings that might tell me if he really is part of the clergy. "You're not really a…" I can't even bring myself to say it, not after I ground myself onto his thigh in the hope of orgasm. He just stares, not one hint of truth or honesty belying anything useful. He can't be. He's too handsome for priesthood. Good looking guys don't turn celibate, not that he has done, obviously. "Because that's just not right, if you are. What we did, this whole situation. I mean, you can't do this sort of thing and be…" He just turns away, his chinos leaving the car the moment he decides our conversation is finished.

I scrabble at my belt, my legs removing me from the car quickly so I'm not left behind with unanswered questions. "Priest?" He doesn't answer as he walks the steps up to the frontage, an easy gait rendering the holy ground beneath him of no concern. I glance around as I try to keep up, noticing the lack of anything in the vicinity. It's just this white stone church, acres of land, a few small graveyards and nothing else. "Where are we?" Still there's no response. And as he enters the church, swinging the massive wooden gate wide for me to follow, I find myself scanning the grounds again, a sense of foreboding creeping up behind me. I turn, trying to fathom the feeling and gazing out into late afternoon sun. There's nothing there, only the car we left and the driveway into the grounds. Yet still the eerie sensation comes, making me think someone, or something else is here. I'm not so easy with my own pace as I navigate the last few steps. My hurried feet scamper the stonework, stubbing my toe on them as I go and swearing without thought to the venue.

"Fuck." The word makes me gasp, my hand immediately shooting to my mouth for fear that God heard, not that I'd normally care. Maybe I still don't. Maybe it's just the thought that Blaine might slap me for it. I'm not sure why that doesn't piss me off more than it does. Who is he to tell me what I can or can't do? No one. A no one who has very talented hands, no doubt, but he's not someone I should bow down to.

I wander through the door, looking up to the rafters and smiling at the architecture. Whatever my feelings for God, or lack thereof, churches are lovely structures. They dominate effectively, providing that sense of power people of God must need for their blind following. I never understood that. It makes me think about my time beneath the water at Blaine's house as I gaze around. Perhaps it's the same visions that keep their faith intact. Perhaps they just believe that no matter what, God will rescue them, keep them safe. I suppose if it's half the feeling I got, and it's more of a constant in their lives, then that's exactly why they come here. Maybe that's why I write books, hoping to disappear into worlds I create to escape the organisation of my hectic but tidy life. Maybe it's a way of lightening the load and relaxing, listening to another voice to clarify intent. Not that it's been all that enjoyable of late.

Old pews surround the outskirts of the interior, the floor in the middle of the chapel devoid of any covering. It seems odd to stand in a place like this that has been wiped of familiarity. It's not that it's not here, it is. Same structure, same gilded leafing on ornaments and objects, same stained glass windows surrounding the walls, but with the main floor being empty other than the inlaid, cold stone beneath it, it all feels less welcoming somehow.

"On your knees. Middle of the space." My head swings round at the sound of Blaine's voice, echoed from the top of the building somewhere. He can't be serious. I walk towards the front instead, glancing around for his frame, but all I find is the gilded balustrades as I enter the area. It seems to encompass the space, providing a barrier around where the pews used to sit.

Steps clatter the floor behind me, light and rushed, making me swing back in that direction to peer between the cloisters. A man crosses quickly, carrying something and skirting the peripheries of the walls. It's only when he comes into full view that I realise it's Tyler, carrying a large box and hurrying towards where you'd imagine a priest would change his clothes. The vision makes me think of priests again, which leads me into wondering where Priest has gone to as I scan the corners of the place.

"I'd like a shower first," I call out, hoping it might give me a ten-minute reprieve. I need to acclimatise to the options around me, not that I seem to have many, other than asking to leave. I think that would work. Priest said it would, although I haven't heard it directly from Blaine's lips yet, not that I've asked. "And a change of clothes." We might discuss kneeling after that.

Steps sound the floor again, this time in front of me making me look up in their direction. They're Blaine's; I can tell by their cadence. They're unhurried, heavy, and affirmative, just like his whole demeanour. He walks out from behind a tall column, his body framed by the wide sweep of steps up to the chancel. I stare, suddenly focused entirely on him. Something changes in me, but I don't know what. He just appeared and he's all I can see. The room evaporates around him.

And just a slight lift of his lip as he glances me over is enough for my insides to churn. My heart races, making me clamp my arms tighter around me for fear it might fall out of my chest. It's something about the way he moves, or maybe just the fact that he's had his hand inside me, which is preposterous given how many other hands have had that privilege, but his, well, they seemed to own being inside me. Like he has a right to touch me however he chooses. And I so wish he would again. I do. I can feel the need to move towards him engulfing me, no matter how much I try to stop its spread across my skin. It's like I'm on fire all of a sudden, and he's the only one who can put out the flames. Possibly with a bucket of water again, but I'd take anything for another shot at those orgasms he produced.

    He smiles, truly illuminating the church with an open offering of pleasure. It's quite beautiful, complementing his dark eyes and making them sparkle with undisclosed humour. It makes the need to run to him grow stronger by the second as I imagine some kind of relationship with a man I hardly know. The man who's brought me out here into the middle of nowhere to show me something I've asked for, begged for really.

    "Take your clothes off." I glance around, wondering why he's not answering my question about showers. "And kneel. I've now asked twice. I won't ask again." I'm not sure what that means. What's he going to do, force me to kneel? I thought all this kneeling was made up for the stories, showing submission by way of bowing and scraping. Okay, I did see some of it in the club I met him in, but not much. I can't see why it's relevant to me at all.

"No. I came to learn, but that's idiotic," I reply, stepping forward again and making my way towards him. "And why? What am I supposed to kneel for? You've shown me nothing in the way of kindness. There's no love here, no sentiment of attachment or connection. I am not bound to you like one of your other things." No matter what the hell this feeling is winding its way around my heart. His stare hardens a touch, reminding me of when I called him Daddy and rambled on in my little horny world of excitement. "Surely one needs to prove one's worth before someone submits to kneeling?" He pockets his hands instantly, his foot moving him back a step from my advancement. "Those women in the club you first took me to, what do they kneel for?" I'd actually like an answer to that one, because while I'm not about to do it, I'd like to know why they do. I stare at him again, waiting. I'd rather not wait for anything, to be honest. I want my shower and then I want to get on with whatever's about to happen. I *did* come to learn, and writing on that machine, no matter how incongruous, is definitely finding words and flow in me I've never used before. "And you never did answer me about whether you'd been in love before, did you? Is that why they do it?" He stalls, his eyes narrowing to nothing but slithers and his lips hovering around something that's almost out of them. I wait again, folding my arms and tilting my head for answers that might prove useful to my manuscript, or muddled emotions regarding him.

"Priest says you have a confession." Does he now? That's not an answer to my questions.

"Nothing that's relevant to the two of us, or me learning. Let's discuss the kneeling instead."

"Yet you would have let him fuck you in a corridor?"

"I said no."

"It was hardly a no from what I've heard." It damn well was, because of him I might add. And oh, he likes the avoidance, doesn't he? At least he's intelligent enough to play that game, I suppose. Most men aren't.

"I said I wasn't interested," I snip, remembering the way Priest's fingers dug in less efficiently than Blaine's do. It was lifeless in comparison to the heat I know this man has.

"Which was a lie," he says, his feet inching forward again.

"No. Had I wanted to fuck him, I would have. You've got no hold on me." His brow rises, his lips amused at me for reasons unknown. "Does the thought make you jealous?" Because that would be extremely interesting…and somewhat debilitating now I'm thinking about it. I really could do with not having these odd thoughts of attachment. They're not helpful to my research or any sense of realism. And then he moves again, still smiling, but now managing to turn what was a plausibly amused smirk into irritated charm. "I really wish you'd stand still."

"You have quite the sense of ownership, don't you?" I keep gazing as he halts, his arms mirroring mine as he folds them, his tongue running over his teeth in contemplation.

"I own me. Not you or any other man here. I only came here to find out how you manage to own everyone else you fuck with that dick of yours." He nods and backs away again, his tongue laving his lips until he takes another, then another. Why does he keep moving away? It's exasperating and unnerving. "It's a puzzle I can't work out. You're a puzzle, frankly." I find myself moving forward again, refusing to allow him the space he's trying to create between us.

"I don't fuck, not with my cock." Oh. What?

"Why not?" Because that really is interesting. Why wouldn't a man like him actually have sex using the very organ designed for the experience? "And why did you even tell me that?"

"There's a bucket in the corner. Go wash."

"Okay, but why, and why not?" Another bucket, really? I want my shower. If churches have one. Do they? Frankly, I'm suddenly too interested in the cock thing to give a damn about buckets anyway. "Well?"

"That is as unsuitable as your question about love."

"How is it unbefitting? You've been described as, what was it, a master of deviancy, and yet you don't use your genitals to actually penetrate anything?" His mouth smirks, his hands leaving his pockets as he halts his backwards progression. "Honestly? You can't fuck with it? Or won't? Does it not function properly?" His smirks widens into the most animated version of lovely I've ever seen, and, yet again, my heart rushes for attachment as I gaze at his lips and try to think logically.

"You carry on, Alana, and I'll drive the damn thing down the back of your throat in a minute."

There's a laugh somewhere in the church. I raise a brow at it, trying to suppress my own smile while wondering which of the other two it is. Perhaps we're going to have that gangbang I was discussing with Bree. I move another step closer, enjoying the fact that I wind him up so effectively and searching for the next button to progress this onwards.

"Please do, perhaps then I'll have something to kneel for." There's a look that flashes across his face. I don't know what it is, but it's innocuous compared to the fun face of ten seconds ago. "That's what I'm here for, Blaine. For you to teach me. I need honesty for that, not a re-enactment of some florid club scene." He blows out a breath, stepping back away from me and turning to leave. "I want to learn to love you, if that's what's needed." I'm not convinced that's going to be too hard to achieve in all reality. The man is unfathomably intriguing, slightly exasperating, and gloriously attractive. And this bloody heart of mine keeps interfering with all sense of logic. Unfortunately, rather than answer me, he just keeps moving away again, pointing over towards the other side of the church as he goes.

"If you must, bathe." That's all I get. I'm not convinced it's acceptable to me, and this is confirmed by me huffing my way back to the middle of the church, wrenching at my dress until the slightly crusty remnants of it leave my skin, and then lowering myself to my knees.

"Better?" I snark, staring at his back as he halts, waiting for whatever this will mean. One thing's for sure—no matter how much I wind him up, he always seems to have the ability to back away from me. I mean, even rubbing my own clit in front of him didn't stop him from wandering out. Most men would drool over such things. Maybe his dick doesn't function properly. Although, it did get hard; that's a certainty. I felt it. It was large, and unfortunately not inside my vagina.

"Do I need to do the Daddy thing again?" There's still no movement. "Priest, I'm ready for that confession. Something about rape, wasn't it?" I shouted that rather loudly, hoping that the thought of me near naked in front of another man might spur him into action. It does. His foot slowly spins him round to look at me. He doesn't look at my body, just focuses on my eyes. He just stays like that for the longest time, staring at me. No blinking, no change to the features on his face, which at present seem somewhere between tense and bored, and there's certainly no lovely smile. It gets to a point where I begin to lose any desire to talk about anything. In fact, my eyes begin glancing away for a way of finding comfort. He's so intense, just like he was when he had his hand inside me. His eyes are hard, but with a hint of hidden thoughts, ones I wish I understood. I flick my eyes back, then immediately away again. The moment I do, I notice the grey of his suit trousers moving a step towards me. I look back only for him to halt again so I turn from him once more. It doesn't take long to figure out the game. I look at him, or challenge him, and he leaves me, or turns away. I look away from him, or at the floor, thus not challenging him, and he'll move toward me. Presumably he's trying to train his dog. I'm not a dog, but I play his little riddle anyway waiting for him to get close enough before I start questioning again.

"You see how easy it is when you stop fighting me," he says, his shoe appearing in my line of sight by my knees. Fighting? I'm not fighting. I'm asking questions. What's wrong with that? I'm not sure how anyone's supposed to learn if they don't question reasoning. My mouth opens, the weight of the movement dropping my chin open only for him to close it for me with his fingers and then crouch down to my level. "Just stop fighting me, Alana." I don't understand what that means. Seriously. How have I fought him? "Fighting me will only provoke me. You didn't come here for that." I gaze into softening eyes, ones that seem like he's trying to explain something to me in terms I don't understand. "You came to learn, not to be my toy."

"But…" The word slips through my lips, and before I'm given a chance to get the rest out, he stands up and backs away again, all elements of softness replaced by tough scowls. I hover the train of thought, wondering what response is best. Challenge again, or accept whatever plan he has. Seems I'm not that interested in placating him with mollified offerings of acceptance. I want whatever it is he's not delivering.

I stare at the floor rather than at him, tracing the lines of gauged out rivets that have been formed by the pews over the centuries. I'm not concerned with the pleasantries of the scene, nor the idea that one kneels in some state of obedience. I know that sort of top line information. It's not dissimilar to the way people kneel for God, I assume. What I want is the whys. Why should I kneel? Why should I submit? Why would I want to?

"Tell me why?" I ask, my body pushing itself upright to stand in front of him again. He sighs, his fingers reaching for his brow as he steps half a step away.

"You're not giving me a chance to, Alana. I'm doing it like this for you." Like what? For god's sake this is all becoming farcical. I just want information and a reason why.

"For god's sake, Blaine. Stop with —" He grabs at my arms, swinging me around into his hold so my back is against his chest as one of his hands grasps the side of my g-string. It's immediate and harsh, causing me to gasp at the contact and collide into his frame. I struggle against the sensation, not sure if I'm ready for whatever he's suggesting and confused about the sudden aggressive nature of his hands as his hold increases.

"Is this what you need to stop fighting me?" No, no. I'm just asking questions. I try to turn, my feet tripping over themselves so I can get to his eyes again. He doesn't let me, and his advancing weight behind me starts pushing me down to the ground as he keeps yanking at the g-string. Panic surges through me as I twist in his hold, as if that's just nature's way of retaliation, my body struggling for freedom. "Get on the fucking floor and stop being a brat," he growls, grunting as my elbow connects with his ribs. No, screw him. My arms flail again, grabbing at nothing but air and muscles, as my left knee hits the ground. He pushes again, one of his legs hooking around my shin as his fingers brace the back of my neck and force me downwards again. I have no strength left to fight him with. My own power strains against both our bodies, my arse trying to wriggle free of his grasp as my hands brace the stone below. He suddenly halts his momentum, his frame freezing above mine while his lips drop to my ear. "Pliable is the reaction you should be offering now." I pant out, grabbing some much needed air before rallying my bones for more exertion. "I suggest you try it on for size before I take your unwilling cunt and strap it for disobedience." The image of anything strapping my bits causes my skin to crawl, sending nerves to places they absolutely shouldn't be enjoying the prospect of. His breath warms my neck further as time just stops for a few seconds. I let the sensations travel my veins to help me understand them, flicking my gaze around the empty space and wondering if God's watching the performance unfold. A calm begins washing in, laced with exhilaration. A rush of sorts, making me ache for something to feed the cunt he's talking about. And the fact that same cunt is beginning to rub against his knee, my arse rising higher to accommodate the friction, only confuses the situation more as my nails grate against the stone. "Better," he says, his voice hovering over my ear as he steadies his thigh against my grind. "Fuck yourself on it." I can feel the elastic of my g-string rubbing against my own thigh, digging into it and chafing back and forth as I relay the same motion. I don't even think about why I'm doing it as I stare at the crucifix on the wall. I just do. It seems acceptable, like I've got no choice against the ache that longs to be fed. I feel empty, as if I need filling, desperately. So much so that my arse rises higher, one of my hands daring to move back to grab hold of him. He can fill me in this moment; I know he can, just like he did on the floor we rolled on. Right here, right now, I want nothing more than for him to fuck the boredom out of me while my arse is in the air and his teeth bite into me.

"Fuck," I breathe, the grinding causing so much pleasure I couldn't begin to hold the word in. I'm not sure if I'm asking for him to do it, or just expressing a need. I'm so lost in the abandon of it, blindly allowing desire to take over as my rubbing increases in pace. Back and forth, the pressure escalating as I keep up my momentum and moan out the torment. "I need you to… Oh, god. Fuck." That's all I've got again. There's nothing more. There's only his thigh, the impetus to ride it like a lunatic, and the thought of him filling me with anything.

"What do you need, pretty thing?" My head shoots up, momentarily broken from my train of thought. I see Priest standing in a corner, a woman standing to the left of him dressed entirely in black and smiling at me. Oh god, what am I doing? My whole body stops, recoiling into Blaine and trying to forget the fact I'm nearly naked. Blaine growls, his hand splaying on my back and pushing me forward and back down onto his thigh.

"Keep fucking yourself. You want to play this way. This is your reward." I don't know what that means and try to retreat again. It doesn't work. His splayed fingers just hold me down firmly then creep up to my neck. "Answer him." I can't. I don't know the answer. I'm barely able to keep the sensation I had before going given the sight of another man and woman. And Priest beginning to walk along the alcoves towards us really isn't helping my nerves. There are just long echoed steps heading my way as he drags his fingernails across the wall beside him and smiles. The sound grates through me like a chalkboard, reminding me of discipline in school and teachers who glowered at misbehaviour.

"No spirited comeback this time?" Priest says, his smile spreading into something that shows complete control of the space around him. "Or is that confession confusing you?" He stops five feet in front of me, his hands clamping behind his back as he looks down at my face. And at the same moment Blaine inches my head further to the floor, fully releasing it as my lips kiss the ground.

I'm still motionless, desperately holding my shivering thighs for fear of rubbing against Blaine, as I look up at Priest's hollow eyes. I feel so exposed, belittled. It makes me glance over at the woman, her heels clipping the floor as she sways in Priest's direction and looks over me at Blaine. I don't know what the feeling is, but it's not stopping the ache from willing me backwards onto something solid. My body simply doesn't care that I'm on display, or that this is surreal and peculiar. It wants what these two men are doing to me. It's not even just Blaine or the attraction I have for him. It's Priest, too, perhaps even the presence of the woman. I frown at her, confused yet again by their sudden involvement here which seems to make me feel more inclined to continue, not less. I'm throbbing down there, teetering on the edge of not giving a fuck and grinding backwards without thought. "Tell us what you need, pretty thing."

I want to say nothing. I want to tell both of these men, and her, that I don't want anything, but I do. At least my body does. It calls to Blaine, offers him something of me I've never had before. It's that damned connection again, quieting my argument. I can't say I feel treasured or cherished as my core relaxes back onto his thigh, and certainly not loved. But I do feel desired. Needed. I feel a part of something greater than just me, and as my clit slides over the thick woollen material again, sending a shockwave through me, my gasp confirms what they all already know. I want this. I want him. That's my confession, whether I like to admit it or not. It's nothing to do with rape or any of this. It's about Blaine and my feelings for him, because I am desperate for this in whichever way he chooses to push me into it. I am desperate for him.

Blaine's hand suddenly hits my backside so sharply it sends my face further into the ground and makes me scream out as the sting spreads. I actually gasp for air as I let the burn penetrate my skin, my hands trying to push me up a little to create space between the ground and me. The moment I do, my thighs connect around his again, forcing my clit against the rough material and sending more spasms through my aching body.

"Answer him," Blaine says, his hands nowhere near me as his body folds across my back. "Tell us what you need." Fucking. I need fucking. I know that, much as I don't want to say it.

His tongue is tracing my spine before I know what's happening. It goads me into the next tentative movement, my eyes looking back at Priest and wondering how any of this came to be. Did they plan it? Is this the way it always happens? Is this what kink is? Oh god, the next swipe over his thigh closes my eyes in ecstasy as I let the sensation crawl through me. I rise to accommodate it, levering more purchase against him and hoping another hit comes to spur me on further. Christ. It's never felt like this. It's never had such an intense effect on me. Never sliced through and cut to the very core of me until there's hardly any breath left. My groans further my momentum, hardly able to care that either of them is here, only that Blaine gives me a platform to come against. My body begins to use that without regret even though my mind can't keep it. It begins in earnest as my calves help the movement and I let myself fall into Blaine's lips on my spine. It's so good, and yet so confounding. And something makes me want his teeth rather than his lips, as if some sort of pain is required for finality.

"You've still not answered," he says quietly, his teeth beginning to scrape along my jugular as he smothers me and I keep grinding. "Find the words to ask me for it. Let them come." Oh god, the ache's frantic now. It's surging through me, battling me between the rights and wrongs of this. And I don't care enough to stop anything. I just want this, all of this. I want Blaine inside me. I want Priest watching. I want the woman touching me. Visions even come of Priest handling his own cock as he watches a rape scene I'm thinking about, his fingers wrapping around a present I've yet to see. The thought makes me wheeze, part disgusted at myself and rendering me breathless once more as I groan out in torment. And then it comes, Blaine's teeth bite down for the first time sending me into a frenzy of need, any sense of remorse leaving me the moment they make contact forcefully.

"Please..." The word comes out with no thought. There's nothing here anymore, just sensation and visions and images of unpredictable fucking. That's everything I want as my warm cheek heats the stone beneath me. Fucking. I'm desperate, and now grating myself back and forth like I'll explode if I don't get it. My hands scramble again, the material of Blaine's jacket scrunching into my hold as I feel my orgasm coming. It chases itself through my body, my moans announcing a need I knew nothing about previously. "Please..." Oh god, there it is again. Desperation. Begging. A hysterical and anxious need for something that little bit more to fulfil a moment I can't control, don't want to. My eyes prise themselves open, for some reason needing to see Priest, perhaps hoping that will make me come, or bring visions of the sin I'm wanting more and more by the second. He nods, but not at me. He's not even looking at me. He's focused on Blaine, and in the next breath I'm shunted forward off his thigh. It makes me catch my breath as I land heavily on the stone, my hands trying to brace me away from it. I'm not given a chance to, rather pushed further down against it and manhandled roughly.

"Ask me," Blaine growls, his voice hoarse and sounding as desperate as I feel. I turn my head, wondering what's happening and find such concentration staring back at me it scares me into movement again. His eyes have become pools of black liquid, churning with anything but the control I usually see. My knees grate, the coarse ground scuffing in and causing pain as I reach for Priest, a slight and strangely irrational panic setting in. He just shakes his head and backs away a step, leaving me alone to deal with whatever's coming.

"Ask him, pretty." That's all I get, that and a sneer that would unnerve the gods as he takes another step away from my outstretched hand. I don't even know why I'm reaching to him. He's not on my side. He'll only help Blaine, not me. And then I hear rustling behind me again as hands grab at my legs and drag me back along the ground. It makes my top half spin once more, intrigue and fear mingling together, confusing me further as my core cries out for more and I brace my hands out at him.

"Ask for it." The strain in Blaine's voice is palpable. It matches the tension in his hands as I watch one of them ripping at his belt and the other batting my fingers away from his face. My mouth opens, unsure what my mind's response to this is, but once again my body's panting with need and ready to delve headlong into this hedonism. "You know that cunt needs it." It might do, but I'm still hostile to the thought as my hands lash out again in a display of non-agreement. I don't know why. He's right. I am ready, more than ready. Perhaps it's just the scenario, or maybe it's the thought that I'm enjoying this aggression and I can't comprehend why. I stare at him, my body primed to run and yet wanting nothing more than for him to hold me down and fuck any other man out of me.

"No." The word leaves my lips at the same time as my leg kicks out, renting the side of his thigh and forging me away towards Priest again. I'm confused, unable to make a decision between my needs and thoughts. This isn't right. It's wrong. I'm in a church with two men, another woman watching on, and one of them is about to fuck me because I've been acting like a slut all over his thigh. And I want to ask him to do it. I do. I want to say those words and welcome it, all of it. But now I'm fighting him again because I have the need to run. It makes no sense. I can't breathe. I can't think. All I know is that the sight of him there as I spin my head back again, his fingers attached to one of my ankles as he drags me back easily and smiles wickedly, is the most erotic image of hate I have ever seen.

Chapter 15

BLAINE

"Fuck you," she says, her breath filtering through my skin as she tugs again. Good little brat.

Malice heaves, pitching any thoughts of serviceable training to insufficient memories. The back of my spine tingles, beckoning out all power through my fingers as I latch on to her ankle and pull her backwards into me. She can battle all she wants, but she's not getting away. She's pushed and prodded, focusing all my thoughts on letting loose as she integrates her rebellion into my mind. Most subs stay quiet, bowing down gracefully because they want to learn. Not Alana Williams. She defies, questions, and bleeds every instinct out of me to just show her without conversation or consent. Maybe she doesn't know what she is. Maybe she can't wrap her head around what is happening to her or between us. Either way, I don't give a fuck anymore. I'm too wound up, too aggravated by her ass in my face, her cunt on my thigh, the heavenly stench of come drifting under my nose and the way her mind tries to escape her body's requirements.

Delaney nods again, his arms still clenched behind his back as he watches on carefully and offers a sense of rationality. I'm not convinced it'll work, but again, as her leg heaves and kicks out in confusion, I don't care. She'll understand in a minute. She'll feel it and lick the fucking ground as she does, gasping for breath and screaming at the pain she's about to receive.

I let go as one foot slams against my chest, amused by the notion that she's still not giving in, only to give her three seconds grace to almost get to Delaney before yanking her back into my hold.

"You asked for this," I grate out, welcoming the nails that reach for my hair as I grab at her hands to restrain them. "You pushed and disobeyed." Delaney laughs, the sound of his feet walking away as he gives me room to play.

"Fuck you," she shouts again, her body twisting in my hold as she tries to get to Delaney again. I don't know why. The man will only push her back. And if he doesn't, his current partner in crime certainly will. They might be standing there seeming unaffected, but they aren't. And it will only take one nod in return for this to turn into more than one of us fucking her.

I grip her wrists, tightening my hold without any graduation until she mewls and quietens her explosive frenzy, her body finally coming to a stop in front of me as she pants.

"Finished?" She gives a sudden knock back of her head, perhaps trying to engage it with mine. I let her, leaning my cheek down into hers so she can butt at me as much as she likes. I enjoy the argument, want more of it. She fights like she'll never give in and I don't want her to. I want her scratches and rebellion. It's why I feel like this now. Desperate and ready to drive insanity into the core of her, regardless of how much she denies it. She isn't a general sub; she wants aggressive play, demands it with every question and rallied intent to deny her needs. She wants rape play, holding down and having the life sucked from her until she's a quivering mess of tears and distress. For me, one of the few who require it this way, she's sheer faultlessness. Exactly what I want from a woman and exactly what I should be running from.

My voice quietens as I remove the growl from it and try to calm down, but all the old sensations began flooding me, heightening this fucking mood and pushing me onwards. It fills me with a soundlessness I've not had for so long. And as my fingers crush at her skin, my body leaning her forward and my tongue licking across her face, I know she's what I want and finally accept it. "Just ask me for it," I whisper, scraping my teeth across her jaw and moving her wrists into one hand. "Stop fighting yourself and let me show you what you are."

She shakes her head, her body beginning to struggle against me again. It makes me smile and let my mouth caress her skin, pulling in long cleansing breaths as I make my way around the back of her head and trail her spine with my fingertips. It's the last chance I'll give her to comply willingly. I knew it wouldn't work anyway and barely care anymore. She just needs pushing, forcing as all brats do. Less talk, more action. And for once in all this time with her I just let go, let the inside of myself free and slowly push into my trousers to get my cock out without any more thought.

It rages in my hand, heat spreading through it as I groan at my own touch and tighten my grip on her wrists. Fuck, she smells so good, the heat of her rising beneath me, her body still snaking around.

"Don't you—" she spits out, her body trying to spin as she lowers her ass from my view.

"Too late, pretty thing," Delaney says, cutting her off mid-sentence.

It's the last I hear from either of them. It all becomes about the precious cunt in front of me, the air around me, the sight of her skin panting and the frustration flowing through it. Her ribs pitch and spiral, the perfect surface of them unblemished and so far unmarred. They won't be soon. They'll be scarred with the first indent of my wrath with no real fucking care to the outcome.

My cock aches as I pull it a few times and watch her thrash, then easily transfer my hand's hold to the back of her neck to push her downwards again. The move causes her to shriek and reach for anything she can find to help her escape, but there's nothing there to find, nothing but the cock I'm about to give her to hold onto. It's what she'll learn to lean on. The only thing she'll have. It's the support she needs even if she doesn't know it yet. It makes me grip harder, forcing the fact, to the point of her bellowing out in pain as I feel the crunch of sinew beneath my hand and scrunch her cheek into the floor.

"Can you smell yourself?" I ask, levering the tip of my cock at her and slowly drawing it though the slick opening on offer. Tremors ride through me, tensing the constricting grip on her further and damn near sending me into my own fever of attack. Veins pulse, the ache sending me into desperation to get in and fuck 'til she bleeds. "How much will you take?" She bucks away from me slightly, trying to close her legs, yet still offering her ass with little real objection. I lean down, prolonging the zeal and drawing my tongue, this time, through the same dripping surface, only to continue to the pucker of her ass, too. The taste of her explodes in my mouth as I push at it, widening it and causing a moan to sound from her lips. Good, I'll fuck her there, too, in time, but not now. Instead, I trail upwards again, roaming my taste-buds across her skin, embedding the scent of her into my mouth and imprinting it in my mind. She's so new, so fresh, like an elixir of ramifications and accountability I neither want nor am able to tear myself from. Mine. Something to bind against again. Someone to rent myself on. Someone who will comfort the passion and take it into herself with fervour and demand. A new beginning, perhaps sent to nullify the past.

  The first inch in as I nudge at her is breath-taking, a violent eruption of colour splitting the blackness in my mind to arcs of reds and blacks. Her hair is flung back towards me as I sink in further, her head gaining purchase as my hand weakens a touch, sending an array of purple hues to mingle with the brightness. I groan, sensing her body clamp tighter and try to keep me out. It only spurs me on, forging forward again and leaning over her for when the screams grow louder. Small friction, at first only gently pulsing back and forth, not daring the full penetration for fear it will end. But I'm so desperate for the release, and my hands can't stop but gain more hold. They grasp at skin as I shove her shoulders to the floor, my body smothering hers in the same moment and sending her flat to the cold stone. I wind my hand around her stomach, lifting her frame into mine as I push in again and feel the oncoming sense of relief. She's so soft. So wet. Already dripping with come and waiting to be used by the very cock I'm beginning to drive in and out of her. And she bellows beautifully as my teeth bite through her skin and I shove at her hip, grating the bone into the church floor for more leverage. Then grunts, spit flying from her mouth as I forge in again and watch her eyes ignite to what I knew they'd become when pushed. She becomes fierce, a devil, enough so that I'm desperate to see them and curl her face further towards me, still raging in and reaming out more space inside her cunt. Another snarl growls out of her, her mouth as frenzied as I'm becoming with my cock, her teeth snapping wildly. It makes me latch onto her lips, squashing her chin with my fingers as I keep driving in and she twists beneath me. It's glorious. She's glorious with her venomous little mouth growling hatred through the air between us and winding me further. It's everything I've been hiding, quieting. She beckons it out of me, fuelling the fire with every next attempt at non consent. And then her tongue flicks at me, probably without thought. Fuck knows. I no longer care anyway, I'm becoming too lost to give a fuck, and the grinding she's offering is plenty enough to know that this is now consensual, regardless of where it started. She fucks back at me as good as I'm giving her, her hips rising and forging back as I continue pounding into her flesh. And her fucking noises drive me mad with desire, enough so that I wrench at her leg, flipping her so I can get her on her back and fuck in deeper. The mere thought half halts me, a flash of indecision weighing in to stop the connection I'm still trying to refuse. But those fucking eyes beg me as she swings them straight back to me, asking for more with every heated fuck inwards. They ask for adoration, for a connection I'm not ready for, for something I've pressed to recesses and deprived of air to keep the sadist quiet.

They fucking ask for love.

"What?" she says, panting as she reaches up and grabs at my neck to pull me down. I glare at her, ravenous for those wide lips to suffocate mine with visions of narcissistic delight, and yet infuriated at the scratches that enhance her cheek. The same ones I've shoved her into gaining. And the question fucking bewilders me, increasing the sense of outrage that consumes my thoughts. But the moment her hand curls around my neck and digs in, forcing a link she doesn't even understand, is the moment I know she's with me. Like it or not she is here, in the very place I've put her, daring a life she knows nothing about and, with that, offering something I crave. "Stain me, Blaine. Do it."

It's like a knife slicing through my skin. She speaks the sentiment as if she understands it as she reaches her hold further and drags me downwards. "I want this, please." Shudders build inside my chest as my heart races to propel me into her again, but this time it's my mind that fights, tearing me apart and reminding me of eyes that asked for that once before. I pull out a fraction, increasing the distance between us and staring into her eyes in the hope that she understands that, too. She's just here to learn. She is here to be looked after and shown the correct disciplines. That's all. That's all she asked for.

What the fuck am I doing?

I tip my eyes away from her, glancing at her body and noticing all the reddening that's already there. I can't cope with the picture in front of me suddenly, can't bear the thought of vacant eyes or that lifeless expression of death that seems to mix with this moment, regardless of my need to rip my own clothes off and continue. I did this. I made it happen. Again. I did the same thing to another woman, one who had become as willing as Alana is now. One who's dead. "Please, Blaine. Please."

I close my eyes to the torment, grabbing hold of her wrist and forcibly removing her hand from my neck so I can back away. My fucking cock isn't so willing. It grinds itself in further regardless of my mind telling it to leave her alone. "Don't leave me. Show me." I snarl in response to the plea, pushing at her hands again as they land on my hips and try to draw me back down. I'm furious, livid, defeated maybe. Fucked if I know anymore what I am. I'm fucking insane.

"Get on with it."

Delany's voice shocks me, making me remember I'm not alone. I look up to find the guy leaning on a marble column, one hand rubbing at his lips and the other holding Tabitha's waist. Alana's head turns, too, as if she's just remembered there are four of us as well.

"I…" she stutters, her body wriggling away from me and doing exactly the right thing by both of us. One more minute and it might have been … "This is wrong." She's damn right it was. So fucking wrong.

My head hangs as I pull in breaths to try to dispel whatever the hell my body thought it was doing. I'm greeted by my cock, still rabid with the need to fuck its way through her untainted body and aching to cause the pain it wants to. I hover there, half rooted inside her and staring at the glistening visions of a joining I'm not ready for, but still yearning to cement. Our skin's slicked together, our breaths merged. Our panting, rhythmic and aligned in a glory I know will be soul consuming. It's only my mind stopping me now. Just as I've fucking trained it to do.

I slowly pull out fully, every second of the movement causing an ache so profound my own thighs bellow at the prospect, my muscles cramping in protest. My whole body baulks and hesitates, willing me inward again rather than the exit I'm trying for.

"Blaine, please I…" I shake my head, my hands leaving her skin as my mind finally wins the internal war that's raging and leaves me cold and alone again. She knows nothing. This isn't up to her.

"Take her to the bathroom," I snarl quietly to Delaney, as I lever my body up, turn for the back of the church, and walk away from the one thing I need most. "Then into your suite. Let her rest and clean her up." That's all I can get out as I lift my feet up the steps, barely recognising the direction I'm walking in. Fucked if I know or care—perhaps up to the steeple to throw myself out of the window.

Time's a fucking healer, they say. Is it fuck? All time does is prolong the inevitable. It simply produces a point through which nothing matters, until the inescapable corrects the path forward again, duplicating the old and returning it with brighter blooms than it ever had before. Time just delays the response. Nothing is learnt. Nothing is different. Everything inside me is as savage as it used to be, ferociously asking for release and desperate for its escape. Although, I did stop; perhaps that's what time has achieved. But fuck, my fingers still itch, and as my hand goes to put my cock away, it changes its fucking mind and begins rubbing against the skin instead, all the time imagining a whimper so profound it still resonates. I grunt at the thought, leaning my hand onto the spiral staircase and beginning to tug my cock regardless of the visions coming at me. I'm a sick fucking man. Insane perhaps. But that death stare, and that whimper in the final few seconds, and that final struggle is still all-consuming. The life it offers, the open will that hands itself over, not caring for its demise in my hands as it does? Fuck. My groan echoes against the metal as I think of Alana's pleas and tug again, leaning my head onto the frame to cool my mind down.

"Blaine?" I frown, my hand stopping and my back turning to her for fear of the damage I might do if she does the unthinkable and offers herself again.

"Go with Delaney, Alana. I don't want you here."

"Why?" The sigh that leaves me is sheer hell to maintain. It runs through my body, loosing yet more aggression and dulling my mind's ability to tell my body what to do.

"I swear, if you ask that one more time, I'll…"

She moves, carefully creeping into my space and then my face, her body ducking under my braced arm until she's right here, pinned between me and the metal of the stairs. I stare, yet again trying to warn her that this isn't right. She knows it; she's said it herself. This isn't what she's come for, and no matter how strong the itch to slam her against something and root myself so far inside her she'll hardly breathe, I won't. I've stopped it once, made the correct choice, and regardless of my hand still holding my cock's advance at bay, I won't be goaded again. But something about her smile tears strips from my resolve. Or maybe it's her eyes. Or maybe it's the way those colours in her hair match the stripes of ink and purple beginning to shine on her skin from bruising. She just waits there, neither confirming nor denying that any of my thoughts are the right ones. She just waits, and then her hand moves to my chest, flicking one of the buttons on my shirt open and slowly lowering to the next. I watch it move, inwardly begging her not to go any further.

"Stop." It's barely audible, just a pretence at the right thing to do, and my own hand confirms it by beginning to pull the skin on my cock again.

"You're extraordinary," she whispers, shy eyes now looking at my chest rather than at my eyes anymore. "This is all extraordinary." Mmmm. It certainly is unusual, and becoming more so as she flicks another button and pulls the rest from my pants to slide her hands onto skin. "I thought you were teaching me. Why did you stop?" She makes her way past the waistband on my pants as she speaks, slipping one hand down to reach for the base of my cock and pushing on my own fingers to get them to move. "It's okay," she says, a softness to her tone that only furthers the need to fuck in deeper. No it isn't. None of this is okay. I should know better. Should *be* better. "Do you like it deep throated?" My brow rises, perhaps enjoying the way her smile quirks the dirtier her mouth becomes. I nod in reply, unable to keep the thought of those pretty lips gagging out of my mind. "Shall I then?" she asks, her eyes coming up to mine at last so I can stare back into them and forget the right thing to do. "Or should I…" She points back at where she's come from, presumably at Delaney, who should be taking her away, not letting her come back. I probably should shout at the dick, but the sight of her here, quivering slightly and gently touching me is consuming any appropriate reaction. I do want her mouth around me. And I do want to fuck her. And I do want the one thing I shouldn't even be considering. And she's asking, blatantly now. She's standing here offering. Begging.

I lick my lips at her, waiting for her to make whichever fucking decision she wants to. I'm tired of making the choice for her, which is exactly what I should be doing. That's what men like me are supposed to do. Be in control. Hold the process and teach with clarity and informed decisions. But in so few meetings I've struggled to control it every time with her, and this last time, the one that happened mere minutes ago, I've been nearly untameable. Egged on by Delaney maybe, but it's all down to me and the way she makes me feel about touching her, about connecting with her. I'd kill for her now. I'll smother any man that comes with ten feet of her, seeing him as a threat to my possession. My precious little toy. I know it in this second more than I have before. I know because of the itch still consuming my fingers and the second sigh that leaves my lips as she flutters her eyes. I'm done with care. Done with denying it. Done with trying to hold everything inside and keep her safe. She's just there, offering herself and showing me her willingness. Still, I should take her home; that's what I should do, isn't it? Give her her life back before I take it away.

"Do what you want to do."

It's the best and only response I have. Done. She'll either suck my cock, bathing me in something I don't fucking deserve in the slightest, or she'll leave. Either of which is probably an exceptional response to the near beating I've just given her. Tension rattles the air between us. Not from me. I'm done with it. I just grip the metal tighter, relaying my strength into it in hope that it will keep it from her skin, and hover my arm across her shoulder as her soft fingers stroke against my cock. I don't remove my eyes from her, and I don't stop my other hand from reaching up and drawing a finger along her face either. I don't want to. She's such an unspoiled little thing—beauty personified and drenched in as much sin as I need. All I have to do is set it free. I just have to show her and let her feel her own way through the turmoil to come. I just have to let her come with me.

"Like this?" she asks, her fingers glancing the side of me with nowhere near enough pressure. It drives me crazy, causing my teeth to grit at the involuntary shunt that shoves my cock harder into her hand.

"Tighter." Perhaps single words will be better. There's less connection in the singular. She giggles softly, her smile amused at the primal response. It rallies more visions of pain to collide in my mind, ones that stop brattish giggles dead in their tracks. But as she increases her grip, her fingers compressing securely and her mouth smiling sinfully, she begins to pump it back and forth exactly how I need it. I feel the spasms begin in my balls, causing my own mouth to grimace at the oncoming bliss she will deliver. She works the fucking thing with the precision of a trained sub, something I've not imagined as achievable the first time around.

"Fuck you." I grunt the words, not really at her, more at my own lack of discipline. This is so far past wrong its lunacy, and yet not one part of me is stopping her this time. My body actually steps into her, squashing her backwards into the metal and sighing at the screech that echoes from her lips. Fuck her sucking me. I want inside her cunt again, where I might even spill my load and watch her eyes beg for more of what I have to offer. The need is indescribable, more so than it even used to be. So much so that I drop my hand and ram it inside her instead, causing another bay of discomfort to come from her mouth. Then she gasps as I let go of the metal and drop my other hand to her thigh, spreading her legs and lifting her to rest against the metal staircase.

"This will hurt you," I bark, little care as to whether it will or not, just letting her know it will as I pull my hand out of her and hitch her weight. She nods, her tongue tracing her bottom lip as she keeps my cock in her hand and guides it exactly where I want it to go. "And I don't fucking care."

Rather than gasp again, or show signs of fear, she takes me straight to the place I crave and then lifts her hands to grip the metal behind her. I gaze at the movement, hovering an inch inside her and trying to let whatever emotions are beginning to take hold come. The sense of urgency still ravishes my entire frame with perseverance and need, but there's something more happening now as I watch determination firm her brow. Something about taking her out to dinner. About walking with her. About sharing a bed with her and waking up to her smile so I can replace it with groans and whimpers. And as I slowly push in a little more, the ache barely restraining itself as my fingers grip her ass, I realise I simply want to be *with* her. Joined. Irrevocably and permanently.

The weight of that thought alone drive's my cock so far inside her she shrieks at its impact and tries to back away from it. I just watch on as her eyes widen and her body squirms against the grate behind her, mesmerized at the mere thought of love and trying to push in deeper. It enthuses my cock tenfold, sending a harmonic lilt to the battered fucking I thought I'd be giving her. It somehow pulls me in closer, making me crawl my hand up her back to prop her spine off the metal and support her against the pain. My ass rallies, the muscles in it tensing and unfurling, driving my cock forward again as I lower my head to her tits and let them mingle in my mouth. The moan that comes from her as I bite down on one nipple sends more quivers across my frame, beating shocks against my clothes and making me wish we were both naked. I want her fucking love. Crave it. I can feel the need for it emanating out of every damn pore as I keep sending my cock home and listen to her groans.

"Yes," she hisses out, tensing as I ram the next drive in at her and crawl my mouth up to her throat. Fuck she tastes good. Sweat and sin, the slight mask of disinfectant still lingering between the sweet smell of come and florid juices as I bite in again. I can even sense her breathing alter as her back slams against the rails, the hitch in it as I dig my fingers in deeper almost like a call of primeval requirement. She mewls then, her body grasping onto me as she lets go of the rail behind her and grabs at my cheeks to pull my lips to hers. It becomes nothing but continued bellows of pain and as her nails scratch in to anchor her to me. Perhaps it gives me the ability to drive in harder with every next fuck, her offering of acceptance forcing me closer than I knew possible.

I couldn't last any longer if I tried. The come begins shooting from me the moment her tongue drives into me, a sigh swirling our breaths together. She might as well be the one fucking me with it. It churns and probes at me, her lips slathered with saliva and her teeth mangling with my own. It's hungry, animalistic. Fucking feral if truth be told as she groans into me and then breaks free to bawl out more screams. It causes my cock to rear into her with more fever, the come already channelling its way towards her cunt in a show of ownership. She just lets me increase the pace, her legs wrapping around my waist and her hands gripping onto my face so fiercely I feel her own explosion coming through them. She digs her nails deeper in as her heels tighten, making her thighs lock, and she finally stills at the same moment as my own come shoots from me and oozes out into her warm, willing cunt. It's fucking heaven. Sent from fuck knows where and offering itself with nothing but brutal fucking need. I growl out with it through our mouths, entrenching the taste of my own blood as she bites into my tongue, and remembering the sound of her still wild tone as she sucks it into her.

Quiet takes over then, a sense of tranquil contemplation. For my part, I'm just content to keep slowly fucking into her, letting the sensation of coming in someone wash through my mind as my hips push against her. Her lips lave mine again, the trace of her tongue like a slither of acceptance for my act, burnishing me with thanks for the nature of it. I sigh, exalting in this new coupling and trying to simply savour the moment rather than chastise myself for it. The sum of our parts becoming one has been, still is, indescribable. Something to be honoured for a few moments, respected, certainly with regard to her exquisite nature and devilish perfection. Not many women take this. They can't. Or don't want to, but she does. My new little toy will be everything I need. But then clapping begins in the background, reminding me of Delaney's involvement. It instantly makes me scowl as I continue licking my own tongue with hers, trying to dismiss the comment that will come. It'll ruin our moment of clarity, my moment, denouncing its effects as something to be amused by or jeered at.

"See, not dead at all," the guy says, his footsteps getting closer by the fucking second, a pair of heels following them. Alana's head rears back weakly, breaking me of my hold on her mouth and violating our intimacy. It annoys me further, causing me to grab her closer. I'm simply not done with letting the feeling of her wrapped around me embed itself further. Now isn't the time to contemplate matters like that, let alone discuss them. She doesn't know what she's done here, hasn't felt the effect of it yet. Her body's still warm, labouring under the misconception that it's handled the battering she's just taken. She needs bathing and soaking. The lacerations that are more than likely on her back need tending to and servicing. She'll be bruised and raw for days, her cunt barely able to piss without it searing pain into her guts, and if she isn't, I'll damn well be making her feel more of what she's just taken from me. Gladly.

"You should rest," I say quietly, with one final quiet shove of my hips sending her into the rails. She groans beautifully, filling the air with violent undercurrents and dirty beginnings. The sound makes me smile into her neck and hoist her higher so I can walk with her still attached to me, hopefully joining us back together rather than letting Delaney interfere with our thoughts.

"Come one step closer, and I'll break your fucking neck," I snarl, keeping my back to the guy and starting to walk towards the suite. The chuckle in response isn't as acceptable as it's been prior to her, not that I can remember ever telling the guy to leave me alone before, but it grates my nerves, perhaps telling me something I can't quite comprehend at present.

The walk to Delaney's suite takes an eternity. Not because it's far or because she's heavy, simply because with every forward step I watch her in my arms and wonder what the fuck I'm doing. I also find myself trying to hold still when she groans again, somehow hoping to lessen the pain I'm causing by holding onto her back. Her eyes remain closed the entire way, making me notice the length of her lashes for the first time. They're as long and lush as she is, showing more of her natural beauty now that the mascara had been wiped from them. And her mouth simply rests with a sense of exhaustion etched into its position, dragging my mind back to times when I'd slept with a woman and woken up to lips waiting to be ravished.

  I smile at the image, grinding my teeth at the thought of more and yet knowing I should tell her this is finished. It isn't until I walk through the old cloisters and arrive at Delaney's doorway that I abandon any thought of not going forward with this. The bed beckons me, its new swathes of clerical whites draped around the four posts akin to that of a devil in disguise. It makes me snort quietly, entertained by Delaney's sense of humour as I slowly move her towards it and lower her down. She groans again as my hands scrape across her skin, the sound making me both wince and smile as I roll her to her front.

  I've seen the damage I've caused on skin before, know its effects punish effectively, but for some reason the sight of her raw flesh troubles me. The vision of it makes me frown, questioning realism for the first time since Eloise. She'd let me drive headlong into pleasure-seeking escape, urging me forward with every new dissolute liberation as she moaned out my name. I can still see her now, in this moment, lying just as Alana is now. Although, the blood was thicker as it spread over her, unlike Alana's barely weeping wounds.

  "Blaine?" I smile as the tone of her drained voice penetrates my heart, reminding me of nights drenched in decadence, ones I don't deserve a second chance at let alone more of. "It hurts." Mmm. I told her it would.

"I'll draw you a bath," I reply, heading for the bathroom and sighing as I tuck my cock back into its confines. The steam starts to fill the small room up within seconds, heating the space and reminding me of fire play, and of wax, and of the screams associated with both.

"I don't know how to write that." I come out the bathroom and find her looking straight at me, a weary puzzlement on her face as she looks me over. "And I've never seen you naked." I smile at her as she grins weakly, the sassy element of her face returning now that she's resting. I suppose she hasn't, and although what I should do is walk out the door once I've deposited her inside the bath, giving her a chance to realign her mind, I find myself pulling my jacket off and unbuckling my belt again. Unwise, possibly. Unsuitable, certainly. I don't give a fuck. Suitability isn't welcome here for now. It wasn't ten minutes ago when I spilt my seed inside the first cunt I've had for a well over a year, and it isn't now. "Your face seems softer now you've come." I snort at her, amused by her ability to say exactly what she wants to constantly.

"Draining my cock deflates my frustration," I reply, toeing my shoes off and stepping out of my trousers. It also drains the fuck out of me. I feel as exhausted as she looks, perhaps for the first time in months, years even. I feel like I could sleep for a week, preferably with her body adorning me and her mouth available should I choose to push my cock into it. She smiles again, her blue eyes sparkling as if she understands exactly where my mind is heading. It won't take much more of her glancing her eyes over my body, licking her lips as she does, and neither of us will be getting any sleep at all. Something that, even in her fatigued state, I would quite happily venture into without care for the effect. But then she winces as she tries to move off the bed.

"Stay," I snap, walking to get to her and lifting her before she falls. "You've got no idea what you just took yet." I continue, hoisting her up into my arms again, and relishing the feel of her skin on me now that I'm naked.

"Pretty sure I do," she says, her head lolling back over my arm while her body lounges in my hold.

I walk her towards the bath rather than reply or disagree, hoping that after a soak, some ointment, and a night's sleep, she might still want to keep researching her book because now the thought of not having her here is annoying, weakening even. And fundamentally no, she doesn't know anything at all. She knows nothing other than the fact that she enjoys being fucked by a monster, one who'll ruin her if I get a chance to, regardless of the love that seems to be hovering in the air. By the time morning comes, and she feels the pain that will come with it, she might realise that, dissect it maybe. She might choose to leave and carry on with normality, relegating all this to a nightmare of experience, one that's as insane as the night I murdered a woman. Which is probably the logical choice for her to make, regardless of how infuriated that thought makes me.

Chapter 16

ALANA

Dawn breaks somewhere in my mind long before I open my eyes. I feel it wakening before I'm ready to catch up with it. Thoughts start circulating, almost surreal as they curve their way into corners and mingle with screams. I don't know what they are or what they mean. I'm barely able to make sense of the shifts in colour, or the bends suddenly haunting recesses and fractures. It's like something splitting in me, making me shake my head at them as I try pushing something away. I'm scared, my hands thrashing in front of me, hoping to dislodge the pressure that's coming at me from all directions. It's everywhere, wrenching at my skin, trying to tear me apart and rip my insides out of me. I can't breathe. I'm drowning again. I'm underwater and fighting for air, desperate for help.

Another scream sounds out somewhere, making me shift and buck against the weight all over me. It's overwhelming, suffocating, and I can't reach the shore. I can't swim to it. I can see it not far away, behind the scream, waiting for me to get to it and pull myself back together, but I can't reach. It's all blues and greens, and the sand's spraying at me, lashing my skin and causing more pain to erupt in my mind. It burns like fire, shredding what's left of my rationale as it begins pushing inside my mouth, stifling my yells for help. And still I can't breathe. I can't get free. Someone's grabbing at me and slashing, my bones crunching under the knife with every other yank and pull. My legs thrash out madly, trying to get it off me. Trying to break free. Just trying to find a route through all the sensations and…

"Alana, shhh." I don't know who that is. Who is that? "Shhhh." Still my body thrashes, whipping itself around under whatever's clamped on top of me. It's smothering me, purposely. It won't let go, won't let me get away. "Wake up." Wake up from what? "You're dreaming." Blaine?

The sound of his voice soothes me slightly as I prise at my lids, hoping that will get me to the shore. I instantly feel my stomach drop as something warm douses my insides with real sensations. The groan that leaves me makes me truly open my eyes, barely recognising where I am as another swipe of consciousness renders me incoherent with need. My legs are hooked over his shoulders before I've thought, grabbing him to me for a solid grounding as my mind still swirls endlessly. My hips rise, grinding themselves into his face for something to cling on to, something that's real. And tears are coming. I can feel them. They're winding their way through me, making me beg for something to end them before they erupt. I'm so confused. I don't know what's real and not real. I don't know why I want to cry, why I'm scared, why the incessant screams keep raging in my head. It's all so loud, so vivid. It's brightly lit and scraping at my neck, stopping me from breathing.

"Please, Blaine." It falls from my lips, almost like a prayer. I don't even know what I'm asking for, much less how he's going to give it. I can just feel him here. He's dense and physical, a mountain of strength. One who can be my foundation, harnessing reality with his strong shoulders holding me off the bed, and his tongue lapping at me. It's just... He's just... Oh god.

The scrunch of the covers in my hands becomes painful as I claw at them, making me release them and look down at him as he carries on. His head's buried there, his tongue constantly roaming in and out of me, the occasional bite forcing yet another groan to leave my lips. And then he lifts his head, just enough for me to see his eyes as he carries on. It's too much. Watching his lips suck across me, seeing the way his eyes are dark and untamed with each draw of his teeth across my sensitive clit sends me spiralling upwards. The tremors start in me with only that vision. He's truly the sexiest fucking thing I've ever seen, and the connection here is like I've never felt. It's more than strong; it's blinding me, making me feel him rather than just watch on. He's inside me. With only his tongue, he's managing to take me higher than anyone ever has. And as his shoulders pitch me higher, his fingers suddenly scratching the forbidden area and probing for acceptance there, I do nothing more than close my eyes to let him do whatever he wants. It's all him. He can fuck me, take me, climb me higher up this spiral and throw me to the wind if he chooses.

"Fuck me," I breathe. It's all I've got as he pushes a finger inside my backside and keeps on with his endless sucking. It builds a momentum I can't begin to understand as I search my breath for help, grabbing the headboard for support against it. It's all so different than ever before. He's so different. His forcefulness might be everything I hate to admit to needing, but I do. I felt it last night when he hurt me, frightening me and yet making me beg for more of it. And I want that, too, now. I can feel that in the way I'm grating my own bruised back into the bed, hoping for the pain to intensify. I want it right now. I want to feel scared by him. I want unprepared, unrehearsed. I want to feel what I haven't before. Get lost in it. Have myself taken to this very point with no ability to stop him so I can fly and truly understand what he can do.

My hand reaches for him, scratching out to get his fingers and dragging them towards my breast, needing more of his weight on top of me, perhaps mimicking the dream I had. At the moment I want to be consumed. I need it. I want to be suffocated and drowned. That's his position here. On top of me. On top. Above me so I can languish beneath him and stop thinking so much.

There's a chuckled growl as he crawls over me, his eyes crinkling slightly as if he's amused at my state of disarray, all the time his finger continuing to widen the hole he's digging out.

"Ask me," he says, his lips brushing the side of my jaw as he sinks his thumb into my pussy. Oh god, the feeling is so full, like I'm replete with only those two digits fingering me. And still I climb, the thrust of my own hips giving him the concord he's asking for. He knows exactly what he's doing, with little to no help from me. And ask him for what? For more? I just close my eyes again, letting my body own the moment, or letting him own it. I couldn't care less. I'm so far past caring he could pull a whip out and I'd take it. I'd bend over, be shackled. I'd live in a cage as long as this sense of freedom was offered, relishing its empty vacuum of beauty and rolling in its degradation of self-opinion. "I want you to ask me this time, Alana. Beg." I don't want to open my eyes or tell him what to do. I don't even want to talk. I just want to lie here and be used in any way he sees fit. I want him to take without any of my questions or consent. I want horizons and early morning storms. I want them crashing over my skin and pulling me into a place of safety and harmony, just like this is. Everyday.

I just want him.

"More, please."

I'm rolled, the creak of the bed frame alerting me to the movement rather than the action itself. I'm too immersed in him to know where I am or what I'm doing, but the sudden wrenching of my hand up to the headboard makes me gasp in surprise. Metal clicks so quickly I hardly recognise the sound, barely registering it while his other hand still works his fingers harder inside me. It's so forceful it directs my attention straight back to it, my arse still grinding against it as he manoeuvres my other hand to another cuff and drags his teeth up my lacerated back again. My yelled shout echoes in the room, somehow hastening the thought of orgasm as I keep chasing it.

"Oh God, please…" Fuck, I want him inside me. That's it. That's all.

My wrists rattle the cuffs as he shoves me forward, causing a sense of disorientation to creep in and focus me back on being bound to something, but his scent drifting by soon makes me greedy for him again. It's heavy, rich, as dense as he is and somehow drenched in a primitive intoxication, one that feeds me with the need to give in, give up. Submit.

"Make yourself come," he says quietly, pulling his thumb from my pussy and asking me to grind on nothing but his finger. And just as I begin questioning the thought, just as I start letting my mind evade his wishes, his hand slaps my battered skin. The first lands sharply, making me gasp in surprise. The second lands so heavily my hands wrench me to the headboard to get away from it, shards of pain firing across my back. My eyes fly open, the sensation making me bellow out against it and scratch into anything I can grab on to.

"See how much you enjoy it? Use the pain. Fuck yourself with it," he says as he sinks another finger inside me, widening me further and licking across the very place he's just slapped. It increases my frenzy, enough so that I grate his finger in deeper, sensing the stretch and not caring for the pain associated, welcoming it even. The third smack is delivered harder still, making tears prick my eyes as I pitch forward once more. He just increases his force behind me, his other hand wrapping around my hips to hold me in place and making me question why any of this feels right. It does, though. My hips speed up once more as I increase my grip on the headboard, desperate to come and keep the sense of pain attached to it, just like last night. "You fuck like a coward," he snarls, his fingers scissoring inside me as he grabs my chin and wrenches my head around to look at him. "Fuck yourself harder." He shouts it in my face, his lips contorted into a monster's guise as he stares me down, watching me pant and drool for something I can't achieve. "You want this from me? More of this. Prove it, Alana."

Something about his face drives me onwards. Maybe it's the way he laves his lips, slowly bridging the distance between us and finally landing them where I want them to be. The draw is instant, sending shockwaves through me as I keep grinding down. My body's wild and free as I search for stars and eventually let them come. I can see them. They're coming, driving me into another sensation I've not had before him as his tongue urges me on. It's not painful or debilitating. It's clarifying. A rush, breaking through the hollow ground of monotony and making me insane with need for more of his touch. My mouth breaks from his, the pain finally building to something I would have thought unobtainable, but it's not. It's a prospect breached, a new perspective, and it crashes though my skin, exploding as I feel it hastening through my veins, darkening the blood within them.

It takes me a minute to assimilate the thought as my insides clamp eagerly on nothing but air, leaving me aching and unfulfilled. They throb for something more, no matter how volatile the orgasm. I feel empty, as if I've been punished and not given a reprieve for good behaviour even though I came.

"Fuck you," I cry as I open my eyes and gaze into his, my breath stuttering out around the words as he does nothing but smile in response. It's wicked and evil, and infinitely more fucking debilitating than any orgasm could ever be. It's a smile built on facts I don't want to admit. But his voice, the way he uses it, dirtying every fucking thing he does, it's all consuming. It makes me filthy. It makes me want to be. It forges him into me whether I like it or not, unable to deny his strength nor try to. His perversions are exactly what I require for now. And as I let the come drip from me, salivating at the thought of more of it and flexing my fingers in the restriction of the cuffs, I glare at his amused face. I'm part ready to scratch it off of him for showing me this, and part adoring him for the emotions he's produced with only ten minutes worth of work. "Fuck you."

His smile just increases as I pant in front of him, turning to something some would die for and lessoning my sense of hatred for his arrogance.

"I'll let you have that one," he says, his finger still driving in slowly. "You're cunt's dirtier when you swear." Fuck him again. I don't have a dirty cunt. Actually, perhaps I do at the moment, and just as I'm remembering that, he leans in and lets his mouth linger near mine again. "You're truly beautiful," he whispers, his finger slowly pulling from my arse and running gently over the length of my sensitive clit. I snatch my body away before he inflicts more aches, still infuriated, or humiliated, or confused. Perhaps I just feel left hanging, even though I'm not and could quite easily get more if I asked for it. I don't know. It's all a riot of reactions I can't process right now. "You're a beautifully twisted mess, Alana Williams."

I still haven't got much more than a fiery, if not exhausted, 'fuck you', so I don't bother responding to his arrogant claim. I'm not a twisted mess. Well, maybe I am. I don't know about that either. I just keep glaring until his smile makes me want to smile, too, and then turn my head to look at the handcuffs and my stained fingers in them rather than acknowledge any of his superiority.

"I can't write this," I mumble, uneasy at the thought of articulating my feelings.

"Mmm." It's not a supportive insertion into my musings.

The bed slumps under his weight, making me tip my eyes back to watch him lying there. His cock flinches on his ridged stomach, probably at my perusal, which makes me want to eat it. And then his hand starts roaming his own skin as he shifts himself about, tempting me further with my blowjob fantasies that I was diverted from last night. I just stare for a while, wondering what he has that I'm drawn to. It's not just the pain, although that will most definitely take some thought, but it's more than that. He's more than that because the rush kept coming, didn't it? I couldn't stop my constant pull back to the sordid and dirty he was opening up as acceptable. It was all I could think of in the moment, all I could feel. It was him. He did this. He has perverted me, turned me into something barely resembling human. He's shown me a new path, something above my comprehension. People don't do this to each other. They don't cause pain in the exploration of pleasure. They don't rip shreds out of skin and smile as the blood seeps from battered flesh, licking the crimson drops away before replacing them again. We should have mewled and moaned our way through this now, the same last night, not growled and groaned under the strain he asked for, increasing the ache with every fucking drive into me. And it'll only get worse. I know that. I can tell by the way he seems unaffected by his work, as if it was only partway done, hardly scratching the surface of his capabilities. There might be emotions involved in all this, love if I'm honest, but it's tainted with filth, or maybe enhanced by it. All the thoughts make me start questioning everything again. Why? When? Who? I mean, how does this sort of thing start? Is there an introduction to the underground world? How does one even know that's what you need?

"When did you know?" I ask, perhaps searching for validation that this feeling I now have is okay, that I've not turned insane in the short time he's been handling me.

"Hmm?"

"How old were you when you knew you were different to all the other boys?" Because I am now, too, aren't I? Different. He's shown me I am. Maybe I always was and I didn't know. Normal doesn't come close to this. It's probably why all other men have been non-descript, reasonably easy to leave. Perhaps this is why all my other relationships haven't worked.

He rests his hand under his head and looks at me, relaxed in his open offering of sexuality and completely immersed in his own superiority. It's effortlessly intriguing, enough so that I feel the need to let him lead me all the more, regardless of what that could mean.

"Are we having a conversation for your research, or do you genuinely want to know?" he replies, as he looks away from me towards the ceiling.

"Does it make a difference?"

"Yes."

"Why?"

"Ah, the questions again." He chuckles a little, his hand dropping to his cock and beginning to roam it casually. "Because if you genuinely want to know, I'll take you out for dinner and tell you all the gory details so you can learn, but if you just want research options, I'll test your cunt's reflexes first. You can learn that way instead."

Well, what a decision. And, frankly, dinner? We don't do dinner.

"Are you talking about a date? I've told you. I don't need that." Although, for whatever reason, I am intrigued with the thought of just talking, especially given my current lack of clothing. It would be nice for this to seem more normal. That thought alone scares the shit out of me as I watch him smile at my confusion, knowing I'm falling with little hope of recovery.

"No. I'm aware you don't want that." He rolls onto his side, gazing at my arse as I try to get comfortable. It's not easy given my wrists are still handcuffed to the bed as I twist and turn about. "But you should eat."

I frown, wondering when the last time I actually ate was. It makes me look away from him and try to put some context to the last few days, where I've been, how long it's been. I hardly recognise the time of day, let alone how long I've been here. And I haven't texted Bree to let her know I'm okay. In fact, I haven't contacted my publisher. No one. It's been like a void of time missing from the real world. I don't even know what day it is.

"How long?"

"What?"

"The party? Was that yesterday?" Because now he's mentioned it I want to know. I've lost time, not even caring for where it's gone. And I haven't typed anything. Not a word since that room. I need to get this all down on paper so I remember. "I need to get back to writing."

He stands up without another word and walks around the other side of the headboard to unlock the cuffs on my wrists, a casual smile adorning his face.

"Shower and get changed. Your bag's in the corner of the room."

"How did that get here?"

"Delaney brought it in last night."

"Oh." Seems he's got everything covered, not that I know who Delaney is. "Okay."

I rub at my wrists as he shrugs on a pair of trousers and leaves without another word, my stare following him. I suddenly feel odd in the room on my own. The feeling leaves me cold. It's not the standard sensation delivered when I leave a man. Normally I feel happy to be on my own again after a session, but this time I feel like I'm absolutely alone. Like a part of me just left, leaving me empty.

I shake my head at the perception, trying to dismiss it as ludicrous. I hardly know Blaine, regardless of the joining we seemed to share when he was inside me last night. It wasn't the same just now. It was less linked, but it still lingers in the air nonetheless, showing me the something I asked for.

The shower revives me a little as my body aches beneath the jets. But yet again it makes me question the sanity of any of this. I hurt, a lot. Everything. Not only do my muscles not know what to do with themselves, my back stings. It's not until I get out and try to get a glance at it in the mirror that I realise why. Part of it is cut and others are scratched, reddened lines scattered across its surface. Nothing seems deep or permanent, but it's there anyway, staring back at me and reminding me of the battering I took. It seems strange to me that I'm smiling as I gaze at it, perhaps remembering the passion involved in the act, or the way I spurred him on so that I could come underneath the pain. It's more likely the memory of him rubbing cream into me when we got back in here last night. His hands were tender, devoted even, offering a softer side of his persona for me to think about as I relaxed further into them and drifted, exhaustion taking over. And then, I suppose, I must have fallen asleep in his arms, his hands still stroking at my back in an act of care. It's all so bizarre to my mind that I quickly get changed into some jeans and a shirt rather than staring anymore, and then rifle through my bag for a notebook and pen.

In no time at all I'm sitting on the bed, my hands scribbling furiously again and searching for a way of explaining what I've been through. There's so much to write since I last typed, so many words and so little time to get them down, but it slowly begins flowing regardless of the mass of information assaulting my mind. It's a complete mess if I'm honest, with no clarity of structure, but it's hammering out again nonetheless. Within a few minutes I feel lightheaded, a slightly sick sensation wracking me. It makes me realise I haven't had any happy pills for the last few days, something I assume I'm going to need given the amount of material my brain has to cope with. It's exhausting trying to formulate this in my mind. Drawing maps seems harder without their help clearing the way. The realisation makes me reach into my bag again and begin to rifle through it for the little plastic container. It's not there. Nowhere to be seen. Anxiety sets in, my heart racing at the thought of them not being available for use. I feel it climbing through me as I frantically search again. I'm not addicted, but I need them. I do. They make everything make sense. They clear the chaos, helping me see straight through all the information coming at me daily. The stories stay contained. The meetings, easy to manage. The constant social media easier to engage with, showing my willingness to please everyone. I can't be without them. I can't function properly without them. I definitely can't deal with Blaine without them. I need my story straight. All my ducks in a row. I need to be controlled and able to manage all this so I can see all the answers. Oh god, where are my pills?

"Stop," his voice suddenly says from somewhere. I look up, shocked, and find him standing in the doorway, apparently showered and changed into jeans and a jacket. I didn't even hear him come in. It takes me a minute to find my voice, or perhaps reinstall myself back into reality given my almost hysterical searching, my hand still hovering in my bag. And when I do, I realise I've never seen him look so casual. It's still quite formal, but he looks so much softer. It reminds me of his hands last night. His whole body seems more relaxed, too. And then he smiles, breaking me of my meander around his body and highlighting an extremely handsome face. "Food?"

Oh yes, food. Although, we could always do the handcuff thing again. I turn to face them still dangling on the bed, their sliver glinting in the sunlight, and my mind is suddenly focused on anything but my pills. That was... "Now."

I find myself smiling at his aggravated tone, suddenly feeling comfortable with its expression, as if it's simply an extension of his hands. The sensation makes me pull my hand from my bag to scribble the thought immediately, almost ignoring the command so that I can get the facts straight in my head. Well, try to.

"You don't scare me, Mr. Jacobs," comes from my mouth, my hand rushing the notes. Not through need to do as I'm told, just because he's right. I am hungry, ravenous actually.

He mumbles to himself about something as his feet cross the floor to me, but I don't really hear it. Perhaps it was something about the fact that I should be. I don't know or care. I'm still too busy scrawling down my path, mind maps beginning to emerge again as I turn the pad sideways and listen to his breathing.

The sudden lifting of my body does make me look up at him, though, yet again smiling as he shrugs me up with little care for my weight.

"Charming," is my chuckled response, watching the way his frown descends the moment my body settles into place.

"Trouble," is all he says as a reply, his frame walking us off though the door and out into the church again. The sight of the place floors me, my mouth hanging open in amazement as I flick my eyes around to gaze at the halos shining in through the stained windows.

"Wow." There's light everywhere. It bounces off the stonework, striping its way along the floors and creating patterns. Reds, golds, blues and greens. It's everywhere, dowsing the huge interior with crescents and shimmering off the metallic statues of saints. "He's not really a priest, though, right?"

Blaine snorts, moving his arm to accommodate my twisting body as I try to arch around and look behind his back.

"Why, have you sinned?"

"I think I probably have." He just smiles at me as his fingers dig in to carry me straight through the middle of the space I was kneeling in last night. "Just about there," I say, pointing at the floor and remembering the way Priest gazed at me as the man carrying me held me down. It brings a frown onto my face, confusing me and making me question why I'm being carried in some show of gentlemanly intent once more.

"Don't analyse it," he says, his arms relaxing as he keeps walking. "You overthink it and you'll drive yourself mad." Oh. Right. "It's not like you didn't enjoy others watching us, is it?"

Mind reader. I don't suppose I did. Maybe at the time, when it first stated happening, but then it became another part of the experience. And when Blaine backed off from the moment, choosing to walk away from me rather than carry on, it had been Priest that sent me back to him, telling me to goad him back into action.

"Show him what you need," he'd said, as I looked lost in the middle of the floor and tried covering myself. *"Remember your confession. Don't hide."*

He said that as the woman stood slightly in front of him, her body cinched into a perfectly fitted black dress, and her smile as open as her intent to join in. I'd stared at her, half in amazement at my own thoughts and half ready to walk the length of the building and leave. But she'd smiled again, nodding her head at Blaine and somehow telling me to go back, perhaps to just be honest with myself and stop over thinking my situation.

"What made you walk away last night?"

"You did," he says as if I should understand the answer. I don't, so I stare at him as we make our way through the tall pillars lining the entrance route, watching the way he tries to avoid any more conversation. As far as I'm aware, I was asking him to carry on, begging actually.

"That's not true, though. Because if…" He abruptly deposits me onto the church steps as we finally break out into fresh air. The light makes me squint, my hand rising to shelter my eyes from the sun pouring down onto us.

"If you had even the slightest comprehension of what I want to do to you, you'd be thanking me for the chance at escape, not stirring me into delivering more." I wish the sentiment made me scared, but it doesn't. If I'm honest, it enthuses me to some degree, my crotch already readying itself for more than it damn well got this morning. "And Delaney should have known better than to send you back to me." Oh, Delaney is Priest. Okay. And, well, maybe he should have, but that's not getting my story written, is it? Or furthering whatever this feeling is that Blaine produces in me.

"I don't see what you think the problem is. What are you going to do? Break my bones?" For god's sake. This is only kink. Sure, pain's obviously involved, something I appear to be taking astonishingly well regardless of my aching frame, but it's not like people die because of it. Not that I've heard of anyway. I stare at him for clues about that, nothing's forthcoming other than a slight frown that I guess is because of the conversation. No, that's silly. Dies? Stupid. This is just a practical lesson, that's all. One I appear to be falling head over heels for, possibly stupidly, but he's just providing a service of sorts, isn't he? A dirty one, true, but it's nothing he should be ashamed of or concerned about. "I came to you because I trust you to offer me something I've not experienced before. You're doing it. I don't know what you're beating yourself up about. I'm asking." This is all just something that needs doing. An exploration into the unknown for me, and nothing too arduous for him. If a little emotion comes into it then I'll just deal with that, chastising myself along the way because it can't be real. None of this can. Mystical encounters or not. Beautiful or not. "It's just a job of sorts." I nod at myself, trying to remember that fact. "For both of us," I say, turning and walking down the steps, not really sure I believe my own thoughts in the slightest but searching for whatever car we're getting into nonetheless. It's not like he wants anything other than this. Me either. "Are we going? Which car?" There's no response. Nothing. I swing to see why not. He just stands there at the top of the steps leading into a church. It's the most incongruous vision possible, even more so than Priest was last night. It makes me giggle like a child, wondering if men like this should ever be able to go near a church. "Well, look at you, Mr. Jacobs. You just need a dog collar and you'll fit right in."

Five minutes he stands there, or at least it feels like it to me as I fold my arms and wonder what the hell he's doing. He's not doing anything, actually. He's just standing, staring at me, his stance as rigid as I've ever seen it. He's not smiling or giving off any of the relaxed impression he gave only a few seconds ago. He's changed. Uncomfortable with something I've said maybe. And he's boring his bloody eyes into mine, giving me no room to breathe without him allowing me to. It's overwhelming, almost making me shake, just like he did last night as he drove himself inside me and showed me something new. It's more than it was ten minutes ago and less than my heart tells me it should be. The thought makes me catch my breath as watch him start to walk down the steps, his legs travelling the ground comfortably and closing the space between us. I don't know where it's come from. My heart isn't included in this arrangement. It never was, regardless of how much I've been feeling it weaken for him. It's not part of the bargain. It's an entirely ludicrous notion, one that fills me with trepidation as it keeps interrupting logic with every step he makes. I back away, refusing to acknowledge the way he's crawled into my chest and desperate to keep the distance as far reached as possible. He's Blaine Jacobs. My project. Research. He's not to be reflected upon with any implication of attachment or romance. He's just a man who's good with his hands and lips, and everything else. Oh god, I'm really falling, aren't I? No. I can't.

I end up flicking my hair around, twiddling it under his gaze and pretty much letting him own every thought I'm having. That infuriates me enough that I eventually huff out a small breath and turn, reprimanding myself for many reasons, one of which is the fact that I'm becoming more involved than simple professionalism dictates, if fucking someone can be considered professional, anyway.

"What are you running from?" he says, his voice too close for comfort and his words sinking in more than I want to admit. Him, that's what I'm running from. This isn't romance. It can't be. I didn't ask for that and he doesn't offer it. He knows it as well as I do. Whatever this little connection or interlude in our professional relationship is, it's not happening again. Love inducing lips or not.

"Whatever that look was." It's the only thing I've got, because the thought scares me to death.

I'm walking away from his eerie impression on my skin before he has a chance to speak again. I have to, need to. Although, that's going to be a tad difficult given the food we're heading out for. Still, I'll just find a way to manoeuvre my way around any conversation that involves feelings, because I don't have any, and nor does he. It's all about work. My book. And him having some fun with his over-zealous hands and my enthusiastic response to them, I suppose. We'll talk about that instead.

So I wait by a car, unsure whether it's the right one or not but hoping that if I seem uninterested in the discussion, he'll just give it up.

"That's why I backed away from you last night," he says, his face arriving in my eye line on the other side of the car. And I'd like to act like I don't know what he's talking about, nullifying my heart's inclination as I do. "To stop this before it started, Alana." I'd also like to pretend those words go straight over my head, keeping me, us even, on track with the professional thought I'm attempting, but they don't, because I do know now. I feel it in his walk, his brown eyed stare, and the way he smiles so sadly as he gazes at me. It seems we both know exactly what's happening here.

Chapter 17

ALANA

The restaurant, for want of a better word, isn't at all what I thought it would be. I assumed we'd go to some reasonably high-end place, one full of affluent people. It's actually just a small side street eatery, full of people chattering and eating their lunch. It makes me smile, reminding me of times spent with Bree when we just opened up the laptops and started writing with little concept of time or the amount of drink consumed. Or of times long before her when I struggled to keep up with my studies, but somehow always managed to write words down regardless of tests and timetables. Writing was more important then than it is now. It was real. It evoked a passion I'm only just beginning to feel again because of the man opposite me. It meant something to my being. My soul bled into the scribblings, elongating the minutes drafting to hours, the hours turning into late evenings hammering the laptop, midnight occasionally creeping in to exhaust me further before I carried on again anyway until I was thrown out. Some of my best work has been written in places like this, the noise of the other people simply providing a monotone drone to lead me into whatever world I'm writing about. It's not happened for a while, as we tend to write outdoors through the summer months. Actually, the real writing hasn't happened forever, but this reminds me of the winter coming and the long sit-ins we do. The same ones I used to do all the time. It brings a hope into my mind again, one filled with memories of times gone by and true thirst. My smile grows wider as I realise the one thing I'm trying to deny. They're hopes filled with the man in front of me, aren't they? It's all about how he's making me feel. They're dreams filled with Blaine.

"What's made you smile?" he asks, sipping his water and then forking another mouthful of pasta.

"This place," I reply, placing my cutlery down and pushing the plate away slightly. "It's not very you." It's true. He portrays something other than this. Something higher-end. And I'm not about to discuss feelings I shouldn't be having anyway. Neither of us are.

"You wouldn't know what me is." My smile turns to more of a flattened smirk as I watch him raise a brow at me, his tongue running over his lower lip. It's the most disconcerting moment of my life, because he's got a point. It's odd that we've done as much as we have in the bedroom, or out of it, and yet I know so little about who he is. It makes me feel awkward, as if we're not connected regardless of the link we have in any form of sexual encounter. Not that I'm interested, because that would mean a closeness I'm not discussing. It quiets me again as I stare out of the windows into the road, my fingers fiddling with my napkin as I search for something else to talk about other than the one thing I real want to ask. It's all felt a little odd since we've been here. Stilted, as if conversation about the average and ordinary is hard work, proving that we are obviously not average and ordinary at all.

"I was fourteen the first time I knew something was different," he says, his own cutlery clunking the ceramic as he finishes his meal and picks up his water again. I reach for my notebook immediately, ready to scrawl information down and feel a sense of safety in that function again, but his hand reaches for mine, asking me not to without a single word. "Just for you." I nod in reply, my own hand letting go of the leather and slipping from beneath his. "It might help you understand who you are. Who I am?" Good, because at this precise moment I don't know anything about who I am, who he is, or what the hell I'm doing, let alone why my heart keeps interfering in conversations it has no business thinking about.

"Alright. What wasn't normal?" He looks around him a little, noting the lack of tables nearby and signalling for a waiter.

"Do you want a drink?"

"Will I need one?" He snorts, laughing at my question and lighting up the room with his smile as he shrugs. The movement makes him seem younger, softer again, uncomfortable in his display of ambiguity maybe, but seemingly more beautiful because of it.

"You might. I certainly do. Hesitant is not my forte."

"Really? I never would have guessed," I quip, remembering every grab, slap, and hold that he has. Although, there are always those backwards steps. They're always there, making him hesitant in my mind anyway, irrespective of his forceful ways.

"It's not something you'll see again in a hurry, so make the most of it." I smile again, watching the way he seems nervous, his eyes locking with anything but mine.

"Well, I best have a drink, too, then."

He orders something from the waiter, barely looking at him as he mouths out the order and then sends him on his way. I don't know what it was. I'm suddenly transfixed in thought at the suggestion that something's just for me. I don't know why, especially given that we are not doing emotions in any way. Christ, I wish I could believe that.

"I'd slept with a range of women by then, and wasn't able to finish successfully." The words shock me, breaking me of my uncooperative emotional gaze. So much so that my mouth hangs open in surprise, unable to process the thought of Blaine not being able to come. That leads to visions of a younger Blaine, one who perhaps wasn't as confident in his demeanour. It's as inconsistent as seeing him on church steps. He laughs again, his hand reaching over to close my gaping jaw. "We were all young once, Alana. Don't be so surprised."

The waiter returns, depositing something on the table as I continue to stare at Blaine's smiling mouth. I still don't understand. What fourteen-year-old male can't ejaculate? Assuming that's what he means.

"I don't understand. I mean, why?"

"I've never really known why. I only know how I overcame it."

"Which was?" He sighs, suddenly looking remorseful. "It's okay. It's not like I'm going to write it."

"I can't do this here." What does that mean? His eyes look around, once more searching the interior as if he's bothered by the people milling around. It makes me look around, too, suddenly so interested in this information that I'm ready to go wherever he wants to so he can tell me.

"Somewhere else?" He nods, picking up his drink and turning from me to walk towards the end of the restaurant. I get up and follow him, happy to swipe my drink, too, and take a sip as I grab hold of my notebook and handbag. We swerve our way through the people, him occasionally looking back at me to check I'm still there, and then the unthinkable happens. He reaches his hand for mine, making me frown at it and stand still. I don't know what's so shocking about it. It's not like we haven't been intimate, but something about it seems more intimate than any amount of nakedness. It's personal, showing a sense of ownership or possession. My mouth falters around my hand's movement, unsure whether to say no or accept the offer. It's everything I'm trying to avoid. It's neither professional nor sensible. It's probably stupid, but it doesn't stop my need to reach forward and take hold of it. And he just holds it there, his body as solid and dependable as his ability to cause pain.

"What does that mean?" I ask, unsure what he's offering and even more insecure about the answer that might leave his lips. Why is he doing this? He did it at the steps. The same thing. He's trying to force a connection that neither of us should acknowledge. Why? Why would he even think about it?

"It's just a hand."

"You know as well as I do it's not just a hand, Blaine."

He doesn't move, and he doesn't remove the hand, rather leaves it hovering there, waiting for me to admit the inevitable. He doesn't even look confused by the offer, which is completely juxtaposed to the way I'm feeling. In fact, he looks absolutely resolute, challenging every thought I'm trying to rebuff as he waits.

"I'm just offering the truth, Alana. That's what you came for, isn't it?" Does he mean that hand is the truth? Because if he's trying to suggest that taking his hand will lead me to information relevant to my book, I think he's wrong. It'll lead to me falling fully in love with someone who is not for falling in love with. I know it and so does he. I've felt it too many times in the stars that rattle my mind when he touches me, pushing it away each time in the hope that it doesn't encroach on the facts. This is not love. It isn't. It's lust. Infatuation. Obsession maybe, but it can't be more than that.

I stare at it some more as a woman knocks into me, barely registering her weight until I feel myself wobbling around for balance. It makes me reach for him. I see it happening in slow motion, my fingers stretching to close the distance between us as I stare uselessly into his eyes. He doesn't move, rather lets me fall, but just as I feel the floor coming at me, his name leaves my lips, a call for help maybe. I don't know. It feels more than that, though, like something else is happening here, like there's a pause, an epiphany running through the moment. The grip on my hand is instant, his arm wrenching me upright again and pulling me into him with little care for comfort. It's simply a case of catching me—that's all. A show of strength. A dependable show of strength maybe, but it's just help. It's nothing to do with the look in his eyes as his arm wraps around my back and presses me further into him. It's also nothing to do with the fact that my lips are desperate to kiss him. It's certainly not the fact that he's looking at them as if they're all he wants and the rest of the world doesn't exist. He just caught me; that's all. Nothing more.

"You caught me," I splutter out quietly, unable to keep my eyes off his lips now. This is stupidity. He's a sadist. Research. I'm not doing this. Oh god, I can't do this.

"You asked me to. I've told you, all you have to do is ask." The tone of his voice makes my stomach swirl. It's soft, unlike anything I've heard from him before now. It's not demanding or demeaning. It's quiet, and filled with a velvet I'm unused to. It's debilitating to any sense of rationalism I'm trying to hold onto as it fills me with sentiments I don't want. "You just have to ask, Alana."

"What for?" He smiles, his long wide lips suddenly moving towards mine and filling our air with an intimacy I can't avoid.

"Whatever you want." He's not suggesting what I'm thinking, is he? Surely not.

My head rears back as I shrug from his hold, part desperate to take him up on his conversation, probably allowing myself to fall hopelessly into the hands of a sadist as I do, and part ready to run for the hills at the thought. It's an outrageous idea, one that fills me with excitement, escapism maybe, but it's got no sanity to it. There's no marriage here. No dreams of children and love ever after. He is a man who does what for a living? Creates pain? How would he know reality?

"That's not what this is, Blaine." The words stutter from me, trying to travel their way back inside the moment they've left my lips, proving I'm not even sure I believe them myself.

"Isn't it?" I shake my head, trying to tell my brain to harden up. To remain professional.

"No."

He smirks, arrogantly lifting my hand to kiss it. The move throws me completely off kilter, rendering me useless as I desperately try to picture the look in his eyes when he hurts me rather than this offering of a gentlemen. A beautiful one maybe, but he's not suitable for anything other than what he does. I've seen it, felt it. Enjoyed it. Oh god, I've enjoyed it. And I've begun to fall for it in a way, am still falling if truth be told as his lips linger on my hand, but it's not real. It's all a lie, or a distraction. I don't know, but it must be, regardless of my hearts continued flutter.

I snatch my hand from his fingers, irritated I've let myself become a mush of emotions and frantically squashing the thought of anything but research, regardless of how comfortable my fingers feel under his lips. Men like Blaine have nothing to offer but smut and deviance, no matter the unparalleled thoughts that are currently filling me with anything but those visions. Fucking man.

"Why are you doing this, Blaine? We were talking about you, not us. There is no us. There can't be."

He just raises a brow at me and turns away to start weaving through the crowd again, leaving me without an answer and questioning if my opinion is even relevant to how he thinks.

I watch him go for a few moments, considering what the hell he's playing at, even if I can't deny the pull I feel to him. Why would he push that? Why? It must be a ruse, something that his kind do perhaps. Something to lull us mere mortals into submission or servitude. Actually, maybe it's just a way of him showing me something that I've asked for. Not that I'm sure what, unless he's trying to make me fall in love with him, which, quite annoyingly, appears to be working.

A snort leaves my nose at the thought of it all. Alana Williams in love with a sadist. Blaine Jacobs at that. It's preposterous, regardless of the way his hands tightening on my body makes me crazy, or this strange sense of love that keeps infiltrating coherent thought. I'd call the whole venture a story if I could, a woman, me, being swept off her feet by the big bad monster. Little red riding hood springs to mind. It's annoying, making me think about things I have no right thinking, including romance that he clearly won't know anything about. I don't even know who he is. Christ.

I eventually flick my eyes around the restaurant to see a selection of eaters just gawping at me as I hover in the middle of the floor like an idiot. I'd almost forgotten where I was. The thought of professional ineptitude makes my feet move, springing me forward into action instead of labouring in this wistful state of irrational thought. It's the sort of endeavour that might just go and spank a sadist for confusing this further than it needs to be. Stupid man. Beautiful, but stupid.

The words don't entirely ring true when I finally find him again. He's outside on the deck, overlooking a view of the town and staring at it like the weight of the world is on his shoulders.

"Where are we anyway?" I ask, not necessarily interested in the answer but needing to say something to get conversation flowing again.

"I think you should go home." His words stop me in my tracks, barely able to move my feet for the sudden loss that strikes my heart. It pierces the core of me, rendering me near speechless as I attempt to stay strong and in control. "I can't do this with someone like you."

"Why?"

"You know why," he says, his head dropping a little as he turns to look back at me. My heart flounders further at his inspection of me, casing a flurry of foreboding to crawl over my skin. "I should never have started with you. I should have protected you from this, not advanced it."

"I don't know what you're talking about," I reply stupidly, knowing full well what he's talking about and neither ready to disband the feeling, nor amass it further. "You're just confusing this into something it isn't. We can carry on as is. There's no need to …"

"Stop, Alana," he says as he starts walking towards the door of the restaurant, his body moving as efficiently as it ever does but with a sense of hesitation that shows me I'll only have to speak to stop his momentum. But why should I? It's not like this is a love affair; it's not. It's a mission of intent, one that shouldn't involve feelings or sentiment. He knew it when we started, as did I. Unfortunately, the sight of his hand grabbing the handle to walk away, pressuring me into an answer, almost forces words from my mouth I haven't got my head around. "This should finish before it goes wrong. You know I'm right."

"No." It's out of my mouth before I've got a sensible reason for saying it, my own fingers reaching for his back without any understanding of why. "Blaine?" He turns his body around fully to look at me, waiting for me to confirm the rest of my thoughts, but I've got nothing else to say. What am I supposed to say? I think you're right? He can't be, and neither can I. Neither one of us should be letting any of this emotion in. It's just sex and kink. The things I needed to know about to write my book. It's not …

"What, Alana?"

"I…" Nothing. No sense. No opinion. I can't find anything to make this seem plausible as my head confuses itself further and sends me spiralling into mouthfuls of illegitimate ramblings. I can't even spit them out under his gaze, already knowing he'll see through the lies anyway. It's the lack of my pills. It must be. I'm confused and irrational. Unable to make a coherent decision for all the possible repercussions of such idiotic thoughts.

"I can't fuck unless you are in pain. Do you understand that?" Oh god, what a thought. It only adds to the muddle of my mind, making me gaze at his face and wonder what life with that would be. It's overwhelming, regardless of his beauty and the fact that I see the insecurity in his eyes as he says it. He's as lost in this as I am, barely holding enough rational thought in his own mind to help me make up mine.

"I know, but what if..." What if he changes? What if us being together changes that? I mean, he's normal as well. A human. A man. And does it matter anyway? I like the way he handles me. I enjoy its tension, no matter how much I'm trying to suggest it's just for my book.

He shakes his head.

"It will never go away. It will never subside. It will only get worse."

The statement makes me chastise myself as I look at the floor, considering any option available and remembering the pain already imprinted on my back. There aren't any, and he's right. If this goes any further than it already has I will fall in love with him hook, line and sinker. If I'm honest, I'm already skating down that slippery slope full tilt, my fingers grasping onto my book in the hope that it offers me a reason for being so stable against him. This, us, is something so much larger than simple words. I know that when I'm writing it. I can feel it in my chest when I scrawl the scenes, relaying them as love rather than fucking, regardless of Priest's revelations.

"Yes, I know," I reply eventually, my eyes meeting his and searching for a sense of clarity.

"I won't promise you anything." That's his clarity. It's crystal clear and full of such candour that I know I'm winging my way into hell's embrace, barely giving sense to the worry of it and hardly bothered by the consequences.

"Yes."

"I'm a fucking asshole." He says it as if it should make a difference. And it should. I know it should, but something about the way he caught me makes me know there's more than just that. There has to be, doesn't there? "If you come with me, Alana, you come with no hope of more than it is."

He stares, his mouth flat and solemn, as if this should be enough warning of the unending storms that will batter my body. The thought makes me realize that catching me requires me to fall first, possibly without thought or consideration to the rights or wrongs of leaping. It was the same beneath the water, the same on my knees. It's the same all the time. But he always catches me, doesn't he? Whether he likes it or not. It's inbuilt in him, maybe only for me, I don't know, but he will catch me if I ask. He might be an asshole, but he's an honest one. One I want to spend more time with. One I'd like to enjoy outside the bedroom, too, learning about him and myself in the process. He's the most handsome thing I've ever seen and as debilitating to regularity as I've ever encountered. He electrifies me, rendering anything other than this thing between us near inconsequential.

"Why aren't you running, Alana? What do you want?"

"I..." Love, that's what I want, no matter how much I'm standing here trying to dismiss it or argue about it. The thought scares me to death as I finally acknowledge its depth inside me, my legs backing me away from him shakily as I do.

"That's exactly what you should be doing," he says, holding the door open and nodding at it as if I should use it. "I was wrong to start any of this with you. I knew in the beginning." Did he? That means he must feel the same way. He wouldn't have continued if he didn't. In fact, he tried to stop it, didn't he? He said no, tried to put me with someone else. He did it after the pool, after the bedroom, after whatever was starting on the stairs. It makes me stop, and look at him again, barely restraining the need to kiss him and tell him how I feel.

"But..."

"No. I won't push you further. It's already been enough," he says, tension flowing out of every part of him as he slams the door he's holding open and pockets his hands.

"But I think..." It leaves me unconsciously, my brain unable to stop my mouth's movement.

"What? You think you love me?"

Fuck.

My tongue licks my lips, trying to contain the need to tell him. It's irrational and unreasonable. It's hardly even a recognisable emotion to me, having barely touched on the thought before him. I've never felt its complexity, never felt its draw, I've only written it, but I know it's more than I've ever felt before. It's a consuming energy, binding me to him without any lucidity. We haven't dated. We haven't talked. We haven't even just had a drink together, walked along a beach holding hands. Nothing. And it's only been such a short amount of time. People don't fall in love like that, do they?

I glance at my fingertips, searching the ink stains for clarification of feelings I can't quite explain. Perhaps that's what the staining does—perhaps it blindly opens up windows and avenues for more, little care for wellbeing or safety recognised as they come. But try as I might, and regardless of my acceptance of the facts, I can't get the words out. Does anyone love someone like him, and if they do, are they considered sane? They can't be. It's madness. Utter lunacy.

"I do."

My hand shoots to my mouth, trying to recall the words or at least search for other ones to counter them. Instead of finding anything, I just stand here wondering what might come back at me. For once in my life I'm in my own story. It's one filled with confusion and a myriad of reasons to run. I know that. It's turbulent, and will be filled with a passion I know nothing of nor hardly dare entertain as acceptable. I shouldn't be doing this. I should be running backwards, or forwards, or anywhere rather than into his hands, but I can't stop myself.

He looks as shocked as me in some ways, his frown descending to counter my words. It only emboldens my thoughts, making me realise he's as tangled about the right thing to do as I am. We should both walk away, shouldn't we? I should leave him in his world and head back to my own, remembering a time when I dipped my toe into unknown waters and enjoyed its strange romanticism.

"I can't..."

He doesn't finish the sentence, or perhaps it wasn't a sentence to finish. I don't know because he just turns, opens the door again, and leaves me, the flash of his hand the last image I see as the door swings closed behind him. My own body turns from the vision, my eyes searching the skyline of the unknown town for answers I haven't got, as my arms wrap around me. There's nothing there to help or guide me. No answers other than the one I just announced out of my own mouth. I love him, or am certainly falling in love with him. It might be unreasonable, and of no use to my emotional well-being, but I do, or I am. And having told him that, he's left me here alone, giving me nothing in return for my offering other than the sight of his back. Perhaps that should be warning enough. Perhaps I should lock that image into place and remember that he does not feel the same, and that he will not give me any compassion or love, but I don't because I know he will, irrespective of the fact he's left me here. I wish I understood the instinct that tells me that. I wish I could explain it to myself and let it hold me in its warmth, but I can't, and yet nothing stops a smile from spreading onto my face at the erratic thoughts. He's out there somewhere, thinking of me. It doesn't matter that he's left, and it doesn't matter that he's confused, because I know he'll come back. He hasn't finished with me yet. I am uncompleted business, a work in progress. Try as he might, he won't be able to abandon whatever this is. He would see it as a journey incomplete, a venture uncontained. He's the one who has run, not me. It will irk the living hell out of him as he searches his own emotions, trying to deny them, just as I have done. Well, no more for me. This is what it is, and will be whatever it will become. My story will play out one way or another, either finishing with grand gestures of commitment or relegating itself to clandestine adventures alone. I will not control its destiny like I do everything else in my life. He will.

    I sit eventually, my feet propped up on the balcony as I relay the thoughts in my head into my notebook. It's cleansing in some ways, chaotic no doubt, especially without my pills or his aura to stabilise me, but it's instinctual to write it regardless. And all the time I do, I feel my mind willing him to walk back through the doors and rescue the moment from its unclear ending, my body screaming for the same resolution to its new ceaseless ache for him. But nothing happens as I continue writing, scribbling each and every jumbled thought that enters my head to try to find sense in it all. It comes eventually, though—the melancholy, the sense of abandonment in a moment of beauty. It flows so well after a while that I begin to lose myself in it, hardly thinking of Blaine at all in the present tense, rather imagining a love story unfold in my imagination that endures countless barriers, breaking through them with only one destination in mind. It makes my smile grow wider as I scrawl the words, imagining a future for a pair such as these. It reminds me of the beach at his house, and of the waves crashing in the background, two lovers walking together and overcoming whatever rationale keeps them separated. Sadism be damned. There is hope in these words, love that connects beyond the reality of the average existence. It binds in a more truthful way.

    I lift my head from my scribbles, gazing over the rooftops to the far side of the small town and remembering his words. He was right. It's full of honesty and trust, more so perhaps than the normal pronouncement of love. To give yourself to someone who wants to cause pain, needs to even, to offer them that with no recriminations and bathe in the glory of their honesty, too? That's a love unencumbered by restriction or temptation. It's a love offered without thought for its boundaries, but it's also something one needs to truly delve into to appreciate. It's something I have not yet done, not with any real sense of attachment, anyway. The thought makes me frown, my back rubbing against the metal chair to sense him there. I might have taken him inside me, felt him on my skin, and I might have had my hands chained, but I'm quite sure I haven't felt what he knows he can do, will do even. He knows the end of this journey, doesn't he? He's been there, knowing what he'll do to someone who offers themselves freely. That's why he's left. It's why he won't answer the question about loving before. He's scared. And because of that, it's all in his hands to bring himself back to me.

I'm not sure how much longer I sit here writing, but by the time I finish the last page of my notebook, I realise night's drawing in around me. Dusk settles over the town like a low fog, clouding what was sunny a short time ago and making me shiver against the evening chill. I pull my cardigan around me for protection against the cold. Maybe he's not coming back. Maybe he really has left me here alone to imagine fantasies that aren't real. I delve into my bag, searching for my phone in the hope that maybe he's sent a message, only to find that I have no power. Well, I suppose if he's not coming back then I need to find a hotel, or maybe even think about getting myself home somehow. I don't even know where we are. It's a town called Braysville. That's all I've got. The roads here were just back lanes, all off the beaten track giving me no idea where I am in relation to big cities, certainly not

Manhattan. I've done no travelling in America since I've been here, only the signings that the publishers pay for. I'm usually whisked there in whichever manner is quickest, not giving me any time to actually see any of the locations or ponder their merits. It's yet another thing that troubles me lately. For all my wealth, I'm not allowed time to discover the reason why I work so hard? It's as tiresome as the monotony of the same book after book I've been producing, draining what little of my soul I have left.

    I stand up, looking over the barrier down onto the street to see if there are any motels around. There are none that I can see from here, but there has to be one somewhere, so I resign myself to that fact and scoop my notebook into my bag, ready to head on with my life to some degree and leave, but I can't. My feet don't want to. They want to stay here and wait, still trying to tell me that he will be back. It's the same sensation that told me he'd rescue me. It's in my guts, low down, somehow connected to my feet at this moment and refusing to let me move. I snort out a laugh, amused at my inability to control my own body because of Blaine. It's ponderous, making me forget all my questions and eventually just try to accept the instinctual pull. It's here, buried inside me and urging me to do the right thing by my body. A cocktail of both insecurity and advancement, rising though my veins and linking me to something I neither appreciate nor am quite ready for. It's wondrous really, a defining of something other than the norm. Almost reminiscent of past lives, telling me I'll find the path eventually regardless of my current confusion.

    The door opens behind me. I hear it and tilt my head as I keep staring out at the view, my arms resting on the rail's edge. It's him. I know it is. I can tell by the quake that flutters my skin regardless of the space between us. It intensifies the feeling inside my bones, wakening them and reminding me of the feel of him holding them. Such strength lingers in his grip. Some would call it bruising, maybe even define it as simply a murderous touch, but having listened to my insides, having registered the bond that's happening, I can't say it's to do with the pain he causes. No, it's the holding that's more relevant this time. I can feel it, as if it wants to engulf my torrid mind, emptying it of its concerns and trials. It's releasing in some ways, elevating me past the constancy of multiple names and words. It calms me, making me see only him inside there. Him and his mind.

"I need to know more about you," I say softly, wanting nothing more than for him to accept that and let me find my way inside him too.

"Push, push, push," he says, two of his footsteps easily closing the distance to nothing at all.

His aftershave wafts past my nose, the scent of wood smoke immediately flooding me with ideas I have no right to consider, but I do anyway. I imagine the ability to lie with him and talk of futures together, smiling as I do and remembering his tone when he came inside me. And then again when he wiped my back, his hands as soft as velvet when he remedied the pain he'd caused.

"I need to be inside your head, Blaine. Let me in or take me home."

There's silence for a few minutes as I keep looking out across misty old buildings, some near to crumbling with the town's weight upon them. It seems to go on forever as I wait for him to reply, but I've said all I will. For this to continue, for me to get my story and invest myself in whatever this is as well, I want more than a teacher now. I want him. He feels it as much as I do. And I know it without doubt now because he has come back. He's right here, his hands probably lodged in his pockets as he weighs up what to say next. I don't need words from him, not ones that intend to play games or toy with me. I want the truth, all of it, whatever it might be. I want whichever Blaine Jacobs he doesn't release to any other women.

    His fingers suddenly slide around my waist, drawing me back to him as he leans to rest his chin on my shoulder. The relief that shudders through me is palpable, surprising me, and making me gasp for air as he increases his hold. It's a thud of contact, his groin lined up perfectly with my backside, his chest smothering my back again and making me feel tiny in his arms as the other wraps around me, too. And then his lips brush my cheek, the softness of them only helping me conceive more ideas of warmth and love. They sigh out of me, as whimsical as the images of beaches and dreams. As heartfelt as they've ever been.

Chapter 18

BLAINE

" I want her to watch me," comes out of my fucking mouth as Delaney walks the length of his bar and then fiddles with one of his sub's outfits.

"What?" I'm not surprised by the blatant expression of astonishment that looks back at me, but it's the right decision whether he thinks it or not.

"Bring one of the pain sluts in, or several. Make her watch." The guy half hesitates, then refocuses on his task of tightening a corset.

"Interesting technique," is the eventual response, hardly audible above the classical bass blaring out into the room. I swivel on the bar stool, trying to find a better option than the one my fucked up brain is considering.

"It's not a witticism, Delaney," I mumble, wandering to the other side of the room in thought.

Three women pass me in the twenty-five foot distance, any of whom should be useful for the kinds of things I'm thinking about. And I half turn for the third, ready to deliver what my hands have been thinking about the entire journey here.

"It sounds like it to me."

I sigh and continue walking, remembering the way Alana looked at me as I take a seat by the far wall, her eyes begging for something she neither understands nor will be able to handle when the time comes for niceties to be dispensed with. I barely recalled the need to choke her where she stood at the restaurant, both in awe of her offering and disgusted with my reaction to it. Fuck, she'd smelt so good, her chest heaving under the realisation of the love between us. And it is fucking love, too. Always has been, right from that moment beneath the water. I saw it then as I let her feel herself drowning, and I feel it now, even though I've tried every technique to deny it. I fucking hate it. It stinks of moral obligations and responsibilities I'm barely ready for, let alone happy about. And yet it floods me with hope, too, reminding me of Eloise and her open soul, waiting for me to destroy it with both hands should I choose to.

"Why would you make her watch?" Delaney eventually asks, sitting himself opposite and flicking the top button on his collared shirt.

"She needs to know. I'm not doing it again unless she knows." I'm not. It doesn't matter the way her eyes plead, and it doesn't matter that she's wound her way into my heart, leaving me no ability to fight the thoughts that circulate there.

"Eloise knew. What difference does it make?" I laugh at the idea of Eloise knowing anything. She was young, in love, and addicted to pain. What happened between us was neither right nor honest. I never loved her, never made the promises I'm considering with Alana, and I never gave her the chance to see that what she was falling into was wrong on so many levels.

"I never gave Eloise a chance to make a choice, and you know it. She was too young, and so was I. She didn't know what had hit her until it was all too late." Delaney smiles, his drink sinking down his neck as he watches on and waits for more explanation. "She was my student. One I should have looked after. Instead, I took every opportunity to use her with no regret or thought for the consequences." The thought saddens me as her eyes still glint in my mind softly, regardless of my constant attempt to quash them. "It's not something that will be happening again. Alana deserves better than what I did to Eloise."

"Why?"

I'm not shocked by the question. It is Delaney after all. The man's a never-ending torrent of confessions, but I am surprised by my own inability to give a succinct answer as I stare at prying eyes. I turn my gaze out into the church to avoid the inquisition, considering the depravity of the small gathering in full swing instead and wondering why the air seems thin. Lacking. It makes me smile to myself, realising its lacking her as I remember her breath mingling with mine.

"See, good man." Hardly good. Perhaps better than previously, certainly older and wiser, but these hands are still as aberrant as they've always been. They might even be worse now they've been contained for so long, something I try not to concede to as I watch them turn over in front of me.

Delaney snorts and leaves me, his frame owning the floor as he wanders away, barely acknowledging the sub who crawls by his feet the entire way.

"Where is she now?" he calls back, as he picks up a chain and hooks it onto the little sub's collar. "Pretty thing, aren't you?" he says, cooing at her and then slapping her face so hard she tumbles to the floor, groaning with desire. The whole scene makes me gaze for a second, assimilating the vision and trying to understand its lack of transparency. I don't. I may have tried to fit into its diversity and find a place in its hierarchy, but I've never been truly at ease with it. Dominants and submissives. A woman or man on their knees, happy to concede and admit their needs beneath hands willing to help them through it. I understand its phycology intimately, proving its definition has a right to exist. And there isn't a thing, substance, tool or art form within the scene that I haven't mastered, but all this isn't what I am. I'm neither Dominant nor a Master. I know that. I'm not interested in the process nor do I deserve the title. Delaney does. He's everything a good Master should be. Sane, lucid in his requirements and precise in his delivery, turning his hand to whatever someone needs from him. The man works for the harmony of his subs, resolutely resurrecting them to something more than before. What he doesn't do is fly free within their destruction, ready to demolish with only selfish endeavours in mind. And, unfortunately, at base instinct, and regardless of the years confining it, sadistic predilections still explode inside my mind rather than the want or need to reconstruct. It just waits there, ready to humiliate and shame someone. Hurt them, purposely, with a sentiment only comparable to abhorrence. Of what, I don't know, still, even after years of scrutinising and analysing the thoughts. Nothing is kind as a result of whatever it is that continually lays dormant inside me, though. Nothing is done with a purpose to allow love to shine. It's only ever about the decimation of someone's frame, the need to watch them bleed and scream. "Blaine? Where is she?"

"I sent her home," I murmur, still too far inside my own mind to care what Delaney thinks. "Tyler took her." All I can suddenly see are her eyes looking back at me, her ass in the air as she struggled to pull herself from my grasp and get to what she believed was the safety of Delaney's hands. Perhaps they are safer in some way, certainly more restrained, anyway. I look at the floor area leading into the main nave, gazing at the lectern with a small spiral staircase behind it, then follow the turn of the metal as it snakes down to the floor again. Of all the places for love to eventually complicate me, Delaney's church is the last place I thought it might happen.

"And you thought that was practical, why?" For escape. So she can realise what she's doing and remove her need to return if she wants to. Love is a connection she doesn't understand in this instance. She doesn't know what it will mean for her skin or her state of mind when she lets me on her, telling me she loves me for it.

"You know exactly why I'm doing it this way. You know what happened with Eloise. You want it to happen again?" Delaney immediately seems affronted as he walks back, his hackles rising and ready to fight his own defence. He needn't bother. He's not the one who killed someone. I shake my head at him, signalling my own contrition before an argument starts.

"That was before, Blaine. You're different now," the guy eventually says quietly, sitting and tumbling his glass around in his hands as he watches the liquid spin, irritability written all over him. "And it never would have happened had I been there." I hold up my hand, defusing my friend's irritation before morbidity takes hold and sends the whole discussion to an emotionally driven diatribe. It seems I'm quite capable of doing that on my own anyway, my eyes still roaming the spot she'd screamed on as I remember her strength fighting at me. "Can you at least give me a reason?"

"What?" I have, haven't I?

"A reason why you shouldn't just tell her what happened last time?" I remove my eyes from the floor, levelling them at Delaney and considering the virtues of just telling her and seeing what she does with the facts. "Why don't you? I'm assuming, given the way you backed off from her, that you think this is love. Love conquers all." I doubt it does in reality, but Delaney does have more experience with the emotion, so perhaps there is an element of truth to his words. "You came inside her, Blaine. You never come in anything. I heard the fucking groan from the back of the church." I sit back, suddenly ready, for some reason, to rip the guy's body from his head at the thought of him listening to something private. "When was the last time? At all since Eloise?" The thought alone rallies more visions of intimacy, including the way Alana kisses me. It's so much more than Eloise. She's vibrant, assailing me with an acceptance and longing Eloise never rivalled. And the way her delicate fingers grip into my back as she takes another battering, pulling me closer and warming something inside that doesn't deserve any attention, it's incomparable. Nothing like Eloise.

My gaze travels to the lectern again, the eagle at the top branching its wings in a display of open acceptance to its congregation. "If you admit you love her, I might help. Why you didn't tell me in the first place, I don't know. I thought she was just another toy, an amusement."

I sigh again and close my eyes, willing one of these women dancing around to cause enough curiosity to challenge Alana's hold over my mind. Not one of them does. Not the slut grinding on another one. Not the one by Delaney's feet. There's nothing in here but the sound of her voice, the resonance of her groans, and the sight of her barley able to articulate her words as she told me she loved me.

"You haven't answered."

"I don't have to answer anything," I snarl out, wondering how much she'll ask of me. She wants inside my mind. She said that, said she wanted to know more, that she won't carry on without access to the haunting memories.

Delaney sighs this time. It's loud enough to cause another one of his subs to come running to the rescue, presumably offering an ass to spank should the need arise. I wish it were that simple.

"Will she sub?" he asks, his hand flicking at something on the table.

"With enough patience from me, yes." Something I'm not entirely sure I can handle, or even want if I'm honest. It makes me look at the brown haired girl at Delaney's feet again, considering the inclination and wondering if that's the only route forward for us.

"Do you want her to?" The direct question is enough to make me stand and point at the exit, my feet narrowly avoiding the woman beneath my own feet offering up services I'm not the least bit interested in. Delaney nods, not bothering to avoid the hand of one of them as his foot lands. There's a small scream, which only results in her being glared at for inanity.

"I want the fight. You know that. The brat is always more inspiring to me. It's immaterial whether she bows down or not." I pocket my hands and walk, unconcerned with the fate of anything in this building. "That's why she needs to see before she makes a choice to go further. I need her to see the truth." Because the only thing of any relevance is my purple haired madam, one who's shown enough reverence to offer herself into the unknown for me. Even if it is for a story she doesn't know the ending of.

We continue through the nave, heading along the route I carried her through, desperate to get some food inside her so she could rebuild her strength.

"Delaney, why did you end your relationship with Flick?" The man chuckles as he wanders along beside me, more than likely amused at my need to discuss love's endless turmoil.

"Flick ended it, not me."

"Why? You never did tell me."

"She wanted more than I could give her. All things I wasn't prepared for at the time."

"Still?"

"Still. Tabitha is more manageable. And I'm not grown up enough."

Hmm. The thought makes me imagine Alana and her future, wondering if she has a view to where it's heading. Presumably it has never been imagined under the hands of a sadist, let alone becoming part of a community she deems revolting. I picture her fingers typing, her hands furiously scribbling her notes and relaying her version of a story. She's probably there now, continuing to depress levers and stain her fingers further with the ink I've provided for her. Maybe she'll be remembering the reality of life without me, relishing it and enjoying her sense of freedom again. Or perhaps she's as lost as I am now, simply remembering the feel of our skin together and sighing.

"Where then?"

"What?" I reply, as we walk out into the fresh air, the dull sounds of the beat dispersing behind us as Delaney closes the doors to his home.

"Where do you want this meeting to happen?" I don't know, and the vision of the church suddenly fills me with thoughts of anything but dirty meetings, rather offering a saintly glow that shouldn't be anywhere near the fucking place.

"Why the hell do you live here?"

"I'm a priest," he replies, mock shock encompassing his face. "Where else would I live?" I suppose the man has a point—not that he is, but the place does suit him nonetheless. "It's the same reason why you have a home on the coast. It suits your disposition." I frown at the man, not understanding the likeness. "Destructive." The word makes me snort, conceding the analogy as I begin walking down the steps to leave. "You could make a home there, Blaine. You could be at one with her if you choose to be. It only takes an element of concession. And frequent confessions, obviously." I smirk back at the guy, wandering the path towards his car. "Go on holidays. Walk in the sand. Forget the rest of the world exists?" The thought is more appealing than I've previously given credence to, making me turn back to look at Delaney's smiling face. "It's alright to fall, my friend."

Is it?

I scan the cemetery, reminding myself of Eloise again and wondering if I should go and visit her grave, the same one I've banned myself from. Perhaps she'll have the answers.

"Find a club, the dirtier the better, somewhere I haven't been before," I call back. Alana hates the dirt, and that will show her the whole sordid monstrosity of what she's about to become a part of. It *is* obscene in some respects, and it *is* vile in its own way, and she *is* leagues above those levels of depravity regardless of how much I want to debase her.

"Sable?" Delaney asks, his feet slowly coming down the steps, as if the emotive conversation isn't finished with. It is. But Sable Jennings? I raise a brow in thought, still surveying the grounds and imagining Eloise's haunted eyes staring up at me from beneath the ground. Sable is something I've had plenty of fun with on occasion. Someone who laps up every strike and cut with the precision of a wild banshee in heat. I muse the memory of her body, somehow merging both her and Eloise, thinking of the scars crisscrossing their frames, ones they'd both begged for. The thought hardens my cock in its confines, making me wish Alana was within feet of me, not the hundred kilometres I've purposely put between us.

"Or something like her. As long as it bleeds, Delaney. You choose." I turn from the continued advance of emotion related questions, ready to leave the ground exactly where it currently is, and suddenly far too absorbed in my own state of fucked up arousal to talk over the topic any more. "In fact, bring five of them. Just organise it."

~

The image of Eloise's body didn't leave me as I got in the car, nor did it leave as I travelled the distance back to my house. It didn't leave me when I got there either, and it hasn't left me as I've tried to sleep, no matter the come I've splattered into the shower hoping to rid myself of the thought. It just keeps taunting me with blurred imagery, morphing Alana's head onto the Eloise's skin, the tone of the two completely contrasted to each other and raging recklessness into an otherwise levelled mind. It makes me toss and turn, my fists balling the sheets and ready to rip shreds out of anything that comes within feet of me.

Eventually, I sit upright, scrubbing my face and watching the moon hover over the ocean as I slide to the end of the bed. A drink might help, one with half a tonne of Temazepam in it to soothe the visions away. I move further forward, my bare feet hitting the hardwood and reminding me of reality at last. Here is real. The moon is real. The light splintering in and reflecting off the walls is real. It makes me pull in a deep breath, searching for more shards of reality as I gaze around. Nothing is any more relevant than the moon and the vast expanse of the ocean before me, causing me to get up and wander towards it. It cleanses me, rendering all other images to nothing but distant memories while reminding me of my own control. I've managed this, contained it. I still can.

The water crashes against the cliffs below as I slide the door open quietly and step out onto the deck, a bolt of wind wakening my body further as it hisses across exposed skin. I just stand still, letting it whip over muscles and revive them from their languished dreams. But try as I might, and regardless of the moon filling the sky with nothing but light, I can't rid myself of Alana's darkening eyes or the feel of her in my hold as we'd slept. She's uplifting, bolstering. How, I can't grab hold of. The words escape me. It's simply an irrational thought, satisfying me with a sense of comfort in a loneliness I've not felt before her. I miss her.

The realisation makes me smile as another wave crashes against the steps leading to the beach. That I miss someone is enough to broaden my smile, her offering seeming to give me a purpose other than just a memory of the dead.

I turn for the house again, padding the boards and then hesitating as I grab at my jeans, wondering what I might say should I just arrive unannounced in the middle of the night. The thought alone makes me laugh to myself, more than intrigued at the sense of boyish charm radiating out into the open from depths unknown. Anxiety and trepidation, both things I've never felt before now, neither of which are either comfortable or endearing, and yet in some ways, both of which are enamouring because of her. I snatch up some clothes, slowly pulling them on and challenging every fucking movement because of what the suggestion means. Commitment. A joining I should be scaring her away from, not persuading her into. I've already organised it with Delaney and had her driven home so she can think clearly, and now I'm going to turn up in the middle of the night and hold her closer? It makes me stop altogether, discarding the shirt before I've slid my arms into it and looking around the house in search of reason. It's as silent as ever, the only sound the low rumble of the sea and the occasional crash of the winter ravages coming for its structure. It all feels cold, the same sense of cold I normally enjoy. Its barren echo is usually more than enough to silence my mind. It condenses thought, making me immobile within the confines of its walls, quieting the animal inside. Why an entirely new feeling is currently diffusing the air around me, I don't understand. It makes me walk away from the bedroom, wandering the darkness in search of whatever has changed. Nothing has. The rooms still pass by, one by one displaying their heartless interior. I touch the wall by the second lounge, slowly looking around the doorframe and remembering her inside there. I can still hear the tapping of the machine. Still smell her arousal. Still see her look of horror as I drenched her, and then the unadulterated bliss that followed, as I'd put my fingers inside her for the first time. And I can still sense my own rage as I backed the steps away from her, her body taunting me as it writhed, broaching a subject I'm still not ready to show her, regardless of my need to do so.

I hover, part listening to the ocean and part wanting to go back into the bedroom, put my clothes on, and get to her as fast as the car can get me there. The only thing keeping my feet planted in place is the correct thing to do. Some semblance of honouring a hierarchy I don't want to respect in the slightest, even if I have employed the sentiment myself. The thought of her burns my skin, making any element of the control I'm hanging onto near impossible to maintain. Love burnishes; it appears. It glints and throws relevant thought into chaos, as does my own normally deviant mind. The two will be catastrophic, akin to the sea outside as it batters shores and then bathes the glorified in its fucking painful salt. *Eloise.*

I suck in air and turn from the hall, intent of heading back to bed for an attempt at some rest. Now is not the time for adolescent trips of sentiment or love. She can make that decision afterwards, perhaps honouring me with one more chance at her lips before she withdraws and makes the right choice for her. But the stars from the large redundant den stop me as they shine in the sky, making me check my own mind for something to cling on to. They fill the darkening sides of the skyline, reminding me of paths as I trace the lines of constellations with my eyes and walk into the space. They all lead back to her. It makes me smile again, thinking of the way she crossed her legs on the bed, announcing that she wasn't afraid of me, that she was just writing a story. And how scary could I be anyway? I'm just a man. *"You're just a man, Blaine."*

I don't deserve it. I know that, but it doesn't stop me drawing back the sliding wall, exposing the dusty armoury as I do and thinking of her in here. Lines and lines of implements, all crafted to inflict the greatest pain. Each one used. Each one worn well against flesh and still bloodstained, long after they've been cleansed of the physical evidence. I flick my gaze to the stars again, immediately seeing Eloise alongside the moon, her frame hovering in the open doorway ready to descend to the sea for comfort after the event. The thought wakes my fucking cock further as I turn back to the wall, my fingers dragging casually along the display of riggings and tools. *Push, push, push.*

I turn and cross the room to the opposing wall, turning the screws to bring the hooks out of their sanctuary, readying them for use without thought perhaps. I don't know, but the calm that falls over me as I methodically ratchet them into position is purgative, ridding me of any concern other than Alana and her body. Love, it appears, is a challenging dilemma. I back away from the wall, staring at the hooks now embedded into steel and the drawers open for play. A multitude of sin, diverse in its array and yet so unfathomably simple to a sadist's mind. The thought of her fingering objects, her body swaying between each one as she tests everything for its reasoning, makes me smile wider. I'm almost damn well grinning at the image of it, her responding confusion making her ask all the whys she has in her vocabulary. And I'll answer this time. Not by simply showing, but by talking it through with her, by explaining so she understands the depths of sadism. I'll reward her offering with an insight few have so she can write it, use it, understand its merits and harness them into written verse for the world to see should they want to.

    I press on the safe, carefully punching in the numbers and letting the doorway swing open. Her reward, the thought makes me chuckle as I step inside and glance round at the shelves piled with money. She can have this, too, if she gives me what I need. She might as well. I don't use it. I haven't touched it since my parents' deaths. I neither value it nor levy it for anything other than its grimy positioning within these walls. It's simply paper, something to be used as a necessity not enjoyed. No holidays, no frivolous spending. Perhaps it will help Alana enjoy the journey, help her see it as acceptable. I can both teach, train and care for her, giving her all that I have along the way and honouring her for the love she offers. Perhaps learning how to do the same in reply.

The realisation makes me back out of the room and turn to move faster along the corridor toward the bedroom again, my hand reaching for my shirt as I keep looking upward and hold her smile in my thoughts. She's there, in a bed, waiting for someone to show her her story, perhaps give her a surprise ending. Maybe I can, with time. Maybe we'll find a route through what is to come. And maybe this time I'll control it, maybe not even need it. I've worked hard enough on it, and I won't know unless I try. I won't know unless this feeling inside me is given a chance to engage something other than just the sadistic thought process I normally live within. Time is what we need. A chance to try at something new. For the first time, and because of her, he want a love I've never considered rational before now. I want the normal other people live in. I can taste its effect on me already as I remember her lying in my arms, her body breathing in sync with mine and her smaller hand linking her fingers into mine as she slept. I knew then, and I knew in the pool, and I know now.

I watch my reflection in the mirror as I button the last of my shirt, still questioning what the fuck I'm doing and not giving a fuck about the answer anyway. I'll sleep with her, hold her, tell her how beautiful she is and then fuck my way through her, forging us closer and not allowing her escape. Maybe I'll need to break her for that to happen, decimate her even, but she is as much a part of this as I am. And when she holds me, when her lips meet mine and she rolls her tongue, her nails digging in at the same time, she fucking knows, too. Kink be damned. This is about so much more than kink, or sadism. It's about love, and about a feeling so reflective I don't know why the fuck I've been denying it. It wrecks me, tearing my insides around and making me crazy for her. I haven't been tossing and turning because of what I want to do to her, or what I've been dreaming of. I've been restless because she simply isn't here to hold me still, just as she had done last night.

Snatching my keys from the table, I walk out along the corridor towards the door, wondering how long it will take to get there and considering phoning her in case she isn't even there. Then I carry on regardless of whether I should phone her or not. I know where she lives, and she will either answer the door or not. If she isn't there, I'll call her and make her come back. Or find her. I don't give a second thought to the way I look as I slam the car door and began the journey, swigging at a bottle of water and wishing it were a bottle of Jack instead. Fucking nerves. I laugh, letting them crawl over my skin and remind him that I'm as human as the next man. If not a little more fucked up than most. The sensation makes me laugh so much I nearly miss the turning, my feet slamming on the brakes as I haul the wheel around the corner. Christ, it's like being in senior year again, although only barely the same. Senior year, in reality, had been nothing more than studying and fucking my way through anything that registered as motivating, hoping that I'd be able to come in it. I hadn't come in anything, not in a cunt anyway. But I can in hers, and it's waiting there for me to do it again, making me speed my foot further onto the peddle and picture a reason to use the wealth accumulated. Maybe Delaney is right. Holidays and private islands. Walks along a beach for no other reason than the walk, holding hands. Laughter, the sort that makes the air rattle and stomachs convulse. It's so long since I've been a part of that, if ever.

The thought makes me frown, remembering the way Eloise had tittered and giggled at me when I gave her just a small piece of my soul, mainly to keep her coming back for more of what I wanted her to take. It slows my acceleration, making me, once again, question the merits of what I'm doing as the houses begin to drift by. I hardly see them, choosing to focus on the blue eyes staring into parts of me I've not allowed viewing before. My lips tug upwards again as the drive slows to a quiet meander, sensing her crawling in deeper somehow. It makes me look at my hands, the tension in them as strong as it always is, but they suddenly hold a softer yield to them, one that wants to caress. They tap lightly on the wheel, feeling the leather in my grasp and remembering her quivering beneath them. It isn't simply a memory, though. It affects me, my heart already stretching the distance between us to feel her again. I want her wrapped around me, for no other reason than the feeling of her warmth against my skin.

The sound of a man's dulcet tones drift around me as I turn on the music, as much as the surroundings do. It appears that no amount of concentration on anything makes her eyes disperse, nor her smile. She glows in my mind, radiating inside it and shining something new at me rather than the normal clarity of everyday mundanity. And the moon still hangs low in the sky as I gaze at it, reminding me of the one night we've had in bed together as I watched the light filter in on her. I'd hardly slept, choosing to watch her instead as her frame settled back into me, her purple stripes irritating my face and her stained fingers making me frown. I'd put that staining there, just as I will continue to do, opening her up to a world filled with unimaginable immorality. And in this moment, and probably because of the way my heart reacts to the thought of not having her, I couldn't care less. She will either enjoy my tainted ethics, immersing herself in them and dwelling with a transparency she's never known before, or she won't. Either way, I won't let her go. I can't. Not now I've felt a pull towards sensations never set free before. She'll be made to watch and then make her choice, the latter of which will mean nothing to whether we see each other again or not. I'll fucking sit on a beach just to spend time with her, not touching her for fear of breaking this connection if that's what it takes. But I won't lie about what I am. Not with her. Not this time.

Eventually, the rumble of the bridge pulls me from thought, a car horn blaring out as I drift over the lines and narrowly avoid crashing against the barriers. It makes me snort out as I straighten the car, considering the last time anything had made me deviate from sound, level-headed thought. Nothing has for some time, nothing after Eloise, anyway. And I can't remember ever being coerced in thought by her, either. She simply existed to be used. Toyed with. She was my exploration into what my hands could achieve when something was willing enough to comply. She debased herself willingly, allowing me every deviance I could amass with a trust I didn't deserve.

The sight of the funeral emerges in my mind, something finally managing to push Alana's smile aside for a few moments. One hundred and sixty guests, all dressed in black, her mother wearing a veil, her father crying, and Eloise's young sister staring blankly into the ground. I'd cowered a long way back, skulking between trees in an attempt at apology as I watched them lower the coffin. No one knew who I was, the family barely recognising anything other than the sight of their precious child being taken from the earth long before her time. They all cried and wailed, some of them murmuring prayers and nodding at the Preacher in thanks for the service. Morbid was the only consideration I'd given the show. A pretence at sorrow and grief. Eloise wasn't happy in life. She'd longed for death, chartering me further into her murder with every offer of submission. She lathered her old scars with concealer daily, hiding the truth from those who loved her while begging me to wipe it away so she could show the world how miserable she was. Fake parenting, both of them with little to no desire to see the truth staring them both in the eyes. The best schools, pushing her to achieve their dreams rather than her own. The finest clothes so she could keep up with appearances needed for a family such as theirs. The hour I'd stood there had filled me both with rage and regret, part wanting to tell them it was their fault she was in that ground, and part wanting to throw myself on top of her coffin and have them all stab me for her murder. They'd sent a troubled young girl straight into the hands of a young, fucked up sadist, telling her everything would work itself out when she graduated, and not having the slightest idea what they'd sent her to. I was supposed to guide her through her psychology degree, offering her a path out of her own screwed up nightmare of a mind. Instead, I'd immediately noticed the scars on her inner thighs, a summer's breeze blowing her skirt up in the wind, and then used them for my own depraved compulsions, enjoying her torment as I'd led her further into darkness.

  I'd eventually walked away from the performance quietly, promising myself I'd never touch someone like that again. It might have been a heart attack caused by a weakened valve no one knew about, but I'd still forced the heart under attack, still caused the fucking thing to stop under the pressure I'd put her through. And fuck, I can still feel her skin under these hands now, the leather in my fingers reminding me of anything but Alana. I can still feel her heart thundering away against my chest as she'd taken everything I'd given, her screams bellowing out into the deep, dark forest I'd taken her to until it had eventually just stopped and she'd gone lax in the chains. I hadn't even noticed, too engrossed in her body to care whether she was breathing or not, and too invested in my own amusement to recognise her demise. She'd just hung there, naked and warm. Still offering everything she could with her body, regardless of her death, and winding me further into an adolescent frenzy I should have controlled.

I pull the car over as the sight of her floods me with regret once more, unable to carry on driving for fear of powering straight into the nearest wall. Time might have moved on, the coroner's verdict ruling death by fatal heart incursion when she was found in her room days later, but it still didn't remove the facts. I killed her, accidently maybe, but it was still murder. A life taken.

The torment makes me stare vacantly into the blazing lights of Manhattan, hardly recognising streets or passing traffic. It doesn't matter how I've controlled it since, or how I've protected countless others from the same fate. And it isn't relevant how often I've trained new versions of myself, guiding them from their deviance and channelling it into something they can use efficiently, hoping to contain their mind's advance at the same time. I'm still a killer. A man who has killed under the delusion of pleasure, actually enjoyed its resonance until I noticed the death dangling in chains before me, and only then because the come spat inside her prone body ended the release.

Nothing's changed. I deserve nothing, certainly not happiness.

Chapter 19

ALANA

I wish I was sleeping well. I really wish I was, but I'm not. I'm up and pacing around my apartment at five am, not able to concentrate on anything, let alone write. I started the moment Tyler dropped me off, relaying as much logic into the words as I could fathom on a real laptop, but then Blaine started to creep into my bones, stopping my flow without any reason. It was all there, all coming so easily and drawing my story out to another level of brilliance and then, just nothing. It was as if the story just halted, maybe unfinished, or as if some part of it was yet to be mapped out. So I tried to sleep, thinking that maybe a night's rest would clarify the story. It didn't.

I stirred and pitched, barely snatching minutes with my eyes truly closed. I showered instead and scrubbed at every orifice I own, my own fingers tracing holes only he's touched lately as I tried to rinse him away. That didn't work either. It only amplified the way his hands move, making me follow the same lines until I made myself come by just imagining him on me again. Sounds emanated in that cubicle, ones that came from my own mouth, the one I was trying to reoccupy as my own voice, as in, not belonging to him anymore. And even after that was finished, my feet stepping out of the shower so I could stare into the mirror at the wounds on my back, I still felt empty. It's like my own orgasm wasn't mine. It was lost, haunted because he wasn't inside me. Perhaps if I wasn't quite so concerned with why I wanted him inside me again it might help, but I am. It's all I can think about, as if some part of me is missing and barely holding on to reality without him here. It's horrendous, affecting areas within me I can't even compute as real.

It's a loss, deep down, as if the very essence of me has been taken away leaving me lonely and vacant of life. It's also the single most unhealthy feeling I've ever encountered, making me wish he was here and not knowing what to do with myself because he isn't. I'm actually enraged by its hold on me, maddened that I suddenly can't control my own thought process without some kind of guidance from him. And it's not like he tells me what to do, well, maybe he does, but it's as if my ability to make a decision is absent, just like my story. Do I want to go out, stay in? Walk, sit, stand? I'm not even sure if I know what I want to drink as I stare at the old typewriter, nibbling my inky fingers, let alone if I even want a drink.

He was right, I suppose. Sending me home with Tyler has given me time to think. Although, it was the last thing I expected up there on that roof. He didn't push me away. He didn't create a space between us again. He just kept holding on to me, eventually pushing me against the rail to hold me still as he whispered things, dirty things. Deplorable things. Things that made my eyes widen and my crotch clamp closed. He just held me and talked, listing all the activities, for want of a better word, that he wanted to do, more than likely withholding countless other endeavours inside his mind. They were terms I'd never heard before, objects I'd never conceived as useable, and then there were blood and liquids. He mentioned them so many times, as if they were the embodiment of what he needed from a woman who lay beside him. And he said all these things as he kissed my cheek and let his breath flurry over my skin, reminding me of the peace associated with such acts. He said it as he forged his cock against my arse, levering it against me and softly groaning as he carried on elaborating on his desires. Crosses, whips, canes, cuffs. A bench, blades, shackles and rope. He whispered in such a way that my heart beat faster with his cadence, the roll of his words becoming like a litany of lust against my skin. And then, after his mouth stopped offering information, after he'd both aroused me and disgusted me, making me question everything my own mind was trying to regard as rational and love induced, he told me to go home and think, truly think about what I was proposing. I suppose it was his way of letting me go. His way of saying, 'don't come back unless you truly want this, all of this. All of me'. His way of releasing me back into the ordinary.

I'd just stared out into the town as dusk turned to the black of night, feeling like the very ground beneath me wasn't real. He made it feel that way with his hushed obscenities in my ear and his solid frame tugging me backwards against it. Blaine Jacobs, in those few minutes, made the abhorrent seem plausible. He made the vile seem enlightened, enjoyable even. He made me envision fingers delving and screams resounding, the lash of a whip connecting with flesh. Even the smell related to it lingered in my nose, regardless of his aftershave drenching me some clouded fog of lust. And he did it with nothing but his satin tone and his sense of ownership around me as he kept me still. He made the distasteful more believable than normality could ever be with just his words.

"Never fuck like a coward again, Alana."

Those had been his parting words as the car pulled away, Tyler behind the steering wheel and me in the back. I'd watched him stare at us leaving as the large, modern complex faded into the background, his eyes narrowed and his mouth restrained, as his jaw clamped closed. For once he didn't back away, but took steps after us, after me, his long legs clad in jeans as they moved and his jacket tossed over his shoulder. He looked so handsome, just like any other wealthy man. His dark hair tangled about in the wind, his clothes probably as expensive as money could buy, hanging in perfected falls on his frame, but we both knew better than to think he was just any other man. He stood there as a man quite alone in his irregular thoughts. A man who had just told me only a few of them, letting me into his unorthodox world and yet offering me a way out at the same time. The vision had made me smile, my hand resting on the window as if trying to reach him until he disappeared from view, the dust kicking up from the car the only thing left to see.

Alone.

And that's how I feel now. Alone. My adored apartment feels empty. My writing seems devoid of compassion or empathy, perhaps even commitment to its plot now I don't know where it is heading. It's as if the place, the writing, even I need filling with music or laughter, or any emotion rather than this cavity that reverberates around the space. Perhaps that's what I should do, just put some music on and let the sound lull me back to the words, hopefully forgetting his hold on me as it does. That's what I need to do. Try to do this again without him. That's what he sent me away for, isn't it?

It's exactly what I do, regardless of the fact that it's five am. I've put on a mix before I've thought any more about it. And now I'm dancing as I look out into the early morning sun that's rising, considering just throwing my clothes on, grabbing my laptop and heading out to the nearest coffee shop, because this isn't working. It doesn't matter that the music's loud, and it means nothing that I've chosen bright songs, hoping to lift my mood and flood myself with happiness. Nothing's changing. I'm still standing with an unfulfilled sensation as I slow my erratic jig to a more relaxed sway, imagining his arms wrapped around me rather than the sense of freedom I was aiming for. Fuck.

"Screw you." It's not a helpful proclamation. It's a lie, and if he were here he'd be smirking at me as I try to denounce his effect on me, probably offering his hands at me as an enticement as he slowly drew his clothes over his head. Why do they do that? Showing their muscles and their ripples. It's mesmerising. Hypnotic. It makes women stupid. It makes me stupid.

I huff out to myself, quickly crossing the room and flicking off the music with tuts coming from my lips. I don't know why I thought that would work. As if I could turn off Blaine Jacobs with some music. All it's done is paint the atmosphere with yet more visions of fucking and fingers. It's simply charged the air again, intensifying the sense that I'm alone, or more importantly, without him. It's enough to rile me further, making me cross into my bedroom to get dressed and find a way to write this all down. I'll go to the coffee shop on 42nd or maybe to the plaza and listen to the traffic. Maybe that'll push it back inside my head so I can put some sense into it all. Make my story work again without it affecting me personally so much. In fact, I'll call Bree. I've been meaning to do that anyway. I sent a text on the way home telling her I was travelling back, so she knows I'm about. And it's not like she'll be sleeping anyway. She's more than likely got a release going on, several probably.

A few minutes later and I'm out the door, leather laptop bag in hand and my phone plastered to my ear as I catch up on messages and emails. Several from the publisher. The first telling me about all the changes that have been made to covers on the Fidelity series, why, I don't know. They were perfect the way they were in my opinion, not that my opinion means anything to those people. Some of the others give me more meeting dates, probably so they can heap on more pressure for something I already haven't got time to achieve, let alone have more added to. One from my lawyer, something about clause 17, article 4b being in renegotiations. Good, it's about time they gave me some more leeway on who I have editing. And the last one asking why I haven't checked in with edits on the two Valerie books I should have handed over by now, from the very editor I can't stand. Well, screw her. I'm too invested in this new story to bother with that. And with the whole Barringer Fuckwit the Third thing going on, I couldn't give a damn anyway. What are they going to do? Tell me it's over? Unlikely. They make far too much money off my exhausted back for that. They took too much last year. I might have held an element of power at the negotiations, but it's still too much in my opinion. The thought is irritating enough for me to delve into my bag and pop some happy pills, searching for the energy I'm going to need to make it through another day on little sleep. Honestly, those visions of walking and talking with

Blaine seem more appealing by the minute. Holidays, beaches. Dipping my toes in that water that crashed against the beach at his house. Oh, that was lovely. It looked inviting, refreshing. He was different in those thoughts, his brow softer, his smile warmer. Shorts and a t-shirt, relaxed. A margarita in my hand as I lay on a towel, more than likely waiting for him to lift me up and toss me into the water. It makes me smile as I walk out onto the pavement, imagining him stripping off layers and showing me who he is, mind and body. Another huffs pouts through my lips as I turn and head for coffee shop, stabbing my phone as I do to end messages and phone Bree instead. I'm in love, aren't I? Properly. With someone who was not for falling in love with. And it's not like normal love, not that I really know what that feels like, but I'm sure it's deeper than that, something more than just average. I'm head over heels for someone I hardly know, and why? Because he's had himself inside me and shown me something? That's just lust. It's not that. It's something else.

"Sore?" is Bree's opening gambit, as I hear furious clattering in the background. A snort leaves me, my head nodding irrespective of my answer.

"Not at all."

"Liar." Maybe, but if I can't explain all this to myself, there's no way in hell I'm going to be able to explain it to her. I'm in no way ready to discuss the merits of aggressive fucking, because let's be honest, I've not even really entered the realms of BDSM yet. Well, apart from that strange sling I was put into to type, and the handcuffs, and being watched by others, which was stimulating in its own respect, but… "Whippy dick, or not?" Something dick. Beautiful, definitely, but whippy? Not yet.

"Bree, please. Professional," I reply, tugging my bag strap and looking through the traffic as I dodge it to cross the road, a smile plastered on my face at the thought of anything whippy.

"Seriously? You're not gonna give me all the deets?" No. "Because you can fuck off if you think I'm meeting with you so that you can sit in self-righteous smugness and not tell me all about Blaine's whippy dick." I smirk again, imagining the two of them meeting, maybe seeing Bree's face as he walks into a room and blows her mind apart with his never ending filthy mouth.

"Well, that's up to you, but I'm going down to Bluties," I say, still amused at the vision and dreaming up a scene in my mind. "I need to write somewhere that'll drown me in noise." Actually, thinking about it, the restaurant come coffee shop I met Blaine in originally would be good. It's nearer for her and there are booths at the front there. We could tuck ourselves away and watch the world go by in the window. It makes me wonder if it's open this early. "Do you know Carlucci's on Livingston Avenue?"

"Yep."

"Is it open for breakfasts?"

"Think so."

"Okay, well I'm heading there then. You want to come?" I ask, sidestepping a mother and her pram and changing direction, my eyes focused on my new destination. It's him again, isn't it? Making me do things without thought. I roll my own eyes at myself, trying to ignore the twitching down below as I stride on. Maybe it'll help, god only knows how, but something's got to.

"Okay. I'll be an hour."

And as usual the phone goes dead, indicating that Bree is either too busy to continue the conversation any further than she deems necessary, or fifteen messages need answering as she continues working three WIP's. It's probably all of the above at the same time. She'll be surrounded by her screens, having had about as much sleep as I have and desperately trying to make her life, if it could be called that, work. There's no life in this anymore. It's just a manic delivery of words, lobbed into the fold and then expertly teased until it leaves the reader gagging for more. I've been back in my world for only a short time and I can already feel my stress levels rising, winding me up into delivering more, achieving more. *More words, more words.* It's like a chant in my mind as I keep walking on, suddenly desperate to get to my destination, as I think about all the words necessary. My word count has been sorely lacking the last few days, and not only on this story. I can be as pompous as I like about the Valerie books, but I do need to do them, as well as Peter's. I have deadlines coming at me from all directions now I'm thinking about them again. None of which are being helped because of all the half ended stories backing up in my brain, as well as backed up on this laptop. I've at least three that need to be finished by the end of next month, ready for next spring. Those two that do need editing, regardless of my irritation with the fucking editor, and then there's this one in my mind, the one that won't bloody come anymore for reasons unknown. I'm running out of time, aren't I? I don't know what I've been doing taking a few days off for research purposes, if that's what I can call them. Falling in love? Being swept off my feet, sort of. Well, not really. Oh God, whatever. I haven't got time for it. Bree's right. My life is in this laptop, not out chasing strange dreams of romance, no matter how lovely they might be.

The thought halts my increasingly manic mind, as if Blaine's chastising me, making me stare into morning traffic and remember the sound of fabric tearing instead, and his voice tempting me into the unknown. It's a blind quiet. One just filled with him and his mouth again. A minute of calm. One that instantly nullifies the honking horns and engines revving as the garbage trucks start their daily jobs. I just keep walking towards the blue Carluccio's sign I can see, hoping to push him from my mind again, but I can't. It's a constant in there now, isn't it? He is. Nothing appears to be able to glide along without his voice commanding the thought, and the skies above me, the ones full of thunderclouds forming, are only asserting that sensation further into me. I feel like texting him and telling him to fuck off out of my head, or get back in it to full effect. I just want him to tell me how it's going to be. Sending me home? Bastard. Perhaps sensible, but it's not what I expected, or wanted, because all this other noise, the type that continues whenever he's not around, is deafening me again. It was quieter when I was with him, more focused on just him and me. Noiseless.

When I eventually head into the restaurant, I'm taken straight to exactly where I want to be sitting. The last booth on the left of the restaurant overlooks the road and through to the park beyond, the small offering of woodland a nice distraction from the grind of the daily commute. Yellow cabs pass by, the exhaust fumes beginning to be visible as traffic increases and slows the speed to barely a crawl.

Frankly, it would be quicker for most of these people to walk wherever they are going. It makes me groan at the thought of more walking as I relax back and dig into my bag, wondering if it's too early for a glass of wine to calm my frenzied thoughts. It's not something I've ever done. Normally my pills get me by and keep the momentum going, but a large glass of red seems more than useful at the moment. What harm would it be? Frankly, I deserve one after the last few days anyway. It's not everyone who goes under the hands of a sadist for research purposes. I stare around the restaurant, feeling slightly naughty for even thinking the thought, let alone asking the question of the rather hassled looking waiter who's busy running orders around. It doesn't stop me hailing him in the middle of his run back to the kitchen, though, and it doesn't stop me ordering a large glass of Sancerre either. He looks slightly stunned, but nods nonetheless, returning with it quickly and then scampering off to carry on with his other duties.

  It leaves me staring at the glass next to my laptop as if fires up again, my tablet laid alongside it and my phone adjacent to that as wifi begins hooking me up to the Internet and SM again for the first time in a few days. I can already hear the ping of emails and notifications coming at me, the flash of messenger going off constantly and announcing the delivery of, no doubt, dick pics galore.

  I sigh, already feeling the anxiety flowing through my soul and reminding me of the endless efforts I'm made to endure. I just want to write what I want to write. Talk to who I want to talk to. Be like I was when it all started. I want to love it again, enjoying it for what it is rather than this sense of business that's become all consuming and debilitating to creativity. And the longer I look at these machines endlessly beeping at me, the flurry of notifications increasing with every second passing, the more I want to close it all down and walk away. Less than twelve hours I've been back in my world and I'm already back to where I was before, albeit this time admitting it and realising there is something more to be sought after. It makes me reach for the wine, turn the sound off on all my technology and cross my legs to stare out into the road again as the rain starts to patter against it. Tired, so fucking tired. And the one story I want to write, the one that excites me, is not presently available, it appears. Blaine's made that happen. I don't know how, but he has. He's not here with me and therefore nothing's sparking my brain back into life. I should just shut all this off and get drunk. Perhaps then all this would change and transport me back to the young girl who dreamed of being an amazing writer. The one who made it with nothing more than late night ramblings as she tried to make her way through college, working Wattpad as if her life depended on it. She's the one I need, not this grown up version who pays bills and apparently has everything she needs. I have nothing. I have an apartment and clothes, but that's it. No life. Not even a sense of companionship other than Bree, and she's so lost in her own world, just like me, that she's barely present at all. I want whimsical again, like I was in college. I want love and creative flow. I want to dream and live, counting my blessings every day and remembering what life is for. Not this – my hand flicks at the machinery - whatever this is. Christ, we're just multiple personalities, manically driving forward and neither engaging in nor dreaming of reality. Well, I wasn't until Blaine Jacobs came along and tilted the world for me, proving its axis pretty fucking redundant without him controlling the spin of it.

I might be a bit blotto by the time Bree arrives and dumps her bag down on the floor, phone still attached to her ear and a shit eating grin spread across her face for some reason.

"What?" I spit out, unamused by her happy face and already signalling the waiter for more wine before he leaves. Apparently I've entered morose enthralment, choosing to deliberate the entirety of my ineffective existence rather than deal with changing it in any way. She flaps a hand at me, her nonplussed expression focused on her conversation with someone other than me.

"Really?" she says, her body slowly lowering to the booth seating as she drags out her laptop and starts setting up. I don't know why she's bothering. I've written zero words in the last hour or so while I waited for her, choosing rather to stare blankly at the world and imagine Blaine staring back at me with his dirty mouth ready for use. "That's phenomenal." The word sparks my interest a little. Nothing has ever been phenomenal in Bree's world, irrespective of the fact she makes a fortune. In fact, I don't think I've ever heard her use the word. "Yes. Okay." She listens some more, now smiling and writing something down on her notepad. "Okay, I'll see you then." She hangs up the phone, her body leaning back as she chucks the pen on the pad and keeps smiling at me.

"What's phenom…" I can't get the word out, so try again having swigged another gulp of wine and inched myself more upright. "Phonimal…" Oh, balls to it. What's the point? I give up, choosing to carry on with the wine drinking until she expands rather than attempting speech.

"Drunk, are we?" I blow a raspberry at her, unsure whether it's the effect I'm after or whether I've given up on speech altogether. The latter's probably better given the mood I'm in. "The fuck's up with you?" Life. Life is what's wrong with me, and the lack of Blaine Jacobs in it. Which is ludicrous. I've known him all of five fucking minutes and now I can't exist, think, or do anything without him? It's tragic. I'm a tragedy. My hands are trembling as I hold this fucking glass and I feel like Shakespeare is about to spout forth, listing some ode to missing hearts that beat only for the function of love. Perhaps I should leap from a balcony, hoping someone will catch me and make the hole in my heart stitch back together.

"Fuffing." I'm assuming that meant 'nothing', but I can't be bothered to change it, and she'll get the point anyway. All I want is this alcohol and some sleep, maybe mixed with some Blaine fingering for enlightenment of some kind. I could balance on his finger. It'd be nice, spinny. A snort leaves my nose, followed by some wine that must have still been in my mouth.

"The fuck, Lana?" Bree exclaims loudly. I look up to find her brushing the front of her cream sweater off, blobs of red dotting the surface of it. Whatever.

She looks at me for a while, not really saying anything other than what her eyes are attempting to communicate. I don't know what that is. I'm still too busy trying to say the word phenomenal in my head, occasionally attempting to mouth it. She might as well just get drunk with me and then we can all go to hell together, soulless and friendless, certainly loveless and weeping for things we shied away from rather than embraced as new and fulfilling. Oh god, why do I miss him so much?

"Well, did you at least get everything you needed?" she says, "'Cause it's clearly fucked you up, whatever it is." Fucked me up? No. This fucks me up. This unending noise that comes at me, this pressure and constant want for more from me. I haven't got any more. I can't do it anymore. It's all too much. There's not enough me time. There's no time for me or my life.

I nod at her anyway, thinking of all the things he has shown me and wanting nothing more than more of it.

"Did he hurt you?" Yes. No. Absolutely and irreversibly. He's changed me with pain, and his fucking eyes, and that mouth of his. I'm all changed with no ability to contain what I was anymore, or real enthusiasm to do so anyway. I'm a mess of confusions. Unfortunately, it's not something I can convey, though. I can't even speak, let alone tell her any of this at the moment.

"Come on," she says, closing the laptop she's only just opened and closing mine, too. I gaze at the move, agreeing with it entirely. Yes, close them all down. Stop the noise and just be. We should both just do that. We could sit in a bar somewhere, here even, for at least three days. I might need a bit more energy for that, though. The thought makes me reach for my happy pills, my body pitching as I try to aim for my bag and delve inside it. Two more should do, not that I know how many I've already had, but fuck it. What does it matter? I've got no one waiting for me anyway. I'll sleep it off eventually. Perhaps we could go dancing and sweat these shakes out of me. It's not like I can finish this fucking story anymore, is it?

The lid pops unpredictably, sending my pills sprawling across the floor as I stare at their spread, terrified at the thought of losing them. Before I know it I'm down on the floor, the wine glass launched and my hands picking at the little white things as they roll about, desperate to get them back in their container.

"Help me, Bree," I cry out, my fingers trying to reach each and every one of them. My pills, I need them all. They're mine. They help me contain it all. They keep me focused. I can't do this without them, and they're everywhere. People are here, covering them, possibly stealing them. Nothing happens but me still scrabbling about, banging a man's foot out of the way in case he's standing on one. It's just me and the floor, a sea of little white tablets scattered out in front of me as I crawl around between people's feet. Where have all these shoes come from? I can't see my pills. I need to. "Get out the fucking way," I snap out, slapping out at a pair of red Manolo's and growling when they don't get out of the damn way. I'll bloody throw up on them in a minute if she doesn't move. I swear I will. I glare up at her, my body pushing itself upright as I scoop another handful and try to steady myself. "Can't you move?" I snap, wondering if she's a mannequin or simply dense. She slowly turns, a look of utter disgust directed at me. I don't know why. Bloody woman. "My pills?" I say, pointing at the floor.

"Lana?" What? I swivel to see Bree, all our bags loaded onto her arm as she starts to walk out. "Time to go." I'm not going anywhere. I've got to get my pills. I'm straight down to the floor again, my chin colliding with the floor as I search under the chairs, finally finding another one, reaching for it and then crawling off towards another one before it gets trodden on. Something tugs my jeans, making me shoot backwards and bash my head on the table as I scuttle to get out. "You're making a fool of yourself," Bree hisses, her hand still attached to my belt and her voice as harsh a whisper as I've ever heard. What? I look around, scanning the crowd that seems to be looking directly at me.

"But my pills, Bree," I reply, slurring slightly but still not moving from all fours as I look around again. "I need them. You understand, don't you?" She doesn't answer, but she does. She takes them as much as me. We have to in order to keep going. I can't do it without them. It'll all fall apart if I don't get them inside me. They're the only reason I can keep going through the night. The schedule will collapse without them to help and I won't be able to keep up with the pressure. There are too many words needed. And too many people to be nice to. And too many stories to keep dreaming up. There are contracts and calendars. Timings. Distribution dates. Functions. Signings. Meetings and edits. The constant emails, the noise. It's all so fucking noisy. I need my pills for it all. I do.

"Lana, come on," Bree says again, her hand touching my shoulder. I shrug her off, irritated with her lack of help because no. I won't 'come on'. I need my pills. She should know. She should.

My hand slaps out at another leg as my head spins, moving it so that I can get to another shiny tablet that gleams from across the room at me. I must have nearly all of them now, some stuffed in my pockets, others being scooped into the little pot, my fingers trembling each time I try to keep them inside. They keep falling out. They keep dropping, tipping out again and making me scoop them up again. It's hard keeping them all contained, and the constant crawl round, all the time bashing people and trying to reach another one, keeps making me drop them all again. But I've got them all now, I think. They're all back with me. I'll be okay when I get the last one. My eyes scan the floor again, frantically searching the wood for any other pill that I've missed. I can't see any. There's only a sea of shoes and that one last pill that's rolled to the far side. The thought calms me a little, my head beginning to slow its spin as I crawl the final few feet to reach it. But before I get there, a hand picks it up from between a pair of black brogues. My knees stop crawling, annoyance and fear mingling as I watch the fingers lifting it up and away from me. Who's taking my pills? I'll scream. I will. They're my pills. Mine. It makes my eyes slowly creep up the legs, ready to fight for what's mine if necessary. The hand hovers by his side, a silver cufflink glinting in my eye line that pokes out from a blue tweed jacket. And it's only when I take a few seconds to stare at it, my own tongue licking my lips at the thought of the pill, that I realise who it belongs to. It imprints itself faster than the pill does, my lips licking again for no other reason than the hand slowly turning the pill between finger and thumb. I'm part dumbstruck he's here, part relieved he *is* here, and part infuriated he's anywhere near me.

    And then the knees bend, his body lowering to a crouch and bringing the pill between his legs to rest in front of me. I don't look at him. I just keep focused on the pill, for some reason unable to lift my body from the floor nor able to speak all of a sudden as lucidity begins rushing back.

"What are they, Alana?" he says, his voice flooding me with a calm I've been lost without. It's so mesmerising I'm immediately drawn back to my quiet again, my hand instantly relaxing its death grip on the pot as I remember the soundless times with him. But there aren't any words yet, not ones that can explain my need for these pills anyway. And the very fact that *he's* asked the question makes me feel ashamed of them for some reason. I look away from the tablet, my knees itching to move me away from him and it. And my head shakes, unable to think rationally about the whole situation as I snatch glances at the rest of the crowd. "Would you rather I forced it?" I still don't look at him, and the reason I don't is because I know what's coming. It's something about the way his tone lowers, grating itself rather than asking politely. It causes everything inside me to remember the way he fucks, and the way he grips, decimating what's in his hands and opening up a truth I didn't understand before him.

"Lana, get the fuck up." It's Bree. I can hear her faintly, but it's nothing like the continued sound of his voice in my mind. "Who the fuck are you?" The ferocity of her manner makes me look at him, my head continuing to shake in the hope that he doesn't go back at her. I'm floored the moment I do, my arms almost giving up the desire to hold me aloft. He seems furious, his face etched with harsh contours that are entirely focused on me. We just stare at each other, my own mouth trembling around words I can't get out as I look between his lips and eyes.

"I suggest you follow me," he eventually says, his knees pushing him upright as he crushes the pill in his fingers, probably amplifying the way my bones will crumble in his hold should I follow, and then lets the remnants of white dust fall to the floor.

"Jesus, Lana. The fuck is that asshole?" Bree says, her hands trying to pick me up as I watch him leave. His legs cover the floor with little thought for the people in his way, somehow owning the building by being in it as everyone starts moving for him. I still don't speak as he stands in the doorway, his back facing me as he holds the door open and waits. He knows I'll follow, doesn't he? And I don't even know why I want to, but I do. I want to more than I want my pills, more than the need to speak to Bree, more even than the need to get up from the floor. I could easily crawl from him to him, for some reason knowing he'll help me up when I get there.

"Blaine." I don't even know why I answered Bree. It's so quiet I doubt she even heard it. Perhaps I just wanted to say the name out loud so someone else could hear it and know who he is. His head turns slightly, barely moving really, but he heard me say it and it connects me to him again so quickly I stand without thought. Bree grabs my arm, spinning me to her so that she can get in my face.

"That's him?" she says, her body getting in front of me to distract me from him. I stare into her eyes for a moment, deliberating her face and wondering if I should sober up and talk this through with her rather than accept the hand he's offering. "The fuck are you doing, Lana?" She's right. What am I doing? He sent me away. Told me to think. I should be thinking, not flicking my eyes to him again, salivating, and craving everything he whispered at me on that roof. But it's so quiet when he's about. There's no noise, no incessant needling inside my brain.

"I'm going with him, Bree," I reply, drawing my bag from her shoulder and taking my other things from her grasp. "He's right. I should go with him."

"You're not. You've done what you needed to," she says, snatching at my laptop bag again and stopping me from walking forward. "It's just a book, Lana. This isn't real." But it is real. This is more real than it's ever been before him. This is what I need. It's love.

"I have to." I do. It's proved now. I can't function without him, horrendous as that might sound. I know it and so does he. It's inbuilt. Some kind of draw that only happens inside *my* mind, bridging something I can't describe, no matter how much I want to explain it to my best friend.

"But look at the state of you, Lana. He's done this, hasn't he?"

She spins away from me, her feet storming across the room to him and ducking beneath his arm as she walks out onto the pavement. I don't know why but I smile at the thought, knowing she's about to meet someone who'll pay little care to her mouth as it tumbles out frustrated ramblings.

He still doesn't move as I watch her lips begin to move, her hand waving as if she's trying to threaten him as she stands there in the rain, not giving a damn who he is. He just stands stock still, his arm continuing to brace the door open under the shelter of the doorway until I walk through it and accept his request. And it is a request. If there's one thing I've learnt about Blaine it's that he doesn't force anything, not until he's given permission to do so, and he somehow knows that even if I don't. He knows it in the way my body moves.

I slowly walk over, slipping the bottle of pills into my pocket and readying myself for an argument with Bree. This isn't a discussion he'll have with her. Her opinion will mean little if anything at all to his decisions about me. She'll be as relevant as shit on the pavement she's standing on.

Chapter 20

ALANA

"Why are you here?" I ask quietly, looking at him and walking out to join Bree as she keeps shouting about something. I can't hear it, and nor can he. He's uninterested in anything but me and what's going on. He lets the door swing shut and just stares at my face, his hands lowering into his suit pockets as he steps forward two paces into the rain with me. There's no answer, and he doesn't seem happy, making me feel uneasy about how he's portraying himself to Bree. But he's angry because I lied about medication, and he has a right to be, I suppose.

"Deal with this so we can leave," he says sharply, probably giving me only minutes to calm Bree down, or explain it to her somehow before we leave anyway. "Or she can come, too, learn some fucking manners herself." No, that's not happening. Although, the thought does make me smile a little, which appears to make his eyes crinkle, showing he's not quite as mad as I thought.

"And I can't fucking believe this is acceptable to you, Lana. People worry, you know? What, you're just gonna run off again with him and fuck some more? No phone calls, emails?" Oh yes, I never did text while I was away. And, well, yes, but it's more than that anyway, and the way the corner of his mouth lifts just slightly as she carries on only proves the irrelevance of fucking. "You're not. You told me you'd got everything you needed." I've got nowhere near enough from him yet. I want his heart.

I turn to face her and step forward, slightly unsteadily, my body wanting nothing more than to wander back into his arms and let him hold me still again.

"I have to, Bree. It's more than just…" I can hardly finish the sentence, for some reason feeling the word debases what this will become given the proper involvement. "It's…"

"It's what? A fucking bully hurting you for fun?" she snaps, her eyes glaring at Blaine behind me as if she might launch at him any minute, her fingers flicking water at me as the rain begins in earnest.

What? My eyes widen, fury rising at what she's suggesting. I've not been forced into anything. I've been asked, been given options the entire way through this, and the only time I wasn't he was fucking right to push me anyway. I snatch my laptop bag back from her, annoyed at her slandering him. She was the one who told me to do it in the first place and now she wants to call him a monster of some kind? "You're a damn mess, Lana. I've never seen you this trashed. And what the fuck's going on with the pills?" she says, grabbing my hand and holding it up to my face. "You're shaking. Look at you. How many have you had? You need to get the hell away from him, not go straight back for more."

My mouth opens, ready to deliver an argument of epic proportions as I snatch my wet fingers from her grasp, but just as I start, his fingers link into my other ones, making me swing to him as he rounds in front of me and pushes Bree away gently. I just stare, dumbfounded at the move and then gaze down at our fingers mingling together. They're so intimate, a true show of closeness, or a completion that hypnotises me out of any rationale I was clinging to.

"You don't have to describe any of this, Alana. Not until you're ready to," he says, his hand drawing ours up between us. "You don't have to explain yourself to anyone. Not yet." He kisses my fingers, his mouth softly lingering there as the rain pours onto his face. It makes me frown at the connotation of a relationship. A real one. Something of substance that means this is all very real, that my life will never be the same again because of him. "You just have to get in the car and trust me. There's something I need to show you before you explain anything to anyone."

"Show me?" Show me what? I don't understand. I brush my hair from my face, the slick feel of it as I wipe it away as irritating as my current confusion. I don't understand where this sudden change of mood has come from. He was angry and now he's being gentlemanly? I stare up at him, watching the way his frown contracts as he says the words, announcing something he's concerned about. And then he lets go of me, his body backing away towards a lamppost to wait for whatever decision I make.

"Never had you down as stupid, Lana," Bree's voice says beside me. Stupid. I gaze at Blaine and watch his suit being drenched as he waits for me. I suppose I'm just deliberating the word now that I'm out here in the real world and trying to fathom whether it's relevant or not. I suppose it might be in some ways. I'm undoubtedly bordering on insane given what he wants from me, but it doesn't stop the way my pulse races as I watch him stare back at me, and it doesn't stop the thought of being without him crucifying something inside. "It's just a fucking body and good looks, Lana. Don't let it fool you." Oh god, it's so much more than that. I don't even care about the looks that much anymore, the ones I'm staring straight through in an attempt to see a glimpse of his core. I care about his hands and what they do to me, and I care about the way he's inside my head, knowing me before I know myself. And I care about the way that same hand just held mine in the middle of this rain storm, showing me an intimacy in all of this, one that's so far removed from simple fucking it's inexpressible. But I care most of all about the fact that when he touches me, when he lays just one finger on me, I'm quiet again and floating in a void of tranquillity no one's ever made me feel before. "Think about what you're doing." I push my hair away again, feeling the water pour along my cheekbones. Oh, I am thinking. I'm thinking about it all, a near sober head suddenly dowsing me with reality and making me question things again now that he's here because she's right to some degree. He is Blaine Jacobs. A sadist. A potentially unpredictable force who could end me for amusement once I let him free on my skin. He told me that, regardless of his attempted decency so far. He told me and let me listen to the words that fell from his mouth so easily it brought with it visions of unimaginable pain. And we both know he's still not for falling in love with, no matter how much I already have done. But there has to be more inside him, doesn't there?

"Why should I?" I ask, willing him to mention love and make this all seem tangible in some way that fits into society's embrace. He smiles as he pushes himself off the lamppost and walks towards his car, the puddles echoing with every step he makes.

"You know the answer to that, Alana," he replies, his head shaking to sluice the water away as he bleeps the alarm and opens a door for me. "You have from the first time in the pool." Mmm. The pool. My own smile increases, my feet wandering closer without any help from me. "The feeling you wanted from me then, I'll give it to you if you ask. It's all yours." Mine. "Just for you." The words are as mesmerising as his face as he holds a hand out again and watches me moving closer. He smiles wider, showing me the beauty he has to offer and letting me into those eyes that are solely directed at me and what I need. It's as immersing as it was from beneath the water, as focused, and just as filled with a kind of love I'm beginning to comprehend as acceptable. It's all just for me, isn't it? I can have it if I ask. "You just have to ask."

"Lana?"

I don't turn at Bree's question, rather keep walking where my feet want to take me, listening to my heart's rumble pushing them there. It's all so quiet, so very peaceful and hopeful in there. There won't be any chloroform this time. No surprises. I'll take what's offered and do it for me, not for any form of research. I'll ask because my own body and mind need to know. And he'll show me all of it, won't he? He'll be true to who he is and we'll find a way forward, somehow.

"You're sure, Alana?" he asks, taking my bags from me as I lower into the seat and stare back at him. Oh god, I hope so because I've just burnt my bridges with Bree. I've just walked away from her and straight into his hands because of a feeling. He's not professing love. He's not offering me a lifetime commitment. He only offers what he's said he wants to do to me. And while I hope she understands what

I'm doing, while I hope I'll be able to come back and discuss it with her when I have more understanding of it, no amount of her telling me it's wrong is enough to stop me. It's not wrong. It's the truest version of right I've felt for a long time. My nod at his question confirms it to myself if nothing else. But as the door closes on me, I switch my gaze back to her to find her still standing there, the rain falling on her as she glares at me. It saddens me instantly. I wish I could find the words to help her see reason, to make he see that this is right for me, but I can't. I haven't got them yet. For once, and because of him, I'm without words effective enough to show her how this feels.

The car pulls away with me still looking at her, my hand touching the window to somehow hold us together regardless of the distance I'm about to put between us. She's my best friend, the only one I trust with everything. She knows it all, has been with me through all these years. She's helped, cried, argued and laughed with me, but I can't take her with me this time. The vision of her face retreating, still standing stock still with surprise and anger etched all over her face, is one that I'll never forget.

"Bree…" Her name creeps out of my lips, barely audible but filled with so much love for her that I feel tears pricking my eyes. "This is your fault," I say to him, eventually turning back to gaze at the road instead of her and trying to stop my tears. It is. I'm arguing with my friend because of him, something I never would have thought possible of any man, regardless of how I felt about them.

"Fault is an accessory after the fact, Alana. You make your choices, not me. You are solely to blame for any emotion you're currently having." I swing my head to him to find him smirking, his fingers tugging his tie off as he weaves the car through traffic and stares out into it. It makes me question the heart I thought might be there waiting for me. My eyes flick back behind us to see if Bree's still there, wondering if I've made the right choice. "If you want to replace the sentiment with something useful, get my cock out and wrap your mouth around it."

The very thought makes me turn back again, part disgusted at his appraisal of the situation and part infatuated with the imagery of it. "The gag should enthuse the tears further. Which is probably what you need to do." I've got nothing to answer that with. "And you should consider what the fuck you're weeping for anyway," he says, his fingers ratcheting his belt and undoing the buckle as he chuckles a little. "A friendship that bears no ability to understand is irrelevant to where you're going." My eyes open further, trying to find a reason for accepting that as okay. It's not okay. She's my friend and she cares about me.

"You've got no right to talk about her," I mumble, my eyes trying not to look at what he's doing with his hand as it continues working the belt.

"I've got every right. The only reason I want to see tears is because I've caused them, not someone else." Wonderful, what a lovely thought. It makes me huff out in exasperation, my hands folding in my lap as I try to understand what the hell I'm doing and look away from him. His hand slaps my cheek, making me turn and glare. He catches my chin so quickly and yanks it forward towards him that it makes me brace my hands to stop me tumbling over the seats. "Suck it and forget,

Alana. Idealisation will get you nowhere with me." I just stare again, feeling the pinch of his fingers and somehow bending to their will.

"But it's broad daylight."

He nods as he lets go of my chin, reaches inside his pants and draws the thing out. It's already hard, the smooth lines tempting me and making me forget anything other than the sight of it as he palms it a few times. Pre-come seeps from the tip, making me lick my lips at the thought of it in my mouth. I've never sucked him. All this time, the things we've done and yet I've not had him in my mouth. The closest I got was offering to, and he ended up fucking me instead.

"Use the emotion for something other than negativity." Another palm, his thumb rubbing back and forth, a loose groan sounding as he keeps going. "There is nothing sexier than a woman crying as I offload in her throat." I'm entirely sure there is, and it's all about the way he speaks. He's so damn direct with exactly what he wants. I'd like to be affronted by such coarseness as I gape at the cock on offer, but I'm simply not. I'm aroused, just as I always am when he speaks. I flick my eyes to the street as I hover over the middle console, noting all the people milling about, the cars right next to us, the slow creep of traffic not going anywhere. I might be aroused, but I'm not stupid, no matter how tempting the thought.

My nerves get the better of me as I pull back and settle back into the seat again. I'll just watch his little show instead. Besides, this feels manipulative in some way. It's something I'm not comfortable with at the moment.

"Not dark enough for you?" he says, his hand speeding a bit and then slowing again. "Scared?" No, not scared, just not happy to be arrested for indecency. The thought makes me snort given the man I'm sitting next to.

He carries on, one hand continuing to palm his cock as he turns the wheel with the other. The vision makes me realise how relaxed he is using both hands differently, as if even under the pressure of coming he's still in complete control of everything around him. It's under that awareness that I notice the car merging through traffic onto a side street.

"You need to appreciate how trashy you can be when asked," he says, the car pulling up next to a small refuse area. What? He clicks the seatbelt off and grabs at my hands, using his strength to drag me across the seats regardless of my fight. "It'll make you remember who you are." He just gets us out, parts of me knocking off the car and very nearly falling to the floor as he finally lets me go and smiles. It all looks so incongruous. His suit, the area, his hand wrapped around his cock again as I glare at him and lick my lips unconsciously. He tips his head at me, indicating I should follow. I'm not doing that, no matter how much my crotch might be screaming for it.

"Get your ass behind that dumpster before I drag you there." And there's that tone, the one that makes me think all of this is acceptable. It's not. I've been manhandled again. I fold my arms in response, looking directly at him. Whatever this is, ordering doesn't work with me.

"You're lying to yourself, Alana," he says, his feet backing him towards the dumpster, my own feet forgetting I disagree as I try to keep my eyes on his. "Stop withholding. Let's see the tears coming for a worthy reason, shall we?" I lick my lips again as I flick my gaze around, looking for other humans. "No, right here," he says, making me look back at him. "Keep looking right here. Forget all of that. Use my eyes as your anchor if you need to." It's said with a sense of reverence, making something inside me swell with an emotional response to the situation around me. "Come on, Alana. Give yourself to me. That's what you've come for, isn't it?" His feet are still backing away, high-end shoes beginning to crumple discarded rubbish into the puddles beneath his feet. "You know that cunt needs what I've got in my hand." It does. He's right. It's clamping inside me on nothing but air and desperate for filling as the rain keeps coming, irrespective of my hesitation. I wish it wasn't, but the twitching, the emptiness building inside me, the confusion of noise I'm trying to fight with, it's all there, still, and it won't be once I'm in his hands. It'll go away, leaving me quiet again. "It all stops here. Stop questioning and come to me. Let me guide you." It's reverent again, almost romantic somehow, and given the way his black holes shine back at me, a fire dancing in them and beckoning me forward into him regardless of location, I've got nothing to fight with, nothing to question. It's what I want. He's right. *He's* what I want.

"Good girl," he says as my feet move closer to him, the sound of the water pouring down lulling me somehow. "See? So much easier when you give yourself over to the thought." I'm not thinking. I'm just doing. One foot after another, willingly offering myself for anything he wants. Dumpsters, dirty floors, anything frankly. I just want what he's got in those hands of his. I don't care anymore. I'm all out of care or questions.

My body is torn from realty with only one pull of his fingers, my back pushed against a wall behind a dumpster and then pressed down to the floor beneath his feet. There's nothing romantic about it, but it's sensual in some way regardless, a riot of vibrations crisscrossing my skin and making me crazy to have him in my mouth, maybe. The world doesn't exist anymore. Nothing does, only his hand on my chin and the fact that his cock is coming at me, and the feeling when he drives it in? The sense of elation at being able to finally taste him with my tongue and wrap my lips around his girth? It makes my own orgasm chase through me from the knees resting in the wet dirt immediately. My shoulders are pressed back next, my head banged on the wall as he pushes in deeper and holds my cheekbone to keep me from moving. He doesn't need to. I'm not going anywhere. Everything is here. There's nothing else here but what I'm doing and what he wants. It's all evaporating around me as I focus entirely on trying to get more of him in my throat, oppressing my gag reflex to ensure more depth. I feel consumed by him, overpowered and, for once, happily so.

My hands hold on to his legs, giving me support against the friction he's creating with every thrust inwards as he grabs my hair to tip my face to him.

"Watch me come in you." The words, his eyes, the way he groans on the very next breath, it all has me desperate to please him and gain more attention. It's so dark in here, the feel of his hips coming at my face, the occasional brush of the fabric distracting me from his eyes as water sluices, the moment reminding me of the pool again. "Fuck, yes," he groans out, his fingers pinching my scalp as he yanks me sideways a little. And then he drives so deeply I swear it's coming through me into the wall. Tears swell in my eyes, the sort wrenched from pain, not sadness or love, as I snatch at breaths and let him use me. It hurts. Everything hurts. My back's banging against the wall, my head's being strained about, and my knees are scuffing through my jeans and grinding me downwards further as he pounds in again. And I ache so much, my body screaming for attention as he drives in again and again. I want to hate him. I want to tell him this isn't right, that it's filthy, that's its immoral and disgusting, but it isn't. It's filling me with anything but those sensations and I don't understand why. I gag on the thought, bile rising in what little throat I have left as saliva tries to keep him slick inside me. "Fuck, you're good." Oh, god, those words, they fill me with a sense of pride I can't describe as I look into his eyes. It's all about the silence and his voice. It wells inside me as I grip tighter onto his calves, urging him on as the muscles in them pump in time with his cock. And just like that, my own orgasm still climbing inside me with nothing but the friction of my jeans to spur me on, he stills, the length of him lodged in my throat and both his hands resting on the side of my head to keep me in place. The come heats me as it pours in, the quiver of his hips the only real movement I can feel as only a pulse runs the length of his cock. But the groan that follows, the sound of him emptying himself inside me and using me as a vessel as he bores his dark eyes into mine, that's what finally finishes any questions I have. That's all that matters. It's all I care about, because that groan belongs to me, as do the eyes that look thankful for what I've given him.

    I don't let go of his slick trousers as he slowly begins to pull out of my mouth. Rather I feel the need to clutch him to me, needing more contact than the clothes we're both wearing allow. I don't know. I just know that I need him now. I need whatever those minutes were as much as I needed the feeling of him fucking me in Delaney's church. He lets me hang on, his hands softening on my cheeks as he pulls out completely and just stands there in front of me. One thumb wipes beneath my eye, wiping away the rain and collecting the tears he made happen, and then he transfers them to his lips as he watches me watching him. It's a mesmerising sight, something that makes me think of an ownership I hadn't considered possible. I'm here on my knees in the dirt, the rain driving down on us as I've taken his cock raging into me and enjoyed it. And now, with just that movement, with just that collecting of my tears and sucking them inside himself, he's proved all my fears true. He owns me, doesn't he? My heart, my thoughts, and now my tears, too. I'm helpless to deny it anymore even if I wanted too. I'm as lost as I've ever been with only him to guide me forward.

"Don't confuse yourself, Alana," he says, one hand moving under my chin to keep me looking upwards at him, the other pushing his cock back into its confines. "You did what you wanted to do. It's nothing to be ashamed of." I'm not ashamed, surprised maybe, and definitely hoping there's more than just sexual fantasy involved given this love I'm feeling, but I'm not ashamed. Far from it, in fact.

"I'm not ashamed," I reply, choosing to stay exactly where I am and try to assimilate the feelings I am having as I drop my gaze from him and stare at the rubbish lying around my feet. Trash. He called me trashy, didn't he? Am I? I don't know. Perhaps I am. Perhaps this little interlude proves that he can make me do anything for him, because he has, with little fighting on my part.

A thousand dollar suit suddenly sits down beside me, his back leaning against the wall and his ass in the dirt alongside me as his arm opens up to invite me inside.

"We are all as dirty as we want to become," he says, his smile broadening as he pulls me in between his legs regardless of my surprised gaze. "Slutty is useful, on occasion." A snort leaves me, my own smile matching his as he knocks my head into his chest and begins brushing my hair from my face. "You need that ache taking care of?" Yes, I do, and the very thought makes me grin as we sit here on the sloppy wet ground like a pair of lustful teenagers staring out into the road. But I'd rather it was in a bed, or just inside in general really.

"I'm not aching."

"Liar." The reply makes me chuckle as his hand weaves into mine, our fingers mingling again as he holds them up in front of me and turns them around. "I've never done this."

"What?" Sat behind a dumpster? The thought doesn't surprise me at all. Nor have I, frankly. We must be doing something new together. The thought makes me smile more, amused that I've got something he's not done for anyone else.

"Held someone's hand." I don't move or show a reaction to the statement. I'm not sure what to show as I gaze at them still turning in front of me. Anything other than nothing will incite more feelings of hope, ones I don't know worthy of consideration. "Why do I want to with you?"

I don't know the answer to that, but my gaping mouth as I keep staring into the street watching the rain come down, probably doesn't help me think of an answer either. The gape slowly spreads into a smile, though, that sense of hope creeping in as it does and telling me to trust every instinct that's relaxing into his arm across my stomach. And so we just sit here for a while, the rain still tumbling down on us, and the occasional car driving by to distract my thoughts from a place they shouldn't be going towards. It's all as soothing as the stroke of his fingers on my forehead, as tranquil as the feel of his chest rising and falling behind me, and as picturesque as a winter's garden spread out before me. It's raw and unprejudiced. It has a lifetime's worth of iniquity linked into its definitive aura around us, the one that pulls me closer to him with every heartbeat. It's, he's, *we,* are as dirty as the streets we're lingering on and as heartfelt as nature intends us to be.

"I should get you home," he finally says. *Home.* Here is home. It's quiet here. "You're shivering. Up you get." Am I? I don't care. I don't want to get up. I want to stay here and remember this feeling. Labour in it and forget all the other things I have to do. The thought makes me remember all the deadlines coming at me, which brings on the sound of the notifications bleeping and rattling my nerves again. It makes me brace against his movement into me, holding my weight there in the hope that he understands and just lets me stay here with him instead. He does. His body instantly relaxes, only to move and prop me away from him again for a second or two. And then his jacket covers my shoulders, dowsing me in the warmth of his skin as he pulls me back into him once more.

"Tell me about the pills." Oh, the pills. I'd forgotten about them. I dig into my pocket searching for them only to find them not there. "In my pocket." Really? When did he take those? Not that I care.

He might as well know. He's going to take everything anyway. I know that now. I know it because I don't want to move at all.

"You're a thief, Blaine Jacobs."

There isn't a chuckle coming back as I find the small bottle and hold it up in front of me. He's gone quiet again, clearly not amused by the topic of conversation. My mouth opens to fill the void, ready to tell him the truth, ready to tell myself the truth about my addiction to them, actually. It seems a cleansing thought, one that fills me with a sigh as I think of how to word it correctly and stare back into the rain again.

"You wanted to know about my past, didn't you?" he says, breaking me of words I can't find and offering me a chance to just listen again. "About why I became who I am today? How I knew something was different." Yes, I suppose I did, but it doesn't seem that relevant now. It's not like anything's going to scare me away from this anymore. It is what it is. I'm suddenly far too deep to think anything badly of him. "I fucked a guy in college. It was the first time I'd come inside something." Wow. Okay, that shocked me a little. He's gay? My body tries to turn to look at him. "No, stay there. You need to listen to the rest of it." I'm not sure I do in all honesty. "It wasn't him being a man that turned me on. It was that he fought me. I came because I forced him into something. I held him down and fucked him with a smile on my face and little care for his feelings at the time."

I don't know how I feel about that statement. I'd like to be appalled, disgusted maybe, but I'm more interested in him carrying on than judging him because of it. Who am I to judge anything anymore? I've just let him fuck my mouth behind a dumpster, panted for it, actually. I'm hardly saintly now, am I? I just keep staring into the rain instead, occasionally glancing at my pot and eventually resting my head back into him again. "I knew then. Everything needs to be in pain for me to come inside it." He sighs quietly, his hand still relaxed on my stomach as he kisses the back of my head. "I haven't come inside someone for over a year. Until you." It seems like a confession of sorts, one that makes me smile. Not necessarily at the content, more the fact that he's giving me the words he probably hides from others.

"I'm addicted to amphetamines." It's my own confession, and it comes out so easily it surprises me, makes me chuckle even as I blow out a breath and feel the words leave with it. "I'm addicted to amphetamines." My body attempts to push away from him as I try to get to my feet, embarrassment starting to creep in at the thought. "I'm addicted to amphetamines. I... I can't cope without them." He doesn't let me move from him. In fact, he holds tighter, slowly taking the pot from me and flicking the top of it off.

"Do you want to be?"

"No."

"Throw them away then. Use me instead of them." I don't even know what that means, but the thought of those little white pills leaving fills me with dread as I watch him get one out and hold it up to me. "Just throw it away and trust me to give you the same thing." He rolls it in his fingers, the sight of it tempting me rather than doing anything to stop me wanting it, as water trickles along his hand. "You just have to ask, Alana."

"I can't... I mean, I need them, and..."

"Just ask me to help you." Another sigh leaves me as he hands me the pill, wrapping my fingers around it and then wrapping his hand around mine.

"There's drug advice places. I should go and see about..." I don't know what. "You don't understand what it's like. The meetings, the deadlines. All the voices in my head, the stories. I can't keep up with them all, Blaine. It's chaos without the pills. They..." I don't know what they do, but they contain it somehow. They make it better, help me see clearer.

"I do know how it feels, Alana. I'll get rid of the bedlam for you if you ask. You've felt it already." How? By sleeping with him? That's just ridiculous. I can't get over a drug addiction by sleeping with someone. He might be good, and he might have things in his arsenal that other men don't know about, more's the pity, frankly, but he's not rehab. How would he know what to do?

"But I..." He brings our hands to his mouth again, releasing his and kissing mine as his fingers unfurl.

"This conversation needs to happen somewhere other than slutty backstreet avenues, nice as they've been. Come on, get up," he says, his body pushing me upright as he moves and shrugs off the rain that's soaked his shirt. "We'll go back to yours. You can cook something. I want to talk to you anyway." Cook? I don't cook. And where the hell has that come from. I thought we were having a conversation about addiction. I thought we were discussing things and bonding in some way. Now he wants me to cook?

"I don't cook." He chuckles and walks over to his car, barely acknowledging my proclamation, one that means he won't get fed, not by me anyway. "And I thought we were having a conversation? You can't just stop it mid-way through because you're hungry. I've just done this on a filthy sidewalk because you made me and then we're getting all deep and emotional and you're just stopping it? I need to get this out. We need to do this. You can't just …"

It seems he can, because with one final smirk he opens his car door and gets in, leaving me standing by the dumpster part way through my slight tantrum and wishing I didn't want to get in the car as much as I do. The passenger door opens within seconds, forcing me to concede to my soaking wet skin, the fact that I'm shivering, and that I want nothing more than to follow his lead. "Why were you even at that restaurant?" It's the first thing I ask as my soaked frame lands in his seat, my arms folded in sulkiness, and the leather slipping under my backside as I do.

"I missed you, Alana."

Chapter 21

BLAINE

The fifteen-minute drive has been as arduous as watching her mouth around my cock, filling me with all the old sensations and opening up a hope I don't deserve. But she is here nonetheless, her hand still shivering slightly as she tries to unlock her apartment door.

"Here," I offer, taking the key from her hand and watching as she lets my jacket slip from her shoulders. The vision makes me smile, amused by my own reaction to gentlemanly resolve given the garbage bins I damn near fucked her behind. Christ knows where the ability to stem my flow came from. The little fucking madam deserved far more than my confession to help her ease her own.

I push the door wide and show my hand, allowing her to enter before me and then closing the door quietly behind us. I don't know why I sat with her so long. I don't even know why I got down to the floor in the first place. Normal procedure would have involved amusement at her mental distress, and perhaps a slap or two for her dishonesty, but sentiment had taken over. It's the same as the sentiment that appears when I admit to missing her, or the same as the feeling when I hold her hand, and certainly the same as the feeling attached to coming inside her. It warms me, damn near giving me the ability to stay wet and soaked forever in her presence, not feeling one inch of the storm around us as we'd sat there.

"Tea or coffee?" she asks, her hands hanging my jacket over a small chair by a table. "I don't even know what you like to drink." She giggles nervously, running her fingers through her hair to get rid of the rain and crossing the room to the kitchen. "Actually, I don't know anything about you really." No, she doesn't. She isn't supposed to know anything other than what she needs for research purposes. I won't be helping her anytime soon either. That's not my position here. Not now I know about the pills. It's not what she needs anymore. I look around the room, enjoying the way her whole imagined being lives in here. It's juxtaposed to the real version of her that lives inside her body. It's all too tidy, too disciplined. It's sparsely decorated with muted tones, done undoubtedly to attempt a calm she can't produce herself. "Blaine? Tea or coffee?"

"Scotch. And have one yourself."

"Oh, okay."

I finger a blanket over the back of her sofa, lifting it to my nose to smell the fabric conditioner on it. It smells lifeless, its fragrance as pale as the colour she's chosen in the space. I smirk and drop the item, unbuttoning my shirt instead and heading along a small corridor in search of a bathroom.

"Bathroom's on the right," she calls. I turn into the first door I find and am greeted with her study rather than the bathroom. It makes me stand and look around the space, searching for something that resembles her and not the sparingly adorned interior of creams and light woods. The only sense of colour, of her, or what I believe her to be, are some of the books that line the shelves. Valerie Du Font. Peter Halloway. Another smirk rings true as I wander over to them, immediately handling one of three vivid purple toned spines that stand out and remind me of her hair.

"Oh, you're in here," she says, her voice quietly filling the silence in the space along with some ice cubes clinking in the glass. "That's the first trilogy I wrote. In college." Probably the truest version of her there is then. I turn it over, reading the synopsis and smiling as the words talk of heroes and fairy-tale endings. "It still sells well to this day. I wasn't much of a writer then, but I still love the story. Other people, too, apparently." I smile again, my eyes searching the other covers for something else that gives me a sense of her. Nothing does. All the rest seem as bland as the surroundings, to me at least.

"It matches your hair," I say, holding it out to her and taking her offered glass of Scotch, then leaving the room to find the bathroom as I shrug from my shirt. "Like my sea does your eyes."

I wander further, still noting the lack of anything resembling her. It's all so infertile, its soul removed perhaps, certainly covered over and lost. Where are the notes? The scrawl of papers she had on my kitchen table? The expulsion of art, distributed and lingering around so she can chase each dream the moment she thinks of it. I can't see anything here other than perfection and a neatly ordered existence, a pretence of life.

"Shall I call some food in?"

I find the bathroom and switch on the shower, drowning out her voice and waiting for her to come searching for me again. I've got no interest in food. I'm interested in her and her body. I'm fascinated by the way her mind works and why it works the way it does. For once I'm so engrossed in using my own mind to understand hers I can't fathom anything else. I want to hear it from her lips, just like the pills. I want to see her burrowed down with a drink and listing her concerns, perhaps help her find a way through them if she wants. Psychology is, after all, my profession, and rather than destroy another woman with it, rather than use her and relegate her to the reject pile, I feel the need to harbour her, look after her. Protect her maybe.

My trousers peel from my skin, the rest of my soaked clothes following suit as I fiddle with lotions and potions, none of which she needs. She hasn't got one damn clue how beautiful she is stripped bare, that fucking mascara of hers doing nothing but hiding the true splendour that lay beneath it.

"Blaine, food?"

"Get your ass in this shower," I call out, needing nothing more than the feel of her skin in my hands, the bite of her teeth as I grind my cock inside her, and the taste of her cunt in my mouth. How I managed not to fuck it against the wall earlier rather than her mouth, I don't know.

"Ravenous, are you? Good title for the book."

"You've no idea." I grab at her arm as she giggles and yank her into the unit fully clothed. I'll strip her in here. I'll fucking strip her anywhere, starting at the bottom and working my way up until she's nothing more than a vessel to use. The shoes go first, then jeans, peeled from her and slung out into the bathroom where they belong. Fucking jeans. I hate women in jeans. I like skirts and dresses, like the one she wore the first time we met. Summer ones especially, the kind that flaunts a woman's curves without showing off too much. "Don't wear jeans again," I snarl, lifting the shirt over her head and slinging that away, as I crawl down her perfect fucking body and push it against the tiles. "And heels, wear them all the time." I like heels, too, specifically when nothing else is being worn with them other than underwear, corsets, or steel.

She squeals as my tongue makes contact with her, her body beginning to writhe long before I've made any really impact on it. It's enough for her feet to slip, her hands scratching out at the glass for something to hold onto as she continues looking for balance. The wriggling makes me furious, my hands trying to stabilise her as my mouth searches to latch on. Fuck it, I've picked her up and carried her out of the shower before I can think of anything rational. I just want inside her. My tongue, my cock, I don't give a fuck. And I want to strap her disobedient fucking ass for lying to me, something that has me reaching for my trousers as I walk past them and search for a bedroom. She lands awkwardly after I've thrown her on the dull cream sheets, which makes me smile at her discomfort and yank the belt from its loops.

"Blaine?" she says, her eyes as surprised as her body appears, as it scrambles and backs up the bed away from me.

"Turn over," I say, bending the belt in half and considering the buckle end rather than the softer option. Fucking lies. "This will hurt."

"You're not using that on me." Yes I am.

"You lied." It's not a discussion. My hand just reaches for her foot to turn her over myself rather than allow any further comment or struggle. "This will teach you not to do it again." She kicks out at me, her face a picture of hatred as she scrambles out of my grasp again and assemblies the little brat she is. "I can do this all day, Alana. You'll still lose in the end."

"You are not strapping me with a belt," she shouts, her legs scrabbling again and her hands up to stop me. Oh, but I am going to, and I'm going to do it at least ten times, and she's going to count them and realise who the fuck she's been lying to.

I grasp at her ankle again, viciously, tugging and stabilising her as my other hand forges straight up her thigh and into her cunt before she has a chance to get away. Her whole body stops instantly, the curl of my fingers ensuring the presentation of her ass.

"Punishment comes to those who lie to me, Alana," I whisper, as I feel the calm wash over me and take me back to times I crave. She bucks a little, the soft swell of her breast turning towards me as drag her cunt closer to the end of the bed.

"I didn't..." She stops her words as my fingers twist inside her, the other set increasing the pressure on her ankle and willing her to carry on with the lie. She doesn't have a choice here. Not anymore. She will be disciplined. She will be punished and say thank you at the end of it. The only choice is whether she takes it well or whether I'll have to push her further after the event. And then she mewls, her cunt squirming on my hand again as I bend forward and pull in the scent of her. It would be so easy to simply devour, to take and not stick to rules and regulations. Here, now, I could just be free of the restriction. Use the materials available around the room. The glass from the light bulb, crushed and laid beneath her. The knives in the kitchen, sharpened and ready for inducing the quick slash of pale flesh. The ropes holding the curtains back, the bathrobe, hanging lifeless but for its ability to suffocate. And my hands, these ferocious hands, still reserved and yet wanting nothing more than to see the light dim once more. I slowly pull my fingers from her to see if she'll lie still like a good little brat should. She doesn't. She immediately begins to question again, her mind undoubtedly searching the entire scene beginning around her for clarification of facts. The only facts she needs to understand are the ones that leave my lips.

"Do as you're told, Alana, before you piss me off." She pisses me off eternally, has done since the day we met with her snooty disposition and her patronising glances at my people. She's as filthy as the rest of us, more so given her predilection for fucking on church floors and sucking cock on garbage strewn pavements. It's the fucking brat in her, the one I appear to love for my sins.

She stills, her eyes sneaking a glance back and then looking away again. "Good." I stand up again, releasing her ankle slowly and watching the way she presents herself. Natural. Her ass high, and the glistening juices already coating her cunt's waiting lips on display for me. The belt curls the air as easily as a knife through butter, not one part of it, or my arm, hindering the deliverance of the first lash. It strikes with as much force as I care to give, causing a scream to sound the room instantly as she shunts forward and slumps to the bed. "Count it," I snarl out, my cock remembering the sound of a pain solely for my ears. She pants and fidgets, her fingers tightening the sheets in her fingers as she frowns. "You know why. You caused this. This is how we will be. You count it, Alana, and then you ask for the next one like a good little brat should." Her head eventually nods as she steadies her body and pushes up onto her hands again.

"One," she whispers, her breathing as laboured as the slight pink of her ass. "Another one."

"Say please." Her head drops, her lips blowing out another breath as her back dips in defeat. "Say it and the next might not hurt so much." It will. It'll hurt more. I couldn't care less if she says please or not. He care that she understands herself and what she needs from me. What I need from her.

"Another... Another one, please."

I smile at the sound of the words faltering from her mouth and send the belt home without any other thought, causing another shriek of pain to bellow out. Two. Only two, and the feeling enthuses such visions I focus entirely on her ass, barely hearing the words that leave her lips as she keeps counting. Strike after strike land, the sound battering the room and forging me onwards. It might be discipline, a kind that's necessary for her, but I don't give a fuck. All I can feel is her burying herself inside me with every uttered breath and moan. She's as divine as the come that drips from her cunt, and as beguiling as the fingers that I long to hold as the seventh strike lands and I watch the tears start to fall. Her body crumples, her face turning to the side as she pants through the pain and still manages to find enough voice to ask for the next. It makes me move to get a better view of the pretty little tears, casting a glance at the rest of her lithe frame and watching the way it begs for fucking. The mascara I hate runs courses down her cheeks, her eyes as red as her ass as she slowly levers herself up again to look at me and waits for the next.

"Another, please, Sir."

Sir. The sentiment reminds me of Eloise and the way she called me nothing else, but there's anger in Alana's blue eyes, not the desperation of a once echoed voice. She isn't desperate for death or craving the pain as Eloise did. She rallies against it, letting the feeling remind her of hope and forging her ability to latch onto someone else's strength. I smile at her, my hand wanting nothing more than to stroke her head and wipe the tears into my mouth again. Still, I've got two more to deliver. Two more to ensure she understands what our bond will be. Two more to teach her her lesson.

"Higher," I say, watching her quivering lips and shaking frame. "You've dropped your presentation." She moves herself to counter her exhausted muscles, raising herself higher and closing her eyes. The moment she does, I send the belt home again, rewarding her for her good fucking behaviour. And I send it harder than before, relishing the way her body collapses immediately and the tears pour further down her precious cheeks as she chokes out sobs. "You've only had nine. Are you behaving like a coward again?" She croaks out a noise, her hands trying to brace herself off the bed. I gaze at her, flexing the leather in my fingers and considering shoving something inside her to make the pain more bearable. Instead, I turn the belt, my own mind apparently more interested in her response to the metal of the buckle striking her skin. "Up, Alana, and beg for the last one." She sniffs, her weakened fingers clawing at the sheets again as she groans and pants.

"I... I can't," she says, pleads actually. I smirk again, waiting for more pleas to come, ones begging for the pain to stop. Pain doesn't stop with me, not now she's offered me an avenue to release it on again. She needs to feel this, just this slight proposition of what she thinks she loves. She needs to feel it and then watch me go at another woman with more enthusiasm.

"You will. And you'll tell me you love me after it lands." Her eyes widen, her body slumping further into the bed as her body begins to give up. "That's what you think, isn't it? That means you have to love this, Alana. This is what I am. I warned you, gave you the chance to leave."

"I can't do this," she mumbles, her head turning into the covers to get away from the thought. She can. She wants to. I can tell by the way her ass is rising again, the way her fingers stay tight and focused on achieving more, and I can tell by the way she sniffs in her tears, burying them again and trying to be as strong as I need her to be. I just watch and wait, all the time restraining the need to fuck her as I give her the time to assimilate thoughts and remember why she's here. "Another, Sir."

"Hardly begging," I say, still smiling as she pushes herself to her knees and glares at me.

Good girl. That's what I need from her. That fire right there. She needs to dredge it up and bridge the hole I'm creating between us, whether I help her realise it or not. I need that from her. As does she. She'll hold the strength to keep us connected, not me. She'll ground me, helping me find sane thought in the middle of my frenzied ones, and in return, I'll offer a peace she's never felt before. "Beg, Alana. Prove you want me."

"Please," she spits it at me, her arms locking into position after she's wiped her own tears away, and her eyes as poisonous as I've ever seen them. "Please. What else do you fucking want?"

It all happens so seamlessly, as if nothing's between us anymore. The belt swings, aimed solely at the cunt spread wide and on offer, the metal of it clinking though the air before it maims flesh. And her eyes remain focused entirely on mine as I watch her waiting for it to land, the grunt as it finally does sending a shiver through him. Not one other sound leaves her lips as she screws her eyes to the pain and snarls out her frustration. She just tips her head downwards and bites her lip, letting the buckle fall from her skin and absorbing the pain of it into herself. Presumably allowing enlightened abandon to take over, the little pain slut of hers finally free of its confines.

"Fuck you," she snarls, her lips offering the word to the white sheets beneath her rather than to me. I smirk and coil the belt again, enjoying the thought and waiting for the rest to come as I throw the leather away. "Fuck you." She says it again with seethed venom, her hands scratching holes into the sheets as she turns to look at me, her body starting to move with no care for the pain she's in. I watch her crawl, her muscles fluid as they propel her upright and towards me, probably chased with adrenalin and endorphins. It's better than any fucking drug can offer her, always will be. It shines in her eyes, regardless of the still confused hatred there too. "I love you," she says quietly, her feet rounding the bed to get her to the floor. She stands there, her body on display and her face blotched with a pain she refuses to show anymore. "Is that what you want, Sir?"

Yes, it is. She's a perfect offering of everything I hate adoring. Spirited, judgemental, aloof. Regaled indignation contrasted with her own sense of ownership. She is sugar and spice. She is beauty personified and strength weighed down by life's empty conquests. And she will capture a heart I've long since closed down, the same one that already beats erratically at her glare of disdain as she waits for me to continue with my fucked up endeavour.

I reach for her face, the feel of it sinking naturally into my hold as I wipe one last tear away. She feels like a submission of temptation, her skin like a selection of delicacies ready to be consumed as and when I choose. And fuck, I want to kiss those trembling lips. I want to plague them, have them live inside me where they can be used and toyed with, cherished on occasion. I want it so much that my cock doesn't care about sinking inside her anymore, nor do my hands care about creating the pain I've just delivered. I just want her lips on mine, her body in my arms, her warmth wrapping itself around my heart and setting me free of the detachment it normally feels.

"Show me," I say, wondering what offer she will give to express her love. Her eyes shift, nervously, her body suddenly at odds with itself as if all confidence has left it. It makes me drop my hand from her face, leaving her alone to make her choice in the face of confusion. She just hovers, her gaze flicking around as she twitches her sore ass. I smirk at her, amused at the notion that given her free will again, she doesn't know what to do with it.

"I don't know what makes you happy," she murmurs as she steps away and looks around the room for inspiration. "How can I not know that?" Why would she? We've not spent any time together. No dates. No drinking and laughing. "I should know that if I love you, shouldn't I?" I wouldn't know. I've never loved. Not until this feeling I assume must be love. She turns and walks back across the room, her arm reaching for the belt I've tossed aside and grasping it. "Is this what makes you happy?" Very much so, but not as much as the feel of her lips would.

I wave my fingers at her, beckoning her over to me and letting my hand grate into her ass as she walks into me.

"That hurts." Mmm. My other hand winds up through her breasts, reaching for her throat and daring the pressure I crave as I walk her towards the wall. She squeals again as her ass makes contact with it, and more so when I push her around on the doorframe, its edges heightening her discomfort.

"Say it again."

"What?" My mouth hovers over hers, waiting for the words to come so I can swallow them down and feel them near my heart. I just stare, not caring for more elaboration as I gaze into blue eyes that remind me of the ocean at home, and then increase the pressure on her throat. My hand squeezes at the delicate bones, letting my cock remember all the things it wants to do to her. It aches again, desperate to batter something. It can smell her cunt better than I can, probably her love for it, too. "I love you?" I smile, my lips latching to hers as I crush a little more, the sinew of her neck buckling as I apply the restriction further. Her breath hitches, her body beginning to fight against me as I continue delving my tongue inside her mouth, searching for her and her ability to get inside my mind. It's all in there, waiting for me to explore it, work out how it ticks, why it ticks, and for once I don't want to destroy it. Not this one—this one I'll keep and nurture, look after.

Her mouth breaks away suddenly, the kiss lost as she pushes at my chest, her feet kicking my shins.

"Blaine, stop. I can't..." I back a step away, tilting my head at her as she scrambles on the wall, her fingers reaching for my hand at her throat. "I can't..." Speak presumably. But the light is there still, flickering away with her beauty and drawing me into it like a candle slowly dying, its last flames petering away. I stare at her hair, the purple highlights tumbling from the grips she's pinned them with, the colour casting shadows and reminding me of something. "Please..." It's becoming more an obstructed attempt at words, ones I can still taste on my lips. It makes me run my fingers over them as I watch my hand grip her tighter and tighter, my insistent cock galvanising itself for fucking her as she starts slipping away.

"This makes me happy," I murmur, enthralled with the state of her as she bucks and quivers in my grasp. "And this," I continue, letting my hand find its way inside her and shunt her up the wall. "The sight of your turmoil makes me happy, Alana." Her eyes widen. "The feel of your lips trembling as I kiss them." Grasping fingers try to prise mine away from her throat as she keeps panting out short breaths. "You have fallen in love with someone who wants to watch you suffer." She hooks her fingers in, giving her a short reprieve from the throttling, something I allow by the slight release of my hand so that she can hear and breathe her way through the orgasm that's coming. "Listen well, Ms. Williams. I am an asshole. I warned you. I am someone who will use, degrade, and humiliate you." She frowns, her head shaking a little as I began fingering further in. I snort at her, amused at the version of the love she feels. I know I love her, I can feel it haunting every nerve I have, but it makes little difference to what I am, what I have always been. And she's set it free again now, given it permission to be alive once more. "You fell in love with a sadist who constantly controls his tendencies." Her mouth gasps for air as I pinch inwards, my other hand twisting as I do and bringing her closer to orgasm with every inhaled gasp. "Do you understand?" Her head shakes, a groan leaving her lips as I press on her clit and shove her pliable body about. "Your love gives me permission to use this skin how I see fit."

"No," she splutters out, her hands trying to forge into mine again to break the hold around her neck. "Fuck..." I've squeezed the 'you' out of her brattish statement before it leaves her mouth, reminding her exactly who is holding all the power as I stare into her eyes and move in closer.

"I own you now," I whisper, my lips travelling lightly across hers as my hand carries on ramming into her. "And you want me to, don't you?"

She chokes on her lack of air as I pull back fully and watch her for a few more seconds, wondering how long she'll last as the flush crawls across her skin. She writhes, her cunt starting to clamp and constrict, my fingers delving and twisting to bring her off, give her her reward for taking the pain so well. And then she stills, her hands falling away as she rolls her eyes and comes on my fingers, the juice dripping from her like a fucking waterfall of salt. It's something I'd bathe in given a chance. In fact, I will one day because she is perfection. Splendour embodied, and all for me.

Having watched her come, enjoying the twitch of her frame in my hands, I gradually release my grip altogether and pull my hand from her cunt at the same time. She falls to the ground, her back heaving as she tries to get her breath back and claws at the very place I've been holding. She looks stunning. A glorious mess of tears and fear, her face as fraught as the world makes her mind feel. I stare, amazed at her flawlessness in front of such a monster and infatuated with her ability to take me. She will be the strength she once was with me. I'll bring her back. Her creative flare will return with every submission she gives freely. She won't need the drugs to keep her going. She'll use me, just as I will her, and take my offering so I can help her see her truths. Perhaps she'll help me find mine, too. "This all makes me extremely happy, Alana."

"I..."

I wait for the fury to come as I watcher shuddering lips, wait for her fuelled rage to find itself and fly at me. I will it from her as I turn and gaze around the barren room, daring her to argue that she doesn't need what I've just given her a sample of. Nothing comes, though. Only silence and the broken gasps for air.

"Your whole existence is filled with nothing more than a pretence of who you are," I say, wandering over to the dressing table and opening a bottle of perfume. She doesn't argue or speak at all. Instead, she just keeps sniffing a little, letting me focus on the perfume in my hands. It reeks of high-end stores and pretentious social climbing, nothing like the scattered writings of an author in full flow. Another bottle catches my eyes, crystal topped and filled with a concoction of wealth, no doubt. I grab at it, walking it back towards her and twisting the top off. "Where are you, Alana?" I ask, standing above her and starting to pour the liquid into her face. She flicks it off, her fingers smearing the lotion around as she tries to move away from me. I chuckle, throwing the empty container to the floor as I walk away, more interested in the rest of her property and what it has to offer my mind about her pretence. I end up stroking my cock's weight as I wander the apartment, still searching for elements of her I can use to bury in further. Still there's nothing. It's simply an empty shell, barely resembling anything of the woman who fucks on church floors, or the one who called me Daddy and manipulated my thoughts, certainly not the one who sucked me off in a back alley full of garbage. But one thing does catch my attention, a framed picture quietly sitting in the corner on top of a scantly filled bookcase. I wander over to it, glancing out of the window at a pair of curtains that twitch in my eye-line and smirking in reply. The older faces stare back at me as I pick up the gold frame. It's clearly her parents. She's the image of her father, with traces of her mother's femininity curbing the harsh lines, but the lips, the eyes, even the blonde hair is the same. It makes me consider my own parents for a moment, barely remembering their love for the years I've not seen them alive.

"Put it down," she says, harshly, her body suddenly appearing by the back of the sofa, a dressing gown in place rather than the nakedness I prefer.

"Why? It says more about you than this whole place does."

"You know nothing about me."

"Oh, you're wrong, Alana," I reply, stalking the room to get to her. She flinches, backing away a little as she glares and pushes her cream sodden hair back. "I know you. I know what you really are."

"Stay away from me."

"Why?"

"Because I don't want you to—"

"Why?" *Push, push, push.*

"That was... In there... I'm not doing that again."

"Why?"

"It's wrong. This is all wrong." I smile in reply to that, remembering when the word meant anything to us, still carrying the frame in my hand and wondering what Daddy would think of such things. Wrong. What a fucking word. I'm tired of wrong. Tired of fighting it everyone's opinion of it, my own included, and too far down this emotional road to even try anymore.

"Why is it wrong?" She frowns, her body still trying to get away as I keep moving and countering any direction she makes. "Can't you answer the questions, Alana?" She shakes her head, her arms folding around herself. Good, now she knows how it feels to be pushed, and I'll keep pushing. I'll push her resolve, her pain limits, and her ability to defy me. I'll push it all to get that dimming fucking light that eggs me on. "You asked me why I always back away from you. This is why. This is what happens when I move forward. See?" I cross the floor with such speed it makes her jump, frightening her back to a wall again as I stretch my arm out to touch her. "It's always so easy for me to move forward. Are you understanding now?" She quivers again, her eyes flicking anywhere other than at me. "It's the backwards steps that are hardest, Alana. The retreating. And I worked so hard for you. I tried, didn't I?" I discard the frame, choosing to cage her in instead and draw my thumb down the length of her neck. The reddened imprint of my hand still lingers there, making me smile at my version of love. "But backwards stifles me. It all fucking stifles me, Alana. I don't want to be stifled anymore."

It's all so quiet for a minute or two—just the two of us standing here in an apartment that lacks anything real but the two of us. Truth lies in the two of us. Nothing is wrong here. Everything is perfect. She only needs to realise it and we'll both be free. She can come and live with me, be there for me. I'll give her a room she can explore her mind inside. She can sleep with me, let me hold her and cradle the noise away. She can even hold me, tell me it's alright to be as I want to be. We'll evolve into something other than what we currently are.

She says something, but I don't hear it. I'm still too consumed with thoughts of my den and the ocean crashing behind it as I look at her neck, my finger still wandering the artery that pulses in front of me. "Is this for you or me?" she murmurs.

I look up into her eyes, really hearing her voice for the first time in a while. It applies some rationale back into my mind, reminding me of the things I'll do to her, or rather the things I shouldn't do.

"Is there a difference anymore?" She still looks frightened, her lips trembling, something that should turn me on, make me needful, amused even, but it causes a frown to descend as I watch her eyes sadden. The fire's gone from them. Where has the fire gone? My venomous little snake has left me alone again, all the power in her eyes suddenly lost in fear or trepidation. I pull in a breath and look at her as one foot backs away, my fingers leaving her skin at the same time as my second retreating step heaves away, too.

"One more chance," I mutter, my body turning from her as dismay wracks my every nerve. I'll give her one more chance to see before I consume her. I promised myself I'd give her that. Regardless of all this I should offer her that freedom first. Delaney was setting it up, had set it up.

I walk to the bathroom and begin pulling on my sodden clothes, chastising myself for my own erratic thoughts and still remembering the feel of others in my hands. I should tell her something, explain more appropriately. She's given so much already. The need for hesitation infuriates me, riling me into a wreck of balled energy again, one that needs to expunge on something, anything.

"You're leaving?" she says from the other side of the room. I watch her fiddle with her dressing gown, closing the top of it and backing away. It makes me snort, unsurprised at her abhorrence but irritated with her scared appearance. "You do all that and now you're leaving me? I don't understand, Blaine. I don't know what's happening here. I just ... I gave you ..."

I heave in a long breath as I look at her, desperate to show her more and yet holding myself back from the very thing I want most.

"You need to see. Before it begins, you need to see, Alana."

"See what?"

"This. Me. You need to see it and understand what's coming for you. I need to know you've seen it, that you accept it. Love or not, I will not stop because you feel pain. I will not let you in any further than I care to do. I want you aware of that before you profess any more love for me. Because that love you offer, it condemns you. It means I own everything about you. And I'm not sure you're ready for that, or even if you want it. So make your choice," I say, scribbling the address on a piece of paper and tossing it on the table as I back away from her, the room, and her life if she wants. "But make it wisely. Once it begins, it doesn't stop. I don't offer safe words. I don't let up until I'm finished. I'll bask in your humiliation, manipulate it, and enjoy your torment all the more because of it." She looks shocked. I don't know why, she should have felt it in my hold ten minutes ago. "But I do love you, if that makes it easier for you to hear. And I'll help you right yourself again, if that's what you want. We both will." She just stands there, stock still, her eyes as wide as she can make them and her hands holding the belt on her robe.

"What did you say?" she asks, her mouth a line of expectation.

"All of it, or just the words you wanted from me?" I stand as still as her, staring with little remorse and wanting nothing more than for her to drop the robe, walk over and kiss me for being so honest. I simply want honesty, to be accepted. I realise that now. I can feel it all coming together in my mind, winding a path for a future built on trust and love, one filled with pleasure and those fucking walks I crave.

"Just those words again."

I stare, perhaps amused that she only needs to hear those words again, but still too wound up to give them any real credence. They must make the rest seem bearable somehow. It makes me back away again, sneering at the thought of it all, one hand reaching for my jacket and the other reaching for the handle on the door as I watch her reassemble herself. She shines in front of the rain that still pours outside, tempting me, just like the stars I watched when I thought of her last night. She glints, her body framed by a cascade of water tipping down the window's surface. Her eyes as blue as my ocean, more so because of the tears she's cried. And her hair, slicked back, those rebellious purple stripes beginning to match the prints around her throat already. She's stunning in her disarray. More so in her elegance as she stands and waits for honesty, waits for me to help her through the confusion she's caused herself. She's everything I need. Perhaps more.

"Come to the club," I snarl out, taking one final sweep over her neck before I turn and open the door. "See what you're letting yourself in for before you ask me to say it again." Because those bruises, the reddening that lingers just a little under her hair, is nothing compared to what I will do to the bodies Delaney has waiting for me. She needs to see that, needs to understand. I won't lie anymore, not even for her.

Chapter 22

ALANA

I've walked all day, not really understanding where I'm walking to or why. I thought when I started this it would all just be research, something I needed to do to write the story correctly, but it's far from that now. I feel like I'm floating as I wander through all these people, neither caring for nor interested in their lives. Nothing is sparking an idea. No stories unfolding on the streets of New York like they usually do, other than the one that's carrying on in my own mind. Everything just seems pale and insipid now, as if it's bare of taste or flavour, no solidity even. It all feels like my apartment out here, lacking warmth or charisma. It's cold, regardless of the streets flying by and the hustle and bustle of everyday life around me. I haven't even got my laptop stuck to me as usual. For the first time in however long, I didn't want it with me. I just wanted me, on my own, wandering with no sense of timing, no meetings, no notifications bothering me. Just me, whoever that is. Not Val, not Peter, not even this new pen I'm trying to find. I just wanted Alana to walk about, taking in life and seeing how she chose to view it. She's more lost than I thought she was, perhaps pushed aside by the other voices in my head. I'm not sure I ever contained them like I thought I did. Maybe they just all overtook at some point, making me forget who I am.

I didn't follow him or say anything other than a quiet goodbye after the door had closed behind him yesterday. I wasn't sure what to say. He loved me. He said it. But how can someone love like that? How can someone be in love with someone who wants to do that? And irrespective of the confusion in that hour or so we spent together and the way he touched me, hurting me each and every time, it nearly made sense. Something began clicking into place like it had done while I sat on the terrace in that back end town. But then he left leaving me bruised and raw, and within thirty minutes of that happening, I started questioning again, searching for reasons and answers as I waked around the room, examining the result of all my labours in life. He was right. There was nothing of me to find, not the real me. Not the Alana who used to sit in college and scuttle the keyboard furiously, investing her every free moment into a story and letting it rip my soul to shreds. It was as barren of me as he professed it to be, bleak in comparison to the feelings associated with him.

I find myself turning into midtown and heading for, well, nothing really. I'm still just wandering aimlessly, the only consideration of direction aimed at the club he wrote on this piece of paper I'm gripping. I'm not sure why it's in my hand. I know it off by heart. I've looked at it all day, slept with it by my bed last night. It's comforting, giving me a direction to follow, until an hour from now. Eight pm. The address and eight pm. That's all that's written on it. I even looked at the handwriting for a while, having never seen him write a thing before. It's as beautiful as he is. Long positive scrawls. No mess, no fuss. Simple and direct. Not unlike him, I suppose, but I know so little about him. Where he likes to go, what he likes to do. I don't even know what he likes to drink. That's what started it all last night. I didn't know what he liked to drink. And I still don't understand how I can love someone, be in love with someone, without knowing that information. It all seems so backwards. It's as if we've lost our innocence before we've even found it. The thought makes me chuckle as I stare at the traffic, people walking around me on the corner. I'm unsure if he's ever had any innocence to lose. He's so rooted in his being, not deterred by any other interference. I want to know why. I want to know who he is, why he is. His parents, more brothers, sisters? His life before this started—was it happy, loving? I don't even know if he has hobbies. Not that I'm sure if men like Blaine have hobbies, other than the causing pain type, but I want to know. I want to find our innocence. Prove it's there maybe. I need that. We need that.

  I set off again along the pavement, not really thinking anymore, just being. One step in front of the other and following my body's impulses as I watch the people hurrying around me, their bags crashing into each other as they give little thought to anyone else. It's like a primal rat race. Who gets there faster, who wins the most, who gets the better job. None of its real, though. It's not based in sweat and tears. No one feels their footsteps grinding the same pavement. They just continue in their pursuit, but it's all a lie, isn't it? A fabrication of the same story over and over, hoping to better what didn't need fixing. Every fucking race to achieve more is just a screwed up measure of self. Yes, perhaps it's done dressed in a killer suit, but it accomplishes so little other than money. I know that now. I can feel it in the air now he's set me on the road to realizing it. How many of these people have lost themselves in their quest of success? How many left their dreams behind, forgetting them, or seeing them as insignificant as they scaled higher walls and battered doorways for advancement? It makes me question everything as I wander by my publishers and stop to stare up at the building.

Why I wandered this way, I don't know. I should be thankful for them, for the people in this building, certainly for the opportunity they gave me, but I'm not anymore. I feel used by them, degraded. Like they've taken my soul, not allowing me any freedom with it anymore. They've chained it to a desk and wrapped a lock over it, refusing to let me breathe through my words anymore. They've contained me, made me contain myself for them. *I've* contained my whole existence for them. Fuck, I've even made my home as they would need it to be. Clean, edited. A canvas organised and categorised into perfect folders. I thought I was doing it for me, thought it made everything easier, but I didn't, and it doesn't. It stifles me. He used such a good word last night. He said he was stifled. So am I. This whole life has become nothing but stifled and suffocating.

"Where are you, Alana?" That's what he said.

I don't know.

I sneer up at the building, staring at the windows and willing one of them to walk out here now. Especially Barringer. I'd throw the towel in now if he did, tell him exactly what I thought of his attempt at threatening me. What could he do? Fire me? I snort out, amused at the notion that his opinion, his wants, his desires are relevant in any way to me or my existence. They're not. They weren't really before Blaine, let alone now. I'm different now. I can feel it as much as I can still feel his fingers around my neck, and the others inside me, pushing me to an orgasm I'd never had comprehension of before him. Perhaps I should walk up there and let his father know what's happened. I'd barely remembered it all until I stood here. That night seems so long ago now, like a lifetime has passed between it and the present, my mind changing along with it. I'm as new as I can be and as close to the old me as I've ever been. I'm even in a dress and long, heeled boots like I used to wear rather than the jeans I'd usually go for. My make-up's as light as a feather, barely covering the marks Blaine left on me, and this material flows along my skin, relaxing me rather than constricting me inwards. I feel free, my mind wandering as aimlessly as my feet.

My hand scrunches the address in my grip, feeling him there and wondering what he'd do if he knew of Barringer's advances. I'm not sure if he's the jealous type. It seems unreasonable to suggest jealousy has anything to do with this scene I'm falling into, but then Priest said love didn't either. He was wrong, so wrong, from my point of view anyway. It has everything to do with it.

I turn and sit myself on the frontage of the small wall that surrounds the building, just staring again and remembering the way he looked at me as Blaine took what he wanted, forcing me to admit I wanted it, too. He was as invested in the idea as Blaine was. His fingers may have been restrained and his body languid as he stood and watched, but he was in that moment too. We all were, the woman included. And he wants me as part of it, doesn't he? He wants me to love him and tell him it's alright to be the way he is. *"I do love you, if that makes it easier to hear."* What a statement. If that makes it easier to hear? It did, for some ungodly reason. For something that could only be described as reckless, it did. It made the whole explanation seem as pallid as these streets have become, the only relevant thing in it the professing of love and the way his eyes begged for it to be returned in some way. He looked as lost as I felt, still feel.

I check my watch, noting the time and looking back at the building again with more thoughts of going to say my bit. It just stands there looking at me, its looming presence of grey stonework as constricting as my thoughts regarding it. I'm done with them. I'll write my last ones and then I won't sign up again with anyone. Bree's right. I don't have to be with anyone. I don't even need the money anymore. I can be as free as I want to be, choosing what I write, when I want to write it, how long it should be, and for whom to read.

I texted her a while back, apologising for disappearing on her and telling her I was fine. I don't know if she cares or not, or even if she forgives me for going, understands even, but she hasn't texted back. I'm not surprised. It's not in her nature to be undermined. That's how she'll see it, but that's not what I did. I just embraced me again, what I wanted. At the time, and still, I want Blaine regardless of his intentions. I want whatever he has to offer, so I can complete whatever this transformation is. Where it goes after that, I don't know, but I'm going to travel the road nonetheless, let it enthuse Alana Williams again, let him guide me back to where I want to be, or shunt me forward in a new direction, new horizons maybe. Either way, I don't care. I'm going with or without Bree by my side. This recurring life I'm in has to stop. This fucking nightmare that controls my mind, my body and thoughts. It stops. And the damn pills I need to take daily to keep up, that stops, too. It all has to stop. I need control over my life back. I need me.

My dress skips across my knees as the wind picks it up, making me smile as I stand and begin my meander again, this time with more direction than before. I know exactly where I'm going, who I'm going to. I might not know what he likes to drink, or where he likes to eat, but I know him. I already know what he needs to do to my skin to feel complete. I felt a little of it last night, felt the way he hit me with that belt, my body reacting just as he probably thought it would when he climbed me to orgasm. I just have to keep trusting him to take me there, wherever there is. He'll take me further, though. All I have to do is ask. I just need to watch whatever he needs to show me and agree to more. That's all. I just have to love him.

~

"You're early, pretty thing," Priest says, his frame filling the doorway of the nondescript venue I've arrived at. Am I? I hardly know what day it is given this haze I'm in. I don't know if that's what's been happening in my life or the fact that I haven't taken my pills yet. I just walk under his arm, heading in with little concern for what's coming. I'm not scared or worried, maybe a little apprehensive, but the blur around me seems calming regardless of what I'm about to witness.

"Is he here?" I ask, looking around the small deep blue foyer area. It's like a theatre entrance, a tacky, sixties style lampshade at odds with itself near a ticket void on the wall, an equally tacky patterned carpet under my feet.

"He is."

"What is all this, Delaney?"

"First name terms now, is it?" he says, his body gliding past me as he heads into a dark stairwell and begins climbing the steps. "I assumed you knew. He told me you did." I watch him climb, the sweep of the old stairs filtering dust through the air as he carries on. "He's never done this for anyone else. Why you?" I don't know, but I follow anyway, letting the wooden banister beneath my hand ground me a little as I turn. "You look dazed. Are you alright?" Who knows what alright is anymore? A few weeks ago I would have called all these people insane, been judgemental, regardless of my thoughts of equality. Now, this seems more normal to me than the apartment I've spent so long working on or the life I used to lead.

"Fine," I say as I look up at him, his tan suited legs continuing again and then disappearing. "Where are you taking me?"

"To see the show," he calls back. "It's already started."

I hurry up the stairs, desperate not to miss anything as I turn at the top and look around for where he's gone. There's no one here. It's just a maze of doors and little alleyways, all leading off in new directions. I scan them again, searching for clues, but nothing presents itself as useful.

"Priest?" No answer. "Priest?" I shout it louder, hoping for an answer but not expecting one in the slightest. He probably finds all this funny. Poor little, pretty thing that I am. If I wasn't so hazy I'd snarl at his arrogance, but who am I to judge anymore? Perhaps he deserves his egotism for some reason. He certainly knows his scene, I'll give him that. "Delaney?"

"Hello," a woman's voice says from a corner. I swing to look at her and find the woman from the church smiling back at me. "Can I help?" She looks as immaculate as she did the last time I saw her. Lipstick perfected, make-up perfected. Her body strapped into another black, figure hugging dress, calf length and finished with stilettos. "Are you lost? You seem it." Something tells me she's not talking about me not knowing where I'm going. I feel the fidget take over me as I gauge myself against her, hoping I measure up.

"Yes, I'm here for Blaine. Could you—"

"I know you are," she replies, her arms folding as she sways towards me. "He's this way." I follow, almost entranced by the way her backside seems to have its own rhythm. It lulls me after her, making me stand taller in the hope I can achieve the same result. Sadly, I'm not sure I can. Well, not with such an elegant demeanour anyway. It's probably the four-inch heels I'm not wearing, I suppose. That, or the fact that she's a trained something. I can tell by her whole being. She's superior to the others I've seen in clubs, perhaps been given some special status around these people. She might even do what Blaine does for other subs? Or maybe she's a Domme. I don't know. She gives hardly anything away other than perfection in her look.

"Who are you?" I ask, because it would be nice to know given the fact that she's watched me have sex. Not that I mind, clearly. I've become a slut like that. It's just that first name terms would be good really. Helpful.

"Tabitha," she says, without turning as she keeps going forward. "I'm here to help." Right. Help. I'm not sure how. What has she got to do with Blaine and I? "You believe me, don't you?" she continues, her hand reaching back for me as she turns her head and smiles. "That I'm here to help you in any way I can?" I'm not sure I do, but I nod anyway, scanning all the rooms we pass, the noise coming from them making me wonder what's going on inside. "I'll hold your hand if you like, make it seem less frightening. Although, it always is a little. Still."

I've no idea what any of that means, and I'm not inclined to take the hand that's offered either. It seems fake somehow, or maybe it's just that I don't know her, or perhaps it's just that, for now, the only thing I'm remotely interested in holding hands with is about to show me something I'm possibly not going to enjoy. So I frown at her instead as she keeps going, my fingers digging into my own pockets to show that I don't need my hand holding. I'm here of my own accord because I want to be, not because I'm some scared little rabbit blinded by headlights too big for me to bear. I might be new to all this, but I'm not in need of a friend. I've got one of those in Bree, hopefully.

"But what are you here for?" I ask, more interested than I thought I would be as I catch up with her strides and attempt the same rhythm. "And why were you with Priest? When we... I mean, Blaine and I... When we..." I wish I could say these things easily. You'd think I would be able to by now given the company I'm in.

"Fucked?" she replies, a wink causing my insides to flip over. I hate to admit it, but she's stunning. Not that I've ever considered another woman, but she has watched me so it seems natural to go that step further. "Is he very good? He always seems it. He seems more animalistic than most." Well, at least she's not had him then. The thought makes me smile, something akin to pride washing over me as we wander along a corridor and eventually stop in front of a door. "I've felt him once, but not inside me," she says, turning towards me and putting her hand on the door latch. Jealously sears through me, replacing the pride I had seconds ago and making me want to rip her eyes out of her skull. "Potent is a good word for him, I think. Don't you?" I'm so close to pushing her over it's horrendous. I've never felt this kind of sentiment before. In fact, I can't ever remember feeling jealousy before in my life. She giggles softly, looking at me and then putting her finger up to my face at the same time as a thud emanates from the room we're standing by. It makes me jump, my eyes swinging sharply to the sound. "Don't worry, Alana. You're here, aren't you?" Her fingernail travels the length of my cheek, her face moving towards mine as she tips my chin up and inspects my neck for the bruising that I've covered. "You're the one he wants, not me. I hope you're ready for him." Another thud happens, this time against the very door I'm hovering by, making me back away from it again. It's followed by a groan, a woman's voice making the tone seem aroused somehow. "Can I taste you before you run away?" Tabitha says. I look at her, stunned by the question and not moving any further from the thought, but she turns the latch before I can answer, a smile on her face as she giggles again and pulls her finger away. "Too late."

Her hand grabs mine, hauling me into the room and quickly across to the back of it. My head spins, trying to find Blaine, but she hurries me past Priest as he heaves a woman past us, a smile on his face as if he's amused. I'm speechless, my eyes frantically searching the skin as he drags her away from me. She's loose in his arms, her body just hanging there, limp and lifeless. It's covered in welts, large swollen areas all over her, glowing a fucking warning at me, blood even on her back and thighs. He picks her up eventually rather than dragging her, lifting her as if she weighs nothing and closing the door behind him. I stare back into the room again, my nerves creeping back from the depths of me as I wonder what the hell just happened in here.

"What did he do to her?" I ask, my eyes still focused on the door and wondering why Priest, anyone really, would do that to a woman. She looked almost dead as he carried her out. Tabitha giggles again, making me turn back to look at her.

"Still in love?" she asks, her lips curving further up as she takes a seat and pats the one next to her, inviting me. "It's all so primal, isn't it?" The thought makes me scowl at her then turn away, suddenly uncomfortable with what happened in my own home last night, let alone whatever this is.

It's a large room and empty short of the few seats she's sitting in at the back, a stage of sorts at the front. It's lined with three women, evenly spaced, all chained to the walls and as naked as the day they were born apart from blindfolds. Two sets of cuffs dangle free at the end, one set's rattle still audible in the silence that's descended now the cacophony of Priest leaving has gone. I scan the women, looking for bruising or marks of distress, not one of them has any that I can see. One does seem asleep, or barely conscious, her neck strapped back in some rope work not unlike the sling he put me in, but the others seem alive and well, just patiently waiting for something to happen.

"Priest will be dealing with number four. Don't worry about her," Tabitha says from behind me. "Five has already been dispensed with. I watched earlier." I look down, watching her smoke a cigarette as she gazes up at me. Numbers four and five. Is that what they are? Just numbers.

I eventually sit down next to her, regardless of my apprehension, trying to remain calm like the rest of the women here, but I'm not. I don't know what I am anymore, but the haze has cleared. It's been replaced with expectancy or fear, certainly a focused thought progression. I thought I wasn't scared, but I am. I don't think it's for me, though, more for those women up there who are just hanging, waiting.

"Did you know he trains all the sadists in the upper states?" she says, a lungful of smoke puffing from her mouth as she crosses her legs and looks at me. "Of course, you must have known. You'd need to for your book, wouldn't you? For the research." I'm about to ask her how the hell she knows about that when Blaine walks in to the stage area, his top half free of clothing and his bottom half dressed only in blue jeans. There's not a bead of sweat on him, or even a frown marring his face. He seems calm, relaxed even, which is now a complete contrast to the women who dangle around him as they begin squirming in their chains, one of them inching her feet up the wall as if she wants to get away. He doesn't look out to me. He just stands there for a minute, his back on view and the muscles in it relaxed as he twists to look the women over.

"Two," he says, his voice low and gravelly as another woman walks on the stage, her fingers fumbling with number two's locks until she collapses to the floor and looks up at Blaine. She immediately seems frightened, extremely so as she glances around, her eyes wild and frenzied as she blinks. It strikes me the second I look at her that *he* did that to the other woman. It wasn't Priest. Blaine did it. Is this what he wanted to show me? If it is, I don't want any part of it. The thought instantly sickens me, making me question everything I thought I knew about him.

I stand up, ready to call a halt to whatever these proceedings are, but Tabitha yanks me down, her eyes turning aggressive as she curls my arm and shoves me back into place.

"How fucking dare you?" she spits, her hand slapping out at my face and colliding with it so hard tears spring into my eyes. "You stay there and watch what he offers you." I'm so shocked that I just gape at her. "If you behave well enough I'll make you come when it's over." My hand rests on my cheek, unable to process anything. She chuckles again, her mood switching as quickly as the fucking wind. "Look at you," she snorts, disdain levying every feature as she turns back to look at Blaine. "Not having fun anymore, Alana?" No, I'm not. Not that fun was ever anything to do with this, but I thought love was. I thought this was all about love. My love for him, his for me. It's not, is it? "You hardly deserve his time, let alone his emotions. Why this is happening is beyond me." I glare at her, irritated with her opinion but too confused about the situation to do anything. Some of this is repellent. That woman who was dragged out couldn't move. She was either exhausted or dead, I'm still not sure which as I glance back at the door. "Watch him."

I don't want to. I don't know what this is becoming but the thought of turning back to that stage is terrifying. I can already hear a grunt coming from the front, a slapping sound following it. And then her fingers grip my chin, forcing me to turn. Instinct makes me fight her, the tears in my eyes as definitive as my need to walk away from this. It's all wrong again. I don't know what I expected, but this isn't it. This is not my Blaine. It's not.

I struggle, ripping my face from her nails and feeling them tear the skin as they leave.

"I'm not doing this," I say, my body trying to knock her away from me as I stand again and try to leave. "Screw you. Get off me." My hands push at her, my body trying to get her arm from mine as she increases her grip and begins dragging me back to the seat. I can't even believe I'm doing it as I begin fighting with a woman. It seems peculiar, at odds, like my body doesn't understand what it's trying to achieve. My fingers just slap out randomly, in hope if nothing else. I haven't got a hope, not even a small amount of one, and I can see that as her body comes at me quickly, forcing me towards the stage as she easily counters every move I make. She manages to get me into some kind of hold I can't get away from, her body coiling around me and constricting further, her long fingers eventually getting my chin again as she stands behind my back and forces me to look at the stage. I gasp, instantly seeing Blaine in front of me and filling the room with nothing but his eyes. He's turned to that man last night when he near choked me, his black holes narrowed as he stares at me from his crouched position and scowls.

"This is what you asked of him, Alana," she says, her breath barely laboured as I pant in her arms and stare back at him. No, it's not. I didn't ask for this. My mouth opens, ready to disagree, but she pushes again, her leg hooking into mine and forcing me down towards the floor. My knees hit first, my face just about managing to keep itself away from the sticky carpet below me. It's then that I notice the woman he's hovering over. She draws my gaze to her, my eyes following the line of his arm to her body. His fingers are curled around her breast, twisting, digging into the flesh, and his other hand's lodged inside her, the whole hand. I watch him slowly pull a little of it out, my own crotch squirming at the glistening image as his wrist cmerges and then pushes back in again slowly. Disgust and arousal merge inside me, my body relaxing in Tabitha's arms and then tensing again as she begins to let go.

"Just watch it, Alana," he says, his voice as aroused as it was when he fucked me the first time. I look up at him again, my mouth still gaping as I try to process the vision. "Watch it and learn about me."

Oh god, I'm provoked, sexually. I can feel it down there, stirring me up. It's wrong. All of this. And the woman's grunting again, making me look at her to see him crawling his hand up to her neck. She doesn't look scared anymore, she seems like she's enjoying it. Her body's wriggling a little as she's shunted along the floor, but her legs are widening, not closing. My mouth is still open as I eventually return my eyes to him, and try as I might, I can't stop my tongue licking across my bottom lip, my own teeth biting into it and showing my arousal at the vision in front of me.

"Just give in, Alana," Tabitha's voice says, her hands leaving my wrists again slowly. "Become part of it like he wants you to."

I just stare, unable to accept what my own skin craves. I want to watch this—I do—and I'm desperate for it to be my skin under his hands, not this other woman. It's not sensible or logical. I know that, but there's nothing but the filthy air around us and the smell beginning to creep into my nostrils lulling me into him, into it. It's all pure sex, and being driven into my nose by the continued slow drive of his hand inside her as he smiles a little. His face is so peaceful as my heart hammers erratically, winding an excited anxiety up inside me. There's no grimace from him because of his actions, no sense of wrong, no condemnation or sadness as he blinks at me and then turns back to the other woman again to crawl over her. Primal is right. It's exactly the right word for what's happening in front of me. It's not even crazed or uncontrollable. It's slow, considered, measured. His body stalks her skin, his fingers gripping into it like a cat that's already got its prey, caught it and is now beginning to toy with it for nothing more than fun's sake. He slaps her face, hard enough for the sound to course over my own skin, making me gasp at the sensation and sit myself more upright to accommodate it.

"Did you feel that?" he asks me, not her. I know he's asking me. He might be trained on her, but his mind is all on me. I see it in the way he lowers his head and licks her neck, reminding me of last night and the way he held me in the same way. "Do you remember? Is my grip still there?" Oh god, yes it is. So much so that my own fingers travel to my breast without consent, gently teasing the skin as they crawl over me up to the bruises he put there. I finger my pulse lightly, widening my own knees for reasons unknown as I flick my eyes between his face and hands. It's a riot of sensations again, making me shiver as I hear the squelch of liquid again. "Her cunt's nothing like yours," he says, his frame lowering as he licks his way down her stomach, still holding onto her neck. I should be disgusted as I watch the man I love sinking down her body and heading for the one place no other couple would allow, but I'm not. I'm giving in. I can feel it, as I will him further down, readying myself as my own hand travels down my body, too. I want my hand inside myself, or his, but I don't want to feel empty. I don't ever want empty again. Whatever all this is, it applies to a part of me that I've not known about before him. It excites me, regardless of the slight hint of self-loathing still coursing through me. I want it, need it even, and I watch him so intently I don't realise where my own hand is until it's too late. It takes one flick of his tongue against her clit for me to begin touching myself. "She tastes sour in comparison." And then he drives his teeth into her, his other hand releasing her neck to hold her thigh down instead. She screams at the same moment as my own fingers slip under my knickers, two of them sliding inside me as my eyes roll back and a groan leaves me. It's like they're his fingers, his mind making me do it, and I'm not stopping. I'm already desperate to come as I open my eyes again and watch him yank her body so he can face me, his teeth still ripping at her clit and making her scream louder. Her arms flounder in my view, the sound of tears and pleas echoing in the air, but I can barely hear them as my fingers keep driving into myself and I watch him watch me. It's all slow to me as my other hand joins in, my legs widening further still to gain more leverage against myself. And I wish it was him. I do, but the view of him on her, the way his shoulders buck as the weight of his mouth holds her in place, it's the filthiest thing I've ever witnessed, making everything else I've ever been a part of seem unworthy.

"Harder, Alana, scream for me. Let me hear you." The moans come then. They leave my mouth with little care for anything other than what he wants. Dark eyes bore into mine as I hitch my dress further out of the way, his mouth occasionally hovering over the other woman and then returning to biting her again. She glistens on his mouth, a slight hue of red only spurring me on to moan out more and keep searching for my orgasm. I'm as debased as he is, as filthy, irrespective of my lacking education. I want all of this. I'm reactive, wound tightly, my fingers furiously furrowing my insides, seeking an answer to my own attack on my skin. And then it starts coming. It comes as her howls get louder, her body being pushed around like a rag doll as he slaps her again and rolls her onto her side. The hand holding her thigh just moves to her arse, widening it and beginning to drive itself inside there. It reminds me of the bed we laid in, my hands cuffed to the bedstead as he made me fuck myself on his fingers. His tone, the weight of him behind me, the belt I took last night on my own arse, the same one I'm purposely digging into my boots to heighten the pain. Fuck, my eyes roll again, my mouth gasping for air as I keep riding my fingers, hoping, clawing, desperate…

  Hands coil around me, my body hoisted and turned. They're his, and they're at full force, his fingers ripping mine from inside me and shoving me face first into the floor. I don't open my eyes or try to fight him off. I give in, just like Tabitha said, letting him do whatever he wants with me. It feels calming, emptying. Everything disappears other than his weight, his breath in my ear, the continued gravelled tone of his voice, and the way he hauls me around. It's nothing like before. No words of pleasure, no naughtiness. It's like last night was, brutal. My body goes lax, just letting him shunt me into any position as I feel the back of my dress tear open. It's as freeing as his weight on me, my skin finally open to the elements, open to him.

"Do it," I moan, as I try to brace myself up a little, not knowing what's coming and not caring either. I'm so wound up I'll take anything he wants to do. Beg, scream, howl. I'll do anything that woman has done. I know that because as my knees grate the carpet, widening themselves and offering myself to him, I'm smiling at the thought. "Anything you want." Anything to keep this rush going, make it send me higher. I don't care where I am or what I'm doing. I just want him on me, in me. I want his mind holding me down, his hands bracing me into whatever he thinks is right for me. I can stop thinking here, stop all the noise and drift. Be like I was under the water, float in my haze knowing that I've asked for him, so he'll help.

Pain ricochets along my spine, sending me straight to the floor in agony and wheezing out the breath I was pulling in. I just stay there for a minute, unable to process the feeling and barely able to hold in a whimper. It feels like I'm sliced open, a searing heat ripping into my flesh and buckling me in two.

"Another?" his voice asks, amused as I feel his hand slide under my stomach and lift me back onto all fours. I don't know, and these tears springing from my eyes again don't help me understand why my orgasm wants to come again. "I think so."

It happens again so quickly I scream in reply this time, not only buckling under the pain that comes on my right side this time, but pulling my legs up too, trying to ball myself away from it. He doesn't let me. His hold is immediate on my body, his hands dragging me over the floor somewhere, my own feet tripping on the carpet to get me wherever he's trying to take me.

"Arms up." It's an order I don't recognise, and a tone I only remember as angry, not the amused of a second ago, or the calm of minutes before then. My hands curl around my stomach, seemingly still in my haze, barely acknowledging reality as I'm pushed against a wall and his face comes in front of me again. "Up, Alana." I lift them, and watch as they tremble past my face between our eyes. He doesn't acknowledge the move, just keeps staring at me, asking questions I don't know the answers to and making me do things I shouldn't. "Good girl." Oh, but those words coming from him flood me with peace again, causing the pain in my sides and back to disappear as he slowly lifts his hand up to mine, his body caging me against the wall. It's like a dream I'm barely able to discern. Time and distance are evaporating around me. It's all so quiet other than our breaths and the sound of whimpers coming from somewhere. I just stare at his chest, watching the way it surrounds me and keeps me safe. I'm not even sure I truly feel his fingers putting my wrists into the cuffs, although I know it's happened. I just close my eyes, letting the quiet focus me on my orgasm, which is still so close regardless of what's happening. "Turn around," he says, soft hands working along my dress, occasionally touching my skin as he drags the rest from me. Good, he can take it all off me. All of it. He can take it off me, from me. He can pull the insides out and rebalance me again, find me.

"More," I say. It's not stuttered or stumbled. It's a need I don't know, but one I can't deny any more. I won't. I want this. "Please, Blaine. More."

It doesn't take long. The pain comes again twice as fast. And it's levied with harsher strokes this time, ones that rain down on me causing me to bellow out at them as they keep coming. Right side, left side. Thigh, calf. Oh god, it just keeps coming like there's no end to any of it. Over and over again, the snap as frightening as the landing that cuts in sharply. It makes me buck and twist, my fingers clinging to the cuffs for support, desperate to get away and yet wanting nothing more than the next one to strike. I can hardly hear my own screams anymore as tears start falling, travelling my cheeks like rivers of torment. It's like a dark cave filled with agony as I try to say no, or beg him to stop, but the words don't come. They won't. My lips just stay clamped closed, occasionally letting a grunt slip through them to help alleviate the sensation as my legs start shaking beneath me, but I'm not stopping it. That's his job. I trust him to do that. I asked for this, begged him. He'll tell me when enough is enough. He has to because I don't know where the answer is. I'm too lost to understand the questions, let alone find the answers. I'm so tired of everything, and this place, this place I'm falling into is filled with a noiseless cadence, making me focus on nothing but the rhythm of his beating. It's soundless here with him. Spiritual in some ways. Cleansing.

 My tears stop at some point, and my breathing does, too. I'm not panting like I was a minute ago. I'm just still, my body giving in to my wrists holding it up, my frame relaxing into that thought. I'm not in control of myself, nor do I want to be. I'm all in his hands and finally still because of it. I'm as stained as he can get me and as clean as I've ever been. I'm lost or found—I don't know which as I slowly open my eyes and gaze at the wall in front of me, but I do know I feel free, if only for as long as this lasts. I'm naked and free. I'm home.

"You're done," his voice says quietly, an arm wrapping around my waist to lift me a little. I let him, unable to make my body do anything anyway. It's as lax as the body of the girl Delaney carried out of here and as exhausted as it's ever known. There are nothing but clear views and sleepy nights coming for me. I can't even feel the pain as he lifts me from the floor, his hands wrapping mine around his neck after he's taken my wrists from the cuffs. I couldn't hold on if I tried, and besides, I don't need to because he won't let me drop. Not now I've asked for all this.

"I..." I can't find words still. They're lost, too, all my synonyms and dictionaries tossed aside, ridding me of the need to put them on paper, not that I could ever put this on paper. It's a jumbled mess of tranquillity, leaving me with nothing but empty vowels and syllables to relay its message. It's heaven, or hell—I don't know, but it's not earthly. It's...

"Sssh," he says in reply, his arms hitching me higher as he kisses my forehead and walks us by Tabitha. She smiles at me, her finger wiping a strand of hair away from my face.

"Well done," she says. Well done? I can't find any care for what that means or who the hell she is. It's just too nice here in his arms. I'm loved, cherished.

He whispers something to her about the others, I don't know what as we keep moving out of the door Tabitha opens and back down the hallway. I don't care about that either. I don't care about anything. I'm just here, with him, hanging as limply as the last girl was and ready for whatever he thinks is right for me. I'm all in his hands now, happily so.

I just watch his face as he levers me closer to his skin and frowns, his eyes as dark as I've ever seen them and his mouth a slight sneer. It makes me imagine a happier face as I lift my hand weakly to touch him, one filled with laughter and warm summer nights, perhaps the normal kind of love.

"I want dates," I manage to say as he turns us to the left. "Nights out together." He smiles a little, but he doesn't look at me as he keeps walking, a frown still marring the smile. "I deserve them after this, Blaine." I'm not sure what that means. Acceptance? Reliance? It's all just a blur of need, something I only know is essential in some way to bring me back in kilter. He just carries on, his lips kissing my forehead again as we eventually back into an open doorway.

"You can have the world if you want it, Alana," he eventually says, his foot kicking the door closed behind us as he walks us over to a bed and throws me on it. Pain sluices through everything I have, the cold sheets reminding me of all that just happened as I roll into them, of everything I took. It rallies me back upwards, my arched frame trying to get away from the ache assaulting it again as I wearily turn at him. He smirks, his fingers undoing his jeans as he bolts the door and starts walking towards me. "You give me that again," he says, his finger pointing at the bed I'm on, causing me to look at it. "And you can have everything you've ever wanted." It's covered in blood, the white sheets smeared with crimson stains already regardless of the few seconds I've been on them. I scan my body frantically, checking the wounds and realising the damage caused to my skin as I do. It's a mess of colours, all littering me with bruising and welts, ones I hardly felt at the time, or didn't seem to mind. But now I can see what he's done, it intensifies

the pain to the point of sensible reason returning. All this seems so…
"I'll give it all to you. Everything." I look back at him, watching the way his brow hardens and the sneer develops again as he steps out of his jeans.

Everything. I can have everything. "This fucking heart, too, if you want its barren eclipse." Oh god, my knees scramble me backwards as he cricks his neck and draws the belt from his jeans, his feet getting closer with every second that passes. Am I ready for everything? I don't know. And his face now, the one I can see winding itself up to deliver more pain to my skin as he keeps coming, it's savage. It's the animalistic Tabitha said it would be. Full of malice and carnal intent. It's damn well frightening. "If you're asking for it."

I'm not sure if I am or not.
I only have to ask.

THE END
FOR NOW

'The End' is the concluding book in The Stained Duet

Are you ready for more of Alana and Blaine's story?

Find the author at Amazon.

Charlotte E Hart
ONCE UPON A

Acknowledgments

As always I'd like to send out love and thanks to:

My PA - Leanne Cook, without whom I wouldn't survive this booky world. She's the calm in my storm. Mostly.

My beta Readers – Jodie Scott and Katie Matthews. You helped no end. Even if you did make me swear and spit. Yes, Slavey, you also helped with the swearing and will continue to do so, I'm sure.

My Editor – Heather at Heathers Red Pen Editing.
As usual, love you. Thanks for everything. You're still a star.

My other half – Who is my world and gives me this chance. You don't know how much you mean to me or my words. I love you.

Bloggers – You're stunning. All of you. To offer the support you do for no other reason than the love of books, well, I've no words for how awesome that makes you.

And, of course, all of my readers.

You all amaze me with your kind words and encouragement. There will always be a story in me ready to come out, but it's you lovely readers that help me believe the words are worth reading.
I can only hope that I continue to provoke thought with every novel and encourage your minds to search horizons new.

Charlotte E Hart
ONCE UPON A

Also Available by the Author

****

The White Trilogy – Nominated for best BDSM Series of the Year

Seeing White (Book 1)

"OMG. Amazing writer, amazing books. Deliciously dark and deviant."
"Ms Hart's delivery of this genre is inspiring, provocative and ruthless."

****

Alexander White, the wealthy business man with looks to die for. Just like the other colours you'd think.......but no.

He came from a very different place and made some of his money a very different way.

And he keeps it well hidden because the truth would destroy everything he has. All that he's worked for would be gone in an instant if they ever found out what he's capable of, or what he really did and who he did it for. So he keeps people far away with metaphorical games and walls to deceive and confuse.

He doesn't do relationships, he doesn't do emotions and he certainly doesn't do love.

He does money. Making it, manipulating it and spending it whist he plays with women who know what they're signing up for.

Three people shaped who he is today. One damaged him beyond repair, another taught him to control the rage, and a decent one helps him to consider his options more appropriately.

But be under no illusions ladies, Mr White has not been a nice man, and he will probably never be a decent man, but as long as he keeps up his image, and nothing gets through his barriers, no one will ever see the truth.

Life's good for Elizabeth Scott, successful business, happy kitchen and a great sister who deals with all the expensive people so she doesn't

have to. She just cooks, bakes and smiles her way through each day......well most of the time, anyway, that is when her great sister isn't pushing her to, "get out there a bit more," or "sort her shit out."
Then the biggest contract of their lives comes up..... And the ever useless London tube, with her sister in it, catastrophically breaks down. Unfortunately, that means only one thing. She'll have to deal with some of that wealth herself, and that means the devastating Mr Alexander White in all his glory.
Life suddenly couldn't get worse, regardless of his unfairly gorgeous backside.
She has no idea what the hell she's doing.

******

This book is followed by:

Feeling White (Book 2)
Absorbing White (Book 3)

Charlotte E Hart
ONCE UPON A

The VDB Trilogy
(Best read after The White Trilogy)

The VDB Trilogy begins a week after the end of The White Trilogy and is told from new POV's. It is, in some ways, a continuation.

****

The Parlour
Book 1 in the VDB Trilogy

Above all else Pascal Van Der Braak is a gentleman. Devastatingly debonair and seductively charming. Always styled and perfected.
He is also a cad, scoundrel, rouge and kink empire founder.
Tutored in the highest of society, having been born of royalty only to deny it, he found his solace in a world where rules need not apply.
Where he chooses to ensure rules and duty do not apply.
Some call him Sir, others call him master, and no one would dare risk his wrath unless they required the punishment he favourably delivers.
Except one, who has just strapped a collar around his throat, one he asked for. So, now he needs to appropriate his businesses correctly for peace to ensue. He needs to find the correct path forward for everyone concerned, so he can relax, enjoy, and finally hand over the responsibility to someone else.
Simple.
But where comfort and a safety of sorts once dwelled, there is now uncertainty, and a feeling of longing he no longer understands. A need unfulfilled. And as problems arise, and allies scheme, he finds himself searching for answers in the most unlikely of places.

Lilah
It's the same every day. I'd found it odd at first, but I'm used to it now. I was so tired and weak when I got here that it was helpful really. That small woman comes in to help me wash and get dressed. I don't know where the clothes come from, but they're nice enough, and at least they're clean and dry. Not like the rags I arrived in. They were taken from me the moment I took them off to get into the shower, the first

shower I'd had in god knows how long. Nearly a year I'd been running the streets, a year without a real bed or a home of any sort. There isn't a long and awful story to tell about an abusive family member, or a broken home. I suppose I just slipped through the cracks and got lost at some point. I lost my job first, and then I couldn't afford the bills on my apartment, so the landlord threw me out. I don't blame him, he did the right thing by himself. And then it was just a long and never-ending road to nothingness.
So now I'm here, wherever here is.
And I don't know why.

****

This book is followed by:

Eden's Gate (VDB 2)
Serenity's Key (VDB 3)

Printed in Great Britain
by Amazon